MIRABILE

MIRABILE

Janet Kagan

A TOM DOHERTY ASSOCIATES BOOK
New York

This is a work of fiction. All the characters and events portrayed in this book are fictitious, and any resemblance to real people or events is purely coincidental.

MIRABILE

Copyright © 1991 by Janet Kagan

All rights reserved, including the right to reproduce this book, or portions thereof, in any form.

A Tor Book
Published by Tom Doherty Associates, Inc.
49 West 24th Street
New York, N.Y. 10010

Library of Congress Cataloging-in-Publication Data

Kagan, Janet.
    Mirabile / Janet Kagan.
        p. cm.
    "A Tom Doherty Associates book."
    ISBN 0-312-85220-7
    I. Title.
    PS3561.A363M57   1991
    813'.54—dc20   91-19691
                                                         CIP

Printed in the United States of America

First edition: October 1991

0 9 8 7 6 5 4 3 2 1

For MARY MEGSON,
  who read me sf before I was old enough to read,
for FRED MEGSON,
  who let me tell every other chapter of the bedtime
  cliff-hanger,
for SUSAN CASPER,
  who knows why this particular book got written,
and for RICKY,
  of course and as always. . . .

May they never stop scandalizing the kids!

Contents

MIRABILE

1

The Loch Moose Monster

THIS YEAR the Ribeiro's daffodils seeded early and they seeded cockroaches. Now, ecologically speaking, even a cockroach has its place—but these suckers *bit*. That didn't sound Earth-authentic to me. Not that I care, mind you, all I ask is useful. I wasn't betting on that either.

As usual, we were shorthanded—most of the team was up-country trying to stabilize a herd of Guernseys—which left me and Mike to throw a containment tent around the Ribeiro place while we did the gene-reads on the roaches and the daffodils that spawned 'em. Dragon's Teeth, sure enough, and worse than useless. I grabbed my gear and went in to clean them out, daffodils and all.

By the time I crawled back out of the containment tent, exhausted, cranky, and thoroughly bitten, there wasn't a daffodil left in town. Damn fools. If I'd told 'em the roaches were Earth-authentic they'd have cheered 'em, no matter how obnoxious they were.

I didn't even have the good grace to say hi to Mike when I slammed into the lab. The first thing out of my mouth was, "The red daffodils—in front of Sagdeev's."

1

"I got 'em," he said. "Nick of time, but I got 'em. They're in the greenhouse—"

We'd done a gene-read on that particular patch of daffodils the first year they'd flowered red: they promised to produce a good strain of praying mantises, probably Earth-authentic. We both knew how badly Mirabile needed insectivores. The other possibility was something harmless but pretty that ships' records called "fireflies." Either would have been welcome, and those idiots had been ready to consign both to a fire.

"I used the same soil, Annie, so don't give me that look."

"Town's full of fools," I growled, to let him know that look wasn't aimed at him. "Same soil, fine, but can we match the rest of the environmental conditions those praying mantises need in the goddamn greenhouse?"

"It's the best we've got," he said. He shrugged and his right hand came up bandaged. I glared at it.

He dropped the bandaged hand behind the lab bench. "They were gonna burn 'em. I couldn't—" He looked away, looked back. "Annie, it's nothing to worry about—"

I'd have done the same myself, true, but that was no reason to let *him* get into the habit of taking fool risks.

I started across to check out his hand and give him pure hell from close up. Halfway there the com blatted for attention. Yellow light on the console, meaning it was no emergency, but I snatched it up to deal with the interruption before I dealt with Mike. I snapped a "Yeah?" at the screen.

"Mama Jason?"

Nobody calls me that but Elly's kids. I glowered at the face on screen: my age, third-generation Mirabilan, and not so privileged. "Annie Jason Masmajean," I corrected, "Who wants to know?"

"Leonov Bellmaker Denness at this end," he said. "I apologize for my improper use of your nickname." Ship's manners—he ignored my rudeness completely.

The name struck me as vaguely familiar but I was in no mood to search my memory; I'd lost my ship's manners about three hours into the cockroach clean-out. "State your business," I said.

To his credit, he did: "Two of Elly's lodgers claim there's a monster in Loch Moose. By their description, it's a humdinger."

I was all ears now. Elly runs the lodge at Loch Moose for fun—her profession's raising kids. (Elly Raiser Roget, like her father before her. Our population is still so small we can't afford to lose genes just because somebody's not suited, one way or another, for parenting.) A chimera anywhere near Loch Moose was a potential disaster. Thing of it was, Denness didn't sound right for that. "Then why aren't *they* making this call?"

He gave a deep-throated chuckle. "They're in the dining room gorging themselves on Chris's shrimp. I doubt they'll make you a formal call when they're done. Their names are Emile Pilot Stirzaker and François Cobbler Pastides and, right now, they can't spell either without dropping letters."

So he thought they'd both been smoking dumbweed. Fair enough. I simmered down and reconsidered him. I'd've bet money he was the one who sidetracked Pastides and Stirzaker into the eating binge.

Recognition struck at last: this was the guy Elly's kids called "Noisy." The first thing he'd done on moving into the neighborhood was outshout every one of 'em in one helluva contest. He was equally legendary for his stories, his bells, and his ability to keep secrets. I hadn't met him, but I'd sure as hell heard tell.

I must have said the nickname aloud, because Denness said, "Yes, 'Noisy.' Is that enough to get me a hearing?"

"It is." It was my turn to apologize. "Sorry. What more do you want me to hear?"

"You should, I think, hear Stirzaker imitate his monster's bellow of rage."

It took me a long moment to get his drift, but get it I did. "I'm on my way," I said. I snapped off and started repacking my gear.

Mike stared at me. "Annie? What did I miss?"

"*You* ever know anybody who got auditory hallucinations on dumbweed?"

"Shit," he said. "No." He scrambled for his own pack.

"Not you," I said. "I need you here to coddle those daffodils, check the environmental conditions that produced 'em, and call me if Dragon's Teeth pop up anywhere else." I shouldered my pack and finished with a glare and a growl: "That should be enough to keep you out of bonfires while I'm gone, shouldn't it?"

By the time I grounded in the clearing next to Elly's lodge, I'd decided I was on a wild moose chase. Yeah, I know the Earth-authentic is wild *goose*, but "wild moose" was Granddaddy Jason's phrase. He'd known Jason—the original first generation Jason—well before the Dragon's Teeth had started popping up.

One look at the wilderness where Elly's lodge is now and Jason knew she had the perfect EC for moose. She hauled the embryos out of ships' storage and set them thawing. Built up a nice little herd of the things and turned 'em loose. Not a one of them survived—damn foolish creatures died of a taste for a Mirabilan plant they couldn't metabolize.

Trying to establish a viable herd got to be an obsession with Jason. She must've spent years at it, off and on. She never succeeded but somebody with a warped sense of humor named the lake Loch Moose and it stuck, moose or no moose.

Loch Moose looked as serene as it always did this time of year. The water lilies were in full bloom—patches of velvety red and green against the sparkles of sunlight off the water. Here and there I saw a ripple of real trout, Earth-authentic.

On the bank to the far right, Susan's troop of otters played tag, skidding down the incline and hitting the water with a splash. They whistled encouragement to each other like a pack of fans at a ballgame. Never saw a creature have more pure *fun* than an otter—unless it was a dozen otters, like now.

The pines were that dusty gold that meant I'd timed it just right to see Loch Moose smoke. There's nothing quite so beautiful as that drift of pollen fog across the loch. It would gild rocks and trees alike until the next rainfall.

Monster, my ass—but where better for a wild moose chase?

I clambered down the steps to Elly's lodge, still gawking at the scenery, so I was totally unprepared for the EC in the lobby. If that bright-eyed geneticist back on Earth put the double whammy on any of the human genes in the cold banks they sent along (*swore* they hadn't, but after the kangaroo rex, damnify

believe anything the old records tell me), the pandemonium I found
would have been enough to kick off Dragon's Teeth by the dozens.

Amid the chaos, Ilanith, Elly's next-to-oldest-not-yet-grown, was
handling the oversized gilt ledger with great dignity. She lit up when
she saw me and waved. Then she bent down for whispered
conversation. A second later Jen, the nine-year-old, exploded from
behind the desk, bellowing, "Elleeeeee! Nois-eeeeee! Come quick!
Mama Jason's here!" The kid's lung power cut right through the
chaos and startled the room into a momentary hush. She charged
through the door to the dining room, still trying to shout the house
down.

I took advantage of the distraction to elbow my way to the desk
and Ilanith.

She squinted a little at me, purely Elly in manner, and said, "Bet
you got hopped on by a kangaroo rex this week. You're *real* snarly."

"Can't do anything about my face," I told her. "And it was
biting cockroaches." I pushed up a sleeve to show her the bites.

"Bleeeeeh," she said, with an inch or two of tongue for
emphasis. "I hope they weren't keepers."

"Just the six I saved to put in your bed. Wouldn't want you to
think I'd forgotten you."

She wrinkled her nose at me and flung herself across the desk
to plant a big sloppy kiss on my cheek. "Mama Jason, you are the
world's biggest tease. But I'm gonna give you your favorite room
anyhow"—she wrinkled her nose in a very different fashion at the
couple to my right—"since *those two* just checked out of it."

One of the *those two* peered at me like a myopic crane. I saw
recognition strike, then he said, "We've changed our minds.
We'll keep the room."

"Too late," said Ilanith—and she was smug about it. "But, if
you want to stay, I can give you one on the other side of the
lodge. No view." Score one for the good guys, I thought.

"See, Elly?" It was Jen, back at a trot beside Elly and dragging
Noisy behind her. "See?" Jen said again. "If Mama Jason's here,
I won't have to go away, right?"

"Right," I said.

"Oh, Jen!" Elly dropped to one knee to pull Jen into one of her

full-body-check hugs. "Is *that* what's been worrying you? Leo
already explained to your mom. There's no monster. Nobody's
going to send you away from Loch Moose!"

Jen, who'd been looking relieved, suddenly looked suspicious.
"If there's no monster, why's Mama Jason here?"

"Need a break," I said, realizing I meant it. Seeing Elly and
the kids was break enough all by itself. "Stomped enough
Dragon's Teeth this week. I'm not about to go running after
monsters that vanish at the first breath of fresh air."

Elly gave me a smile that would have thawed a glacier and my
shoulders relaxed for the first time in what seemed like months.

I grinned back. "Have your two monster-sighters sobered up yet?"

"Sobered up," reported Ilanith, "and checked out." She giggled.
"You should have seen how red-faced they were, Mama Jason."

I glowered at no one in particular. "Just as well. After the day
I had, they'd have been twice as red if I'd had to deal with 'em."

Elly rose to her feet, bringing Jen with her. The two of them
looked me over, Jen imitating Elly's keen-eyed inspection. "We'd
better get Mama Jason to her room. She needs a shower and a
nap worse than any kid in the household."

Ilanith shook her head. "Let her eat first, Elly. By the time
she's done, we'll have her room ready."

"Sounds good to me," I said, "if the kids waiting tables can take
it."

"We raise a sturdy bunch around here. Go eat, Annie." Elly
gave me a kiss on the cheek—I got a bonus kiss from Jen—and
the two of them bustled off to get my room ready. I frowned after
them: Jen still seemed worried and I wondered why.

Ilanith rounded the desk to grab my pack. Standing between
me and Leo, she suddenly jammed her fists into her hips. "Oh,
nuts. Ship's manners. Honestly, Mama Jason—how did people
ever get acquainted in the old days?" With an expression of tried
patience, she formally introduced the two of us.

I looked him over, this time giving him a fair shake. The face
was as good as the reputation, all laugh lines etched deep. In
return, I got inspected just as hard.

When nobody said anything for a full half second, Ilanith said, "More? You need more? Didn't I get it right?"

Leo gave a smile that was a match for Elly's. Definitely the EC, I thought. Then he thrust out a huge welcoming hand and said, "That's Leo to you, as I don't imagine I could outshout you."

That assessment visibly impressed Ilanith.

"Annie," I said. I took the hand. Not many people have hands the size of mine. In Denness I'd met my match for once. Surprised me how good that felt. He didn't let go immediately and I wasn't all that anxious for him to do so.

Ilanith eyed him severely. "Leo, there's no need to be grabby!" She tapped his hand, trying to make him let go.

"Shows how much you know about ship's manners," Leo said. "I was about to offer the lady my arm, to escort her into the dining room."

"Perfectly good old-time ritual," I said. "I can stand it if he can."

Leo held out his arm, ship's formal; I took it. We went off rather grandly, leaving Ilanith all the more suspicious that we'd made it up for her benefit.

Leo chuckled as we passed beyond her earshot. "She won't believe that until she double-checks with Elly."

"I know. Good for 'em—check it out for yourself, I always say. Have *you* heard any bellowing off the loch?"

"Yes," he said, "I have heard a couple of unusual sounds off the loch lately. I've no way of knowing if they're all made by the same creature. But I've lived here long enough to know that these are new. One is a kind of sucking gurgle. Then there's something related to a cow's lowing"—he held up a hand—"*not* cow and *not* red deer either. I know both. And there's a bellow that'll bring you out of a sound sleep faster than a shotgun blast."

His lips flattened a bit. "I can't vouch for that one. I've *only* heard it awakening from sleep. It might have been a dream, but it never *feels* like dream—and the bellow Stirzaker gave was a fair approximation of it."

The lines across his forehead deepened. "There's something else you should know, Annie. Jen's been acting spooked, and neither Elly nor I can make any sense of it."

"I saw. I thought she was still keyed up over the monster business."

He shook his head. "This started weeks ago, long before Stirzaker and Pastides got everybody stirred up."

"I'll see what I can find out."

"Anything I can do to help," he said. He swung his free hand to tell me how extensive that "anything" actually was. "On either count."

"Right now, you watch me eat a big plate of *my* shrimp with Chris's barbecue sauce on 'em."

Loch Moose was the only source of freshwater shrimp on Mirabile, and they were one of my triumphs. Not just the way they tasted when Chris got done with them, but because I'd brought the water lilies they came from myself and planted them down in Loch Moose on the chance they'd throw off something good. Spent three years making sure they stabilized. Got some pretty dragonflies out of that redundancy, too. Elly's kids use 'em for catching rock lobsters, which is another thing Chris cooks to perfection.

By the time I'd finished my shrimp, the dining room was empty except for a couple of people I knew to be locals like Leo. I blinked my surprise, I guess.

Leo said, "Most of the guests checked out this morning. Let's take advantage of it." He picked up my glass and his own and bowed me toward one of the empty booths.

I followed and sank, sighing, into overstuffed comfort. "Now," I said, "tell me what you heard from Stirzaker and Pastides."

He obliged in detail, playing both roles. When he was done, I appreciated his reputation for story telling, but I knew as well he'd given me an accurate account, right down to the two of them tripping over each other's words in their excitement.

Their description of the chimera would have scared the daylights out of me—if they'd been able to agree on any given part of it aside from the size. Stirzaker had seen the thing reach for him with two great clawlike hands. Pastides had seen the loops of a water snake, grown to unbelievable lengths, undulate past him. They agreed again only when it came to the creature's bellow.

When all was said, I had to laugh. "I bet *their* granddaddy told *them* scary bedtime stories too!"

"Good God," said Leo, grinning suddenly. "The Loch Ness monster! I should have recognized it!"

"From which description?" I grinned back. Luckily the question didn't require an answer.

"Mama Jason!"

That was all the warning I got. Susan—all hundred pounds of her—pounced into my lap.

"They were *dumb*struck, both of them," she said, her manner making it clear that this was the most important news of the century. "You should have seen them eat! Tell her, Noisy—you saw!"

"Hello to you too," I said, "and I just got the full story, complete with sound effects."

That settled her down a bit, but not much. At sixteen, nothing settles them *down*. Sliding into the seat beside me, she said, "Now you tell—about the biting cockroaches."

Well, I'd have had to tell that one sooner or later, so I told it for two, ending with Mike's heroic attempt to rescue the red daffodils.

Susan's eyes went dreamy. "Fireflies," she said. "Think how pretty they'd be around the lake at night!"

"I was," I said, all too curtly. "Sorry," I amended, "I'm still pissed off about them."

"I've got another one for you," Susan said, matching my scowl. "Rowena who lives about twenty miles that way"—she pointed, glanced at Leo (who nudged her finger about 5 degrees left), then went on—"*that* way, claims that the only way to keep from raising Dragon's Teeth is to spit tobacco on your plants whenever you go past them." She gave another glance at Leo, this one a different sort of query. "I think she *believes* that. I know she *does* it!"

"'Fraid so," Leo said.

"Well, we'll know just what EC to check when something unusual pops out of Rowena's plants, won't we?" I sighed. The superstitions really were adding to our problems.

"Mama Jason," said Susan—with a look that accused me of making a joke much too low for her age level—"How many authentics need tobacco-spit ECs to pop up?"

"No joke, honey. It's not authentic species I'd expect under conditions like that. It'd be Dragon's Teeth plain and probably not so simple." I looked from one to the other. "Keep an eye on those plants for me. Anything suddenly flowers in a different color or a slightly different form, snag a sample and send it to me fast!"

They nodded, Susan looking pleased with the assignment, Leo slightly puzzled. At last Leo said, "I'm afraid I've never understood this business of Dragon's Teeth . . ." He broke off, suddenly embarrassed.

"Fine," I said, "as long as you don't spit tobacco on the ragweed or piss on the petunias or toss the soapy wash water on the lettuce patch."

Susan eyed me askance. I said, "Last year the whole town of Misty Valley decided that pissing on the petunias was the only way to stabilize them." I threw up my hands to stave off the question that was already on the tip of Susan's tongue. "*I don't know how that got started, so don't ask me. I'm not even sure I want* to know! The end result, of course, was that the petunias seeded ladybugs."

"Authentic?" Susan asked.

"No, but close enough to be valuable. Nice little insectivores and surprisingly well-suited for doing in ragmites." The ragmites are native and a bloody nuisance. "And before you ask," I added, "the things they *might* have gotten in the same EC included a very nasty species of poisonous ant and two different grain-eaters, one of which would chain up to a salamander with a taste for quail eggs."

"Oh, my!" said Susan. "Misty Valley's where we get our quail eggs!"

"So does everybody on Mirabile," I said. "Nobody's gotten the quail to thrive anywhere else yet." For Leo's benefit, I added, "So many of our Earth-authentic species are on rocky ground, we can't afford to lose a lot of individuals to a Dragon's Tooth."

Leo still looked puzzled. After a moment, he shook his head. "I've never understood this business. Maybe for once I could get a simple explanation, suitable for a bellmaker . . . ?"

I gestured to Susan. "My assistant will be glad to give you the short course."

Susan gave one of those award-winning grins. "It goes all the way back to before we left Earth, Leo." Leo arched an eyebrow: "'We'?" Susan punched him—lightly—on the arm and said, "You know what I mean! Humans!"

She heaved a dramatic sigh and went on in spite of it all. "They wanted to make sure we'd have everything we might possibly need."

"I thought that's why they sent along the embryo and gene banks," Leo said.

Susan nodded. "It was. But at the time there was a fad for redundancy—every system doubled, tripled, even quadrupled—so just to make *sure* we couldn't lose a species we might need, they built all that redundancy into the gene pool too."

She glanced at me. She was doing fine, so I nodded for her to go on.

"Look, Noisy. They took the genes for, say, sunflowers and they tucked 'em into a twist in wheat helices. Purely recessive, but when the environmental conditions are right, maybe one one-hundredth of your wheat seeds will turn out to sprout sunflowers."

She leaned closer, all earnestness. "And one one-hundredth of the sunflowers, given the right EC, will seed bumblebees, and so on and so forth. That's what Mama Jason calls 'chaining up.' Eventually you might get red deer."

Leo frowned. "I don't see how you can go from plant to animal . . ."

"There's usually an intermediate stage—a plant that comes out all wrong for that plant but perfect for an incubator for whatever's in the next twist." She paused dramatically, then finished, "As you can see, it was a perfectly *dumb* idea."

I decided to add my two bits here. "The *idea* wasn't as dumb as you make out, kiddo. They just hadn't worked the bugs out before they stuck us with it."

"When she says *bugs*," Susan confided grimly to Leo, "she *means* Dragon's Teeth."

I stepped in again. "Two things went wrong, Leo. First, there was supposed to be an easy way to turn anything other than the primary helix off and on at will. The problem is that information was in the chunk of ships' records we lost, and it was such new knowledge at the time that it didn't get passed to anyone on the ship.

"The second problem was the result of pure goof. They forgot that, in the long run, all plants and animals change to suit their environment. A new mutation may be just the thing for our wheat, but who knows what it's done to those hidden sunflowers? Those—and the chimerae—are the real Dragon's Teeth."

Leo turned to Susan. "Want to explain the chimerae as long as you're at it?"

"A chimera is something that's, well, sort of patched together from two, maybe three, different genetic sources. Ordinarily it's nothing striking—you'd probably only notice if you did a full gene-read. But with all those hidden sets of genes, just about anything can happen."

"Kangaroo rex, for example," I said. "That one was a true chimera: a wolf in kangaroo's clothing."

"I remember the news films," Leo said. "Nasty."

"Viable, too," I said. "That was a tough fight. I'm still sorry I lost." It still rankled, I discovered.

Leo looked startled.

"I wanted to save 'em, Leo, but I got voted down. We really couldn't afford a new predator in that area."

"Don't look so shocked, Noisy," Susan said. "You never know what might be useful some day. Just suppose we get an overpopulation of rabbits or something and we need a predator to balance them out before they eat all *our* crops. That's why Mama Jason wanted to keep them."

Leo looked unconvinced, Susan looked hurt suddenly. "Just because it's ugly, Leo," she said, "doesn't mean you wipe it out. There's nothing pretty about a rock lobster but it sure as hell tastes good."

"I grant you that. I'm just not as sure about things that think *I* taste good."

Susan folded her arms across her chest and heaved another of those dramatic sighs. "Now I know what you're up against, Mama Jason," she said. "Pure ignorance."

That surprised me. I held my tongue for once, waiting to see how Leo would take that.

"Nothing pure about it," he said. "Don't insult a man who's trying to enlighten himself. That never furthered a cause." He paused, then added, "You sound like you take it very personally."

Susan dropped her eyes. There was something in that evasion that wasn't simple embarrassment at overstepping good manners. When she looked up again, she said, "I'm sorry, Leo. I just get so mad sometimes. Mama Jason—"

This time I had to come to her rescue. "Mama Jason sets a bad example, Leo. I come up here and rave about the rampant stupidity everywhere else. Susan, better to educate people than insult them. If I say insulting things about them when I'm in family that's one thing. But I would never say to somebody who was concerned about his kids or his crops what you just said to Leo.

"Yeah. I know. I'm sorry again."

"Forgiven," said Leo. "Better you make your mistakes on me and learn from them than make 'em on somebody else who might wallop you and turn you stubborn."

Susan brightened. "Oh, but I *am* stubborn, Leo! You always say so!"

"Stubborn, yes. *Stupid* stubborn—not that I've seen."

Again there was something other than embarrassment in her dropped eyes. I tried to puzzle it out, but I was distracted by a noise in the distance.

It came from the direction of the loch—something faint and unfamiliar. I cocked my head to listen harder and got an earful of sneezes instead.

"S-sorry!" Susan gasped, through a second series of sneezes. "P-pollen!" Then she was off again, her face buried in a napkin.

Leo caught my eye. He thought the sneezing fit was as phony as I did.

"Well," I said, "you may be allergic to the pollen"—she wasn't, I knew very well—"but I came hoping I'd timed it right to see Loch Moose smoke. And to get in some contemplative fishing"— meaning I didn't intend to bait my hook—"before it gets too dark."

Susan held up her hand, finished off one last sequence of sneezes, then said, "What about your nap?"

"What do you think contemplative fishing *is*?"

"Oh. Right. Get Leo to take you, then. He knows all the best places."

"I'd be honored," Leo said.

We left Susan scrubbing her face. Pausing only to pick up poles in the hallway, we set off in silence along the footpath down to Loch Moose. When we got to the first parting of the path, I broke the silence. "Which way to your favorite spot?"

He pointed to the right fork. I'd figured as much. "Mine's to the left," I said and headed out that way. If Susan didn't want me in my usual haunts, I wanted to know why. Leo followed without comment, so I knew he was thinking the same thing.

"Keep your ears open. I heard something before Susan started her 'sneezing fit' to cover it."

We came to another parting in the path. I angled right and again he followed. Pretty soon we were skidding and picking our way down the incline that led to the otters' playground.

When we got to surer footing, Leo paused. "Annie—now that I've got somebody to ask: will you satisfy my curiosity?"

That peaked mine. "About what?"

"*Was* there such a thing as the Loch Ness monster? I always thought my mother had made it up."

I laughed. "And I thought my granddaddy had, especially since he claimed that people came to Loch Ness from all over the Earth hoping to catch a glimpse of the monster! I looked it up once in ships' records. There really was such a place and people really did come from everywhere for a look!"

He was as taken aback as I'd been, then he heard what I hadn't said. "And the monster—was *it* real? Did it look like any of the stories?"

"I never found out."

"Pre-photograph?"

"No," I said, "that was the odd thing about it. There were some fuzzy photos—old flat ones, from a period when *everybody* had photographic equipment—that might have been photos of anything. The story was that Nessie was very shy and the loch was too full of peat to get sonograms. Lots of excuses, no results."

"Smoking too much weed, eh?"

"Lot of that going around," I said. "But no, I suspect Nessie was exactly what granddaddy used her for—a story. What's always fascinated me is that people went to *look!*"

Quite unexpectedly, Leo chuckled. "You underestimate the average curiosity. I don't think you appreciate how many people stayed glued to their TVs while you folks rounded up those kangaroo rexes. A little thrill is high entertainment."

"The hell it is," I said indignantly. "I oughta know: I do it for a living. *They* didn't get their boots chewed off by the damn things."

"Exactly my point," said Leo. "Scary but safe. Elly's kids would be the first to tell you what a good combination that is. They watch their kangaroo rex tape about twice a week, and cheer for you every time."

Some things I was better off not knowing, I thought. I sighed. Turning away from Leo, I got the full view of Loch Moose and its surroundings, which drew a second sigh—this time pure content.

The secret of its appeal was that despite the vast sparkle of sunlight that glittered off it, Loch Moose always felt hidden away—a place you and you alone were aware of.

It took me a while to remember that Leo was beside me. No, I take that back. I was aware that he was there all along, but he was as content as I to simply drink it all in without a word.

Sometime—when we were both done admiring the scene—we headed for the boats, by some sort of mutual agreement. I was liking Leo more and more. For another thing, the whistling of the otters made him smile.

The slope down to the boats was dotted with violets. Most of them were that almost fiery shade of blue that practically defines the species, but once in a while they came out white just for the surprise of it. Some were more surprising than white, though. Almost hidden in the deep shade was a small isolated patch of scarlet.

For the life of me, I couldn't remember seeing any material on scarlet violets. I stooped for a closer look. Damned odd texture to the petals, too, like velvet.

"Pretty, aren't they?" Leo said. "Stop by my place while you're here, and I'll show you half an acre of them."

I stood up to look him in the eye. "Popped up all at once? First time, this year?"

"No. I've been putting them in when I found them for, oh, three years now."

"Oh, Leo. Half of Mirabile thinks everything's going to sprout fangs and bite them and the other half doesn't even take elementary precautions. Never *ever* transplant something red unless somebody's done a workup on it first!"

He looked startled. "Are they dangerous?"

"Don't *you* start!" Dammit, I'd done it—jumped on him with both feet. "Sorry. I'm still fuming over those red daffodils, I guess."

"Annie, I'm too damned old to worry about everything that flowers red. I took them for what my grandmother called 'pansies.' Much to her disappointment, she never could get any started on Mirabile. Maybe they aren't, but that's how I think of them. I'm going to hate it if you tell me I have to pull 'em out because they're about to seed mosquitoes."

And he'd never forgive me either, I could tell.

"We'll get a sample on the way back, Leo. If there's a problem, I'll see if I can stabilize them for you." He looked so surprised, I had to add, "Practical is not my only consideration. Never has been. 'Pretty' is just fine, provided I've got the time to spare."

That satisfied him. He smiled all the way down to the edge of the water.

Two hands made light work of launching a boat and we paddled across to the sheltered cove I had always favored. I tied the boat to a low branch that overhung the water, dropped a naked hook into the loch, and leaned back. Leo did the same.

What I liked best about this spot, I think, was that it was the perfect view of the otters' playground—without disturbing the play. It also meant I didn't have to bring along treats for the little beggars. Susan had been feeding them since she was—oh—Jen's age. They'd grown so used to it that they hustled the tourists now.

I didn't believe in it myself, but as long as she didn't overdo it to the point they couldn't fend for themselves I wasn't about to make a fuss. I think Susan knew that too. She had a better grasp of the principles than most adults I knew, aside from those on the team, of course.

The hillside and water were alive with the antics of the otters. Some rippled snake-like through the water. One chased one of those king-sized dragonflies. Two others tussled on the ridge and eventually threw themselves down the incline, tumbling over and over each other, to hit the water with a splash.

Leo touched my arm and pointed a little to the side. He was frowning. I turned to take it in and discovered there was an altercation going on, just below the surface of the water. This one was of a more serious nature.

"Odd," I said, speaking aloud for the first time since we'd settled in. He nodded, and we both kept watching but there wasn't anything to see except the occasional flick of a long muscular tail, the wild splash of water. A squeal of anger was followed by a squeal of distress and the combatants broke off, one of them hightailing it towards us.

I got only a glimpse as it passed us by but it seemed to me it was considerably bigger than its opponent. Biggest otter I'd seen, in fact. I wondered why it had run instead of the smaller one.

The smaller one was already back at play. Leo shrugged and grinned. "I thought mating season was over," he said. "So did she, considering how she treated him."

"Ah," I said, "I missed the opening moves."

We settled back again, nothing to perturb us but the otter follies, which brought us to laughter over and over again. We trusted nothing would interrupt that by tugging at our lines.

Shadow was beginning to lengthen across us. I knew we had another half hour before it would be too dark for us to make our way easily back up to the lodge. "Leo," I said, "want me to head in? Your way will be in shadows long before mine."

"Staying the night at the lodge. I promised Elly I'd do some handiwork for her. Besides, I could do with another of Chris's meals."

There was a stir and a series of splashes to our right, deep in the cove. That large otter, back with friends. There were two troops of them in the loch now. I made a mental note to make sure they weren't overfishing the shrimp or the trout, then I made a second note to see if we couldn't spread the otters to another lake as well. The otters were pretty firmly established on Mirabile but it never hurt to start up another colony elsewhere.

I turned to get a better look, maybe count noses to get a rough estimate of numbers. I counted six, eight, nine separate ripples in the water. Something seemed a little off about them. I got a firm clamp on my suspicious mind and on the stories I'd heard all day and tried to take an unbiased look. They weren't about to hold still long enough for me to get a fix on them through the branches and the shadows that were deepening by the moment.

One twined around an overhang. I could see the characteristic tail but its head was lost in a stand of water lilies. Good fishing there, I knew. The trout always thought they could hide in the water lilies and the otters always knew just where to find them. Then I realized with a start that the water lilies were disappearing.

I frowned. I untied the boat and gestured for Leo to help me get closer. We grabbed at branches to pull the boat along as silently as possible. To no avail: with a sudden flurry of splashes all around, the otters were gone.

"Hell," I said. I unshipped the oars and we continued on over. I was losing too much of the light. I thrust down into the icy water and felt around the stand of lilies, then I grabbed and yanked, splattering water all over Leo. He made not a word of complaint. Instead, he stuck a damp match into his shirt pocket and tried a second one. This one lit.

It told my eyes what my fingers had already learned: the water lily had been neatly chewed. Several other leaves had been nipped off the stems as well—but at an earlier time, to judge from the way the stem had sealed itself. I dropped the plant back in the water and wiped my hands dry on my slacks.

Leo drowned the match and stuck it in his pocket with the first.
It got suddenly very dark and very quiet on the loch.

I decided I didn't want either of us out here without some kind
of protective gear. I reached for the overhang and shoved us back
toward the sunlit side of the loch. It wasn't until I'd unshipped
my oar again that I got my second shock of the day.

That branch was the one I'd seen the otter twined around.
That gave me a belated sense of scale. The "otter" had been a
good eight feet long!

I chewed on the thought all the way back to the lodge. Would
have forgotten the violets altogether but for Leo's refusal to let
that happen. I put my pole back in its place and took the scarlet
violet and its clump of earth from him. Spotted Susan and said,
"Leo wants to see a gene-read. Can you have Chris send rock
lobster for two up to my room?"

"It's on its way." She paused to glance at the violets. "Pretty,"
she said, "I hope—"

"Yeah, me too."

"Hey!" she said suddenly. "I thought you were here for a
break?"

"How else can I lure Leo up to my room?"

"You could just invite him, Mama Jason. That's what you're
always telling us: Keep it simple and straightforward . . ."

"I should keep my mouth shut."

"Then you wouldn't be able to eat your lobster." With that as
her parting shot, Susan vanished back into the dining room. I
paused to poke my head around the corner—empty, just as Chris
had predicted.

We climbed the stairs. I motioned Leo in, laid down the
clump of violets and opened my gear. "Violets first," I said, "as
long as we're about to be interrupted."

I took my sample and cued up the room computer, linked it to
the one back at the lab. There was a message from Mike waiting.
"The daffodils have perked up, so they look good," it said, "and
the troops have returned from the Guernsey wars triumphant.
We'll call if we need you. You do the same."

"You forgot to say how your hand is, dummy," I growled at the screen—then typed the same in, for him to find in the morning.

The first-level gene-read on the violets went fast. The hard part was running it through ships' records looking for a match or a near match. I could let that run all night while I slept through it.

Susan brought the rock lobster and peered over my shoulder as she set it down. "Mama Jason, I can keep an eye on that while you eat if you like."

"Sure," I said, getting up to give her the chair. Leo and I dug into our lobster, with an occasional glance at the monitor. "Watch this part, Leo," I said. Susan had already finished the preliminary and was looking for any tacked-on genes that might be readable.

Susan's fingers danced, then she peered at the screen like she was trying to see through it. Mike gets that same look. I suppose I do, too. "Mama Jason, I can't see anything but the primary helix."

"Okay." Neither did I. "Try a match with violets." To Leo, I added, "We might as well try the easy stuff first. Why run the all-night program if you don't have to." I ducked into the bathroom to wash rock lobster and butter off my fingers.

"No luck," Susan called to me.

When I came out, Leo had disappointment written all over his face. "Buck up," I said. "We're not giving up that easily. Susan, ask the computer if it's got a pattern for something called a 'pansy' or a 'pansies.'"

"'Pansy,'" said Leo and he spelled it for her.

It did. Luckily, that wasn't one of the areas we'd lost data in. "Oh, Mama Jason!" said Susan, "Will you look at *that?*"

We had a match.

"Leo, you lucky dog!" I said. "Your grandma would be proud of you!"

His jaw dropped. "You mean—they really *are* pansies?"

"Dead on," I told him, while Susan grinned like crazy. I patted her on the shoulder—and gave her a bit of a nudge toward the door at the same time. "You bring Susan a sample of the ones you planted around your place, just so she can double-check for stability. But I think you've got exactly what you hoped you had."

I pointed to the left side of the screen. "According to this, they should come in just about every color of the rainbow. We may have to goose them a bit for that—unless you prefer them all red?"

"Authentic," said Leo, "I want them Earth-authentic, as long as you're asking *me*."

"Okay. Tomorrow then," I told Susan. She grinned once more and left.

I sat down at the computer again. Wrote the stuff on the pansy to local memory—then I cleared the screen and called up everything ships' records had on otters.

They didn't eat water lilies, and they didn't come eight feet long. Pointing to the genes in question, I told Leo this.

"Does that mean there *is* a monster in the lake?"

"I can't tell you that. I'm not terribly concerned about something that eats water lilies, Leo, but I do want to know if it's chaining up to something else."

"How do we find out?"

"*I* snag a cell sample from the beasties."

Again his lips pressed together in that wry way. "May I offer you what assistance I can?" A sweeping spread of the hands. "I'm very good at keeping out of the way and at following orders. I'm also a first-rate shot with a rifle and I can tell the difference between a monstrosity and a monster. I promise no shooting unless it's absolutely necessary."

"Let me think on it, Leo." Mostly I wanted to ask Elly if what he said was true.

He must have read my mind, because he smiled and said, "Elly will vouch for me. I'll see you in the morning."

That was all. Except maybe I should mention he kissed my hand on his way out. I was beginning to like Leo more and more.

After he left, I did some thinking on it, then I trotted downstairs to talk to Elly. I leaned against the countertop, careful not to get in the way of her cleaning, and said, "Tell me about Leo."

Elly stopped scrubbing for a moment, looked up, and smiled. "Like you," she said.

"That good or bad?"

The smile broadened into a grin. "Both. That means he's stubborn, loyal, keeps a secret *secret*, plays gruff with the kids but adores them just the same."

"Any permanent attachments?" It popped out before I knew it was coming. I tried to shove it back in, but Elly only laughed harder at my attempt.

"Why, Annie! I believe you've got a crush on Leo!" Still laughing, she pulled out a chair and sat beside me, cupping her chin in her hand. "I shouldn't be surprised. All the kids do."

I gave one of Susan's patented sighs.

"Okay, okay," she said, "I'll leave off. I like it, though. I like Leo and I like you and I think you'd get along together just fine."

"Is he as good a shot as he claims to be? And as judicious about it?"

That sat her upright and looking wary.

"No panic," I said firmly. "You *have* got something in the loch that I want a look at—but it's an herbivore and I doubt it's dangerous. It's big enough to overturn a boat maybe, but—"

"Are you calling in the team?"

"I don't think that's necessary. They could all do with a break—"

"That's what *you* came for. That's hardly fair."

I waved that aside. "Elly, you should know me better by now. I wouldn't have taken this up as a profession if I weren't a born meddler. And I asked about Leo because he offered to give me a hand." I know I scowled. "Money and equipment I can always get—it's the hands we're short."

"You're going to make off with half my kids one of these days."

I couldn't help it. I jerked around to stare at her. She was smiling—and that laugh was threatening to break out all over again. "Annie, surely it's occurred to you that half those kids want to be just like you when they grow up!"

"But—!"

"Oh, dear. Poor Mama Jason. You thought I was raising a whole passel of little Ellies here, didn't you?"

The thing was, I'd never given it any thought at all. More than

likely I just assumed Susan and Chris and Ilanith would take over the lodge and. . . .

Elly patted my hand. "Don't you worry. Chris will run the lodge and you and the rest can still drop by for vacations."

I felt guilty as hell somehow, as if I'd subverted the whole family.

Elly gave me a big hug. "Wipe that look off your face. You'd think I got chimerae instead of proper kids! The only thing I ask is that you don't cart them off until you're sure they're ready."

"You'll worry yourself sick!"

"No. I'll worry the same way I worry about *you*. Do I look sick?"

She stood off and let me look. She looked about as good as anybody could. She knew it, too. Just grinned again and said, "Take Leo with you. Susan, too, if you think she's ready. I warn you, *she* thinks she is, but she'll listen to you on the subject."

And that was the end of it as far as Elly was concerned. I walked back to my room, thoughtful all the way.

Damnify knew how I could have missed it. And there I'd been aggravating the situation as well, calling Susan "my assistant," letting her do the gene-read on Leo's pansies. Then I thought about it some more.

She'd done a damn fine gene-read. If she'd heard Leo talk about the pansies, she'd have no doubt thought to try that second as well.

The more I thought, the more I saw Elly was right. It was just so unexpected that I'd never really looked at it.

I crawled into that comfortable bed and lay there listening to the night sounds off the loch and all the while I was wondering how soon I could put Susan to work. I drifted off into sleep and my dreams were more pleased by it all than I would have admitted to Elly.

I woke, not rested enough, to an insistent shaking of my shoulder and opened my eyes to see a goggle-eyed something inches from my face. Thinking the dream had turned bad, I mumbled at it to go away and rolled over.

"Please, Mama Jason," the bad dream said. "Please, I *gotta*

talk to you. I can't tell Elly, and I'm afraid it's gonna hurt her."

Well, when a bad dream starts threatening Elly, I listen. I sat up and discovered that the bad dream was only Jen, the nine-year-old. "Gimme half a chance, Jen," I said, holding up one hand while I smeared my face around with the other, trying to stretch my eyes into focus so I could see my watch. My watch told me I'd had enough sleep to function rationally, so I levered myself up.

Jen's eyes unpopped, squinched up, and started leaking enormous teardrops. She made a dash for the door, but by then I was awake and I caught her before she made her exit. "Hold on," I said. "You don't just tell me something's out to hurt Elly and then disappear. Ain't done."

Still leaking tears, she wailed, "It's supposed to be a secret . . ."

Which she wanted somebody to force out of her. Okay, I could oblige, and she could tell the rest Mama Jason *made* her tell. I plopped her firmly on the edge of the bed. "Now wipe your nose and tell me what this is about. You'd think *I* was the chimera the way you're staring."

"You gotta promise not to hurt Monster. He's Susan's."

I did nothing of the sort. I waited and she went on, "I didn't know he was so *big*, Mama Jason!" She threw out those two skinny arms to show me just *how* big, which actually made it about three feet long tops, but I knew from the fingertip-to-fingertip glance that went with the arm fling that she meant *much* bigger. "Now I'm scared for Susan!"

"What do you mean, he's *Susan's*?"

"Susan sneaks out at night to feed him. I never saw him, but he must be *awful*. She calls him Monster and he gurgles." She shivered.

I gathered her up and held her until the shivering stopped. Obviously all this had been going on for some time. She'd only broken silence because of Stirzaker's panicky report. "Okay," I said, still patting her, "I want you to let me know the next time Susan sneaks out to feed this Monster of hers—"

She blinked at me solemnly. "She's out there now, Mama Jason."

"Okay," I said. "Out there *where?*"

The bellow off the loch cut me short and brought me to my feet. Unlike Leo, I knew that hadn't been part of a dream. I was already headed for the window when the sound came again. I peered into the night.

Mirabile doesn't have a moon, but for the moment we've got a decent nova. Not enough radiation to worry about, just enough to see glimmers in the dark.

Something huge rippled through the waters of the loch. I stared harder, trying to make it come clear, but it wouldn't. It bellowed again, and an answering bellow came from the distant shore.

Whatever it was, it was huge, even bigger than the drifted otters I'd seen earlier. Had they chained up to something already? There was a splash and another bellow. I remember thinking Elly wouldn't hear it from her room; she was on the downside of the slope, cushioned from the loch noises by the earth of the slope itself.

Then I got a second glimpse of it, a huge head, a long body. With a shock, I realized that it looked like nothing so much as those blurry flat photos of "Nessie."

I turned to throw on some clothes and ran right into Jen, scaring her half to death. "Easy, easy. It's just me," I said, holding her by the shoulders. "Run get Leo—and tell him to bring his rifle." I gave her a push for the door and that kid moved like a house afire.

So did Leo. By the time I'd got my gear together, double-checking the flare gun to make sure it had a healthy charge left, he was on my doorstep, rifle in hand.

We ran down the steps together, pausing only once—to ask Jen which way Susan had gone. Jen said, "Down to the loch, she calls it your favorite place! I thought you'd *know!*" She was on the verge of another wail.

"I know," I said. "Now you wait here. If we're not back in two hours, you wake Elly and tell her to get on the phone to Mike."

"Mike," she repeated, "Mike. Two hours." She plopped herself down on the floor directly opposite the clock. I knew I could count on her.

Leo and I switched on flashlights and started into the woods. I let him lead for the time being—he knew the paths better than I did and I wanted to move as fast as possible. We made no attempt to be quiet at it, either. In the dark and shorthanded, I've always preferred scaring the creature off to facing it down.

We got to the boats in record time. Sure enough, one of them was gone. Leo and I pushed off and splashed across the loch, Leo rowing, me with the shotgun in one hand and the flare gun in the other.

Nine times out of ten, the flare gun is enough to turn a Dragon's Tooth around and head it away from you. The shotgun's there for that tenth time. Or in case it was threatening Susan.

A couple of large things rushed noisily through the woods to our far right. They might have been stag. They might not have been. Neither Leo nor I got a look at them.

"Duck," said Leo, and I did and missed being clobbered by one of those overhanging branches by about a quarter of an inch. Turning, I made out the boat Susan had used. There was just enough proper shore there that we could beach ours besides it.

"All right, Susan," I said into the shadows. "Enough is enough. Come on out. At *my* age, I *need* my beauty sleep."

Leo snorted.

There was a quiet crackle behind him, and Susan crawled out from the undergrowth looking sheepish. "I only wanted it to be a surprise," she said. She looked all around her and brightened. "It still is—you've scared them off!"

"When you're as old and cranky as I am, there's nothing you like *less* than a surprise," I said.

"Oh." She raked twigs out of her hair. "Then if I can get them to come out again, would you take your birthday present a month early?"

Leo and I glanced at each other. I knew we were both thinking about Jen, sitting in the hallway, worrying. "Two hours and not a minute more," Leo said.

"Okay, Susan. See if you can get 'em out. I'll want a cell sample too." I rummaged through my gear for the snagger. Nice little gadget, that. Like an arrow on a string. Fire it off without a sound, it snaps at the critter with less than a fly sting (I know, I had Mike try it on me when he jury-rigged the first one), and you pull back the string with a sample on the end of it.

"Sit down then and be quiet."

We did. Susan ducked into the undergrowth a second time and came out with half a loaf of Chris's bread. She made the same chucking noise I'd heard her use to call her otters. She was expecting something low to the ground, I realized. Not the enormous thing I'd seen swimming in the loch.

I heard no more sounds from that direction, to my relief. I wish I could have thought I'd dreamed the entire thing but I knew I hadn't. What's worse, I picked that time to remember that one of the Nessie theories had made her out a displaced plesiosaur.

I was about to call a halt and get us all the hell out of there till daylight and a full team, when something stirred in the bushes. Susan chucked at it and held out a bit of bread.

It poked its nose into the circle of light from our flashes and blinked at us. It was the saddest-looking excuse for a creature I'd ever seen—the head was the shape of an old boot with jackass ears stuck on it.

"C'mon, Monster," Susan coaxed. "You know how much you love Chris's bread. Don't worry about them. They're noisy but they won't hurt you."

Sure enough, it humped its way out. It looked even worse when you saw the whole of it. What I'd thought was an otter wasn't. Oh, the body was otter, all eight feet of it, but the head didn't go with the rest. After a moment's hesitation, it made an uncertain lowing noise, then snuffled at Susan, and took the piece of bread in its otter paws and crammed it down its mouth.

Then it bellowed, startling all three of us.

"He just learned how to do that this year," Susan said, a

pleased sort of admiration in her voice. The undergrowth around us stirred.

Out of the corner of my eye, I saw Leo level his rifle. Susan looked at him, worried. "He won't shoot unless something goes wrong, kiddo," I said as softly as I could and still be heard. "He promised me."

Susan nodded. "Okay, Monster. You can call them out then."

She needn't have said it. That bellow already had. There were maybe a dozen of them, all alike, all of them painfully ugly. No, that's the wrong way to put it—they were all *laughably* ugly.

The one she'd dubbed "Monster" edged closer to me. Nosy like the otters, too. It whuffled at my hand. Damn if that head wasn't purely herbivore. The teeth could give you a nasty nip from the looks of them, but it was deer family. The ugly branch of it anyhow.

A second one crawled into Leo's lap. It was trying to make off with his belt buckle. Susan chucked at it and bribed it away with bread. "She's such a thief. If you're not careful, she'll take anything that's shiny. Like the otters, really."

Yes, they were. The behavior was the same I'd seen from Susan's otters—but now I understood why the otters had chased one of these away this afternoon. They were recognizably *not* otters, even if they thought they *were*. Like humans, otters are very conservative about what they consider one of them.

Pretty soon the bread was gone. Monster hustled up the troops and headed them out, with one last look over his shoulder at us.

I popped him neatly with the snagger before Susan could raise a protest. He grunted and gnawed for a moment at his hip, the way a dog would for a flea, then he spotted the snagger moving away from him and pounced.

I had a tug of war on my hands. Susan got into the act and so did a handful of Monster's fellow monsters.

Leo laughed. It was enough to startle them away. I fell over and Susan landed on top of me. She was giggling too, but she crawled over and got up, triumphant, with the sample in her hands.

"You didn't need it, Mama Jason," Susan said, "but I've

decided to forgive you. Monster thought it was a good game."
She giggled again and added impishly, "So did I."

"Fine," I said. "I hate to spoil the party, but it's time we got
back to the lodge. We're all going to feel like hell in the
morning."

Susan yawned. "I s'pose so. They lose interest pretty fast once
I run out of bread."

"Susan, you row Leo back."

"You're not coming?" she said.

"Two boats," I pointed out. Susan was sleepy enough that she
didn't ask why I wanted Leo in her boat. Leo blinked at me once,
caught on, and climbed into the boat with his rifle across his
knees.

By the time we reached the lodge, we were all pretty well
knocked out. Jen gave us a big grin of relief to welcome us in. But
two steps later we ran hard into Elly's scowl, not to mention
Chris's, Ilanith's, and a half dozens others.

"I found Jen sitting in the hall watching the clock," Elly said.
"She wouldn't go to bed and she wouldn't say why. Once I
counted noses, I discovered the three of you were missing. So
you"—that was me, of course—"owe me the explanation you
wouldn't let her give me."

"There's something in the loch," I said. "We got a sample and
I'll check it out tomorrow. Right now, we all need some sleep."

"Liar," said Chris. "Who's hungry? Midnight snacks"—she
glanced at the clock and corrected—"whatever, food's waiting."

Everybody obligingly trooped into the kitchen, lured by the
smell of chowder. I followed, knowing this meant I wasn't going
to get off the hook without a full explanation. That meant no way
of covering Susan's tracks.

We settled down and dived ravenously into the chowder. Chris
poured a box of crackers into a serving tray. "There's no bread,"
she said with finality, eying Susan to let us all know who was
responsible for this woeful state of affairs.

Susan squirmed. "Next time I'll take them crackers. They like
your bread better, though."

"If you'd *asked*," Chris said, "I'd have made a couple of extra loaves."

"I wanted it to be a surprise from Mama Jason." She looked around the table. "You *know* how hard it is to think up a birthday present for her!" She pushed away from the table. "Wait! I'll be right back. I'll show you!"

I concentrated on the chowder. Birthday present, indeed! As if I needed some present other than the fact of those kids themselves. If Susan hadn't opened her mouth, Elly would've assumed I taken her along with us, as Elly'd suggested earlier. Glancing up, I saw Elly rest a sympathetic eye on me.

Well, I was off the hook, but Susan sure as hell wasn't.

There was a clamor of footsteps on the stairs and Susan was back with a huge box, full to overspilling with papers and computer tapes. Chris shoved aside the pot of chowder to make space for them.

Susan pulled out her pocket computer and plugged it into the wall modem. "I did it right, Mama Jason. See if I didn't."

The photo album wasn't regulation but as the first page was a very pretty hologram (I recognized Ilanith's work) that spelled out "Happy Birthday, Mama Jason!" in imitation fireworks I could hardly complain. The second page was a holo of a mother otter and her pups. The pup in the foreground was deformed—the same way the creatures Susan had fed Chris's bread to were.

"That's Monster," Susan said, thrusting a finger at the holo. She peeled a strip of tape from beneath the holo and fed it to the computer. "That's his gene-read." She glanced at Chris. "I lured his mother away with bread to get the cell sample. The otters love your bread too. I never used the fresh bread, Chris, only the stale stuff."

Chris nodded. "I know. I thought it was all going to the otters, though."

"More like 'odders,'" Leo put in, grinning. "Two *dees*."

Susan giggled. "I like that. Let's call 'em Odders, Mama Jason."

"Your critters," I said. "Naming it's your privilege."

"Odders is right." Chris peered over my shoulder and said to Susan, "Why were you feeding Dragon's Teeth?"

"He's so ugly, he's cute. The first ones got abandoned by their mothers. She"—Susan tapped the holo again—"decided to keep hers. Got ostracized for it, too, Mama Jason."

I nodded absently. That happened often enough. I was well into the gene-read Susan had done on her Monster. It was a good, thorough piece of work. I couldn't have done better myself.

Purely herbivorous—and among the things you could guarantee it'd eat were water lilies and clogweed. That stopped me dead in my tracks. I looked up. "It eats clogweed!"

Susan dimpled. "It loves it! That's why it likes Chris's bread better than crackers."

"Why you—" Chris, utterly outraged, stood up so suddenly Elly had to catch at her bowl to keep from slopping chowder on everything.

I laughed. "Down, Chris! She's not insulting your bread! You use brandyflour in it—and brandyflour has almost the identical nutrients in it that clogweed has."

"You mean I could use clogweed to make my bread?" The idea appealed to Chris. She sat down again and looked at Susan with full attention.

"No, you can't," Susan said. "It's got a lot of things in it humans can't eat."

Leo said, "I'm not following again. Susan—?"

"Simply, Noisy. Clogweed's a major nuisance. Mostly it's taken care of by sheer heavy labor. Around Torville, everybody goes down to the canals and the irrigation ditches once a month or so and pulls the clogweed out by hand. When I saw Monster would eat clogweed, I figured he'd be worth keeping—if we could, that is."

"Not bad," said Ilanith. "I wondered why the intake valves had been so easy to clean lately." She leaned over to look at Monster's holo. "Two years old now, right?"

"Four," said Susan. "Only one wouldn't have made much difference. Mama Jason, I did a gene-read every year on them.

Those're on the next pages. In case I missed something the first time."

I saw that. The whole EC was there too, along with more holos and her search for matches with ships' records. There were no matches, so the thing was either a Dragon's Tooth or an intermediate. Just this year, she'd started a careful check for secondary and tertiary helices.

She saw how far I'd gotten in her records and said, apologetically, "There's a secondary helix, but I didn't have a clue where to look for a match in ships' records, so I had to do it by brute force."

I handed her the sample I'd gotten from Monster little over a half hour ago. "Here, a fresh sample is always helpful."

She took it, then looked up at me wildly. "You mean me? You want me to keep working on it?"

"You want *me* to work on *my* birthday present?" I might just as well have given *her* a present, the way she lit up.

I yawned—it was that or laugh. "I'm going to bed. But nobody's to go down to the loch until Susan's done with her gene-read."

Elly frowned. "Annie? We've got to net tomorrow or Chris won't have anything to cook."

So there was no escaping it after all. "Take a holiday, Elly. There's something in the loch that isn't Susan's clogweed-eaters. Leo and I will do a little looking around tomorrow—armed."

"Oh, Mama Jason!" Susan looked distraught. "You don't think Monster chained up to a *real* monster, do you?" Her eyes squinched up; she was close to tears.

"Hey!" I pulled her into a hug. For a moment I didn't know what else to say, then I remembered the first time Mike had gotten a nasty alternative instead of what he wanted. "I'll tell you just what I've said to Mike: sometimes you have to risk the bad to get the good."

I pushed her a bit away to see if that had worked. Not really. "Listen, honey, do you know how Mike and I planned to spend our winter vacation this year?"

When she shook her head I knew I had her attention, no

matter how distressed. I told her: "Cobbling together something that would eat clogweed. If all we have to do is stabilize your monsters, you've saved us years of work!"

I pulled her to me for another hug. "Best birthday present I've had in years!"

That, finally, brought a smile from her. It was a little wan, but it was there.

"So here's the game plan. You load the sample tonight while it's fresh, then get a good night's sleep and do the gene-read tomorrow while *you're* fresh. Leo and I will do a little tracking as soon as it's light enough. Everybody else gets to sleep late."

That did nothing to take the worry out of Elly's or Chris's eyes but I could see they'd both go along with it, though they were still concerned somebody might decide the kids should be evacuated. "Elly," I said, "we'll work something out, I promise."

That eased the tension in her eyes somewhat, even though I hadn't the vaguest idea *what* we'd work out. Still, a good night's sleep—even a short one—was always guaranteed to help. With a few more hugs, I stumbled off to bed.

Morning came the way it usually did for me this time of year—much too early. Leo, bless him, was up but quiet. The first thing I wanted was a good look at the otters' playground. That was near enough to where I'd seen the creature that maybe we could find some tracks. This side of Loch Moose got its sunlight early if at all. Luckily, the day was a good one and the scenery was enough to make you glad you had eyes and ears and a nose.

I stood for a moment trying to orient myself, then pointed. "Somewhere around here. I'm pretty sure that's where I heard it." We separated.

Something that big should have left visible evidence of its passing. The popcorn tree was my first break. Something had eaten all the lower leaves from it and done some desultory gnawing at its bark into the bargain. That was several days earlier, from the look of the wood, so I didn't find any tracks to go with it.

Now, the popcorn tree's native to Mirabile, so we were dealing with a creature that either didn't have long to live or was a

Dragon's Tooth suited to the EC. Still, it was an herbivore, unless it was one of those exceptions that nibbled trees for some reason other than nourishment.

But it was *big*! I might have discounted the height it could reach as something that stood on its hind feet and stretched, but this matched the glimpse I'd gotten by nova light.

Leo called and I went to see what he'd found. When I caught up with him, he was staring at the ground. "Annie, this thing weights a ton!" He pointed.

Hoofprints sunk deep into the damp ground. He meant "ton" in the literal sense. I stooped for a closer look, then unshipped my backpack, and got out my gear. "Get me a little water, will you, Leo?" I handed him a folded container. "I want to make a plaster cast. Hey!" I added as an afterthought. "Keep your eyes open!"

He grinned. "Hard to miss something that size."

"You have up to now," I pointed out. I wasn't being snide, just realistic. I'm happy to say he understood me.

I went back to examining the print. It was definitely not deer, though it looked related. The red deer survived by sticking to a strict diet of Earth-authentic, which meant I couldn't draw any real conclusions from the similarities. I was still betting herbivore, though maybe it was just because I was hoping.

I was purely tired of things that bit or mangled or otherwise made my life miserable. Seemed to me it was about time the Dragon's Teeth started to balance out and produce something useful.

By the time we mixed the plaster and slopped it into the print, I'd decided that I should be grateful for Susan's clogweed-eaters and Leo's pansies and not expect too much of our huge surprise package.

"Leo, I think it's an herbivore. That doesn't mean it isn't dangerous—you know what a stag can do—but it means I don't want it shot on sight."

"You wouldn't want it shot on sight if it *were* a carnivore," he said. "If I didn't shoot the first beastly on sight, I'm not likely to shoot *this* without good reason."

I fixed him with a look of pure disgust. The disgust was aimed at me, though. I knew the name Leonov Denness should have rung bells, but I'd gotten distracted by the nickname.

Back when he was Leonov *Opener* Denness, he'd been the scout that opened and mapped all the new territory from Ranomafana to Goddamn! He brought back cell samples of everything he found, that being part of the job; but he'd also brought back a live specimen of the beastly, which was at least as nasty as the average kangaroo rex and could fly to boot. When Granddaddy Jason asked him why he'd gone to the trouble, he'd only shrugged and said, "Best you observe its habits as well as its genes."

The decision on the beastly had been to push it back from the inhabited areas rather than to shoot on sight. Nasty as it was, it could be driven off by loud sounds (bronze bells, now that I thought of it!) and it made a specialty of hunting what passed for rats on Mirabile. Those rats were considerably worse than having to yell yourself hoarse when you traveled through the plains farmlands.

"If you'd jogged my memory earlier," I said, "I wouldn't have bothered to check your credentials with Elly."

"Annie, I didn't think bragging was in order."

"Facts are a little different than brags. Now I can stop worrying about your health and get down to serious business."

Leaving the plaster to harden, I headed him down to the boats. "Two boats today, Leonov Opener Denness. You stake out that side of the loch, I'll stake out this. Much as I'd enjoy your company, this gives us two chances to spot something and the sooner we get this sorted out, the better it'll be for Elly. Whistle if you spot anything. Otherwise, I'll meet you back here an hour after dusk."

We'd probably have to do a nighttime wait too, but I was hoping the thing wasn't strictly nocturnal. If it was, I'd need more equipment, which meant calling Mike, which meant making it formal and public.

There's nothing more irritating than waiting for a Dragon's Tooth to rear its ugly head, even if you're sure the head's herbivorous. After all these years, I'm pretty good at it. Besides, there were otters and odders to watch, and it was one of those perfect days on Loch Moose. I'd have been out contemplative fishing anyhow. This just took its toll of watching and waiting, which is not nearly as restful. Somewhere in the back of my mind, the plesiosaur still swam sinisterly in Loch Ness.

Susan's odders, as ugly as they were, proved in action almost as much fun as the otters, though considerably sillier looking. And observation proved her right—several times I saw them dive down and come up with a mouthful of lilies or clogweed.

A breeze came up—one of those lovely ones that Loch Moose is justly famous for—soft and sweet and smelling of lilies and pine and popcorn tree.

The pines began to smoke. I found myself grateful to the Dragon's Tooth for putting me on the loch at the right time to see it.

The whole loch misted over with drifting golden clouds of pollen. I could scarcely see my hand in front of my face. That, of course, was when I heard it. First a soft thud of hooves, then something easing into the water. Something big. I strained to see, but the golden mist made it impossible.

I was damned glad Leo had told me his past history, otherwise I'd have worried. I knew he was doing exactly what I was doing at that moment—keeping dead silent and listening. I brought up my flare gun in one hand and my snagger in the other. Even if it was a plesiosaur, a flare right in the face should drive it off. I couldn't bring myself to raise the shotgun. Must be I'm mellowing in my old age.

I could still hear the splash and play of the otters and the odders on either side of me. That was a good sign as well. They'd decided it wasn't a hazard to them.

My nerves were singing, though, as I heard the soft splashing coming toward me. I turned toward the sound, but still couldn't see a thing. There was a gurgle, like water being sucked down a drain, and suddenly I couldn't locate it by ear anymore. I guessed it had submerged, but that didn't do a thing for my nerves. . . .

The best I could do was keep an eye on the surface of the water where it should have been heading if it had followed a straight line—and that was directly under my boat. Looking straight down, I could barely make out a dark bulk. I could believe the ton estimate.

It reached the other side. I lost sight of it momentarily. Then, with a surge that brought up an entire float of lilies and splattered water all over me, it surfaced not ten feet from my boat, to eye me with a glare.

I'd thought Susan's odders were as ugly as things came, but this topped them without even trying. Even through the mist, I could see it now.

Like Susan's Monster, it had that same old-boot-shaped head, the same flopping mule ears, streaming water now. What I'd taken for its head in the glimpse I'd gotten the previous night was actually the most unbelievable set of antlers I'd ever seen in my life, like huge gnarled up-raised palms. What Stirzaker had taken for grasping hands, I realized—only at the moment they were filled to the brim with a tangle of scarlet water lilies. From its throat, a flap of flesh dangled dripping like a wet beard. It stared at me with solemn black eyes and munched thoughtfully on the nearest of the dangling lilies. The drifting pollen was slowly turning it to gold.

I swear I didn't know whether to laugh or to cry.

For a moment, I just stared, and it stared back, looking away only long enough to tilt another lily into its mouth. Then I remembered what I was there for and raised the snagger. I got it first try, snapped the snagger to retrieve.

The thing jerked back, glared, then let out a bellow that Mike must have heard back in the lab. It started to swim closer.

"BACK OFF!" I bellowed. Truthfully, I didn't think it was angered, just nosy, but I didn't want to find out the hard way. I raised the flare gun.

From the distance came the sound of splashing oars. "Annie!" Leo yelled. "I'm coming. Hang on!"

The creature backpedaled in the water and cocked its head, lilies and all, toward the sound of Leo's boat. Interested all over again, it started that way at a very efficient paddle. I got a glimpse of a hump just at the shoulders, followed by the curve of a rump, followed by a tiny flop of tail like a deer's. The same view Pastides had gotten, no doubt.

Suddenly, from the direction of Leo's boat, there came the clamor of a bell. The creature backpedaled again, ears twitching.

With a splash of utter panic, the creature turned around in the water, dived for cover, and swam for shore. I could hear it crash into the undergrowth even over the clanging of the bell.

"Enough, Leo, enough! It's gone!" He shut up with the bell and we called to each other until he found me through the mist. I'm sorry to say, by the time he pulled alongside, I was laughing so hard there were tears streaming down my cheeks.

Leo's face—what I could see of it—went through about three changes of expression in as many seconds. He laid aside his bell—it was a big, bronze beastly-scarebell—and sighed with relief. He too was gold from all the pollen.

I wiped my eyes and grinned at him. "I wish I could say, 'Saved by the bell,' but the thing wasn't really a danger. Clumsy maybe. Possibly aggressive if annoyed, but—" I burst into laughter again.

Leo said amiably, "I'm sure you'll tell me about it when you get your breath back."

I nodded. Pulling in the sample the snagger had caught, I waved him toward the shore. When we were halfway up the hill to the lodge, I said, "Please, Leo, don't ask until I can check my sample."

He spread his hands. "At least I know it's not a plesiosaur."

I had the urge again—and found the laughter had worn down to hiccupping giggles.

When we got to the lodge, I didn't have to yell for them—we got surrounded the moment we hit the porch. Elly did a full body check on both of us, which meant she wound up as pollen-covered as we were.

"Susan," I said through the chaos of a dozen questions at once, "run that for me. Let's see what we've got." I held out the sample.

"Me?" Susan squeaked.

"You," I said. I took Leo's arm, well above the rifle, and said, "We want some eats, and then I want to see Susan's results from this morning."

I cued the computer over a bowl of steaming chowder, calling up the odder sample Susan had been working on. She'd found some stuff in the twists all right.

All the possibilities were herbivorous, though, and I was betting that one of them would match my silly-looking friend in the loch. I giggled again, I'm afraid. I had a pretty good idea what we were dealing with, but I had to be sure before I let those kids back out on the loch.

By the time we'd finished our chowder, Susan had come charging down the stairs. She punched up the results on my monitor—she was not just fast, she was good.

I called up ships' records and went straight to my best guess. At a glance, we had a match but I went through gene by gene and found the one drift.

"It's a match!" Ilanith crowed from behind me. "First try, too, Mama Jason!"

Everybody focused on the monitor. "Look again, kiddo. Only ninety-nine percent match." I pointed out the drifted genes. "Those mean it can eat your popcorn trees without so much as a stomach upset."

Ilanith said, "That's okay with me. Elly? Do you mind?"

"I don't know," Elly said. "What *is* it, Annie? Can we live with it?"

I called up ships' records on the behavior patterns of the authentic creature and moved aside to let Elly have a look. "I suspect you'll all have to carry Leo's secret weapon when you go down to the loch to fish or swim, but other than that I don't see much of a problem."

Leo thumped me on the back. "Damn you, woman, what *is* it?"

Elly'd gotten a film that might have been my creature's twin. She looked taken aback at first, then she too giggled. "That's the silliest thing I've seen in years! Come on, Annie, what is it?"

"Honey, Loch Moose has got its first moose."

"No!" Leo shouted, but he followed it with a laugh as he crowded in with the rest to look at the screen.

Only Susan wasn't laughing. She caught my hand and pulled

me down to whisper, "Will they let us keep it if it's only ninety-nine percent? It's not *good* for anything, like the odders are."

I patted her hand. "It's good for a laugh. I say it's a keeper." I was not about to let this go the way of the kangaroo rex.

"Now I understand why I found her in that state," Leo was saying. He pointed accusingly at me. "This woman was laughing so hard she could scarcely catch her breath."

"You didn't see the damn thing crowned with water lilies and chewing on them while it contemplated the oddity in the boat. You'd have been as helpless as I was."

"Unbelievable," he said.

"Worse," I told him, "in this case, seeing isn't believing. I still can't believe in something like that. The mind won't encompass it."

He laughed at the screen, then again at me. "Maybe that accounts for your granddaddy's monster. It was so silly-looking anybody who saw it wouldn't believe his own eyes."

I couldn't help it—I kissed him on the cheek. "Leo, you're a genius!"

He squeaked like Susan. "Me? What did I do?"

"Elly," I said, "congratulations! You now have the only lodge on Mirabile with an Earth-authentic Loch Ness monster." I grinned at Susan, who caught on immediately. I swear her smile started at the mouth and ran all the way down to her toes.

Feeling rather smug, I went on, "Leo will make bells so your lodgers can scare it away if it gets too close to them, won't you, Leo?"

"Oh!" said Leo. He considered the idea. "You know, Annie, it might just work. If everybody went to Loch Ness to try to get a glimpse of the monster, maybe they'll come here, too. Scary but safe."

"Exactly." I fixed him with a look. "Now how do we go about it?"

He grinned. "We follow our family traditions: we tell stories."

"You think if I hang around for a week or so that'll make it a safe monster?"

"Yeah, I think so."

"Good," I said. "Susan? What's the verdict? Are you going off to the lab? If I'm going to stay here, *somebody*'ll have to help Mike coddle those red daffodils."

No squeak this time. Her mouth dropped open but what came out was, "Uh, yes. Uh, Elly?"

Elly nodded with a smile, sad but proud all in one.

So while they bustled about packing, I had a chance to read through all the material in ships' records on both moose and Nessie. By the time they were ready to leave for town, I had a pretty good idea of our game plan. I sent Susan off with instructions to run a full gene-read on both creatures. Brute force on the moose, to make sure it wouldn't chain up to something bigger and nastier.

Then we co-opted the rest of Elly's kids. Leo gave each of them a different version of our monster tale to tell.

Jen, I thought, did it best. She got so excited when she told it that her eyes popped and she got incoherent, greatly enhancing the tale of how Leonov Opener Denness had saved Annie Jason Masmajean from the monster in Loch Moose.

Leo brought bells from his workshop. They'd been intended to keep beastlies away in the northern territory, but there was no reason they wouldn't do just as good a job against a monster that was Earth-authentic.

Two days later, the inn was full of overnighters—much to Elly's surprise and delight—all hoping for a glimpse of the Loch Moose monster.

In my room, late night and by nova-light, Leo got his first peek at the creature. Once again it was swimming in the loch. He stared long and hard out the window. After a long moment, he remembered the task we'd set ourselves. "Should I wake the rest of the lodgers, do you think?"

"No," I said, "you just tell them about it at breakfast. Anybody who doesn't see it tonight will stay another night, hoping."

"You're a wicked old lady."

I raised Ilanith's camera to the window. "Yup," I said, and, twisting the lens deliberately out of focus, I snapped a picture.

"Hope that didn't come out well," I said.

If I'd thought that was the end of it, I'd thought wrong.

Aklilu crawled out from under the covers and bounced once on the edge of the bed. "Now tell me another story, Mama Jason," he said.

"Another? You want another?" I gave a sidelong glance at Elly.

"Another!" shouted Aklilu. "Another!" The bed squealed in time as his bounce got insistent. "Come on, Nikolai," he coaxed. "You ask her, too!"

Good thing all the furniture at Loch Moose Lodge is childproof or there wouldn't be any. Of course, if he managed to get Nikolai to join in, there'd be nothing left of anything.

Nikolai looked from me to Elly, then laughed and swept Aklilu into his lap. "Settle down, kiddo," he said. "I want to hear another story."

"Go ahead, Annie," Elly said. "I know the symptoms."

And I know when I'm licked. "Back under the covers with you," I told Aklilu and, to my surprise, he burrowed back into bed on the spot. "Which one?"

"You pick," Nikolai said to Aklilu.

Aklilu just grinned and cocked his head at me. "You know, Mama Jason. . . ."

"Yeah," I said, grinning back. "Same one you always want to hear. But, since Nikolai hasn't heard it, I guess I could stand to tell it one more time."

2

The Return of the Kangaroo Rex

I'D BEEN STARING at the monitor so long all the genes were beginning to look alike to me. They shouldn't have, of course—this gene-read was native Mirabilan, so it was a whole new kettle of fish.

That's an American Guild expression, but it's the right one. At a casual look, had the critter been Earth-based, we'd have classed it as fish and left it at that. The problem was that it had taken a liking to our rice crop, and, if we didn't do something quick, nobody on Mirabile'd see a chow fun noodle ever again. So I went back to staring, trying to force those genes into patterns the team and I could cope with.

Moving the rice fields didn't guarantee we'd find a place free of them. In the first place, it encysted in dry ground, meaning you never knew where it'd pop up until you flooded the area. In the second place, it could leap like a salmon from the first place *to* the second place. It had already demonstrated its ability to spread

43

from one field to the next. Susan had measured a twelve-foot leap.

The prospect got dimmer when Chie-Hoon caught them making that same leap from dry ground. Their limit was some five or six leaps until they hit water again, but that gave them quite a range.

It was as pretty a piece of native bioengineering as I've seen, one I could appreciate even if the rice growers couldn't. Wiping 'em out wholesale was not an option on *my* list, but I knew the farmers would be thinking along those lines if we didn't come up with something by next growing season.

I don't mess with the Mirabilan ecology any more than I have to. We don't know enough about it to know what we're getting into. Even if I thought we could do it, we'd be fools to try to wipe out any native species. The Earth-authentic species we've imported have played havoc enough with the Mirabilan ecology.

I wasn't paying much attention to anything but the problem at hand, so when Susan exclaimed, "Noisy! You look *awful*," I practically jumped out of my skin and busted my elbow turning my chair.

She wasn't kidding. Leo did look awful. His white hair looked like something had nested in it; he was bleeding—no, had bled profusely—across the cheek; his shirt hung in tatters from the shoulder and there were raking claw marks along his upper arms. Mike went scrambling for the emergency kit.

The only thing that spoiled the impact of all this disaster was that Leo was grinning from ear to ear. "Now, is that any way to greet an old friend?" he said to Susan. "Especially one who's come courting?"

He turned the grin on me and it got broader and brighter. Then he made me a deep formal bow and started in: "Annie Jason Masmajean, I, Leonov Bellmaker Denness, beg you to hear my petition."

I got to my feet and bowed back, just as deeply and formally, to let him know I'd be glad to hear him out. He made a second bow, deeper than the first, and went on: "I have brought you a gift in symbol of my intentions. . . ."

Mike had the medical kit but he stood frozen. Chances were

neither he nor Susan had ever seen a ship's-formal proposal except in the old films. The novelty of it kept either from interrupting. Just as well. I was enjoying the performance: Leo has flair.

Besides, I wouldn't dream of interrupting a man in the process of cataloguing my virtues, even if some of those "virtues" would have raised eyebrows in a lot of other people. I especially liked being called "reasonably stubborn."

At last Leo got to the wrap-up. "It is my hope that you will accept my gift and consider my suit." He finished off with yet another bow.

Seeing he was done spurred Mike and Susan into action. Susan held Leo down while Mike worked him over with alcohol swabs. "No respect for ritual," Leo complained. "Back 'em off, Annie, can't you? I'm not senile yet! I *did* clean the wounds."

Leo had spent years as a scout, so I didn't doubt his good sense. He'd hardly have lived to the ripe old age he had if he hadn't been cautious about infection in the bush.

To the two of them, he protested, "The lady hasn't answered yet."

"Back off," I told the kids.

They didn't until I advanced on them. Mike took two steps away from Leo, put his hands behind his back, and said to Susan, "*Now* he's going to get it." Susan nodded.

Leo just kept grinning, so I gave him a huge hug hello to make sure nothing was broken. The rest of him looked just fine, so I stepped back and bowed once more to meet the requirements of the ritual. "Leo Bellmaker Denness, I, Annie Jason Masmajean, am sufficiently intrigued to view your gift."

He crooked a finger and led me outside, Mike and Susan right behind. "In the back of the truck. Don't open that door until you've had a good look!"

So we climbed the back bumper and all crowded to the window for a good look. We didn't get one at first. Whatever it was was mad as all hell, and launched itself at the door hard enough to rattle the window and make the three of us jump back en masse. The door held.

Leo said, "It's been doing that all the way from Last Edges. Hasn't gotten through the door yet, but I'm a little worried it might hurt itself."

"It's not itself it wants to hurt," Susan said.

"You'd be pissed, too, if somebody wrestled you away from your mama and shoved you into the back of a truck headed god-knows-where," Leo said.

The door stopped rattling. I got a foot on the back bumper and hoisted myself up for a second try. Leo's present glared at me through the window and snarled. I snarled back in the same tone.

Since it was a youngster and I was an unknown, it backed off with a hop, letting me get a good look. In overall shape, it was kangaroo, but it had the loveliest set of stripes across the hips I'd ever seen—and the jaw! Oh, the jaw! It opened that jaw to warn me to keep back, and the head split almost to the ear, to show me the sharpest set of carnivore teeth in history.

"Oh, Leo," I murmured, stepping down from my perch. "That's the nicest present anybody's ever brought me." I gave him another big hug and a thorough kiss for good measure. "Leonov Bellmaker Denness, I accept both your gift and your suit."

He beamed. "I knew I got it right."

"Oh, shit!" said Mike, from behind me. "Susan! It's a goddam kangaroo rex!" He stared at Leo in disbelief. "Are you telling me this man brought you a *kangaroo rex* as a courting present?"

Susan, in turn, looked at *Mike* in disbelief. "It's perfect, you idiot! It means Noisy knows exactly what kind of person she is, and how to please her. Don't you understand anything?"

That would have developed into a squabble—that's the usual outcome when those two get going—but the kangaroo rex slammed against the door of the trunk again and brought them both back to their senses.

"Leo," I said, "go on over to my house and get yourself cleaned up. We'll wrestle the thing into a cage. Then I want to hear all about it."

He nodded. "Sure. Two things first, though. Pick the right cage—I saw that thing jump a six-foot fence—then contact Moustafa Herder Kozlev or Janzen Herder Lizhi in Last Edges.

I told Moustafa I'd make the official report on his Dragon's Tooth but I doubt he believes me." He examined a set of skinned knuckles. "Not when I punched him to keep him from shooting it."

"My hero," I said, meaning it.

He kissed my hand and vanished in the direction of my house. I turned to my available team members and said, "Don't just stand there with your eyes hanging out of your heads. Let's get to work."

BY THE TIME we'd gotten an enclosure ready for the creature, Chie-Hoon and Selima had returned from up-country, where they'd been watching those damned hopping fish in the act. Just as well, because it took all five of us to maneuver the kangaroo rex safely out of the truck and into captivity.

Most of us wound up with bruises. It was still mad as all hell. It slammed each side on the fence in turn (didn't take it but two hops to cross the enclosure either) and once shot up and cracked its head on the overhead wire. That settled it down a bit. I sent Selima to get it some meat.

I couldn't take my eyes off the thing. I hadn't seen one for nine years.

"Another outbreak of kangaroo rexes," said Chie-Hoon. "Just what we needed. I assume it sprang from the kangaroos around Gogol?"

"Last Edges," I said. That didn't surprise me, the EC around Last Edges being almost identical to that around Gogol. "Contact Herders Kozlev and Lizhi up there. Tell them we've been notified. Find out if they've seen any more—"

"The usual drill," said Chie-Hoon.

"The usual drill."

Selima came back. She'd brought one of the snaggers Mike invented and let him do the honors of getting the cell sample while she distracted it with the meat. Or tried to. The snagger doesn't do more than pinprick, but that was enough to rile the rex into slamming against the fence again, trying to get at Mike while he reeled the sample through the chain link.

Mike jerked back but the sample came with him. He held it

out to me. "Hardly necessary," he said. "I know what we're gonna find."

So did I. There was no doubt in my mind that the sample would match those from the last outbreak gene for gene. The kangaroo rex had settled down, wolfing at the meat Selima had tossed it. "It eats gladrats," said Selima, looking surprised. "It can't be all bad."

Not as far as I was concerned, it couldn't be all bad. If it was a Dragon's Tooth, it was a beautifully constructed one—completely viable.

It was possible that the kangaroo rex was just an intermediate, a middle step between a kangaroo and anything from a gerbil to a water buffalo. Right now, however, it was a kangaroo rex, and impressive as all hell.

"You watch it, Mama Jason," Susan said. "I'll do the gene-read." She reached for the sample as if she had a vested interest in the beast herself. She figured she did, at least. Must have been all the times she'd made me tell the story of the first outbreak. I handed the sample over.

Then I just stood there quietly and appreciated it. About three feet tall (not counting the tail, of course), it was already quite capable of surviving on its own. Which meant, more than likely, that its mama would very shortly move its sibling out of storage and into development. Chances were pretty good that one would be a kangaroo rex, too. Since the mama hadn't abandoned this one, it seemed unlikely she'd abandon another. I wondered if there were enough of them for a reliable gene pool.

The rex had calmed down now that it had eaten, now that most of the excitement was over. It was quietly investigating the enclosure, moving slowly on all fours. Hunched like that, it looked a lot like a mythological linebacker about to receive. With those small front legs, you never expect the thing (even a regulation kangaroo) to have the shoulders it does.

As it neared the side of the fence that I was gaping through, it yawned—the way a cat does, just to let you know it has weapons. I stayed quiet and still. It didn't come any closer and it didn't threaten any further.

That was a good sign, as far as I was concerned. Either it was full or it didn't consider me prey. I was betting it didn't consider me prey. Still, it was nasty-looking, which wasn't going to help its case, and it was still a baby. Adult, if it were a true kangaroo rex, it would stand as high as its kangaroo mother—six or seven feet.

In the outbreak of them we'd had nine years back near Gogol, they'd been herd animals. There had been some twenty-odd, with more on the way, of course. Chie-Hoon tells me kangaroos come in "mobs," which seemed appropriate for the kangaroo rexes as well, if a little weak-sounding. And we'd wiped out the last group wholesale.

Oh, I'd yelled and screamed a lot. At the very least, I'd hoped we could stash the genes so we could pull them out if we ever needed the creature for some reason. I got voted down, and I got voted down, and finally I got shouted down.

This time would be different.

The kangaroo rex sat back on its tail and began to wash, using its tongue and paws as prettily as any cat. In the midst of cleaning its whiskers, it froze, glanced up briefly, then went back to preening.

That was the only warning I had that Leo was back. He hadn't lost the ability to move softly with the passage of years. He put his arms around me and I leaned into him, feeling a little more than cat-smug myself, though I hadn't done anything to deserve it. Maybe *because* I hadn't done anything to deserve it.

"Pretty thing," Leo said softly, so as not to startle it. "Now I understand why you wanted to keep them."

"This time we *are* keeping them," I said.

There was a clatter of the door behind me. The kangaroo rex bounced to the furthest side of the enclosure, hit the fence on the second bounce, and froze, jaws agape and threatening.

"I know what you're thinking, Annie," Mike said. "You'd better come talk to these guys first. You're not going to like what you hear."

HERDERS JARLSKOG and Yndurain were not inclined toward leniency, especially not Jarlskog, who had worked himself up into a fine sense of outrage. To hear him tell it, you'd have thought a mob of rexes had eaten his entire flock, plus several of his children. So the entire town was already in an uproar.

I halfway agreed with their sentiments. I like the occasional lamb chop just as much as the next guy—especially the way Chris cooks them up—and this was one of only seven flocks on all of Mirabile. Sheep here are labor intensive. They can't be trusted to graze unattended: forever eating something native that'll poison them. So we keep only the seven flocks and we keep them on a strict diet of Earth fodder.

All this means that they have to be kept behind fences and that the plant life in there with 'em has to be policed regularly. That's one of the reasons all the flocks are on the fringes of the desert—it's easier to irrigate the plant life into submission.

The result of all this is that we eat a lot more kangaroo tail soup than we eat lamb curry. The kangaroos fend for themselves quite nicely, thank you, and there's no shortage of them.

Jarlskog wanted me to arrange an instant shortage of kangaroo rexes. So did Yndurain. In an hour's time, the rest of the town would start calling in with the same demand. I soothed them by telling them I'd have a team up there by the end of the day. In the meantime, they were to shoot only if they saw a rex actually in with the sheep.

They grumbled some but agreed. When I canceled the call, I turned to Leo. "What do you think? Will they go right out and shoot every kangaroo in sight?"

"No," he said. "Janzen and Moustafa are good kids. I think they can put a damper on the hysteria. Once I convinced Moustafa the rex was mine, he was even willing to help me catch it."

"It took a bit of convincing though." I glanced significantly at his skinned knuckles.

He grinned and shrugged. "In the heat of passion." His face turned serious and he added, "He'll shoot any roo that jumps that fence today, though, so if you want to head up there, now's the time."

Mike handed me a sheaf of hard copy. It was the list of everybody who lived in a hundred-mile radius of the spot where the rex had turned up. "Good news," he said. "We only have to worry about twenty families."

That is the only advantage I know of being underpopulated. For a moment, I considered not issuing a general alert. After all, for all we knew, there was only one kangaroo rex and it was in our backyard.

Mike read my mind and shook his head. "If you want to keep them, Annie, you better not risk having one of them eat some kid."

"It was only an idle thought," I told him. "Put out a notification. Keep the kids in, keep the adults armed. But add that I don't want them shot unless it's absolutely necessary."

Chie-Hoon said, "Annie, we're not going to go through this again, are we?"

"Damn straight, we are," I said, "and this time I intend to win! Who's coming with me?"

"Me," said Leo.

"And me," said Susan, looking up from her monitor. "It *is* the same kangaroo rex as last time, Mama Jason, only I've got two secondary helices here. They're both marsupial, but more than that I can't tell you offhand. It'll take the computer all night to search."

"Let me have a look first," Chie-Hoon said. "Maybe I'll recognize something. I have a vested interested in marsupials, after all."

Everybody's got to have a hobby. Chie-Hoon's is the Australian Guild, meaning Chie-Hoon knows more than anybody could ever want to about the customs and wildlife of Earth's "Australia," which includes about ninety percent of the marsupials found in ships' records.

"Help yourself," I said. I'd never found the time to join any of the Earth-authentic Guilds myself—if I were looking for a hobby I rather thought I'd make it Leo—but this was the sort of thing that came in handy. "Since Leo volunteers to come along, we'll leave you to it."

Since I'd worked with Leo before, I knew he and I could handle just about anything that came up. As for Susan, well, Earth-authentic wild horses couldn't have kept her away.

Mike looked glum. "I get stuck with the fish, right?"

"And Selima," I pointed out, which brightened him up

considerably. (I'm rather hoping those two will decide to help alleviate our underpopulation problem one of these fine days. I'm giving them every opportunity.) "We'll be in touch."

"We'll argue," Mike assured me.

WE TOOK MY SKIMMER. Leo, being retired (hah!), no longer rates up-to-date equipment. We let Susan drive and scandalized her by necking in the back seat. When we'd caught up a bit on old times, we broke the clinch.

"Why will you argue?" Leo asked.

"You remember, Noisy. Mama Jason wanted to keep the kangaroo rexes the last time they cropped up. Mike and Chie-Hoon didn't."

"A lot of people didn't want them kept," I said. "I lost that round."

"It's not going to be any easier this time," Leo said. "Both those herders were—if you'll pardon the expression—hopping mad."

Susan giggled. So did I.

"I know. But I'm older and meaner this time around."

"'Meaner'?" That was Susan. "Mama Jason, last time one of the damn things almost chewed your foot off!"

"D'you think I could forget something like that?" I leaned on the back of the seat and glared at her in the mirror. "That had nothing to do with it."

"'You never know what might be useful in the long run.' I know," Susan said. "It's not as if we're going to pick up and go back to Earth if we run out of sheep, either."

I gave a sidelong glance at Leo. "Just what I needed: somebody who quotes my own words back at me. . . ."

"You've only yourself to blame," he said.

"Thanks," said Susan, to let us both know she took this little routine as a compliment. "Now tell me who took what side last time around, and what you expect them to do this time."

"It was me against them," I admitted. When Susan whistled, I stuck in, "I almost got Mike to go along with me, but in the end, that wouldn't have made any difference. Mike didn't have much pull then."

"Meaning he was about the same age I am now," said Susan, "so my opinion won't swing much weight either."

"I had intended to be tactful."

Leo raised an eyebrow at me. "That's not like you, Annie. Do you need the allies that badly? It occurs to me that you swing a bit more weight these days yourself."

"Oh, considerably. But that won't do me a lot of good unless I can convince people like Jarlskog and Yndurain that the rexes are worth keeping. For god's sake, Leo! What's to stop them from simply shooting down every one they see? We certainly haven't the hands to police every bit of territory, especially not Last Edges or Gogol or the like."

Last Edges has a total population of fifty. That's minute, but it's five times the number of people I've got to work with.

"Most people understand enough about ecological balance to follow the guidelines you folks set," Leo said, but with a bit of a rising inflection.

"If I tell them it's 'Earth-authentic,' sure. But this one isn't. Furthermore, nobody in his right mind likes it."

"I like it," Susan said. When I didn't respond to that, she said in a small amused voice, "Oh," then giggled, then sighed in resignation. "So what do we do?"

"Nothing, until we check out the situation locally."

THE LOCAL SITUATION hadn't simmered down while it waited for our arrival. Not that I'd expected it to, but I could see that both Susan and Leo had. A third of the adults were guarding the sheep field with guns. Another third, I imagine, was guarding the kids likewise. The rest turned out to be a combination welcoming committee and lynch mob. Read: we were welcome, the kangaroo rexes were most emphatically not.

I listened to the babble without a word for all of twenty minutes, motioning for Susan and Leo to do the same. Best to let them get as much of it out of their systems as possible while we waited for a couple of leaders to sort themselves out of the crowd—then we'd know who and what we were actually dealing with.

In the end, there were two surprises. The first was that

someone was dispatched to "Go get Janzen. Right now." When Janzen arrived, Janzen got thrust to the fore. Janzen was about Susan's age. He looked at me, cocked an eye at Leo who nodded and grinned, then he grinned at me and stuck out his hand. That was when I noticed the striking resemblance the kid had to Leo. I cocked an eyebrow at Leo, whose grin got wider.

Janzen took care of shutting down the general noise level and introducing us to the population at large. Leo got introduced by his previous job description—as Leonov *Opener* Denness—and, yes, Leo was Janzen's granddad. Both of which upped our status exactly the way Janzen had intended them to. At a bet, a lot of the local kids had been through a survival course or two with Leo.

The second surprise wasn't nearly as pleasant. The other speaker for the populace—read "loudmouth" in this case—was none other than Kelly Herder Sangster, formerly a resident of Gogol. She'd wanted the kangaroo rexes near Gogol wiped out, and she wanted the same thing here and now.

I knew from experience how good she was at rousing rabble. She'd done it at Gogol. I could talk myself blue in the face, put penalties on the shooting of a rex, but I'd lose every one of them to "accidental" shootings if I couldn't get the majority of the crowd behind me.

Sangster squared off, aimed somewhere between me and Janzen, shoved back her hat, bunched her fists on her hips, and said, "They eat sheep. Next thing you know they'll be eating our kids! And cryptobiology sends us somebody who loves Dragon's Teeth!"

She pointed an accusing finger at me. "When they attacked us in Gogol, *she* wanted to keep them! Whaddaya think about that?" The last was to the crowd.

The crowd didn't think much of that at all. There was much muttering and rumbling.

"I think," I said, waiting for the crowd to quiet enough to listen, "I'd like to know more about the situation before I make any decisions for or against."

I looked at Janzen. "You were the first to see it, I'm told. Did it eat your sheep?"

"No, it didn't," he said. That caused another stir and a bit of a calm. "It was in the enclosure, but it was chasing them, all of them, the way a dog does when it's playing. To be fair, I don't know what it would have done when it caught them. We caught it before we could find out." He looked thoughtful. "But it seems to me that it had plenty of opportunity to catch a sheep and didn't bother. Moustafa? What do you think?"

Moustafa rubbed his sore jaw, glowered at Leo, and said, very grudgingly, "You're right, Janzen. It was like the time Harkavy's dog got into the sheep pen—just chased 'em around. Plenty of time to catch 'em but didn't. Just wanted to see them run." He glowered once more. "But for a kangaroo, it's an adolescent. Maybe it hasn't learned to hunt yet. That might have been practice."

"I concede the point," I said, before Sangster could use it to launch another torpedo. "The next thing I need to know is, how many of them are there?"

As if prompted (perhaps he was, I hadn't been watching Leo for the moment), Janzen said, "For all I know, only the one." He looked hard at Sangster. "You seen any?"

Sangster dropped her eyes. "No," she muttered, "not since Gogol." She raised her eyes and made a comeback, "No thanks to Jason Masmajean here."

Janzen ignored that. "Anybody else?"

"That doesn't mean a damn thing, Janzen, and you know it," someone said from the crowd. "For all we know, the entire next generation of kangaroos will be Dragon's Teeth—and that would be a shitload of kangaroo rexes!"

"I say we get rid of them while there's only one," Sangster put in. "I'm for loading my shotgun and cleaning the roos out *before* they sprout Dragon's Teeth!"

"Now I remember!" I said, before the crowd could agree with her. "*You're* the one that's allergic to roo-tail soup!"

"I'm not allergic. I just don't like it," she snapped back, before thinking it through.

"Well," said Janzen, "I like roo-tail soup, so I'd just as soon consider this carefully before I stick myself with nothing but vegetable for the rest of my life."

"Rest of your life. . . ." Sangster sneered at him. "What the hell are you talking about?"

"I'll take that question," I said. "If you've a genuine outbreak of kangaroo rexes here, instead of a one-shot, then you'll have to destroy all the kangaroos. That's what was done at Gogol. Gogol can never let the kangaroo herds—"

"'Mobs,'" corrected Sangster. "Kangaroos come in mobs, not herds."

"Gogol can never let the kangaroos *mob* again. Any kangaroo found in that EC is shot. The environmental conditions there are such that sooner or later any kangaroo around Gogol will produce a kangaroo rex." I gave a long look through the crowd. "I won't lie to you: Last Edges has roughly the same EC as Gogol did. Which means you may have to face the same decision. As for me, I'd wait to find out if the rexes eat sheep before I decide to kill off all the roos."

"Sounds fair," said Janzen, almost too promptly. "How do we go about this?"

"First, I want a good look at your EC. I want to see, if you haven't scuffed it up too much, where you spotted the rex. Then we do a little scouting of the surrounding area." I grinned over my shoulder at Leo. "Luckily, we have somebody who's an old hand at that."

"Luckily," agreed Janzen.

"But I could also use some additional help." I looked straight at Sangster. I wanted her where I could keep an eye on her and where she couldn't rabble-rouse while I was busy. "What do you say, Sangster? Willing to put in a little effort?"

What could she say? She just said it with all the bad grace she could muster.

"Take Janzen, too," came a voice from the crowd. Aha! there were two factions already. "Yes," agreed another voice, "you go with 'em, Janzen. You like roo soup."

"In the meantime," I said, "stick to the precautions we already discussed. However, if anyone spots a rex, I want you to notify us immediately. Don't shoot it."

"Oh, yes, right. Don't shoot it," Sangster mocked.

I looked at her as if she were nuts. "Look," I said, "if there are more than one, it can lead us to the rest of the mob. Or would you rather just hunt them by guess and by golly? I don't have the time myself. Are you volunteering?"

That was the right thing to say, too. So I added one last fillip. "Susan?" Susan edged forward. "Susan will be in charge of collecting the gene samples from each sheep, simply as a precaution."

This did not make Susan happy—she wanted to go haring off after the kangaroo rexes—but I knew she wouldn't argue with me in public. "Sample each?" she said.

"That's right. I don't want a single one lost. After all, who knows what genes they've got hidden in those? Might be, one of them can sprout the Shmoo."

That brought a bit of laughter. The Shmoo's a legendary creature that tastes like everything good and drops dead for you if you look at it hungry. The ultimate Dragon's Tooth, except that Sangster would never use that derogatory term for something she *approved* of.

The crowd approved our plan, especially the part about collecting gene samples from each sheep. It was a nuisance to do, but I knew it would settle them down. Herders know as well as anybody how desperately we need diversity within a species. I was offering to clone any sheep we lost to the rexes in the process of my investigation. That meant they'd lose the time it took to bring the sheep back to breeding age, but that they wouldn't lose any genetic variation.

Moustafa volunteered to help Susan with the sampling. So did a handful of others. Then the rest of the crowd dispersed, leaving us to get down to business at last.

Moustafa led the way to the sheep pen where Janzen and Leo had bagged my baby rex. The enclosure looked like every single one I've ever seen, identical to those at Gogol, identical to every other one in Last Edges as well, no doubt. The sheep inside *sounded* like the crowd had—lots of milling, scuffling, and bleating.

The moment we rounded the corner and *saw* the sheep, I had

to clamp my jaw hard to keep from laughing. The sheep were an eye-popping sky blue, every single one of them! Susan did burst into laughter. I elbowed her hard in the ribs. "Don't you dare laugh at Mike's sheep," I told her.

Mike had been trying for a breed that could eat Mirabilan plant life without killing itself. What he'd gotten was a particularly hardy type that tasted just as good as the original, but sprouted that unbelievable shade of blue wool. Mike had promptly dubbed them "Dylan Thomas sheep," and offered them out to the herders. Janzen and Moustafa had obviously taken him up on the offer.

Susan simmered down, just barely, to giggles. "But, Mama Jason," she said, "all this fuss because a Dragon's Tooth might eat a Dragon's Tooth. . . ."

And at that Janzen laughed too. He looked at Susan. "I hadn't thought of it that way, but, now that you mention it, it is funny." He cocked an eyebrow at Moustafa, who sighed and said, "You always were nuts, Janzen. Yeah. It's funny."

Moustafa looked at me more seriously, though. "But we can't afford to lose many. It's not as if we've got a high population to play around with. We don't even dare interbreed them with the Earth-authentics until we've built up the flock to twice this size or more."

I nodded. The kid was as sensible as Janzen. I wasn't surprised he'd taken a shot at the rex. In his position, I probably would have too. Hell, I'd have done it if they'd been the Earth-authentics. Why mess around? "Okay, Susan," I said, "Start with this flock. Make sure you get one of each."

If the artificial wombs were free this winter, I'd see Mike's pet project doubled, whether we needed them or not. Pretty damn things once you got over the initial shock. They smelled godawful, of course, but what sheep doesn't? The wool made beautiful cloth and even more beautiful rugs. It was already something of a posh item all over Mirabile.

"All yours," I said to Susan, and she and Moustafa set to work.

I followed Leo along the fence, watching where I put my feet. When you've got an expert tracker, you stay out of his way and let him do his job. Janzen knew this just as well as I did, so he was the one, not me, who grabbed Sangster to keep her from overstepping Leo and messing up any signs of the rex.

It wasn't long before Leo stopped and pointed us off across the sheep field. I shouldered my gear and we set out to track the kangaroo rex.

TRACKING A KANGAROO isn't as easy as you might think, even with the help of a world-class tracker like Leo. (I'm not so bad at it myself. Neither is Janzen, as it turns out.) These kangaroos were reds (I don't mean the warning-light red that signals that some critter is about to chain up to something else; I mean a lovely tawny animal red) and *they* are world-class distance jumpers, especially when they're panicked. They had been by Moustafa's rifle shot, which meant they'd been traveling in leaps of fifteen to twenty feet. So it was check the launch spot, then cast about for the landing and subsequent relaunch.

It was only guesswork that we were following the rex's mother anyway. We wouldn't know her to look at her. Only a full gene-read could tell us that. I'd have to sample most of the roos in the mob to find out how many of them were capable of producing baby rexes.

Sangster bent down to uproot a weed or two. When I frowned at her for taking the time, she held out the plant to me and said, "That'll kill a sheep as sure as a kangaroo rex will."

Janzen looked over. "Surer," he said. "I still don't know if kangaroo rexes eat sheep." To me, he added, "But that will poison one. That's lambkill."

I almost laughed. Like any Mirabilan species we've had occasion to work with, it has a fancy Latin name, but this was the first I'd heard its common name. The fancy Latin name is an exact translation. Sounded like Granddaddy Jason's work to me.

Sangster stooped to pull another. Curious how small they were. Must mean they policed the fields very carefully. These were newly sprouted. I spotted one and pulled it myself, then stuck my head up and looked for Leo again. He'd found the next set of footprints.

Good thing the roos have such big feet. In this kind of wiry, springy scrub we wouldn't have had much chance otherwise. Leo wiped sweat from his forehead and pointed toward the oasis in the distance. "Chances are they'll be there, including our rex's mother. In this heat, they'll be keeping to the shade to conserve water." He glanced at Janzen. "Is that the only natural source of water in the area?"

Janzen nodded.

I squinted into the shimmer. The plants had that spiky look of Mirabilan vegetation. There was a distinct break between the Earth-authentic lichens and scrub, then a fence, then a broad strip of desert, then the dark green of the Mirabilan oasis. The broad strip of desert was maybe twenty hops for a roo, or looked that way from this angle.

"Even the roos are a problem," Sangster observed. "They can hop the fence—they bring the lambkill seeds in on their fur."

"It'd blow in from there," I said. "Same as it did at Gogol." I couldn't help it. I'd been wondering ever since I first spotted her in the crowd. "Herder Sangster, what made you leave Gogol?"

Sangster scowled, not exactly at me. "It's Crafter Sangster now. I lost my flock, seventy percent of it anyway."

Leo said, "To the kangaroo rexes?"

She just about glared him into the ground. "To the lambkill," she said. "After we got rid of the rexes and the roos that bred them, the lambkill was still there. Worse than ever, it seemed."

"Yes," Janzen put in. "When Moustafa and I were deciding where to raise Mike's flock of Thomas sheep, I did some checking in the various areas available. Something in the EC here makes the lambkill less prevalent . . . or less deadly perhaps. The death count attributable to it isn't nearly as high here as it is around Gogol." He cocked his head, which made his resemblance to Leo all the stronger. "Say! Maybe you could find out what the difference is?"

"Maybe I could," I said, making it clear I would certainly look into the problem. "But for now let's find those roos. I'll put Susan on soil and vegetation samples as soon as she's done with sheep."

To my surprise, he frowned. "Isn't she a little young . . . ?"

"When's your birthday?" I asked him. When he told me, I said, "Yeah, I guess from your point of view she is a little young. You've got two months on her."

"Oops," said Janzen. "Sorry."

"No skin off my nose," I told him.

Leo grinned and slapped Janzen on the shoulder. "Would be skin off *his* if Susan had heard him, though. Rightly, too." Leo put an easy arm around Janzen's shoulder. "Susan's the one who developed the odders, Janz. You know, the neo-otters that keep the canals around Torville free of clogweed?"

Janzen looked rightly impressed. Good for Leo, I thought, rub it in just enough so the lesson takes.

"Besides," Leo said, "if age had any bearing on who gets what job, Annie and I would be sitting in the shade somewhere sipping mint juleps and fanning ourselves. Now, could we get on with this before we all, young and old alike, melt?"

So we did. The strip of desert was wider than I'd thought. We'd need that spring as much as the roos did. Of course, they were quite sensibly lying in the shade (drinking mint juleps, no doubt, whatever *they* were—I'd have to remember to ask Leo about that later), going nowhere until the cool of evening.

We'd lost our specific roo (if we'd ever had her) on the broad rocky flat that lay between the strip of desert and the oasis. We paused in the first bit of welcoming shade.

Without a word, Leo signed the rest of us to wait while he moved further in to scout the location of the mob without panicking it. I handed him the cell-sampler. If he saw anything that looked like a rex, I wanted an instant sample. I needed to know if more than one mother was breeding them.

For a long while, it was quiet, except for the sound of running water and the damned yakking of the chatterboxes. Every planet must have something like this—it's simply the noisiest creature in the EC. It keeps up a constant racket unless something disturbs it. When the chatterboxes shut up, you know you're in trouble. Most people think the chatterboxes are birds, and that's good enough most ways—they fly, they lay eggs, what more could you ask of birds?

I, for one, prefer that my birds have feathers. Technically speaking, feathers are required. The chatterboxes are a lot closer to lizards. I guess the closest Earth-authentic would be something like a pterodactyl, except that all the pterodactyl reconstructions in ships' files showed them brown or green. I wonder what the paleontologists back on Earth would have made of ours.

The chatterboxes, besides being noisy, are the most vivid colors imaginable—blues and reds and purples and yellows—and in some of the most tasteless combinations you can imagine. They make most Mirabilan predators violently ill, which shouldn't come as much of a surprise. The eggs are edible though, and not just to *Mirabilan* predators.

We watched and listened to the chatterboxes, thinking all the while, I'm sure, that we ought to bring home some eggs if we lucked onto a nest.

Then Leo was back.

He leaned close and spoke in a quiet voice. The chatterboxes kept right on. "Annie, I've found the mob, but I didn't see anything that looked like a rex—nothing out of the ordinary at all. Just browsing kangaroos."

"Chances are, mine is the first one, then. Do you think we can all get a look without sending them in all directions?"

"Depends on *your* big feet."

"Thanks," I told him.

The whole bunch of us headed out as quietly as we knew how. I'd been worried about Sangster, but she'd obviously taken the kids' training course to heart—she was as quiet as the rest of us.

We worked our way through sharpscrub, dent-de-lion, careless weed, spurts, and stick-me-quick. It was mostly uphill. The terrain here was mostly rock with a very slender capping of soil. Leo brushed past a stand of creve-coeur and collected a shirtful of its nasty burrs, saving us all from a similar fate. I didn't envy him the task of picking them out.

At last Leo stopped us. Kneeling, he slid forward, motioning me to follow. Our faces inches apart, we peered through a small stand of lighten-me.

There was the tiny trickle of stream that fed this oasis. In the shade of the surrounding trees lolled the mob of kangaroos, looking for the moment not so much like a mob as like a picnic luncheon. There were perhaps twenty in clear view, and not a striped hip among them. Still, that meant there were plenty more we couldn't see.

It was also quite possible that the mother of our rex had been ostracized because of her peculiar offspring. That happened often enough with Dragon's Teeth.

Beside me there was an intake of breath. The chatterboxes paused momentarily, then, to my relief, went right back to their chattering. Sangster pointed into the sharpscrub to my left.

I caught just the quickest glimpse of stripes, followed it to the end of its bound. As it knelt on its forepaws to drink from the stream, I could see it had the face and jaw of a red kangaroo, but the haunches were very faintly striped. I nodded to her. Good bet, that one. Different enough to be worth the first check.

Taking the cell-sampler back from Leo, I backed up—still on my hands and knees—and skinned around to get as close as I could. (Skinned being the operative word in that EC. My palms would never be the same.) Just at that moment, two of the adolescents started a kicking match.

Their timing was perfect. I took advantage of the distraction, rose, tiptoed forward, and potted Striped Rump with the sampler. It twitched and looked around but wasn't in the least alarmed. All it did was lean back on its tail and scratch the area with a forepaw, for all the world like a human slob.

Very slowly, I reeled in the sample. (I've startled too many creatures reeling in samples not to be aware of that problem.) Once I had it, I stashed it in my pack, reloaded, and popped a second roo, this time a male—all chest and shoulders, a good seven-footer. If the rexes got that big, I would be awfully hard put to convince anybody they should be kept.

Not that it looked menacing now. It was lying belly-up in the deep shade, with its feet in the air. Just now, it looked like a stuffed toy some kid had dropped.

I knew better: Mike had gotten into an altercation with a red that size once, and it had taken 341 stitches to repair the damage.

Roos use their claws to dig for edible roots. They panic, those claws'll do just as efficient a job digging holes in your face.

Two sampled. I figured the best thing to do was keep sampling as long as I could. I got eleven more without incident. Then I almost walked into the fourteenth.

Its head jerked up from the vie-sans-joie it and its joey were browsing. The joey dived headfirst into mama's pouch.

I knew it was all over, so I shot the sampler at the mother point-blank, as the joey somersaulted within her pouch to stare at me wide-eyed between its own hind feet. Mamma took off like a shot.

Next thing I knew, the chatterboxes were in the air, dead silent except for the sound of their wings, and every kangaroo was bounding every which way.

Janzen and Leo were on their feet in the same moment, dragging Sangster to hers as well. Less chance of being jumped on if the roos were stampeding away from you. Leo bellowed at them, just to make sure.

Trouble is, you can't count on a roo to do anything but be the damn dumb creature it is—so three of them headed straight for Leo and company.

Janzen dived left. Still bellowing, Leo dived right. And there stood Sangster, right in the middle, unable to pick a direction. She took one step left, a second right—that little dance that people do in the street just before they bump into each other.

Striped Rump was still aimed straight for her.

I raised my shotgun and aimed for Striped Rump. "No, Annie!" Leo shouted. But I was thinking of Mike—I sighted.

Three things happened at once: Leo hooked a foot at Sangster's ankle and jerked her out of the path of the roo, Janzen bellowed louder than ever I'd heard Leo manage, and I squeezed the trigger.

Striped Rump touched one toe to the ground and reversed direction in mid-leap. My shot passed over its shoulder as it bounded away from Sangster. By the time the shot had finished echoing off the rocks, there wasn't a roo to be seen anywhere.

I charged over to where Leo was picking Sangster up and

dusting her off. Polite full-body-check, that was. From his nod, she was just fine, so I spared a glance for Janzen, who seemed likewise.

"Dammit, woman!" Leo said. "What happened to 'Don't shoot unless it's absolutely necessary'? That was your likeliest prospect."

"The hell with you, Leo. *You've* never seen anybody mangled by a roo." It came out tired. The adrenaline rush was gone and the heat was suddenly unbearable. "I'm not in the mood to be scolded right now. You can do it later, when I'm ready to thank you for saving old Striped Rump."

I glared at Sangster. "If you're fit to travel, I vote we get the hell out of this sun and let me process my samples."

She opened her mouth, a little round "o" of a shape, as if to say something. Then she just nodded.

We slogged our way back across the sheep range. By the time we reached the shade of Janzen's digs, I was unpissed enough to growl at Leo, "What's a mint julep? Maybe I could use one."

Leo shot a sidelong glance at Janzen, who grinned and said, "You *know* I keep the mixings. You also know you're all welcome to stay at my place." He cocked his head slightly to the side, "If you don't tell Susan what an idiot I am."

"We'll let her find out on her own," Leo said.

Which settled that—and us as well.

I was almost into the welcome shade of Janzen's house when Sangster grabbed at my arm. I turned—the look on her face was downright ferocious. Here it comes again, I thought. Death to the kangaroo rex!

Instead, she demanded, "Why?" That ferocious look was still there.

I blinked. "Why *what*, dammit?"

"Why did you shoot at that damned roo?"

Some people just don't get it, ever. I shook my head and sighed. "Humans are the most endangered species on Mirabile," I said, "and you want to know why I fired?"

That was all I had the patience for. I turned on my heel, yanked away from her, and fairly dived into the coolness of

Janzen's house, letting the door slam behind me as my final word on the subject.

THE MINT JULEP improved my outlook no end, so I keyed into Janzen's computer (rank hath its privileges) and entered the samples I'd picked up. While I was waiting for my readout, I checked my office files to see what the rest of the team had come up with.

First thing I got was a real pretty schematic of my kangaroo rex. It was an even neater bit of engineering than I'd thought at first—the teeth at the side of the jaws (they were two inches long!) worked across each other, like butchers' shears. What with the 180-degree jaw span, that would give it an awesome ability to shear bone. Sheep bone was well within its capabilities.

That still didn't mean it ate sheep, but it didn't help the cause any.

Next I got the gene-reads on the secondary helices. Didn't recognize either worth a damn. Neither had Chie-Hoon, because there was a note appended that said simply, "Annie: Sorry, neither of these looks familiar to me. We're checking them against ships' records now. Let you know what we find."

That'd be sometime the next day. A search and match takes entirely too much time, always assuming that there *is* a match. Lord only knew what was in those portions of ships' records we'd lost in transit.

The gene-read on Striped Rump was about what I'd expected, just a few twists off normal red kangaroo.

"Roo stew?" said a voice behind me.

"Sure," I said, without looking up, "still perfectly edible, despite those." I tapped the offending genes on the monitor.

"Janzen," said Leo's voice, "No point talking to her when she's reading genes. She's not talking about the same thing you are."

That was enough to make me turn away from the screen. I looked at Janzen. "Sorry," I said, "What was it you wanted to know?"

"I just asked if you'd mind having roo stew for dinner. I intend to eat a lot of roo while I still have the option."

"Say yes, Annie." That was Leo again. "Janzen and Moustafa make the best roo stew I've ever had. Even Chris couldn't beat their recipe."

"That's some recommendation! Can I get in on this?" That was Susan. "I put the sheep samples in the truck, Mama Jason; all set for in vitro in case we need them. Is that your rex breeder? Sangster won't talk about what you guys found. What did you do to her? Threaten her with a corn crop that sprouts cockroaches?"

"One thing at a time," I said. "Janzen, yes, thank you. I'm extremely fond of roo myself. Will there be enough for Susan too, or shall I make her eat rations?"

Susan threatened to punch me. Janzen grinned at her and said, "Plenty enough, Susan. Now I know why Leo wants to hook up with Annie. Just his type."

To change the subject, I tapped the monitor again and said, "That's our most likely candidate for rex breeder. I was just about to check for secondary helices. You can watch over my shoulder, unless you want to watch how Janzen and Moustafa make stew. The recipe'd make a good birthday present for Chris . . . ?"

Susan looked horribly torn for a brief moment. Janzen grinned at her again and said, "I'll write out our recipe for you, Susan. You stick here and tell me what I need to know about the kangaroo rexes." The kid had a *lot* in common with his granddad.

While Susan pulled up a chair, I turned back to the monitor and started reading genes again. Yup, there was a secondary helix, all right. I split the screen, called up the gene-read on my kangaroo rex, and compared the two. No doubt about it. "Thanks for saying old Striped Rump, Leo. She's it."

I stored that to send back to the lab and called up the next sample. "Let's see how many other rex breeders we've got."

By THE TIME Moustafa dished out the roo stew, I'd found two more rex breeders in the sample of thirteen. And they were all remarkably consistent about it.

"Hell," said Leo.

"Not exactly, Noisy," Susan said. "That means most likely the kangaroo rex is an intermediate for an Earth-authentic."

I was momentarily more interested in the stew than in anything else. It lived up to Leo's billing. I was still trying to place the spices Janzen and Moustafa used when Leo laid a hand on my arm to get my attention. "Mmmph?" I said, through a mouthful.

"You've got to train your assistants to use less jargon," he said.

I scooped up another forkful of stew and simply eyed Susan.

"Ooops," she said. "Sorry, Noisy. A true Dragon's Tooth is usually a chimera—bits and pieces of the genetic material of two very different species. Even a plant-animal combination's possible. But it's not consistent.

"If we've got three roos that are going to at some time produce rexes, all of which are close enough genetically to interbreed, then most likely it's not a Dragon's Tooth. Most likely it's the first visible step on the chain up to another Earth-authentic." She waited anxiously to see if he'd gotten it this time. When he nodded, she dived back into her own dinner. "Great stew, Moustafa, Janzen. I'd sure hate it if we have to kill off the roos."

"Any idea just how big the roo population is?" I asked the two local kids.

They exchanged a glance. Moustafa said, "Couple hundred, maybe. It never occurred to me to count."

Janzen shook his head, meaning it hadn't occurred to him either, then he said, "You can get some idea after dinner. Once the sun goes down, most of them will be out in the pasture, browsing. If it were crops we were raising instead of sheep, they'd be a much bigger nuisance than they are now."

Susan raised a querying brow at him.

"Given any kind of a choice, the roos prefer their food tender, which means they go for young shoots. That'd play havoc with any food crop. Sheep will browse tough stuff that's inedible to most Earth-authentics, and they'll do it right down to the ground."

"Yeah," said Moustafa, "and they're too stupid to know what's poisonous and what isn't."

That reminded me. "Excuse me a minute," I said, but I took my bowl of stew with me while I went to the computer to call up the home team.

I got Mike, which was good luck, and there were no emergencies in the offing, which was better. "I need an EC workup on Gogol. Can you get me one by tomorrow evening?" At his look, I said, "It doesn't have to be complete. Just a preliminary. Quick and dirty is fine. We'll do a complete if anything interesting shows up." His look hadn't improved, so I added, "Take Selima. With two of you, it'll go faster and won't be quite as dirty."

That fixed the look right up. Ah, young love . . . ain't it handy? "Anything new I should know about?"

"Yeah." This time he grinned. "Your kangaroo rex didn't recognize lamb as edible."

Behind me, someone said, "All right!" on a note of triumph. I ignored that to eye Mike suspiciously. When he said nothing further, I voiced his implied, "But . . . ?"

"But it could learn that trick. Right now its idea of superb cuisine is chatterboxes, grubroots, and gladrats."

Interesting. Those were all Mirabilan, and all pests from our point of view. "That's certainly in its favor," I said. "They're all of a size too—nowhere near the size of sheep."

"Means nothing. There's only one rex on the premises. Who knows what size prey a mob of them will take on."

"I know," I said, "but that gives me more breathing space here." I thought about it a moment then got an inspiration. "Mike? Try it on those damn jumping fish next time it looks hungry."

That brought a grin from Mike. "Annie," he said, "our luck's not *that* good this summer. Besides, the rexes wouldn't do well in that EC."

"Just try it. And shoot me that EC report as soon as you can." I broke the connection, picked up my bowl, and—still thinking about it—headed back for the dinner table. I almost ran Leo down. I looked around me. The whole troop had been looking over my shoulder. "Sit," I said, "my apologies. We will now give the stew the attention it deserves."

Which we did, and when we were done, it was time for Janzen
and Moustafa to see to their sheep for the evening . . . and for
me and Leo to place ourselves strategically in the fields to see
how many roos showed up to browse—and how many of them
were breeding rexes.

We ran into half a dozen of the locals and enlisted three.
Susan dug out two more samplers, but those went to Leo and
Susan herself. (We're short on equipment. I put that on the
docket for winter, making more samplers or finding somebody
who wanted the job.)

Sangster was nowhere to be seen. Despite Susan's earlier
comment, I had no doubt she was off somewhere raising the level
of hysteria. I could have kicked myself for not dragging Sangster
in with us that afternoon, just to keep her out of trouble.

It would have been a lovely evening for hanky-panky. Too bad
Leo was on the opposite edge of the field. With the sun going
down, there was a bit of nip in the air. Dew had started to
condense and I was wet to the knees, but I laid out a bit of tarp
to sit on and to drag around my shoulders and settled down to
count roos.

They weren't much worried about humans, as it turned out. At
the moment, that was a plus. If the rexes had the same
inclination, though, it would be just one more thing to worry
about.

Susan I'd stationed roughly in eyeshot—at least, with the help
of a good flashlight. But pretty soon I was so busy taking samples,
that I had no time for more than an occasional check on her. She
was taking samples just as furiously as I was.

Moustafa's estimate had been in the hundreds, by which he'd
meant maybe two hundred. I'd have guessed more. I counted
nearly a hundred within the ring of light my flashlight produced.
The flashlight bothered them not at all. They placidly munched
at this, that, and the other. About as peaceful as a herd of cows
and about as bright: one of the youngsters nibbled my tarp before
I tapped its nose. Then it hopped back into mama's pouch and
glared at me. Mama went on chewing, while I got samples of
both.

In the cool of the evening, they were much more active. The youngsters chased and kicked each other and a lot of mock battles went down, reminding me of nothing so much as the way Susan and Mike behaved.

More than one of the youngsters had striped hips, so I crept as close as I dared while they were occupied with each other, to get samples specifically from them. Once again, a mock battle— great leaps in the air and powerful kicks from those hind legs—covered my movement.

Three older kangaroos paused to look up from their eating, but they looked up at the antics of the youngsters with the same kind of wearied eye I had been known to turn on activities of that sort from our younger contingent. Satisfied that the kids weren't getting into any trouble, they went back to what they'd been doing, which was grubbing in the ground, presumably for roots.

You wouldn't believe those claws unless you saw them in action. Once again, I appreciated the muscular shoulders. I frankly didn't see why a kangaroo rex should seem any more ferocious—at first glance, anyhow—then a basic kangaroo. Watching them, I got a tickle in the back of my skull. The stuff they were grubbing up looked familiar. Nova light is romantic, but not as good for some things as for others. I debated the wisdom of turning my flashlight on them for a better look.

Being old hands, they would not be so likely to take my intrusion as lightly as the joey had. I didn't want to start a stampede. There were just too many of them in the general neighborhood. I didn't relish the thought of being run down by several hundred pounds of panicked roo.

The elder roos looked up, suddenly wary. I abandoned my plan and followed their point. Some sort of disturbance at the edge of the mob, very near where I'd last seen Susan. And damned if I could see her now. There were too many adult roos between my position and hers.

The nearby roos got a bit skittish. Two of the adult males bounced once in Susan's direction, froze, and watched. A new mob had joined the browsing.

This was a smaller group. Dominant male, two females, and

two matching joeys. Damned if the male didn't have that striped rump. I didn't dare edge closer, not with the nearby roos nervous already. I held my ground and hoped the quintet of likelies would pass near enough to Susan for her to get a safe shot at sampling them.

But they skirted Susan (now that my brain was working again, I decided I was glad they had) and headed in my direction. Closer examination told me that poppa was a roo. Neither of the mamas was, though. To hell with the striped rump—these two were plain and simple kangaroo rexes—and most of the nearby roos didn't like it any more than I did.

Their movements were different. (Well, let's face it—they would be.) Except for the male, they weren't grazing. They were searching the grass for whatever small prey the rest of the roos startled into motion. I could see why they liked to hang around with the browsers. The browsing roos gave them cover and, as often as not, sent gladrats and grubroots right into those waiting jaws.

I couldn't recall when I'd ever heard anything eaten with a snap quite that impressive, either. I eased back down in the grass, hoping they'd get close enough that I could get shots at both the mothers and the joeys. I laid my rifle where I could reach it at a moment's notice and raised my sampler.

To my surprise, the roos around me, after whiffing the air a few times, settled back to their browsing. When the rexes came close, the roos eased away, but didn't panic. Not quite acceptable in public society, I could see, but nothing to worry about so long as they kept to their own table.

One of the rex joeys pounced after something small in the grass. In the excitement of the chase, it headed straight for me. I popped it with the sampler on the spot, and it jumped straight up in the air, came down bouncing the opposite direction, and headed for mama. It made a coughing bark, the like of which I never heard from a roo.

Mama made the same coughing sound, bounded over the joey, and the next thing I knew I was face to face with several hundred pounds of angry rex. The jaws snapped as I brought up my gun. Then something hit me in the shoulder with the force of a freight train. The gun went in one direction, I went in the other, rolling as best I could to keep from being kicked a second time by the papa roo.

A brilliant flash of light struck in our direction, illuminating the mama rex as she came after me. There was a yell and a shot from somewhere behind me. I may have imagined it, but I swear I felt that bullet pass inches from my right ear.

The mama rex stopped in her tracks—stunned, not shot. The rest of the mobs, roos and rexes alike, took off in all directions. The ground shook from their thundering kickoffs and landings.

I scrambled to my feet, the better to dodge if dodging was possible in that chaos. It was only then that I realized that some damn fool of a human had the kangaroo rex by the tail, hauling it back as it tried to bound away.

A second damn fool of a human grabbed for the rex's feet, dragging them out from under it so it couldn't kick.

Dammit! They'd forgotten the teeth!

I was moving before I even put a thought to it. Dived, landed roughly on the rex's head, and grabbed it about the throat, pulling the jaw closed toward my chest and hanging on for dear life while the thing struggled for all it was worth. It had the worst damn breath of any creature I'd ever gotten that foolishly close to.

Through the haze and the brilliance of the artificial light, I saw somebody race up and plunge a hypodermic needle into the upturned haunch. The rex coughed its outrage and struggled twice as hard. I almost suffocated. I don't even want to think how close its snap came to my ear.

Somebody else was trying to loop a rope around those thrashing hind legs and not being very successful about it. I'd have let go, if I could have thought of a safe way of doing it.

Then all at once the struggle went out of the rex. It kicked weakly a few more times, then went limp, for all the world as if it was too hot a day to do anything but lie around in the shade.

The fellow with the rope said, "Took long enough!" and finished his tying—as neat as any cowboy on ships' film. He whipped another length of rope off his hip, came round to me, and wrapped the length about the jaw, sealing it temporarily shut. Then he stood up, dusted off his hands, and said, "Kelly, you're gonna have to come up with a better mousetrap. Damned if I'm gonna do that again!"

Sangster uncrimped herself from the rex's tail and stood to face him. "Thought the Texan Guild would be a damn sight better at hog-tying." The challenge in her voice was unmistakable. "I guess the Australian Guild will have to handle the rest alone."

"Hell," said the Texan, in that peculiar drawl that identifies members of the guild, "just give us a chance to practice. These things move a sight different than a fence post."

"You're on," said Sangster. "Now let's get this into the cage before the valium wears off." She turned to me and said, "We'll catch the rest of them for you."

Four of them hefted the limp rex onto their shoulders and started back toward town.

None of it was making sense, least of all Sangster's parting shot. Maybe that roo's kick had caught me in the side of the head after all and I just didn't know it. I felt like walking wounded.

Must have been stunned, because it wasn't until Leo and Susan picked up my gun and my cell sampler and caught my elbows on either side that I even remembered to make sure they were okay themselves.

Leo looked about like I felt. Susan was fine, bounding along, half in front of us, half trying to carry me by my elbow, as if she'd caught the bounds from the roos. "Mama Jason," she caroled as she bounced, "I'm so glad you're okay! That was about the most exciting thing that's ever happened to me, *ever!* Wasn't it, Noisy? Have you ever *seen* anything like that in your *life?* Just wait until I tell Chris and Elly and Mike. . . ."

None of that seemed to require any response from me, so I saved my breath for walking.

"*Are* we going to catch the rest of them?" she demanded at last. "What about the rex's joey? Shouldn't we find it? Maybe it wasn't weaned yet."

From the brief look I'd gotten at the joeys, chances were Susan

was right. If the rex they'd shot full of valium lived, we'd still lose
the rex joey.

But when we rounded the corner, we found a makeshift
cage—a big one, much to my relief—built onto a transport trailer
that sat right next to Sangster's house. In it was the mama rex,
still groggy but unmuzzled now, and her joey. At least, I hoped
it was hers. It was pretty damned angry, but was expending most
of its energy trying to get a response out of mama.

The entire town of Last Edges and then some had turned out
to gawk. Sangster lounged against the cage like she owned 'em
both. When she saw us coming, she nodded and took a few steps
to meet us.

"Earth used to have zoos," she said, with no preamble.
Glancing at the Texan Guilder, she added, "Ramanathan
checked out the references for us in ships' files." She folded her
arms across her chest and, with an air of pronouncement,
finished, "We've decided we don't mind if you keep them in a
zoo. We'll catch the rest of them for you."

That was not what I'd had in mind at all. Still, I wasn't going
to make any objection as long as it kept Sangster and her crew
from shooting them on sight. "Who's funding this zoo?" I said,
"and who's going to catch the grubroots and gladrats to feed
them?"

Sangster and the Texan exchanged glances. "We'll talk about it
later," she said.

I'll just bet, I thought, but didn't say it. I shrugged and turned
to plod back to Janzen's place. I needed a hot soak to get the kinks
out. My shoulder was beginning to stiffen from the bruises I'd
gotten. (At least, I hoped it wasn't worse than bruises.) "Get that
joey something to eat," I said. "They were hunting when you
interrupted them. Grubroots will do just fine. That's what it was
after."

I left. Somebody would see to it—probably Janzen.

Sangster caught up with me at the door to Janzen's place. "I
talked the Australian Guild into cooperating. I can talk them into
funding the zoo, too. Marsupials are *our* jurisdiction. Maybe the

rex is an Earth-authentic that got lost with the missing ships' files."

"Maybe," I said, stopping to consider her. Damned strange woman. I was sure from her manner that she was still mad as all hell at me, so none of this made sense. "More likely an intermediate, ready to chain up to an Earth-authentic."

"We want them *off* the sheep range," she said. "It's this or kill the roos again. We talked the Texan Guild into helping us. We can get them all for your zoo."

What could I say? "Until the next batch chains up from the roos." I shrugged one more time.

Sangster scowled deeper. "I saved this pair for you. I talked them into making a zoo. Now we're even."

She practically spat that last at me, then she turned on her heel and stamped away, raising dust with her fury.

Even for *what?* I wondered. *Damn* strange woman, like I said before.

I WOKE UP stiff all over. Susan was balanced on the edge of my cot, barely able to contain herself. "What?" I said.

"They caught the other mama rex and her joey last night, Mama Jason. We get to keep them after all."

"Zoo is *not* my idea of keeping them, dammit. Just sheer luck they haven't killed any of them yet, between the valium and beating them into submission." I tried to get coherent but I'm not ready for mornings, ever. "Read up on zoos—and I don't mean the cursory reading Sangster and her mates did. Zoos always held the *last* individuals of the species: they were a death sentence."

"Oh," she said. "Mike called. He and Selima are up at Gogol, doing that EC check you wanted. He'll have it this evening."

"Good. I want you to do the same here. I want it this evening, too."

"Betcha I'm faster than Mike."

"Better be cleaner, too," I said, "or faster doesn't count."

She grinned at me, bounded off the cot, and was out the door without another word. Guaranteed her report would be both faster and cleaner than Mike's—unless I called Mike and issued

MIRABILE   77

the same challenge, that is. I dragged myself out of bed. Breakfast first, to get the mind moving, then to the computer to see what, if anything, was new from the lab.

What was new was a note from Chie-Hoon. "Skipped an emergency meeting of the Australian Guild for this, Annie, so you'd better appreciate it." Appended were reconstructions of the two critters our rexes were planning to chain up to.

Chie-Hoon had a gift for that: take the gene chart and draw from it a picture of what the resulting animal would look like. There were no Latin names for 'em, which meant Chie-Hoon hadn't been able to find a gene-read for either in ships' records.

The first one was just a variant on roo. The second was, well, as weird a thing as I'd ever seen, including the Mirabilan jumping fish. It had the same jaw and jaw span as the rexes, but it was a quadruped. The tail wasn't as thick (it didn't need the tail for balance the way the roos did) and the hip stripes continued up to the shoulders, narrowing as they went. Basic predator with camouflage stripes.

The pouch opening aimed toward the tail, instead of toward the head. Took me a moment to figure that out—kept the baby from falling out while the critter chased prey, probably also kept it from getting scratched up on creve-coeur in the same circum-stances. What it boiled down to was a marsupial version of a wolf. Probably wouldn't stack up too well against the mammalian wolf (a species I'm rather partial to), but it was a fine off-the-wall bit of work nonetheless.

Then I went on to the note from Mike. As Susan had said, he and Selima were on their way. Susan *had* forgotten to pass along the final message, which was that my courting present thought the jumping fish were great toys but showed not the slightest interest in eating them. As Mike said, our luck's not *that* good this summer.

"How's the shoulder this morning, Annie?" Leo looked like he'd been up and around for hours already.

"Stiff," I said—and bless his sweet soul, he came right in to massage it—"I appreciate your courting gift all the more, now that I know what kind of fight you went through to catch it for me."

"All in the name of love," he said, and I could feel his grin light up the room all around me even if I couldn't see it. "What can I do for you today?"

"Join me on a long, probably useless, but definitely exhausting walk around the sheep fields. Unless you could pick out the spot the Australian Guild grabbed the rex in the daylight?" Probably too much to hope for.

"I can pick it out," he said. "That big a scrabble left signs . . . and I know about where you were a few moments before."

"What would I do without you?"

So we headed out. The route took us past the caged rexes. Some fifteen people were still standing about staring in at them—some tourist attraction, all right. Safe but scary, as Leo had said once in another context.

I wanted to see how they were faring myself, so I shoved through the crowd. One of the gawkers had a stick and was using it to poke at the baby rex through the bars of the cage. Just to rile it and make its mother charge him.

As I got there, the mother was just rebounding off the wire. I snatched the stick out of the bastard's hand and slapped him a good one alongside the head with it. "You like that?" I demanded.

"Hell, no!" he said.

"Then what makes you think that creature does?"

"I—" He looked sheepish for a moment, then defiant. "I just wanted to see them move around some. They weren't doing anything."

"Roos don't do anything in this heat, either. That's their way of conserving water, you damn fool. Who raised you?"

Stunned, he told me.

"Well, they ought to be ashamed of themselves. They damn sure didn't teach you the sense god gave the rexes there."

"Hey! You can't talk about my raisers—"

"Then you oughta stop doing stupid things that lead me to believe they raised you wrong."

That did it. I watched him go all embarrassed.

"Sorry," he said at last. "Everybody else was doing it."

"Then prove to me that you're a cut better. First, you get the rexes some water, so they can replace what they've lost. Then you get that damned Australian Guild to move this into the shade. Then you can stand here and make sure nobody else beats up on the rexes. Then I'll revise my opinion of your raisers. Got that?"

"Yes, ma'am!"

Yes, ma'am, and he'd do it, too. I was satisfied he'd keep them from being harassed further.

Then I got a chance to look at the rexes. The other joey was dragging a foot. Hellfire and damnation, they'd broken its leg catching it. I roared at Leo, "Get Sangster and get her damned Australians down here right now!"

So we spent most of the afternoon coaxing the injured joey out of the cage so we could splint its leg. Zoos, just love 'em. Hope the guy that invented 'em wound up in a cage all his own—in the sun.

Sangster and her mates were apologetic but clearly had no intention of giving up their plan to catch any more rexes that turned up for their zoo. Oughta be a damned law to protect animals from people.

IT WAS COOLING toward evening when Leo and I finally set out to look for the spot I had in mind. Something was still niggling me about that, but the whole struggle with the rex had shoved it completely out of my head. I was hoping if I saw the spot again, the same thought might come back.

Leo found it for me in record time. Would have taken me twice as long. He stood in the middle of the spot where the first rex had been when that blinding light and stunning shot hit it all at once. "Now you see if you can reconstruct your position from that," he said. "Just pretend I'm a kangaroo rex."

"You haven't got the jaw for it, Leo." I cast about and made some good guesses. They were good enough that I found bits of the broken cell sampler there. I flopped down next to the bits and glanced around. Nothing jogged my memory, so I closed my eyes and tried to see it again.

That worked: the roos (not the rexes) had been digging up plants just there. I hauled myself to my feet and went over to look.

The plants the roos had been grubbing up were still there, shriveled in the heat and utterly unrecognizable. Fine. I could still do a gene-read on them if I did it now. "Okay," I said. "Back to Janzen's. You can make me a mint julep. If this is what I hope it is, we'll toast Mirabile."

WHAT WITH ONE THING and another, I didn't get my gene-read on the withered plants until after dinner. It was just what I expected it to be, so I put in a call to Mike out at Gogol. Mike and Selima couldn't be found for me (aha!) but they'd left their EC run in my file.

"Susan!" I yelled and she came running. "You finish that EC check for me?"

She looked smug. "On file," she said. "Did I beat Mike out?"

I cued up her file. "Mike's was filed roughly the same time as yours but then he had extra hands—Selima was with him."

"Oh," said Susan. "Well, it's only fair to say I had extra hands, too. Janzen helped me." That made her look smugger and set off a second *aha!*, which I did not voice, as much as I enjoyed it.

I read through Susan's EC on Last Edges, then went to Mike's from Gogol a second time, then pulled hard copy on both. "Gotcha," I said, as the reports stacked up in the printer. "Mint juleps all around, Leo!"

I handed Susan the sheaf of reports and said, "Read 'em. Then tell me how this EC differs from the EC at Gogol." I leaned back in my chair, accepted the mint julep from Leo, and waited to see if Susan would see it, too.

After a while, Susan's head came up. She stared at me and her mouth worked, but nothing came out. She handed the sheaf of papers to Janzen, went to the computer, and called up the EC we'd done on Gogol all those years ago, the first time the kangaroo rexes had reared their ugly little heads. She nodded to herself, then pulled hard copy on that, too.

She came back with it and added it to the pile Janzen was reading. Then she sat down and said, "To kill the rexes, they have to kill the roos. But if they kill the roos, the sheep die."

"What?" said Moustafa and tried to wrest the reports from Janzen, who didn't cooperate. "I don't see it, Susan. I don't know how to read these things."

She gave him a pitying look but explained: "There are only two significant differences between the EC here and the EC at Gogol. The first is that Gogol has no roos, or very few—they're shot on sight. And the second is that Gogol is awash in lambkill."

Moustafa made a stifled noise deep in his throat. Janzen said, "Does this mean I don't have to give up my roo-tail soup?"

"It means," I said, "that the roos eat the lambkill, which prevents your sheep from eating it. You may be willing to give up your roo-tail soup, but how many people in Last Edges are willing to give up their sheep—the way Sangster did after the roos were killed in Gogol?"

I raised my glass. "To Mirabile," I said.

IT WAS JANZEN who rang the meeting bell. And what with the Australian Guilders and the Texan Guilders—all of whom were antsy to be back on the range rounding up kangaroo rexes—we had a much larger turnout than expected. There was a lot of jostling and more than one case of bad manners. I had to wonder if the Texan Guild went so far as to call each other out for gunfights, but apparently not, as nobody did.

When they finally all simmered down, I explained the situation to them. I guess I expected them to forgive the rexes on the spot. I should know better at my age.

Sangster said, "Of *course*, the roos eat lambkill! They grub it out right down to the root—anybody could have told you that, for god's sake!"

"You don't get it," Janzen shot back. "Kill the roos and the *lambkill* kills the sheep! That's why you lost your flock at Gogol. D'you want the same thing to happen here? I sure as hell don't!"

There was a good loud mutter of agreement from the crowd on that one. Sangster stamped her foot and yelled for attention. After a while she got it, but it was a lot more hostile than she was used to.

"Stabilize the roos, then," she said. She glared at me. "You've done it before with domestic herds. You stabilized the sheep! Are you telling me you can't do the same for our roos—or can't you be bothered? Might mess up your beloved kangaroo rexes."

I didn't get a chance to answer. From the very back of the crowd came an agonized shout: "No, Annie! You can't stabilize them! You don't know what the rexes are chaining up to! I do! And you can't stabilize the roos!"

I peered over heads and could just barely make out a mop of straight black hair and piercing black eyes. By this time I'd recognized Chie-Hoon's voice, even though I'd never heard the kid quite so worked up about anything.

Before anybody'd had time to react to this, Chie-Hoon was standing on a chair, waving a banner-sized picture. I recognized it even from that distance: Chie-Hoon's own reconstruction of the weirder of the two critters our rexes were chaining up to, the one with the jaws.

"Mates!" shouted Chie-Hoon, and had the instant attention of every Australian Guild member there. (When one of the locals made to object to this interruption from a nonresident, he was swiftly stifled by a menacing look from a guilder.) "D'ya recognize this?" Chie-Hoon spread the picture wide and turned, slowly, on the chair to let every one of them have a good look.

"It's a Tasmanian wolf," said somebody—to which there was general agreement—then a swift reshuffling of the Australian Guild to get closer.

"Good on you, mate," said Chie-Hoon. "That's exactly right! *That's* what our rexes are chaining up to. It was extinct on Earth, but that doesn't make it any the less Earth-authentic. Speaking as a member of the Australian Guild, Annie, I won't have you stabilizing the rexes. Save the Tasmanian wolf!"

With that, Chie-Hoon raised a fist, dramatically, then shouted a second time, "Save the Tasmanian wolf!"

And before I knew what was happening, pandemonium reigned. The entire Australian Guild was chanting, "Save the Tasmanian wolf!" as if their own lives depended on it, with Kelly Crafter Sangster herself leading the chant.

Twenty minutes later, they released the uninjured rex and its mother, with promises to release the other pair as soon as the joey's leg had healed, and I was being threatened with dire consequences if I didn't return Leo's courting gift to the fields within the week.

"They won't let me keep my present," I said to Leo, grinning through my complaint.

"I know," he said, grinning just as much. "But they'll let you keep your kangaroo rexes. That's what counts."

"It was a great courting gift, Leo."

"I know."

"We'll have to see about re-establishing the kangaroos at Gogol, too, before we lose the rest of the sheep there to the lambkill."

"Don't you ever think about anything but work, woman?"

"Occasionally. Call Loch Moose Lodge and book us a room for the week. I need a vacation."

He started off to do just that. I had another thought. "Leo!"

"You're not changing your mind." That was an order.

"No, I'm not changing my mind. But it occurs to me that Chris always wanted to be a member of my team, if she could be the official cook. Tell her I'm bringing her a brace of fish." It was those damned jumping fish I had in mind. "If she can find a way to cook them that'll make them the hot item of the season, she's on the team."

He laughed. "You've just made Chris's day."

He turned to go again, but I caught him and gave him a good long kiss, just so he wouldn't forget to book the room while he was at it. "You made my year, Leo."

Now all I had to do was think of an appropriate courting present for *him*. Which wasn't going to be easy. What do you give a guy who gives you a kangaroo rex?

I'd think of something.

I could smell the hopfish bouillabaisse even before Chris set the tureen in the middle of the table. As a perfume, it's right up there with molasses snaps and roses—though if I ever caught Chris cooking the roses I'd have her liver for dinner, however good it smelled.

"Hopfish!" crowed Aklilu. He made his spoon jump across the table. "Hop!" he said. "Hop! Hop! Hop!"

Chris snatched away his spoon. "Hop!" she said, landing it in the tureen. "You eat the hopfish, Aklilu, and help Mama Jason save the rice crop." She ladled bouillabaisse all around, then pulled up a chair and joined us.

After a first mouthful, she leaned back and smiled, justifiably proud of her work. To Nikolai, she confided, "A dish this size only takes five hopfish, which isn't nearly enough. Next time Mama Jason's telling stories, get her to tell you how Mirabile evens things up with the hopfish."

Aklilu banged his spoon against the edge of the table. "Story!" he chanted. "Story! Story!"

Nikolai grinned. "I'll second that," he said.

"After dinner," I said. "Some things deserve my undivided attention—and hopfish bouillabaisse is one of them."

3

The Flowering Inferno

"ANNIE!" Leo's voice was sharp enough to jab my quiet contemplation to hell and gone. "Fire at five o'clock!"

I hit the brakes, slammed the gear into hover and swung the nose of the craft around to five o'clock for a look. There was a glow on the horizon where there shouldn't have been any. Granddaddy Jason once told me that back on Earth there was always a glow on the horizon—light from the cities—but on Mirabile that kind of light meant only one thing: forest fire.

I looked at the light, looked at Leo. He had that intensity of focus he always gets when there's something needs doing. One damn thing after another—and if this sort of thing kept up, I would *never* have the moment's peace I needed to choose a proper courting gift for that man.

"Fasten your seat belt," I said, even though I knew he always did. Leo doesn't take unnecessary risks.

I threw the hover into forward and gunned it across country. Hovercraft across brush and rocks gets bumpy, especially at the speed I was doing. I don't take unnecessary risks either—so I was careful not to outrun the lights. Still, navigating was tricky and I concentrated on that while Leo picked up the comunit to call in a warning.

I slalomed through a stand of popcorn trees, dipped over a creek, swung wide to avoid a massive old churchill (must have been two hundred feet in circumference), scared the living daylights out of a herd of clashings, dipped down once again for another creek, and came up the rise on the opposite side to a blaze of light.

I hit the brakes again.

Leo whistled. "Somebody's been damn careless," he said.

I knew what he meant—weather we'd been having in this area, there was no chance the fire had been set by lightning.

The wind chased the fire across the meadow. Most of the flame stuck to the ground—usually did in a brushfire like this. But even as we watched two trees crowned out—lit like torches, streaming red, orange, yellow—so bright I could almost feel the heat from them.

Cautious now, I edged the hover closer, lifting it up the rise to overlook as much of the fire as I could. "I make it a couple of hundred acres just now," I said.

"Just now," agreed Leo, meaning he saw what I saw—no natural breaks to put a stop to it. He repeated my estimate into the comunit while I thumbed the transponder button to give the local controllers our exact position.

Then I took the comunit from Leo and said, "We'll skirt it for accuracy. Meanwhile, you check out any families in the area and make sure they're notified."

"Will do," came the reply.

Another tree crowned out just then and there were a half dozen sharp reports as burning bits of it struck the hover. Leo whistled. I backed the hover off hastily then started forward again, this time at a crawl.

After a nod of approval, Leo said, "This is new territory, Annie. There won't be many folks in permanent residence. If the wind shifts, we're in trouble, though. Northwest aims it at Milo's Ford."

I knew the town. "I don't need this," I said.

"Only about fifty families. We can get them out in no time. Just takes fast work."

"It's not the families I'm worried about. As you say, we can evacuate fifty families in no time. But Milo's Ford has our only breeding population of Cornish fowl and I'd hate like hell to lose them!" I picked up the comunit yet again and punched in for the home team.

"Hi, Annie," said Mike's voice. "I thought you and Leo were out dancing. What's up?"

"Forest fire," I said and I gave him the coordinates. "Get on the line to the folks at Milo's Ford, tell 'em to round up the Cornish fowl and get ready to get out if there's a change in the wind. Then phone round to Emergency Services and make sure they've got transport standing by."

"Milo's Ford, Emergency Services, I gotcha, Annie. We're on it." He didn't break contact. There was a moment's pause, then he said, "Susan and Selima are on their way to Milo's Ford. They're taking both of the specimen hovers. They'll meet you there." Then he hung up, before I could order the damn kids to stay out of it.

I snarled but my curses got applied to a series of crown-outs that made a Chinese Guild New Year celebration look like a newborn's birthday cake. I squinted in the afterimage and edged the hover still further away from the leading edge of the fire. It was running faster now; the wind had picked up.

A gust blew smoke our way and, eyes burning, I gunned the hover through it. There was a bit of clear patch on the other side, much to my relief. Leo punched the transponder again.

"Damn kids," I said.

Leo snorted. "You couldn't keep them away if you tried. Everybody likes an excuse to watch a fire."

I took my eyes off the terrain long enough to glower at him. It was the waste of a good glower because he never even saw it.

Proof of his own words, he was watching the fire, all awed

concentration. Reflected light made his dark skin glow like
embers, turned his white hair a flaming orange. Beyond him
another tree crowned out and he said, "Aaah!" with a sound
something like satisfaction. Then he reached over and punched
the transponder again.

I turned my attention back to business. We'd almost completed
our circuit of the fire. "Good enough," I said. "Tell 'em we're
headed for Milo's Ford."

From that spot Milo's Ford was almost dead straight. The only
natural firebreak between here and there was the river. This time
of year the river would be low—not much help if the wind should
change.

Even as the thought struck me, I could feel it in the way the
hover handled.

"Wind's changed," Leo said. Same tone of voice he'd used to
tell me about the fire. He twisted in his seat, fighting the belt to
look back the way we'd come.

I spared a glance in the mirror and saw the wind chase the line
of fire down the hill, hot on our trail. "Sit, Leo, dammit!" I
gunned the hover again. If he hadn't been sitting, he was now.

We left the fire behind, but we were riding the wind now and
I knew it wasn't far behind. I had some hope, I think, of reaching
Milo's Ford before Susan and Selima did.

Fat chance. The two specimen hovers were right there in the
middle of main street, surrounded by a motley collection of other
craft, everything from hovers to dogcarts, and a milling mass of
people that I could already see were too riled to be useful to
themselves or anybody else.

I grounded the hover with a thump, unsnapped my harness,
and reached for the persuader I keep alongside my seat. Then I
was on the ground and headed for the largest knot of argument,
Leo right behind me.

I paused just a minute to assess the situation. Selima and a
bunch of kids were loading Cornish fowl into the specimen
hovers. There was nothing gentle about the way they were doing
it and the birds were kicking up more than the usual amount of
rumpus. Even that didn't drown out the argument.

"And I say we leave the little bastard here!" This got a howl of agreement from the onlookers. "He started the damn fire, I say, let him roast!" The speaker was a big man. Worse, he spoke for the rest of the mob.

Somebody else added, "Yeah, and let his birds roast, too!"

The middle of the knot was Susan. She looked dwarfed. Hell, she was all of sixteen and a skinny kid at that. She looked exasperated beyond her years. "And I say I won't be party to a murder." She turned on one of the other people in the crowd. "Will you? We leave him here and he dies and then maybe you find out he didn't start the fire. . . . You gonna take that on you?"

She'd gotten through to that one, all right. That one ducked away from the mob and, like a cat playing innocent, went to offer Selima her assistance. Susan turned the same stare on a second person in the mob. "You, Catalan, you gonna be a murderer? Thought I knew you better. Thought Elly'd raised you better, in fact, than to go around accusing somebody without the damndest bit of proof. You gonna leave 'im here to die on just *his* say-so?"

It was good work on Susan's part. She might even have brought it off—but the stabbing gesture she made at the ringleader connected somewhere in the area of his paunch. He turned purple, roared, and reached for her.

I raised my persuader and fired it once into the air. Everybody froze and turned. Nothing like a double-barreled shotgun to get their attention.

Having gotten it, I shouted, "All right, everybody. The wind's changed, in case you were too busy to notice. The fire's now headed straight for the town. If you want to save the buildings, you've still got a chance—*if* you get all the able-bodied adults down to the edge of the river to douse any sparks that land on this side. Meanwhile, let's get the kids loaded and out of here."

Still nobody moved. I lowered my persuader and aimed it at the feet of the ringleader. "You with the big mouth," I said. "Go spit on the damn fire. That, at least, would make you of some use." I went to squeeze the trigger.

The minute he saw I had every intention of blasting him, he put his hands up. "Buckets!" he said. "Harriet, get buckets!"

"And shovels," I suggested.

The whole crowd turned and went for buckets and shovels. I tucked my persuader back under my arm and went over to Susan.

Susan swiped at her forehead with the back of her hand and grinned at me. "Am I glad to see *you*, Mama Jason!" She gave me a peck on the cheek, then delivered a matching one to Leo. "Hi, Noisy," she said, "I guess I didn't do so well, hunh?"

"You had him outshouted," Leo told her, bestowing an accolade. "I'd say all those contests we had paid off pretty well."

"Sorry," I said, "no time to rest on your laurels. Give me the rundown."

Susan twisted to look over her shoulder at Selima, who was just closing up the huge hover doors with an equally huge thunk. Selima gave Susan a thumbs up and climbed into the cab. "That's all the kids and the Cornish fowl taken care of," Susan said. "Selima's taking the kids up to Loch Moose Lodge. Elly said she'd look after them. The Cornish fowl I'm taking back to the lab."

Selima took off in the first hover. I watched for a moment as she angled it out toward Loch Moose. When I looked back, Susan was still standing in front of me.

"Well? What's keeping you?" I said.

Susan shot a quick look around. The glow on the horizon had become distinct flames now—another ballyhoo crowning out, I thought, and realized as I thought it that all the trees I'd seen flame had all had that distinct shape of the ballyhoo tree. You could hear the roar now, too. I glared back at Susan, wondering why in hell she still hadn't moved.

She leaned closer. "The guy they accused of setting the fire. He's in—" Her hand made a covert stab at the second specimen hover.

"Ah," I said, understanding at last. I think I must have grinned, I was so proud of her. "Good. Then get him out of here, too." I handed my persuader to Leo. "Just in case. You go with her, Leo, and ride herd on the suspect."

Susan had recovered enough to cast a scandalized eye on the persuader.

Leo laughed. "It's loaded with rock salt. Stings like the dickens. Why do you think she always calls it her 'persuader'? Nothing quite like a shotgun full of rock salt to convince a man to move ass."

"Then let's," said Susan.

I made them both promise they'd take care of business before they did any more fire watching and saw them off. Then I grabbed a shovel out of my hover and went down to the edge of the river to do what I could.

Now that they had something constructive to do, the townspeople had organized themselves pretty damn well. One of them had disconnected the town pump and hooked it to a few lengths of hose. They used the river water to damp down everything on this side of the river. Another handful cleared brush from the bank, chucking it into the river and letting it slide away downstream. The bend in the river here made the current slow and the water shallow (about waist high because of the drought we'd been having) but the river was wider than I'd remembered, which gave us more of an edge against the fire's advance.

The wind was still blowing it in our direction, though. That made enough light to see by, lurid though it was. What I hadn't counted on was the sound of it. Everybody talks about the roar of a fire, especially a big one, but that doesn't tell the half of it. That *sound* is the sound of a living creature roaring its challenge at you. That sound is a beast straight out of your worst nightmare coming to get you. That sound made my entire nervous system scream panic.

I managed to beat most of the feeling into submission but the hairs on the back of my neck stayed up—and I knew I'd be *hearing* my nightmares for months to come.

Something shot past me about hip high, startling me enough to make me jump back. Somebody else let out a shriek. Then we both realized that it was only a hopfish. A full school bounced by, adding to the general confusion. They were headed away from the fire as fast as their hopping would take them. Weird thing about it was that they were headed away from the river as well. Didn't seem sensible. But then other animals were fleeing as well, and they were more scared of the fire than they were of us.

We spotted the herd of clashings headed our way just in time. Clashings will butt anything their size. Under these circumstances, they might have made an exception, but nobody near me wanted to test the theory. We hit the ground and the clashings sailed over us, neat as you please, and crashed into the wood behind us and vanished, screaming challenges as they went.

There was another sound, too, and I realized why it had earlier put me in mind of the Chinese Guild New Year celebrations. The ballyhoo trees didn't just crown out. When they caught, they went like a fireworks burst, complete with a volley of cracks and a shower of burning coals in all directions. I've seen a pine log burst like that—in ships' records. You hear the same sound when it bursts, come to think of it. Happening for real, it was damn pretty, but those coals were getting flung just too damn far for my taste.

The wind picked up speed. A metallic roar behind me made me jump. I turned and saw that somebody'd been bright enough to bring a chain saw. She was cutting down the trees nearest the bank.

I charged over and shouted at her over the sound of the chain saw and approaching fire, "The ballyhoos! Cut the ballyhoos first!"

Either she didn't hear me or she didn't heed me. By then I had recognized her, though. "Catalan!" I shouted again. "The ballyhoos first—they burst! If one of them starts up this side of the river, we won't be able to contain it."

That did it. I pointed across the river and she spared a look just in time to see another ballyhoo burst. Her eyes went wide. She nodded and left off the tree she'd barely begun to race to the nearest ballyhoo and start on that.

So I followed. The ballyhoo fell with a crash. Catalan sliced off the top and the two of us shoved that into the river and pushed it off. Leaving the nearly branchless trunk for somebody else to roll in, Catalan took aim at the next ballyhoo and brought it down too.

Shovelers followed us, scraping up the duff and tossing it by the shovelful into the river. We were lucky—it wasn't more than two inches thick this close to the river—we could scrape down to bare rock.

We could feel the heat from the fire now. Somebody'd brought a second chain saw. I grabbed him and dragged him to the water's edge and in. He looked at me like I was nuts, but I didn't waste time on explanations, just took the chain saw from him and held it high and slogged across the river with it.

I'd gauged the depth of the water by the clashings charging through it. I *hadn't* counted on coming waist high to a pack of grumblers in midstream. Grumblers are only dog sized but that many of them will take on humans if they're threatened—or think they are. They grumbled at me—I couldn't hear it but I could tell by the way their fringed muzzles were working overtime—but they were too busy treading water to really care, so I bulled right through them.

There were three ballyhoos on the opposite bank. By now, I had all too good an idea how far they could throw those embers. Cutting those three was our only chance to keep the fire on the far side of the river. I attacked the first with a vengeance, not stopping to worry about how I could get it pushed off by myself. As long as the crown was under water I figured Milo's Ford had half a chance.

I dropped that one and went on to the second. I was sweating like a pig now, from the effort and the nearing flames. Some wicked bit of my mind wondered what had ever possessed the Texan Guild to coin such a phrase—pigs don't sweat.

The second ballyhoo hit the water with a crash and a splash and I raced for the third. I wasn't sure I was going to make it—the flames were already too close for comfort. I got it dropped though and then leaned into it to shove the crown into the river.

Something pounded me hard on the shoulder—three times before I could react. I whirled to find the guy I'd taken the chain saw from. "Your jacket was on fire!" he shouted. "Let's get this shoved off and get the hell out of here!"

We did both. As we hit the water, with him carrying the chain saw this time, I realized he'd shoved the other two trees off too. God only knows why he'd followed me across the river—people do the strangest damn things when they're scared—but thank god for the favor!

The grumblers were still treading water in midstream, grumbling irritably into their whiskers as they paddled. Since they were making no attempt to reach the town side of the shore, it was obvious they expected the fire to leap the river. I could only hope my helper and I had at least made that a little more difficult.

He gave me a hand again as we hit the bank—with such a yank that I flopped to land like a beached whale. Then he was helping me up. A tree drifted downstream just that moment, so I realized why he'd felt the need for urgency. "Thanks," I shouted, but I don't know if he heard me—he was too busy stamping out a spark that had landed scant inches from his feet.

And then I was too busy stamping out sparks to repeat myself. I took off my jacket, scarcely noticing the hole burned in it, and wet it down to beat out anything else that landed nearby.

And that was what we did for the next few hours. It felt like days—I know it was hours only because Leo told me what time it was when he dragged me back to Milo's Ford for food and coffee. What I *needed* was a bath—I was covered head to toe with soot and sweat—but I didn't have the energy and, anyway, the town's water was being used elsewhere at the moment.

Still, reinforcements had arrived by the hover full, so I was willing to take a break before my body quit on me. Just sitting took all the energy I had left.

Somebody passed me a cup of coffee and a plate of eggs—Cornish hen eggs, from the size of them. If I'd had the strength I'd've had somebody's heart for wasting the gene pool like that. As they were already cooked, I ate 'em.

When I finished, the same somebody took the plate and handed it back with a second helping. This time I was revived enough to pay some attention to what was going on around me.

The guy who was shoving food at me was the same guy who'd followed me across the river.

"Damned if I know what possessed you to cross that river," I said, "but thanks for the help."

He shrugged and gave me a shy sort of grin. "Least I could do for somebody who threatened to shoot my balls off."

I blinked at him and wiped soot from my face. Sure enough—it was the same guy I'd turned my persuader on, somewhere in the dim dark past. I thought back—in reality, it had only been a few hours earlier. "I was aimed lower," I said. "I don't waste good genes." I stuck out my hand. "I'm Annie Jason Masmajean."

"Pallab Hatcher Brahe," he told me in return. Then he laughed, taking my explanation for a joke. "I thought you looked familiar. No reflection on me, then, that you wanted to save my genes. You saved the kangaroo rex."

"You never know what might turn out to be useful," I said.

He looked suddenly abashed. "Not me," he said. "I screwed up bad."

I knew he was thinking about the lynch mob he'd gotten up. "Good," I said. "If you know that much, maybe you can keep your priorities straight next time something needs doing." I fixed him with as steely an eye as I could manage, given all the smoke in the air. "Fire fighting first, justice second."

Something flashed in his eye and I said, "*Justice*, Pallab, not vengeance, and not blind striking out at the nearest scapegoat. Just because you don't like the man doesn't mean he sets fires. Show a little good sense—that would hurt him as much as it hurts you!"

My throat was hoarse and sore, from all the shouting and the smoke. I poured some coffee down it, hoping that would help some. It did—the coffee was mildly spiked.

Hatcher Brahe looked as if I'd spiked him.

"I saw Jongshik Caner Li set two fires earlier this week. Good thing they were small enough we could just stamp them out. But he was in the right place at the right time to have started that one"—he waved a hand in the general direction of the river—"as well."

"*Saw* him start two fires? Bend down and set fire to the woods with a match each time?"

"No, of course not! Nobody's stupid enough to be that obvious!"

I was more than a little cranky myself, so I matched his tone. "So what did you actually see?"

"First time, we were out about five miles west of here." He paused a moment, took a step back in his telling. "Jongshik is our caner. There's a good stand of goldrushes there. I went along to help him gather a couple of bundles of cane."

All right, I could follow that so far. About time for the town to replace some of the older baskets and chairs.

He went on, "I was bending over to scythe the goldrushes—my back was to Jongshik, I grant you—when I heard Jongshik yell for help. I looked around and he was stamping out flames."

"So you helped him stamp out the flames. And?"

"And not much. He looked scared. Hell, I was scared, too. I know how dry the woods are. But we got it out. I reamed him out for being careless. He claimed he hadn't, and he looked even more scared." Brahe took a sip of his own coffee and said, "At the time, I thought he just didn't want to be blamed for—for his carelessness. But there was no way that fire could have started otherwise."

"And the second time?"

"Just like the first. That was the second trip we made for goldrushes—they're awkward carrying at the length Jongshik needs. Except that this time I spotted the fire. He helped me put it out but. . . ." Instead of finishing the sentence, he glowered into his coffee.

"How far away from the fire was Jongshik when you spotted it?"

"He could have thrown a match that far easily. Or it might not have flared until after he moved away."

"Or he *might* not have had anything to do with it."

"When it just 'coincidentally' happens twice in his presence?"

"Happened coincidentally twice in *your* presence," I pointed out. "I can't think of a better way to avoid suspicion than to cast it on someone else first."

Somebody else might have slugged me for that suggestion. Maybe Brahe was as tired as I was, even though he was some thirty years younger, or maybe he was just fair now he'd had a chance to think about it.

He said, "I couldn't have set the big one. I was in town all evening."

Meaning Jongshik hadn't been. "So Jongshik was out there?"

"Yeah. The goldrushes out there dry up red. He uses them for pattern."

I thought about that for a while. "Awfully stupid of him to admit he was in the vicinity."

"I was just thinking that," Brahe said. His shoulders slumped. "And I was just thinking I could probably rig a device that would start a fire two days *after* I walked away from it. I'm not even very good with technological devices. Lots of people are better. They'd have thought of it first in fact."

He stared into his cup. Got up, got us both more coffee. Then he resumed staring into his cup. "I still don't like the coincidence." He met my eyes. "I know, I know, the coincidence makes me as suspicious as it makes Jongshik, but I was there and I know *I* didn't set it."

He glared at me. "Dammit, there's been no rain, no thunderstorms with lightning—not even heat lightning! If Jongshik didn't set those fires, how the hell could they have started?"

"Good question," I said.

THE FIRE WAS PRONOUNCED "out," which only meant that the area would have to be watched closely for two days or so. There was always the chance that a burning ember could restart it. So the firewatch was on.

Leo drove home. I fell asleep on the way and woke up only long enough to crawl into bed (not caring how sooty and sweaty that got the bedclothes or Leo; to his credit, he didn't care much about how sooty and sweaty I got him either) and fall asleep again.

When I woke up, it was late afternoon. First things first, I showered and changed the sheets. The mirror told me what I was feeling was not just bruises but scrapes as well. My face looked like the end cut of a well-done roast. I smeared on antiseptic with a liberal hand—well, at least I looked well-basted now. The thought made me ravenous.

Downstairs I found sandwiches waiting in the fridge and a note from Leo. He'd gone over to the lab to lend a helping hand. I ate my sandwiches on the way.

The lab was the usual madhouse, which was why I was pleased to see that Leo had acquired an interested onlooker. The more the merrier. . . . Leo was giving him Set Lecture No. 1 and sounding remarkably like Susan while he did it.

". . . When they tried to raise Cornish fowl up near Last Edges, they got everything from bluejay to cassowary. Chie-Hoon thinks it was the higher lime in the soil"—he shrugged—"but it might have been the higher average temperatures. Or it might have been something else. EC can differ even from one *farm* to the next."

The onlooker said, "Oh. So that's why Susan insisted we bring their feed, too."

"That's right." Leo caught my eye, grinned a welcome and went on with his lecture. "Now, hit the right EC to switch on the encrypted genes and . . . well, Chie-Hoon tells me the Last Edges Cornish hens hatched out a bluejay-cassowary chimera that was close to eight feet tall and got its manners from the jay side of the family. The only good thing about it was that it couldn't fly. Lucky thing *those* weren't viable!"

"I dunno about that," I said. "It was tasty."

Should have kept my mouth shut. Now I was officially on duty again.

Mike looked up and said, "Good news, Annie! The ashes from the fire just about wiped out the hopfish population downriver!"

Well, that was a nice surprise. The hopfish were still a damn nuisance. The best we'd been able to do was make them a favorite in soups and dinners. That meant we didn't lose all the benefit of the rice they devoured from our rice fields. They eat it, we eat them. Trouble was, we couldn't eat them morning, noon, and night, which was how they ate our rice.

"Best news I've heard all morning," I told Mike. I gave Leo a peck on the cheek and pulled up a chair to see what Mike was up to. "How'd that work out?"

"The ash asphyxiated 'em, Annie. It got in their gills and smothered 'em." He grinned at me. "Disgusting thought, isn't it?"

I grinned back. "Extremely." That explained the school of hopfish I'd seen leaving the river; they'd known something I hadn't. "And what have we here?"

Mike looked up from the little pile of seeds he was working over. "I had a thought," he said.

"Do tell."

"Fire-stripped land is the perfect EC for lodgepole and longleaf pine. I was thinking now we've got just the opportunity to start a grove or lots of groves. . . ."

I held up both hands. "Before you complicate the issue thoroughly," I said, "I want to do a full workup on the EC around Milo's Ford."

He squinted at me. "We've got one, Annie."

"We've got one from before the fire." We'd done it several years ago, trying to figure out why the Cornish fowl did well in that area and nowhere else. "I need one for the current EC around Milo's Ford. As you've just pointed out with your lodgepole pine seeds, things have changed."

He looked at me glumly. "I suppose so," he said, and made a big deal of scraping his chair back from the bench. I knew a pet project when I saw one. Mike likes pine trees better than just about anything (except Selima, of course). If he had his way, Mirabile would be a forest of pines—all Earth-authentic, mind you—and nothing but.

I patted him on the shoulder. "You do me a full gene-read on the Earth-authentics you want to introduce. I'll go do the EC on Milo's Ford."

"Great!" Mike slid his chair back in a whole helluva lot faster than he'd slid it out.

I glanced at Leo and finished, "If I've got a volunteer to help me?"

Leo nodded, as I knew he would, but then his onlooker spoke up as well. "I'll help. I need a lift back to Milo's Ford anyway. I'll be glad to help any way I can."

Leo was shaking his head vehemently. "Not yet, Jongshik. Give things a chance to shake down a bit first."

"But Leo, I didn't start the fire! I swear it!"

"I believe you. But the entire population of Milo's Ford is a tougher proposition. As of today, they'll likely still be too exhausted and too angry to think straight about you."

If Leo believed Jongshik Caner Li, it was a good bet he hadn't caused the fires. I looked him over, now that I had the chance. He was anxious and thin, and he had the palest skin I've ever seen on a human being other than an albino—took me a moment to realize that part of that paleness was the anxiety. Still, the genes were clearly interesting enough that I wasn't about to risk his ass in his home town just yet.

"Sit," I said to him. "You're going to stay here and gofer for Mike. He needs your hands more than I do just now."

"But—"

"No buts. Sit . . . and tell me about the two previous fires you and Pallab Hatcher Brahe saw start up."

He sat so abruptly I knew it was just as well I'd leaned on him. He was still in shock. The mouth opened but nothing came out.

"You and Pallab went for goldrushes. Tell me what happened next," I prompted.

"I didn't—"

"I didn't say you did. Tell me what happened next, before I get too cranky to listen."

Leo said, "You don't want to see her cranky, Jongshik. Believe me. And she's asking because she needs the information."

I was already cranky. Leo's calmer approach, bless him, worked much better.

Jongshik took a deep breath, frowned a bit, as if thinking back that far was tough work. "I can't tell you much, Jason Masmajean. I know Pallab thinks I was being careless that first time. But I wasn't, I swear it. I know how dry the brush is this year."

"Tell me what you saw, that's all."

"I don't smoke, I hadn't lit any kind of a fire, and there was nothing in my equipment that *I* can figure would have caused a spark—" He stared at me, willing me to believe him. "I looked down and there was a fire at my feet. That's all!"

Leo said, "You were using a scythe for the canes, right? Any chance the scythe struck sparks off a flint outcropping?"

"No, Leo, no chance. I wasn't using the scythe. I was tying up canes I'd already cut."

"Spark might have smoldered a bit before it brought up flames," I said. "I like your theory, Leo. It's a possibility—if there was flint in the area."

Jongshik spread his hands. "I don't know."

"Something to look into," I told Leo. Then I said to Jongshik, "How about the second incident?"

Jongshik slumped. Not much, just enough to let me know he didn't think I was going to believe him this time.

"Try me," I said.

That startled him upright. Again, he took a deep breath. "I was"—he stood suddenly to demonstrate—"bending down to gather up canes. I looked back to see where Pallab was. You . . . please understand that I was looking at things almost upside down. I think . . . I *think* I saw a plant burst into flame. I was so surprised that I couldn't do anything for . . . it seemed like a long time. Then Pallab yelled and I realized I hadn't been imagining it and I went to help him beat it out."

Leo said, "You think Pallab set it?"

"No. No, of course not. Unless it was like you said—sparks from the scythe. Pallab *was* cutting cane when it happened. But it looked to me like the plant just caught fire from nothing." He drew a hand across his forehead and sat down again. "I know this is stupid of me, but all I could think of was those old stories about people who can start fires just by thinking about them? I couldn't tell Pallab that. I don't even believe it myself."

"That makes several of us," I said, noting the dubious look on

Leo's face. "So far I like Leo's theory best. Come on, Leo. Let's go see for ourselves."

Jongshik gave me one last pleading look. "Not yet," I said again. "Mike needs your help." I gave Mike's name just enough emphasis to goose him into looking up, catching on, and saying, "Yeah, I could use it."

Leo and I left Mike to handle that one. When we were out of earshot, I told Leo, "Anybody asks at Milo's Ford: Jongshik's under house arrest until we get this sorted out."

"Right."

I WOULDN'T HAVE RECOGNIZED the place. At least, not the far side of the river. I've seen the results of forest fires before, but it always stuns me. The town side of the river was soot blackened and covered with a two-inch layer of ash. The other side—well, the other side was gone. The fire had burned right to the bank and there was nothing left but ash and charred tree spars. A fog of soot-black smoke still clung to the barren ground.

Seeing that, it's easy to think that nothing's left. I could read that reaction in the faces around me. I couldn't share it, though. I *know* what's happening under that scorched ground— underneath there are millions of seeds just waiting for a chance at sunlight and at all those nutrients the ash puts back into the soil.

Meanwhile, even over the sound of the river, I could hear the cracking noises of charred trees cooling, the flurry of insects come to take advantage of those that had already cooled, the beating wings of the thousands of chatterboxes come to take advantage of the insects. . . . They were wonderfully gaudy against the grey of the burned woods.

"Making out like pirates," I said to Leo, indicating the chatterboxes.

Leo chuckled—one of my favorite sounds in this world—and said, "And you complain Mirabile doesn't have enough insectivores?"

"It doesn't. The chatterboxes won't eat anything Earth-authentic. Just as well. Most of our imports would poison them.

Meanwhile, they do just fine at keeping down the native insects."

"Jason Masmajean! Annie!"

The voice from behind us made us both turn. It was Thomas Finest Irizarry, which meant I could have safely brought Jongshik back with us. Irizarry was damn good at his job, which was seeing that the right person was arrested for a crime and that his suspect made it to trial alive.

With him was Pallab Hatcher Brahe. Given the expression on Brahe's face, Irizarry had read him the same riot act I had.

Irizarry looked from me to Brahe and said, "Here, Annie, you can always use extra hands. He's yours for two months total."

"I'll keep my persuader handy," I said.

"Ouch," said Irizarry. He knows what I load the persuader with—I used it on him once. To Brahe, he said, "Now I *know* you'll mind your manners." To me, he said, "I want a word with you in private."

"Fine. Leo, you and Pallab get started on those samples. This won't take but a minute." I gave Irizarry the look I use to tell people it had better not.

He nodded. Together we retired a short distance away. I sat down on the stump of one of the ballyhoo trees Catalan had cut down so short a time ago. "Pull up a chair," I said, patting the spot beside me. The stump was downright striking, the rings being extremely well defined.

He did. "I hear you spirited away the suspect last night."

"Susan did. I just reminded the mob there was a fire coming their way." I held up both hands. "Before you get stroppy—I'm not convinced he had anything to do with the fires. If you want to talk to him, he's under house arrest, helping Mike out back at the main lab."

He nodded again. That obviously took care of the thing foremost on his mind.

"You don't think he was responsible for the fires, Annie?"

"Leo doesn't think he's responsible for the fires, which is a point in his favor." I grinned and added, "But then I'm biased. Officially, I don't think anything yet. I need to know more. Still, if you'll be staying here for a time, I'll bring Jongshik home." Lest Irizarry give me an argument, I added, "This *is* his home."

"Annie, you're my favorite liar. You *don't* think Jongshik responsible or you'd never have leaned on that 'home' bit."

I had to admit he was right, though I hadn't thought it through. So I took the time to tell him everything I'd heard, both from Pallab and from Jongshik, about the first two incidents. I added in Leo's theory for good measure.

Irizarry looked thoughtful. "I'd like to see both spots they talked about. I like Leo's flint theory, too. First, though, I think I'll go have a talk with Jongshik Caner Li."

"Good. Then I can get back to my job." Figuring the interview was over, I turned my attention to the tree rings. I was gouging out a cross sample, when Irizarry said, "Annie? What on earth is so interesting about a tree stump?" Irizarry's the nosy type—just as well in his chosen profession.

"What is so interesting about this tree stump," I said, "is that this area seems to have gone up in flames about once every"—I paused to count the lighter rings between the darker ones—"fifteen years or so."

He stooped to follow my point.

"And it's been doing it for a lot longer than there have been humans on Mirabile."

"Natural fires," Irizarry began.

"*Regular* fires," I said. "Count 'em for yourself. Every thirteen to fifteen years."

"What's that mean?"

"I'll let you know as soon as I find out. Now scoot and let me do my job."

I HONESTLY THOUGHT that would be my most interesting find until I'd had a chance to analyze the samples we were taking. Instead of slogging across the river, this time we took one of the town kayaks. Using the hover, we'd already found, stirred up too much ash to permit continued breathing. Even a bit of wind added to the sting in the air.

A lot of the volunteer fire fighters from the previous night were still ranging on the far side of the river, checking hot spots. Not my idea of a fun job—they checked hot spots by putting a hand down at the edges of them, to see if they were still so hot as to restart the fire.

I didn't think it likely myself: there wasn't that much left to burn.

Leo and Pallab had already set to work collecting soil samples, so I did my bit with what plant life remained. It was a tricky business—some of the trees were still glowing and you had to keep your eye out for toppling trees and falling branches. More than once I got steered away from sampling a tree because the fire fighters knew from experience that one would come down—and soon.

They may be volunteers, but they are professionals. We've had to reinvent almost every skill locally. Ships' records contained detailed instructions for doing just about anything they knew how to do back on Earth, but that doesn't give the first generation any practical experience at the matter. You don't get practice fighting forest fires aboard a generation ship.

These folks had reinvented fighting forest fires. I've got a great deal of respect for them, you can bet!

So I picked one I've known a bit—another one of Elly's kids, name of Clelie Spinner Belile—and followed her around, gathering my samples in her wake. After about a minute, she caught me at it.

"Hi, Annie," she said, "Bet I'll be spinning tales about *you* again! Crossing the river to the fire side to cut down trees. I wish I'd been here to see it."

"If you'd been here," I pointed out, "*I* wouldn't have been doing it, *you* would have."

She laughed. "Maybe so. But tell me all about it, not leaving out Susan's part, and tell me how you knew about the ballyhoos. That was a stroke of genius."

"That was pure observation."

She shrugged, meaning I wasn't going to get off that easily. Then she said, "Let me show you something." She called to another fire fighter to keep an eye on her position, then she led me much deeper into the burned area.

There were still trees standing. Not that you could tell from one look what kind they were—the charring made everything look alike. But there were groves of trees still standing.

We skirted a tree whose trunk was still burning. From what was left of the branches, I'd've said it had been a popcorn tree. Overdone popcorn, if you ask me.

Clelie led me right up to the grove that was still standing. She sniffed and patted a moment, then thumped it hard enough that a layer of charred bark dropped to the ground, raising ash all around us. "Have a close look, Annie."

I did. The core of tree had not been touched by the fire—it lived still. That made me stoop down to examine the burnt bark. It was maybe three inches thick. How thick it had been before it caught, I couldn't guess.

Clelie had moved on to a second tree in the grove. Again she did everything but taste it—then delivered another thump, with the same result. Living core beneath charred bark.

"Clelie? Get me a chunk of the core?"

"Sure thing." She laid into it with her axe and popped me out a few good-sized pieces. "Enough?"

"Plenty," I said, gathering up the pieces to examine them more closely. The grain was unmistakable—they were my ballyhoo trees—the ones that had gone up like torches. "Ballyhoos," I said aloud.

"Yes," said Clelie. "And just about every one we've found is still alive. So what made you cut down the ballyhoos?"

I opened my mouth to explain but she said, "Never mind, Annie. I know. I saw a couple torch myself. I'd have had the same impulse. I just thought you ought to know—the damn ballyhoos seem to *like* fire."

I closed my eyes and saw it all over again. "What's more," I said, "they do their best to spread it."

Every fifteen years? I wasn't ready to talk about that yet, but it was well worth thinking about.

I paid her back for the samples and information with everything I remembered from the night before. As I talked, I gathered as many samples as I could. We didn't have much time until dark fell.

THERE WAS NO POINT heading back to the lab for the night. Pallab offered to put us up and I saw no reason not to take him up on the offer. Why put the kids at the lab through my general crankiness when there was someone who deserved it more?

The first thing I did was commandeer his computer, linked to the main computer back at the lab, and started to run my samples. Then I got introduced to Pallab's wife and fed at the same time. The wife was anxious. The kids were still at Elly's. She'd talked to them and found them still over excited from the night before. I knew how they felt and said as much.

With some good food in me, I felt much better. I leaned back with every intention of taking a break from the problem, glanced at Leo, suddenly remembering that he'd opened this territory, and leaned forward again.

"Hey, Leo! Tell me what you'd use to build a fire?" I realized belatedly that I was not being too clear and was about to explain the question. . . .

But Leo was right there. "I assume you mean when I was solo and I assume you mean in this EC."

I nodded.

He named some of the local trees. A couple he had to describe to Pallab to learn what common name had been given to them—he'd only learned them by sight or scent in one or two cases. He thought a bit more, then he gave me a startled look. "Annie!" he said, "the ballyhoos!"

"What about the ballyhoos?"

"They don't burn worth a damn!" He gave me a second startled look, for all the world as if I might think him crazy.

I didn't, not in the least, but Pallab said, "That's crazy, Leo. You saw them yourself last night. They burned like—" And then he stopped abruptly. He gave Leo a sheepish look.

Leo said, "If you want to start a fire, you strip the bark from a ballyhoo. Better than any kindling you can name. But you don't put ballyhoo branches on your fire because they don't burn worth a damn."

Pallab nodded energetic agreement. "Jillian—Builder Motwani—is still mad that we wasted the ballyhoos we cut down by tossing them into the river."

"I'd like to talk to her," I said, "and maybe to your town carpenter too." I meant when next we had the chance, but Pallab and his wife were up and out to fetch before I could stop either of them.

I eyed Leo. He eyed me. We had just enough time for a nice round of necking before the house was full of people and I was hearing all about the virtues of ballyhoo wood from a furniture maker and a handful of builders. Ballyhoo wood, it seemed, was virtually fireproof. Oh, you could chop it into small pieces and put in on a raging fire and eventually it would burn, but for all intents and purposes . . .

One of the builders pounded his foot on the floor. "Practically fireproof house," he said, "and a good thing too, under the circumstances!"

"Under the circumstances," I agreed. We were into strange circumstances. That was nothing new for Mirabile.

IRIZARRY TURNED UP the next day with Jongshik Caner Li in tow. Susan had tagged along for the ride. It was hard to tell whether Susan had come to help out with the EC or to protect her interest in Jongshik. Having saved his life once, she seemed ferociously interested in keeping him healthy.

She needn't have bothered. What with Irizarry hovering about and with Pallab and the rest of the townsfolk embarrassed as all hell about their respective parts in the mob action, there wasn't much to worry about on that count.

Still, I knew it wasn't over. Embarrassment would eventually aggravate their suspicion of him. After all, if they could prove something against him, their actions would be—in retrospect—justifiable. Human nature, I suppose, but it's sure one of those things I'd breed out of the species if I had my way. Not a useful trait.

I was just as glad to see Jongshik myself. Pallab wasn't sure he could locate the spots he'd seen the earlier fires start up. That didn't surprise me—the landscape had changed considerably. But between the two of them maybe we could find the places again. Being the caner, Jongshik would have a better idea of where he usually went for his materials, even given the changes in the landscape. At least, I hoped so.

I rounded up Leo and Pallab and headed out to apply to Irizarry for the use of Jongshik. Irizarry pointed across the river: Susan and Jongshik were digging in the thick ash. I hailed them and got back Susan's signal for five minutes.

It was ten, but when they showed up, they were both tremendously excited. The first five sentences (at least) were completely garbled.

"Do you suppose," I said to Leo, "that you could slow her down to my speed?"

Leo gave Susan a long look, up and own. "Don't know which button to push," he said, finally.

That had the desired effect. Susan laughed, took a deep breath and started over. "A whole troop of grumblers moved into the burned area, Mama Jason. They're out there digging and eating as if their lives depended on it. We wanted to see what they were after, so we scared a bunch of them off."

She paused a moment, as if she expected me to read her the riot act. Since she hadn't been mauled, I assumed she'd scared them off carefully, so I didn't say anything.

Having lived through telling me that, she took another deep breath and finished on a note of triumph: "Look what they were eating!" She thrust out two very sooty hands. "Roasted hopfish cysts!"

She poured them into my outstretched hands like so many chestnuts. Sure enough, they were hopfish cysts all right. Roasted and partially gnawed. Even without Susan's eyewitness evidence I might have guessed they'd been chewed by grumblers; the toothmarks were pretty characteristic.

Leo peered into my cupped hands. "Tasty," he said.

"I don't know about that. But it might cut down on how much of our rice they eat next year."

"Mama Jason?" That was Susan. She looked confused as all hell.

Her excitement had been purely intellectual, I guess. The grumblers would eat hopfish cysts. She hadn't taken it the next step. "We do a little controlled burning in the rice fields. Roast the cysts, which kills a lot of them. Invite the grumblers in to eat a lot more. Good work, Susan!" I poured the cysts back into her hands.

"Send Mike a full report and have him pass it around. Meanwhile, I'm going to borrow Jongshik here." To Jongshik, I said, "I want to see the locations of the earlier fires, if you can find them for me."

Susan gave a suspicious glance at Pallab and a proprietary one at Jongshik. "I'm coming, too."

I know that tone of voice; I've used it enough myself. "All right," I said, "but that hasn't gotten you out of the hopfish-grumbler study."

Irizarry raised an eyebrow as we headed for the boats.

I grinned at him and said, "I'll let Susan sit between 'em."

Pallab and Jongshik both looked at their feet. That was good enough for Irizarry—he laughed. "All right then," he said. He followed us down to push us off.

It was a long trek, but that was better than stirring up the ash with the hover. We passed two more troops of grumblers along the way. Each time we stuck around long enough to verify that they were indeed digging for hopfish cysts. Then we went on.

Eventually we found the sites of both of the previous fires. At least, Jongshik was sure we'd found both spots. There's not much left of cane after a fire that hot.

No flint outcroppings in either area. That made Jongshik look anxious and Pallab look still more embarrassed. Embarrassed was better than suspicious, I thought. Irizarry was right—I didn't think Jongshik was an arsonist.

Seeing the canebrake cheered me. Life, once it catches hold on a world, is damned stubborn. At the stubby bases of the burnt canes, tiny green shoots had already begun to push their way into the sunlight. In a week or two the whole forest would begin to green up again.

For no reason at all, that made me think of Leo. I turned to say something and found him smiling over the shoots as well.

Then we made the long trek back. Night had already begun to fall when we reached Milo's Ford. There was more I wanted to do, but it would have to wait until the next day. Susan and I spent the rest of the evening passing our information on to Mike and running our samples through the lab computer.

The next morning, I rousted the bunch early and hustled them through breakfast. Then I went to get Jongshik as well.

It was Irizarry that met me at the door to Jongshik's. "Oh, it's you, Annie. Want to borrow him again?"

I cocked my head at him, took in *his* persuader, which I was betting *wasn't* loaded with rock salt. "Trouble?" I asked.

He laid the gun aside. "Just a precaution. Never know when there might be trouble from the neighbors."

Tactful fellow, Irizarry. There wouldn't be trouble from the neighbors as long as they felt Irizarry was guarding Jongshik to make sure they'd have no trouble from him. Economical, killing two birds with one stone like that.

"I'm glad you've got a half dozen kids," I told him. "Ever think of having a few more?"

"Coming from you, Annie, I'll take that as a compliment."

"It wasn't a pass," I said. "Sorry, but you don't get to me the way Leo does."

He gave a mock sigh. "If only I were ten years older."

"Make that thirty. I'm not a cradle robber." By this time, I'd stepped inside the house. Jongshik, still as white-faced as ever, was just finishing his breakfast. "Hi, Jongshik," I said. "I need to see several canebrakes that didn't get hit by the fire. Can you take us to a couple on this side of the river?"

He could, of course, and he would—anything to help—though he didn't understand how it would since there hadn't been any flint outcroppings at the sites of the earlier fires. . . . He got even paler as he spoke, casting worried glances at Irizarry.

For good reason, I suppose, but the lack of flint outcroppings cast as much suspicion on Pallab as it did on him—if we were talking about arson, that is. I said, "I just want a good look at the normal EC."

Irizarry shrugged and escorted us to the hover. He grinned like a Cheshire cat when I gestured Susan into the back seat between Jongshik and Pallab and stayed to wave us off.

Poor boy! Too damn much ash had sifted its way into town. We left him in a cloud of it. After a bit, though, we reached an area that wasn't dusted, and we were out of the swirls of soot and into the forest.

Visually, this was the same EC as the far side of the river. At least, as the far side of the river had been before the fire. I wasn't seeing anything new or different. Both plants and animals seemed to be strictly Mirabilan. It made me all the more peeved that—what with the Earth-authentics and their Dragon's Teeth—we had so little time to devote to the study of native biology. Everything we did was purely catch as catch can.

From the previous EC we'd done, I knew there was nothing poisonous to the touch in an area like this. You just didn't go around putting stuff in your mouth at random. And you went *around* a killquick if you spotted one. The killquick made spotting easy, being lemon yellow, pumpkin orange, or the like. If it saw you first, it inflated to football size and let out a sound like a foghorn straight out of ships' records.

We didn't see a single grumbler as we trudged through the brush. Must have been they were all across the river stuffing themselves on hopfish cysts.

At last Jongshik said, "There! That's the kind I use!"

There was such relief in his voice, I had to stare at him. It took me a minute to realize that he'd also been worried he might be out of a job if all his sources of raw material had burned up.

"All right," I said, "samples of everything. Susan, get a chunk of soil—"

"And don't forget the bugs," she finished for me. "This is me, not Mike, remember?"

When Mike had started work with the team, he hadn't known that a soil sample meant everything in that chunk of soil. He'd spent nearly an hour picking the "extraneous" stuff out of his sample. I considered the whole episode my fault, not his—it's harder to tell what somebody doesn't know than what he does know, especially when to you it's a basic assumption.

"Snotty kid," I said. "I'm going to tell Mike you said that."

"Oh, no, Mama Jason! Please don't!"

"Then think before you open your mouth because next time I will tell Mike."

She nodded emphatically and we all set to business. A little while later Susan was—very politely—showing Jongshik how to take a soil sample, including the bugs. We got leaves and bark, cane and berry, fern and frond. Leo used the sampler gun on a ferret-like creature I'd never seen before that Susan and Jongshik startled out of a burrow with their soil sampling.

As before, there was no flint outcropping in the area. But I did get Jongshik to point out the plant he claimed to have seen burst into flame. It was a new one on me, so I not only took a sample but a specimen as well. Stubborn thing. Two of them came up in a row, then a long underground runner on it with no end in sight, unless it was the specimen several hundred yards to the left of us. We finally settled its hash with the sharp edge of a shovel. Jongshik couldn't tell me what it was called. Not interesting enough to have a common name. I stuck it in my kit and promised Jongshik we'd name it after him, at least in its scientific version.

From there I moved on to the popcorn and ballyhoo trees, so I took samples of both bark and wood. Pallab chopped, I gathered.

We were working on a ballyhoo when I realized I couldn't find any seedpods on the ground around its trunk. I inquired. Pretty soon the whole troop of us were scouting for seedpods. "Maybe it's male?" Susan said.

I pointed up. You could see the seedpods, but every one of

them was well out of reach. "Just the wrong season for ground-falls," I said, "or maybe the ballyhoo is a hoarder."

"A hoarder?" said Pallab.

"Yeah," Susan told him. "Some plants hang onto their seeds until the conditions favor germination."

A perfectly brilliant thought struck me. "Conditions like fire?" I suggested.

From the expression on Susan's face, she thought it was a brilliant idea, too. "I'll get you some," she said. She threw her arms around the ballyhoo's trunk and tried to shinny up it. Her first start was a failure. "Gimme a boost, somebody."

Pallab did, but the result was that Susan was Pallab's height up the trunk when the bark shredded and sent her sliding down in a shower of fibers. "It thought it only did that after the bark had burned," she said dourly.

I couldn't help it. I pointed at the duff on the forest floor. Ninety percent of it had that same fibrous look.

"That's some fire hazard," she said, as she realized what was under her bottom. "Makes a good pillow, though." She got up, brushing herself off, and glared a bit more at the tree. "I'm *still* gonna get one of those seedpods," she told it. "Mama Jason, I'm borrowing Jongshik, Pallab, and the hovercraft."

Jongshik and Pallab looked at each other. Susan fixed them with a steely eye and added, "You can sit on opposite sides. I need you both to lean out the windows, anyway." Again she looked at me.

"Be my guest," I said.

She gave the ballyhoo tree one last hairy eyeball, then stomped off towards the hovercraft trailing Pallab and Jongshik.

Leo said, "Never volunteer."

"If anybody can coax a hovercraft high enough to get those samples, it's Susan. You haven't ridden with her lately, have you?"

"Just a few days ago. Hair raising—but I assumed that was due to the urgency of the situation." He frowned. "Is that a good idea?"

"Letting her try? Sure. She'll be careful. She knows what I'd do to her if she weren't."

We took advantage of the opportunity to neck a bit, at least until we heard the hovercraft head in our direction. We broke our clinch just as Susan skimmed by us and shouted out the window, "There's smoke to the west, Mama Jason! About twenty miles!"

"Call it in and check it out!" I shouted back over the motor's roar. The hovercraft dipped once—Susan's way of nodding without risking her voice further—and headed off.

Leo squinted west. What with trees, neither of us could see anything much, but he was obviously getting an internal fix. "No towns in that area. If I remember correctly, there's one farm. I don't remember if they're raising any of your specialty items . . . Lady's name was Ommanney?"

That did ring a bell. "Experimental farm. She's trying to domesticate half a dozen kinds of Mirabilan animals. At least we won't have to worry about getting them back into a suitable EC." Which was something of a relief.

I gave Leo's shoulders a last hug and said, "Come on. Let's get the rest of the sampling done, so we're ready to go when Susan gets back. I've got a long night of gene-reads ahead of me."

We got back to work. Couldn't have been but ten minutes later, Leo called out, "Annie? Come tell me if I'm crazy . . ."

"I don't have to," I said, "I know you are."

"Annie."

The tone was different this time. I headed over to where he was bent over a sample. "I've got that one," I said. It was the stubborn one with the runner.

"Feel it," he said. The tone was still strange.

Puzzled, I bent down, held out a finger. Leo took my finger and laid it on the base of the plant. It was warm. I thought for a moment that was only from his body heat, but then I realized it was warmer than body heat. I closed my palm around the base. Yeah, definitely warmer than body heat—and the temperature was rising.

"You're not crazy," I said. "Grab a shovel. I want this one

alive. We can put it in one of the soil sample cases. Selima will have a field day with it."

Leo looked at me as if *I* were the crazy one. "Annie, that plant is warm! Either it's not warm or it's not a plant."

"Wrong." I couldn't help grinning. "There are Earth-authentics that do that. Plants that put out heat. Thermogenic, they call 'em."

We hacked through the runner and shoveled plant and soil into a case, Leo still casting a suspicious eye at me.

"Selima came across them in ships' records," I said. "They're something of a hobby with her. She'll love this—she's never had a live one to play with. Just the records." I leaned on the end of the shovel, trying to pull the names out of memory. "One was an arum, I remember. Earth-authentic. The other—hang on a minute—was a philodendron."

"But why would a plant . . . ?"

"Selima couldn't come up with an answer either. Ships' records suggested the heat was a way of attracting pollinators. One of them was supposed to smell like rotten meat."

Leo bent for a sniff of our potted sample, shook his head.

I had to laugh. "Leo, how would *you* know what smells good to a Mirabilan pollinator?"

He grinned and shrugged.

"As I say, Selima will have a field day with a live specimen to play with. One of the Earth-authentics supposedly had the metabolism rate of a hummingbird."

"I believe that," Leo said. He held the flat of his hand a few inches from the plant. "This one's certainly working overtime. I can feel the heat from here now!"

I felt my brow knit. I don't remember thinking at all, I just remember reacting—I shoved Leo back from the plant, hard enough that he sprawled.

"Hey!" he said, then "Hey! Holy sh—!" as the pot burst into flames.

I laid into it with the flat of the shovel. Beating the flames out wasn't easy. Half the soil we'd potted it with was duff and at least two inches of that was shredded bark from the ballyhoos. Leo kept busy making sure none of the sparks reached the ground around the pot.

When we were sure it was out, I remembered to apologize for the shove. Along with the apology, I gave him the full-body check. He returned the favor.

Then I dug through the samples looking for the other specimens of that little goodie I'd collected. "Leo, call for a pickup, will you? This is not a safe place to hang around."

He overlapped. He was already on the hand unit doing just that. "Susan's on her way back," he said.

The uprooted specimens showed no change in temperature. "At least my backpack isn't about to go up," I said. "Jongshik's not our arsonist. And he was close to right when he claimed he saw a plant burst into flames."

I went back for another look at what was left in the pot. "The plant set fire to the duff. Easy to mistake that for the plant itself bursting into flame." I poked around at the remains. "I wonder if the plant survives the fires it sets. I can't tell for sure. I wish I hadn't hit it so enthusiastically. There's not much left."

"*That's* our arsonist?"

"If it's not, one of us is a pyrotic. Have you been setting fires telepathically?"

"Not since I got religion. Which was about five minutes ago." He contemplated the smashed remains of the plant. "Annie? What say we chop down the rest of those while we're waiting for Susan? The one in your pack isn't hot. . . ."

I got the gist. I didn't know if leaving the root left us vulnerable, but it was something to do and it was revenge of a sort, so it felt satisfying.

"Oh, good, there's the hover," said Leo, straightening and turning toward the sound. Only the sound wasn't the sound of a hovercraft. A moment later, I knew he knew that as well as I did—from the look in his eyes.

It was the sound of fire, headed our way.

"We've got a fire headed our way," Leo said into the hand unit. "Marking our position now. Get somebody in to pick us up fast!

We'll leave the transponder on permanent mark and we'll head for the hills."

"Hills?" I said.

Leo pointed north. "I opened this territory, remember? Rocky hills that way. Nothing on them to burn."

I couldn't see the fire, but I could smell smoke now. "Let's go," I said. I dropped my pack, and we both lit out in a run.

Seemed like we ran forever. The roar of the fire was good incentive but neither one of us is young and—adrenaline or no adrenaline—our flat-out run wasn't good enough.

The dense undergrowth had given way to more-or-less grass-land. It might have made the running easier, but it meant we could see what we were up against—at least, those rare moments when the gusting wind cleared the smoke from our eyes.

We crested a small rise and suddenly got a clear view of the way ahead. Leo was waiting for me at the top, which made me realize I was lagging behind, holding him back.

He flung out a hand to show me where we were headed, a chunk of rock sitting in the middle of the savannah. He was right: it would have been a good refuge from the flames. Dozens of animals had already sought its safety.

But in that moment I saw we weren't going to make it. The wind was even now blowing the fire across our path. If we'd been thirty years younger, we *still* couldn't have made it across that plain before the fire swept it.

Leo turned to me and I could see by the look in his eyes that he knew it just as well as I did.

"Next suggestion?" I said.

He took me in his arms and kissed me, putting just about everything into that kiss. Then he leaned me back just a little, just to seeing and talking distance. "Annie, I love you. Marry me."

Under the circumstances, I couldn't think of much to say to that. The wind was ferocious; I could feel the heat of the fire.

Since I didn't answer, he gave me a second kiss, as if that might convince me. Then he pulled the hand unit out of his pocket and said into it, "I want a witness to a marriage agreement. I want a witness now!"

"You're on, Leo. Go," said the hand unit. I could barely make out the words over the sound of the fire, but it was enough to turn me stubborn.

"Marry you!" I said, "I haven't even given you a courting present yet!"

"Under the circumstances," said Leo, with a nod at the flames some two hundred yards from us, "I'll pass on the courting present."

"Well, dammit, I *won't*. I'm too old-fashioned to change my ways at this point."

The wind had changed again. The head fire was aimed straight at us. The slope of the crest gave us a view of the devastation behind the rush of flames.

"I get married," I said, "I'm gonna do it proper, you damn fool. Now, come on. I'll race you. Last one through buys the wine for the wedding."

I grabbed his hand and pulled him back into a run. I'd challenged him to a race but I had no intention of leaving him behind. As long as I held his hand, I knew he'd stick with me.

Down the slope we charged, hand in hand, directly into the smoke and into the flames. I'd made out the head fire to be some twenty yards across—it was the longest twenty yards I've ever done in my life.

Neither of us could see; we were running as straight a line as Leo or I ever could. Couldn't breathe worth a damn because every time I opened my mouth I got a lungful of searing heat. Burning brands struck us on all sides. I could tell my hair was on fire but I wasn't about to stop to put it out.

Once Leo stumbled, but I grabbed with my free hand and kept him up and running.

And then, miraculously, I was running on cooling ash. I couldn't slow yet. I beat at my hair. Burned my hand some, but got my hair put out.

It was Leo who pulled us both to a halt. "Annie," he said, gasping, "we made it through. We can stop now."

The words flicked a switch. My knees gave way and I hit the ground hard. Leo dropped beside me on one hand.

"Ouch!" He lifted the hand and knelt instead. "Watch out, Annie. The ground's littered with embers."

"Find yourself a cool spot and sit," I said.

He did. The cool spot he found was close enough that I could lean against him, so I did.

We sat like that for a long time, simply appreciating each other's company. Once in a while, we had to fling a burning brand away from us, but it was otherwise peaceful. Even the roar of the fire seemed like so much white noise.

A pack of grumblers, maybe the same one for all I knew, foraged in the burned ground behind us. Must have been a river somewhere nearby, for they were coming up with what looked like hopfish cysts. I watched them for a while. What we'd always taken for ornamental whiskers seemed to be much more than that—some kind of heat-sensing organ. They didn't burn themselves once. That would be an interesting thing to look into—later, when I'd caught my breath.

The sound of the fire gradually receded into the distance. The wind swirled hot ash around us, but all things considered we had a peaceful spot to rest our aching bones.

Then Leo said, "Listen!"

For one horrible moment, I thought there was another fire behind us. But there was nothing left to burn. It was the sound of a hovercraft.

Leo cursed. "I dropped the hand unit," he said. "They don't know where to find us." He cursed quite a bit more.

Finally I couldn't stand it. I gave him a big kiss to shut him up and said, "You're the scout, Leo. You can walk us out of here if need be. What the hell are you so irate about?"

I got to my feet and started waving my hands. Leo, no longer cursing, but grinning through a crust of grit and grime, stood up and did likewise.

Minutes after we spotted the hovercraft, the hovercraft spotted us. It put down in a great cloud of ash and ember. A second after that Susan nearly bowled me over in her rush to a hug.

Tears were pouring down her cheeks. I don't know as I've ever seen her in such a state, not even when she was a small child. "Oh, Mama Jason! We all thought you were dead. You were right in the middle of the fire . . . and the hand unit stopped transmitting . . . We all thought you were dead! Oh, Noisy!" With that wail, she gave Leo just as bowl-over a hug as she'd given me.

Jongshik broke up the party. "Let's get them back to town. Those burns need treating."

Susan burst into tears all over again, but that didn't stop her from hustling us into the hovercraft and heading back to town at well beyond the speed I'd have thought possible from a hovercraft.

Leo caught my eye and said, "A nice quiet ride into town. Just what I needed."

We had to skirt the fire, but I'd bet the trip took less time than the straight route would have had anybody else been driving.

When we put down (right in the middle of main street—Susan didn't care how much ash she raised), there was an astonishing amount of chaos. The whole team was there, it turned out—Mike, Selima, Chie-Hoon, everybody. We got a cheer as we eased our sore bones out of the hovercraft. I only realized how many burns I had when somebody (if I ever find out who, he's not long for this world) clapped me on the shoulder to congratulate me on my survival.

There was an undercurrent from the townsfolk I couldn't place and didn't like. Luckily, Irizarry had the good sense to back 'em all off. It took Susan's help to do it, but pretty soon we were bandaged, fed, and resting comfortably—a little drowsy from the painkillers the local medic had pumped into us.

Irizarry sat himself down beside us and said, "Ready to talk yet, Annie? I can hold 'em a little longer, but I'd rather not."

"Talk?" I said. "Yeah, I should turn the team loose on it, shouldn't I?"

Irizarry surprised the hell out of me. "Talk," he repeated. "Name the culprit!" He pointed with his gun—"Pallab or Jongshik?"

Now I knew I'd been in shock. Leo, too, or he'd have spoken up sooner. I hadn't noticed that Irizarry had them both in his sights.

"Neither!" Susan said. "They were both with me at the time!" From the sound of her voice, Irizarry would've had a second barrel of rock salt in his butt if she'd had the persuader to hand.

"Neither," I said to Irizarry, a lot more calmly. I was too tired to get excited, especially when I know Irizarry won't jump the gun. "I could name the culprit for you but I promised Jongshik that privilege, since he was the first to spot it in the act."

Yes, turn the team loose. That was the next step. "Selima, crank up a computer and pull all your files on those thermogenic plants of yours. I've got a Mirabilan analogue that you're just gonna love!"

"All right!" said Selima and turned to do it.

That's what I like about the younger generation—boundless enthusiasm.

"Susan, check the sample boxes you loaded into the hover-craft. I had to leave the second round behind. I'm hoping the cell sample from the pyromaniac plant made it in in the first load. If not, somebody's gonna have to get more—very carefully!"

Irizarry and Jongshik both shouted at me at once. When I sorted it out, the questions were, "A plant set the fires?" and "You mean I really did see a plant burst into flame?"

"Yes and yes," I said, then Leo and I took turns telling them what we'd seen. You could have sorted out who in the room was a jason and who wasn't just by the expressions on their faces. Everybody in the team was intensely interested; everybody who wasn't had a look of such disbelief you'd've thought I'd told them I'd found evidence of previous human life on Mirabile.

Selima took over from there, waving her *Arum maculatum* and her *Philodrendron selloum* at them. "Earth-authentic," she kept saying over their protests, "Earth-authentic!"—as if it were a magic word for believability. "Look, this one hits 114 degrees no matter what the ambient temperature is!"

The rest of the team helped Susan unload the specimen boxes and sorted through for the Mirabilan sample. They not only found the cell sample, but also a few limp leaves from one of the culprits. Susan had collected a specimen too, it seemed. There was a minor altercation over who got to do the gene-read but Selima won.

Irizarry shook his head. "That sorry-looking thing is the arsonist?"

"It looks much meaner when it's not wilted," Leo told him. "You can see the mad glitter in its eyes."

Irizarry got a bit of a mad glitter in his own eyes. "We should be out rooting them up," he said, "shouldn't we? I'm not sure I'd recognize it from this."

"I can draw it for you," Jongshik said. "I know what it looks like in the wild." Without waiting for an answer, he snatched up a sheet of printer paper and went to work.

"I'm not sure we should be out uprooting them," I said. "I want that gene-read first. Pulling them out may set them off." I gave Leo's hand an apologetic squeeze. "Sorry," I said to him. "This hasn't been one of my better days. Pulling them up seemed like the thing to do at the time."

"This one didn't burn," Irizarry pointed out.

"Long root," I explained. "Maybe we set off others at the other end of the root. And the plant didn't actually go up—it just set fire to the ballyhoo bark it was growing in. For all I know, the plant's fireproof."

"Not likely," Selima said. "But I'd bet money the seeds are. Now why"—she handed me the printout of the plant's genetic map—"why would it want to set fires?"

"And why every fifteen years?" I added.

"I like that question, too," Selima said. "It must get something out of a fire."

"Nutrients," said Susan. "From the ash. For its seeds to thrive in."

"Maybe fire wipes out a scale or a fungus that attacks it," Mike suggested. "Fire does that for my pine trees."

"Maybe both. Hey, Mike? Do the hopfish eat this the way they eat our rice?"

"I don't know. But I'm gonna find out." Mike shoved through

the crowd. "I'm going to commandeer another computer. Keep me posted."

"Here's the sketch." Jongshik handed it over. It was better than good. Anybody could have picked the plant out from his work. To the best of my memory, it was entirely accurate. I handed it to Leo, who confirmed it.

Irizarry snatched the paper from Leo's hand. "Now I've got something to work with. I don't need to know the why of it, Annie. All I need to know is, does uprooting one set off others?"

"Sorry," I said, "but you're wrong there. That's not all you need to know."

"I've got my suspect, Annie. If we don't wipe it out, Milo's Ford will go up in smoke sooner or later. Once every fifteen years, if you're right about those tree rings."

"I'm right about those tree rings. We're looking at an ecological cycle. Uprooting the pyromaniacs isn't going to put an end to the cycle, either. Milo's Ford will *still* go up in flames every fifteen years."

"Still? Why?"

"Because the ballyhoo trees make the entire area a fire hazard. Because they're doing it deliberately. Do you think you can police every inch of forest for pyromaniac plants? Even if you could, what about sparks from our equipment? What about lightning? Sooner or later, this whole area will catch, and the later the worse. The longer the ballyhoos shed bark, the higher the hazard."

Irizarry looked as tired as I felt. "Then we can't build towns in this EC. We'll have to relocate Milo's Ford."

"Oh, hell, Mama Jason," Susan said. "What about the Cornish fowl?"

"Chances are the ash from the fire across the river has already done 'em in. You know as well as I do, the EC here has changed enough that the Cornish hens will start hatching Dragon's Teeth. Besides, when it comes down to a conflict between Earth-authentic species and Mirabilan species, we've got to get on with the Mirabilan species or we won't make it on this world."

Even Irizarry, to judge from his expression, could see the truth in that. "So we relocate everybody from Milo's Ford," he said.

"At least temporarily. You want my advice, you get it. Here's what we do. . . ."

IT TOOK A WEEK to relocate everybody from Milo's Ford, along with everything they owned. The fire fighters kept a firewatch going the entire time, of course—that EC made it absolutely necessary. While everybody else moved furniture, we put in twenty-eight-hour days finding out everything we could about our pyromaniac and its partners in crime, the ballyhoo trees.

Susan's piloting got us the seed samples we needed. Leo did a little experimenting with ballyhoo branches and seeds. Clelie supervised, I'm glad to say, because the first thing he learned was the damn things actually explode—highly inflammatory oil in the seed pods—to send their seeds as far afield as possible. Lovely piece of bioengineering.

And, as it turned out, the hopfish did devastate the tender young shoots of the pyromaniac . . . unless there was a fire to cut back on the hopfish population at seeding time.

The pyromaniac plants saw to it there was, of course. The grumblers took care of the hopfish that didn't asphyxiate. Wonderful the way these these things work.

You can't help but admire nature.

At least, I can't. That's what I was doing when Irizarry stuck his head into the lab. "Annie, this was your idea. You're coming with me."

"Everybody's out of Milo's Ford?"

"Lock, stock, and barrel."

"Let me call Leo. He won't want to miss this."

"He's waiting in the hover."

Thoughtful man, Irizarry. He wasn't nearly as scandalized as Susan usually was when Leo and I spent the trip necking in the back seat.

"Heads up, folks," Irizarry said at last. "We're here." He brought the craft to a standstill, hovering just outside the edge of Milo's Ford. The forest around it was still green, but you could see the swollen seeds on the ballyhoos just waiting for their chance. The only thing that'd be left standing after fire swept this area would be the ballyhoos—and the pretty little frame houses in Milo's Ford, all made of that same fireproof ballyhoo wood.

Irizarry handed a box over the seat back. "They're on five-minute timers, Annie. I wanted to make sure we could get safely clear. I'm going to make a long pass all around the town. Clelie will give us the go-ahead when the ground personnel decide the wind is right," He nodded vaguely in the direction of the comunit. He had the damndest look on his face.

"Why are you handing them to me?" I asked.

"Because I don't want to do it. It feels wrong to me. This was your idea—you do it."

"Okay." I glanced at Leo. "Is this going to bother you?"

"Only if you don't share," he said.

So I divvied them up between us, we opened windows on opposite sides of the hovercraft, and we waited. After what seemed like forever, Clelie's voice came over the comunit, "Everybody's clear and the wind is right, Tomas—go!"

He did—and Leo and I dropped incendiaries the length of the run. By the time we reached the river, the first of them had gone up and caught with a vengeance. Irizarry goosed the hovercraft and moved!

At the top of the rise, he brought it to an abrupt halt and swung us around to face the town. He whistled. "Annie, I didn't believe you. I didn't think it would catch that easily."

"Now you know," I said. "This way the hazard gets cleared and townsfolk can move back in safely. At least for another fifteen years or thereabouts. This time a controlled burn was the best solution for everybody and everything concerned. Next time . . . well, next time we'll have to think about it all over again." I leaned back against Leo and watched the fire spread. All around Milo's Ford, the last of the ballyhoos were going up like fireworks.

"You know," I said, surprised at myself, "I think I'm admiring my handiwork."

Leo laughed. "You're my favorite force of nature, Annie."

Leo was back from his survival training trek with Jen and Ilanith, and the three of them wanted nothing so much as to sit on the porch with their feet up and watch nova-rise over Loch Moose. I had a lap-full of Aklilu, who was sleepy and, for the moment, quiet. Elly brought the baby, and Nikolai and Chris came out bearing gifts—molasses snaps and a pitcher of iced tea. For a while, the only sounds were the singing of the cheerups and the munching of cookies.

"Too bad Susan isn't here," I said. "Molasses snaps are her favorite."

"Second only to Janzen." Elly laughed.

"They're pretty mushy, Mama Jason," Ilanith said. "Probably they'd bug the hell out of you. Too busy to talk and all."

"Wait till it's your turn, kiddo," I told her. "Take notes, Jen. You're the one gets to tease Ilanith when the time comes."

"Right," said Jen, smugly.

Ilanith gave her a sideways look and said, "How 'bout a story, Mama Jason?"

That was pure diversionary tactic, but Aklilu roused enough to say, "Story!" So, story it was . . .

4

Getting the Bugs Out

WE WERE DOING a little contemplative fishing out in the middle of Loch Moose. At least, I was. Ilanith had her hook baited, but she was having about the same luck I was without bait or hook, which is to say nothing disturbed the serenity of the loch except the odders.

"Mama Jason?" Ilanith said. "I'm sorry I distracted Noisy. That's the biggest bell I've ever seen him make. I couldn't help hovering."

"Neither could I." I moved enough to pat her hand. "You weren't distracting Leo, kiddo—I was."

She made a scoffing noise loud enough to attract the attention of Pushy, the current head of the pack of odders. He rippled over and lifted his head to bellow at her.

Poor Pushy, he's all grace in the water, but that face is a howler. Looks like an old boot with big warm eyes.

The boat rocked. This time I had to move to compensate as Pushy tried to climb aboard. Ilanith giggled and bought him off with a chunk of stale bread. "Seriously, Mama Jason," she said, as Pushy slithered back into the loch.

"Seriously," I said. "I'm a hot old broad and I can distract Leo from just about anything he's doing. So says Leo—and nice of him to say so, too." I felt the same way about him and if I couldn't think of the right courting present for the man soon I'd start to get cranky on the subject. That was one of the reasons for the vacation (the other being I needed one) and for the contemplative fishing.

I could tell from Ilanith's expression that she didn't believe a word of this. Like most other adults, I took the easy way out. "Wait until you're a little bit older, then you'll understand."

Sensible kid that she is, Ilanith said, "I'll ask Elly."

I thought that over. Elly would find a way to explain it to her—which is why Elly raises kids and I don't. "Do that," I said. "Meanwhile, if you want me to drop you off on shore so you can watch Leo cast the bell, I will. I mean what I say: you're welcome, I'm not."

Well, she didn't understand it but she did believe me. She gave my offer thoughtful consideration and then said, "Nah. I'd rather fish with you."

And *that* was a compliment of the highest order.

Feeling well loved and very smug, I settled back once more. I had plans not to move for the rest of the day, or at least until it was time for one of Chris's dinners up at Loch Moose Lodge. Ilanith settled back too, looking much the same.

It was enough to lean back and appreciate the loch, laugh at the antics of the otters at one end and the odders at the other, and not catch so much as a fry.

Something hovered around us. It had the right amount of legs to be an insect but not one I'd ever seen before so I cocked an eye to watch. I couldn't tell at first glance if it was native Mirabilan or one of our imports. It made an odd kind of whining noise.

Ilanith was watching it, too. She wanted to look at its genes as much as I did.

The object of our mutual interest lit on my arm. The whine cut off just as suddenly. Afraid to disturb it, I moved my head, not my arm, for a closer look—just as it bit me.

I slapped it flat.

"Mama Jason!"

I'd sure as hell shocked Ilanith all right. "Vacation's over," I said. "And you can do a gene-read on a mashed bug just as easily as you can on a live one if you move fast enough. Now, move!"

We did. Rowed like hell for shore, charged up the path to the lodge. Ilanith, being the younger by some, took the lead early on. I could hear her shouting instructions to all and sundry before I reached the first crest. By the time I reached the lodge, half of Elly's kids stood wide-eyed in the hallway.

"You *smashed* it?" said Jen. Her eyes were huge. "Really smashed it?"

"Yes," I said, thrusting out my arm to show her the evidence. "Where's Ilanith?"

Mouth agape, Jen just pointed up the stairs. When I headed up, she trailed behind. The rest of them were too astonished to move that fast. I'd obviously scandalized the whole troop. "Elly!" wailed one of the smaller ones, "Elleee!"

In my room, Ilanith had already brought up the computer and linked it to my lab. My kit was spread out across the bed as if it had been upended and dumped. It probably had, come to think of it.

Scowling ferociously, Ilanith scooped the remains of the bug from my arm none too gently and stuffed a sample into the analyzer.

"You take half," I said. "Run your own gene-read. We'll compare notes when you're done."

That set her face to warring with itself. Disapproval of my outrageous behavior met the sheer delight of being asked to help out. The battle was still in progress when she vanished from the room with her sample.

Freed from the distraction, I got to business. The first step was the computer's. Once I set that going, I took the time to gather my kit back together.

As I packed away the last of my gear, Elly appeared at the doorway, Aklilu on one hip, a fist on the other. Behind her, just visible enough for me to see small child glowers, were the rest of the kids. The faintest of smiles tugged the corner of Elly's lips. "I've had complaints about you," she said.

Jen said, "She *smashed* it, Elly! She even *showed* us!"

Elly laid a reassuring hand on Jen's shoulder and said, "I hope you've got a good explanation, Annie. You're the one who's always telling us not to trash the wildlife unless there's a good reason for it." Elly Raiser Roget is a small woman but her mother tones could stop a kangaroo rex in mid-charge.

Feeling more than a little defensive, I dropped my eyes to my arm. A small bump had raised. I jabbed a finger at it. "I also tell you not to take stupid chances. I don't think I slapped it fast enough."

Elly slid Aklilu down onto the floor beside her, let go of Jen and reached for my arm. "An allergic reaction? Annie, should I phone for Doc Agbabian?"

I shook my head. "A minor allergic reaction. The same as you'd get if the damn thing had bitten you. I don't need the doc, but it'd be a big help if you'd take a sample of that for me so I can analyze it, too. I can't reach it left-handed."

Elly obliged. "If it bit you, it's not Mirabilan," she said.

"Right." Most of the Mirabilan wildlife doesn't like the way humans taste. At least, the native bloodsuckers don't. The swarming horrors only like humans for their sweat, and they're bad enough to give anybody nightmares, which gives you some idea how they got their name. "We need insectivores," I said aloud.

Elly'd heard that complaint often enough that she ignored it. "So whatever bit you was something we brought with us." She narrowed her eyes at me. "And you think you know what or you wouldn't have smashed it."

"I hope I'm wrong. But I couldn't take the chance, Elly."

That satisfied her, but not the kids. The computer's beep for attention gave me a chance to escape their massed frowns. I pulled over a chair and settled down for a look at the gene-read. It was an import, all right.

I keyed for ships' records. Jen had shoved up close to scowl at the screen. I scooped her into my lap and said, "Get me the gene library."

She did. Then she craned her head around and said, "You want insects, right?"

"Right."

She misspelled "insects" on the first try but made it fine on the second.

"Hold it there," I said. "Before you set the computer to searching the whole section for a match, we try a guess." Arms on either side of her, my chin on her shoulder, I keyed in for "mosquito." Then we waited.

"This takes a long time, Mama Jason!"

Well, not really—but at that age they've got a different time sense. "If I remember right, the computer's got some three hundred species to check through," I said. "See how long it would take *you* if you had to do it by hand!" The longer it took, the better, as far as I was concerned: I was hoping the search *wouldn't* turn up a match. From Elly's deepened frown, I could tell she'd recognized the "mosquito" and was hoping just as hard as I was.

No such luck. The computer beeped a potential match. Jen whooped and dived for the keyboard to call up a display.

I called back the gene-read on the thing I'd smashed and laid the images side by side. "Well, Jen? What do you say?"

She took her time considering, touching a fingertip first to one image then to the other. At last she leaned back and said, "I think they're the same, Mama Jason."

"Yes," I said, "I'm afraid they are."

Jen bounced off my lap with a second whoop. "We've got a match!" She caught up Akilu's hands. "We've got a match!" Within moments, the entire troop was dancing about the room to the same chant.

That was what Ilanith walked in on. Give her credit—it didn't disappoint her in the slightest. "I take it I don't have to search insects. Want to compare notes, Mama Jason?" She brought her results up on the screen and made the same careful examination that Jen had between her gene-read and the one from ships' records. "It's a match. That means you had a good idea what it was when you slapped it. And *that* means it's not something we want loose on Mirabile. . . . What's a mosquito?"

Elly stared at her. "I thought you were reading Thoholte this year. Her *Laughing Gods* is downright eloquent on the subject of mosquitoes."

Even as the match dance weaved around her, Ilanith shuffled her own feet for a very different reason. She didn't answer for a long moment, and when she did it was: "I was reading up on genetics, Mama Jason. I don't have time for all this fiction stuff."

Elly cocked an eye at me over Ilanith's head. I knew what was wanted and I obliged. "How do you think I recognized the damn thing when it bit me? I've read *Laughing Gods*. Kiddo, with whole chunks missing from ships' records, we've got to make do with what we've got. Maybe we've got a complete set of gene-reads for the Earth-authentic insects, maybe not. Part of a jason's job is to know the available sources. Fiction's sometimes as useful as nonfiction. If I hadn't read Thoholte, we'd be twiddling our thumbs while the computer spent the night searching for that match."

Ilanith jumped on that as an excuse to change the subject. "So we've got the match . . . now what?"

"Now, if Elly will lend me the troops, we're going down to Loch Moose to see how many of those little fiends we can net."

"Nets," said Elly. "I know. Chris has cheesecloth in the kitchen—that will do for nets."

"I'll go," Ilanith said.

"*You*," I said, catching her before she could make good her escape, "will go read Thoholte. I want you to know exactly what we're up against."

Our sweep of the lake was more enthusiastic than efficient, what with a half-dozen kids of all ages flailing about with cheesecloth nets, but every adult staying at the lodge had come along to join the hunt. No point calling in the team from the lab when I had so many willing hands.

I had my doubts that we'd accomplish anything—not because the hunters were amateurs, but because of the scope of the problem. Any Earth import might have been the source of that mosquito. I knew about half of the water lilies were incubating dragonflies. The other half might be the source of the mosquitoes. Or the dragonflies themselves might be laying mosquito eggs these days. For insects, there are just too many possible sources. We'd have to run gene-reads on every Earth-authentic plant and animal in the forest. By the time we identified the source, chances were the mosquitoes would already have a viable population established.

Having read what I'd read about mosquitoes, the prospect looked downright grim. Aside from their pure nuisance qualities, mosquitoes would be a disease vector. I suppose I should be grateful for small favors that the folks back on Earth hadn't included disease genes on their "keeper" list. But we have diseases of our own to worry about and I could have done without a vector. Up to now, we've been handling Sanoshan fever with a combination of quarantine and a short-lived vaccine—mosquitoes might change that completely.

So the adults and the little ones all caught bugs—to much crowed delight. Kept Jen busy running their samples up to the lodge. I had an evening's worth of gene-reading ahead of me and I was not looking forward to it. For the moment, at least, their good time was infectious. Even the odders stopped their playing to watch.

Filippo managed to fall in the loch not just once but twice, to be fished out each time by his sister Darice. (Luckily, the whole troop swims like odders, but some days I don't know how Elly stands it—just watching them is hair-raising.) Morien insisted on showing each of her catches to everyone—she seemed to be specializing in dragonflies. Even Aklilu caught bugs, with more than a little assistance from Elly, I suspect.

We were beginning to lose the light, though. Elly rowed in close. "Look, Mama Jason!" said Aklilu. "Look bug!"

I looked bug. "Good catch," I told him. "I've never seen one like that before."

His eyes got big. "Oh," he said, clutching his net and staring at his bug, "Dragon's Tooth."

No sense arguing definitions with Aklilu, so I didn't. Elly grinned at me and said, "Time to head in—on a note of triumph." She gave a sharp whistle and heads turned all around. "Head for shore," she shouted. There was some mutinous grumbling but not much. What Elly says goes. We all rowed for shore.

The fun was over; the rest of the evening would be pure and simple grub work. That it really was simple work meant I had Jen's extra hands to help me run samples, though, at least until she got bored with the repetitiveness of the job.

As it turned out, the first tap on my shoulder wasn't Jen's. It was Leo's and I got a real nice set of kisses as a follow-up . . . I sighed, saved everything and switched the computer off. "Break for dinner."

"So much for your vacation," said Leo. "I seem to have missed all the excitement. Between the door and here, I have heard that Mama Jason smashed a bug—an *Earth-authentic* bug, no less, that Aklilu caught a Dragon's Tooth, that Mama Jason smashed a bug, that the entire population of the lodge played jason this afternoon, that Annie Jason Masmajean—defender of the kangaroo rex—*smashed a bug!* But I also see Elly is as close to a worried frown as I've ever known her to be, which means you must have had a very good reason for smashing the bug. Why don't you tell me all about it over dinner?"

If there's one thing Leonov Bellmaker Denness knows, it's the way to a woman's heart: good food, a sympathetic ear and a lot of necking. Not necessarily in that order. After the lot of necking, we went downstairs to the dining room, ordered Chris's special of the day, which was a good spicy hopfish bouillabaisse, and I told him all about it.

I was instantly sorry I'd done it—all those deep-etched laugh lines in his face twisted away as if they'd never been there and his normally brown skin took on an undercast of green that was distinctly uncomplimentary. "Sorry," I said and took his hand in mine.

He shook his head. "I had kin on the *Sanoshan*. They were survivors. I've seen their accounts of the last years aboard, when they weren't sure there'd be enough hands to make a landing—or if they dared even make a landing for fear of killing off the rest of the colonists. The thought of an insect vector for Sanoshan fever scares me silly . . ."

"No," I said. "It had better scare you rational, if we want to do something about it. I've already warned Main Medical, but I think you'd better put in a word, too. Chances are a survivor can really spur them into action."

Made me think how lucky I really was to have Leo. Eight hundred people died in the *Sanoshan* epidemic, and there was nothing the other ships could do to help without infecting their own populations.

He nodded. "Tomorrow morning I break the bell out of its cast. Assuming it came out right, I thought I'd ask you to come along to RightHere and help me deliver it. Bell or no bell, I'll head for RightHere tomorrow and stop by Medical. If we want the entire population vaccinated, it'll take some time for them to gear up production . . ."

"Leo, I'm selfish as all hell. I want Elly and the kids vaccinated *now*—and you, too."

"I'm an immune, Annie. If you doubt me, you can check a cell sample right now. How about you?"

I hadn't even thought of it.

Leo read my expression and said, "I thought not—and you're the one with the mosquito bite. *You* will get your vaccination updated." The laugh lines came back into his face. "Can't have you setting a bad example for Elly's kids!"

I hate vaccinations but he was right. I'd do it. If I worked hard, I might even be able to do it with some sort of grace. I tried to wipe the scowl off my face but I obviously didn't succeed because Leo laughed.

"I don't care how grudgingly you do it, Annie, as long as you do it."

At that point, Susan came out of nowhere, threw her arms around Leo's shoulders and said, "What's Mama Jason doing now, Noisy—grudgingly or otherwise?"

"Getting vaccinated for Sanoshan fever," he told her. "What about you? When was the last time you were vaccinated for it?"

"Me? Two years ago." Susan threw her arms around me. "Elly's a stickler for keeping up on vaccinations."

I hugged her back hard out of sheer relief. Should have known Elly would take care of something like that. I'd double-check for safety's sake, but I felt better already. "Next question," I began.

Susan pushed back and grinned. "Mike found the lab computer searching through mosquito gene-reads. When it signaled a match, he checked the origin of the request. We drew straws over who got to come up to Loch Moose to help you out. I cheated. Now you're asking if I've been vaccinated for Sanoshan fever. . . . I'll go tell Mike we guessed right."

I stopped her. "Tell Mike I want everybody on the team revaccinated by the end of the week."

"Done," she said and vanished as quickly as she'd come. When she reappeared, she pulled up a chair and settled at our table. Chris put a bowl in front of her, gave her a hug and a spoon and said, "Eat up. It's good for the ecology!"

Between mouthfuls, Susan asked questions. Being that age makes them impatient for answers. I did my best, with Leo's help, but when she got to "Where are they coming from?" I had no answer.

"From Leo's pansies, for all I know." That was the hell of it. They could be coming from anything.

Susan, temporarily incapacitated by a mouthful of bouillabaisse, shook her head violently. Leo said, "Not from my pansies. I can vouch for every one of them."

Susan swallowed hastily. "S'truth, Mama Jason. I showed Noisy how to read for secondary and tertiary helices so he could check them. I double-checked the first batch for him, but he was doing fine so the rest I let him handle."

I stared at Leo. It must have been the wrong kind of stare because he shifted in his seat and looked apologetic and said, "You're always complaining about being shorthanded, Annie. Since I was the one who wanted the pansies in the first place, it's only fair I look after them myself." He let it hang a minute, then he added, "Ilanith double-checked them, in case I missed anything."

There was another pause. My fault. I was still too surprised to say anything. Leo and Susan looked at each other. Then Leo said, "I'm not about to apologize for stepping on your turf, Annie. It was fun finding out what's hiding in my patch of pansies."

I threw up my hands. "Fun? I don't need an apology—I'm pleased as all hell. What *is* hiding in your patch of pansies?"

So it was back to the computer, this time to link up to Leo's across the loch, for the list. Most of it was pansy related, which was a relief. The dog-tooth violets seemed like a nice idea, as did the spring beauties. Some insects, but not many, and those in the offing were harmless, except for the one that promised cutworms somewhere down the line. One more demonstration of how badly we need insectivores. I tapped it on the screen.

"Susan told me to pull and burn that one," Leo said.

That would have been my decision, too, and I told him so. "Our rice crop's in enough trouble from the hopfish without adding cutworms to the stew. And I doubt even Chris could come up with a recipe that made cutworms appetizing."

"Just don't let her hear you disparage her talents," Leo said with a grin.

I looked at the list again. "We could do with some of your butterflies. Blue butterfly, okay, but pull the cabbage butterfly—"

"Pulled and burned."

This time I turned my chair to have a good look at him. "You're way ahead of me on this, aren't you?"

He spread his hands. "I'm bored with the bellmaking and I'm too old to go back to opening new territory, but this is a kind of scouting, too. Why do you think I hang around with you all the time?"

I gave him the hairy eyeball I'd learned from Susan in her younger days and said, "And here I thought it was my good looks!"

"It is," he said. He tapped the screen. "This is gravy. The least I can do is keep tabs on my pansy patch. And, before you ask, we tagged every last one of them. You can pull or coddle the rest at your leisure."

"My leisure. . . . Now that would be a lovely thought. You have saved me one helluva lot of trouble. And, if you're serious about this 'fun' of yours, why don't you give us a hand with the insects we caught this afternoon?"

I haven't seen a human being light up like that since I told Susan she could help with the gene-reads. Crinkles of the best kind all over that face and a flash of grin like . . . well, that must be what fireflies were like.

The thought made me reconsider the list. "Still no fireflies." I keep hoping.

"Maybe your fireflies will turn up in this afternoon's catch. Give me a bunch of samples and I'll start looking." He held out those beautiful huge hands of his . . . and I filled them with jars and sent him off to grub through genes with the rest of us.

Shortly after that Ilanith popped in with her fingers stuck into Elly's hardback copy of *Laughing Gods* in no less than three places. "This is terrific, Mama Jason! Listen to this," she said and read me five pages of Thoholte's epic battle with the mosquitoes. Then she added, "No wonder you smashed it! Did she write anything else?"

"Lots," I told her, "check the library index," and shooed her out before she could read me the next five pages she'd finger-marked. Makes me wonder what goes through kids' minds sometimes. Would I make her read a book I didn't like?

Susan, having finished her dinner, stuck her head in the door. "Where's the mosquito you mashed, Mama Jason? I want to try something."

I pulled out the sample for her. "What something?"

"I've been thinking. If it's possible to read the helices to find out what's coming next, shouldn't it be possible to backtrack to see where it came *from?*"

"Damned if I know," I said. "I don't think anybody's ever tried it. You'll have to do it manually—computer's not set up for that—but if it works I'll see you get a bonus week off this year."

"Hah! Like your vacation, I bet." She didn't wait for an answer. Not that she had to—most likely she was right.

I growled something about my lost vacation to the empty doorway. It wasn't Elly I meant to growl at, but Elly's sudden appearance made it seem just that.

"No arguments," Elly said. She jabbed a finger at me and said, "And this one, Suvendi."

Before I could so much as acknowledge Suvendi Doc Agba-bian, he had my sleeve shoved up and was shooting me full of vaccine. I didn't argue.

Except for a sighting of the Loch Moose monster, the rest of the evening was uneventful.

EARLY NEXT MORNING just about everybody at the lodge rowed across the loch to Leo's place to watch him break the bell from its cast. Fancy piece of casting—covered top to lip with relief work. When he'd shined it up a bit, Susan shouted, "Odders! Look, it's all over odders!" That was something of an exaggeration—there were just as many pansies as there were odders—but it was one helluva bell.

Leo strung the clapper, then we tossed a rope over a rafter, hefted the thing up and gave it a try. The bell rang out loud and sweet—a deep, deep bong that must have startled every animal for miles around. We tied the rope off temporarily and retreated outside, holding our ears, while each kid took a turn ringing it. After the first two rings, the odders took to bellowing in response, which seemed about right. Even Aklilu got it to sound, though Jen told us later he'd had to swing from the pull to do it.

It was two hours before we got it packed into my hover and headed for RightHere. From Loch Moose to RightHere it's all upriver, which is nice smooth hovering, and there are plenty of places to stay along the way. We made a four-day trip of it.

Must have signed a dozen guest books along the way—most of them for folks we didn't actually stay with, which was cheating a bit—but how often does a bell that size go by? Everybody wanted a peek at it and a remembrance of the occasion. For once, nobody was disappointed when Leo signed himself "Leo *Bell-maker* Denness" instead of "Leo Opener Denness."

Except maybe Leo. He *had* said he was getting tired of bellmaking.

The second night there was a General Delivery call out for me from Susan at Loch Moose. It was the one I was waiting for but hadn't been expecting, if you follow that. . . . She didn't even say hello, just started out with, "It works, Mama Jason! I backtracked it! And a friend of Elly's volunteered to hack it into the computer so next time it won't take forever to do one."

Leo gave me a sidelong glance and said, "I take it she means she found out where the mosquito came from?"

"And that somebody's writing a program that will let us backtrack fast next time," I said, finishing the translation. "So where did the mosquito come from?" I asked Susan.

"One of Chris's tomato plants. We're doing gene-reads on the whole bed now. So far only the one but. . . ."

I sighed and finished for her, "But we'll have to check every tomato plant on Mirabile, for safety's sake. What did you do with the offender?"

"That's the second thing I called about. Chris wants to hold a ceremonial burning. Any reason why not? It's her tomato plant."

"Fair is fair," I told her. "But I can think of a major reason why not: you know how people get carried away. I don't want every tomato plant on Mirabile roasted. Check the whole bed first, do the same for any other beds in the area, then burn the offenders. Tell Chris to make sure the spinners and gossips see her selecting *specific* plants for the fire."

She'd have done it then and there, but I held up a finger and said, "And remind her she's Chris *Jason* Maryanska in a case like this. She should also cook up one of those stuffed tomato things for anybody who comes for the show. That'd help. They taste something that good, they'll be much less likely to burn the inoffensive plants."

"Right. Chris'll love that, Mama Jason. We'll get on it first thing in the morning." She laughed suddenly. "You know what Chris calls that recipe?"

I shook my head.

"'Tomato *Surprise.*'"

RIGHTHERE is the closest thing on Mirabile to a city in the Earth-authentic style. It has paved roads, stone buildings, and it's home to ships' library. Kind of pretty from a distance, since it sits on an estuary and looks out over Greenglass Sea. A little too constricted for my taste, I think. There's talk of putting in street lights, which means the cheerups will probably move out, and I like to listen to the cheerups carol to each other all night.

Leo dropped me off on a corner and headed on to Main Medical. First things first, he said. He had samples of everything, plus a ten-pound printout of the disease-carrying history of mosquitoes. If that wasn't enough to reinforce our suggestion that medical gear up to revaccinate everybody on Mirabile for Sanoshan fever, he'd hit them with the horror stories his family had passed down three generations, which would most certainly do it.

I went straight to Jason's Hall to see if the past four days had brought them any more luck establishing insectivores on Mirabile than the past three generations had.

Sabah Jason Al-Sumidaie met me just inside the door with: "No, Annie, we haven't had a bit of luck with songbirds here, either."

"I knew it was too much to ask."

So we sat down to compare notes and bitches over tea. Sabah clicked his tongue over my mosquito bite and we both drank a hearty curse to those long-dead geneticists back on Earth who'd caused us this problem.

They'd tried a dozen new kinds of songbird since I'd last checked more than the names and the viability. Not one of them had survived. Looking over their records, I saw the same sort of pattern I'd been seeing in my environmental conditions—Mirabile's native life was so hostile to songbirds that even Dragon's Teeth didn't survive to breed a second generation, not in either EC.

When I said as much out loud, Sabah said, "M-hm. Either the eggs get eaten or the adults do. I think we'll have to put someone on insectivores full-time. I don't see any other way to solve the problem."

I snorted. "Full time."

"You know what I mean, Annie. Full-time except for emergencies."

"We also need somebody full-time on Mirabilan wildlife. That might give us a handle of what birds we *should* be choosing."

"If I get you the salaries, can you get me the bodies? I mean it, Annie, full-time as much as practical."

Makes me nosy when Sabah talks like that. "If you've got the salaries, why haven't you got the bodies?"

Sabah twinkled at me. "We're civilized here in RightHere. It's Mama Jason and her team of Dragon's Tooth hunters that attract the youngsters."

"Get stuffed," I told him, with a smile. I've heard some stories in my time but *that. . . .*

"I'm serious, Annie. I could name you three kids in town that would kill to work with you. But not here and not with us. It's a matter of perception."

"Send 'em to me. I'll read 'em the riot act about a proper apprenticeship—with you."

Sabah put down his glass of tea. "You know, that might just work."

"If it doesn't, at least *I* wind up with extra hands," I said. "And now that we've solved that problem, let's see if we can do something about the damned insectivores."

WE DIDN'T SOLVE that one, of course. Not likely we'd solve in one afternoon what hadn't been solved in the three generations we'd been on Mirabile. But we did know a lot of things that *wouldn't* work by the time we were done.

When we got tired of beating our heads against that particular wall, I checked my mail. Susan had sent along a preliminary program for backtracking the source of a Dragon's Tooth with the note: "Marian says it's not 'elegant' but it ought to hold us while she whips up a better one."

"'Elegant'?" said Sabah.

"Hacker-talk," I explained. "Means, as far as I can tell, the program's not as efficient as it might be. Same use of 'elegant' as in mathematics."

There was a gosh-wow from Chris, too. Then I cast about a bit and found the expected one from Leo. It read: "Scared the daylights out of medical. I'll be at the cathedral." It ended with a whole slew of bare-hug graphics. When I turned back to Sabah, he was grinning like nobody's business.

"You didn't tell me you had a new beau, Annie," he said in mock accusation.

"You didn't ask," I countered. Knowing what would come next, I held up both hands to fend him off. "I've been officially proposed to, and I mean to accept as soon as I can think of an appropriate courting gift. That last is not as easy as it sounds. *He* gave *me* a kangaroo rex."

Sabah's eyes went wide. "I'm impressed. That alone makes it sound like a match. Who is this wonder?"

"His name's Leonov Bellmaker Denness—used to be Leonov Opener D—"

Sabah raised hands to cut me off. "I know Leo, Annie. He's making the bell for our cathedral." His raised hands landed on my shoulders. "Good combination, you and Leo! And I don't mean just genetically."

"Good. Then maybe you can show me where this 'cathedral' thing is. He's there delivering your bell now."

With a shout that he was off for the rest of the day, Sabah hustled me to the door. "'Cathedral' is guild tongue for a large and very ornate stone building used for ritual purposes," he explained, as he led the way. (Only a member of a guild uses the phrase 'guild tongue' without specifying *what* guild. I wasn't about to ask. Tends to set them to proselytizing about how much *fun* you'd have if you joined the Nippon Guild or the Texas Guild or whatever.) "How long has it been since you've been to RightHere?"

"Years, at least."

"Hm, and you don't pay much attention to anything other than Dragon's Teeth."

"Except the kids and Leo," I corrected.

"Then you're in for a surprise."

Well, I have to admit—Sabah was right on that count. I've never seen a building that big in my life, except in pictures in ships' records. You could have stuck the entire population of RightHere inside it with room to spare.

And "ornate" didn't begin to describe it. More than half the damn thing was a solid mass of vaults and spires and carvings. The rest was still rough shaped—blocks holding up the portico where (I assumed) there'd soon be more figures to match those on the other side of the entrance.

I was so busy gawking that Sabah startled me when he grabbed my arm. "Hunh?" I said.

"One thing, Annie. When the guild finds out who you are, they're gonna hit you up for bats. They already did me—I told them we didn't have the time for frivolities—but that doesn't stop them from persisting. So feel free to say no."

"Bats," I said, not taking my eyes off the cathedral. "Say no. Gotcha." And I went for a closer look.

The entire history of Mirabile was carved into the walls of the cathedral. Here was the takeoff from Earth (though some of those plants were Mirabilan, not Earth-authentic) to the generations in journey (including a very authentic and gruesome portrayal of Sanoshan fever) to the landing and the opening. I was fascinated as all hell to find a much younger Leo among the openers and Granddaddy Jason locked in ferocious battle with a double helix. Aside from that first panel, the artist had done a damn realistic job.

"Check the caryatids," said Leo, as he came down the wide staircase from the center doors. I bussed him instead, then I asked him, "What the hell's a caryatid?" He pointed to the figures holding up the roof. Took me a minute to place their faces as those of the ships' captains. They were right, even down to the desperation on the face of that last captain of the Sanoshan. Tiny figures at the feet of each gave further details of shipboard life under each particular captaincy.

"Now look up," Leo said—and pointed.

I craned my neck and stepped back. Glaring down at me, mouths gaping, was the damnedest collection of Dragon's Teeth ever assembled in the history of Mirabile. I was standing, I found, directly under a kangaroo rex—not a face you'd forget if you'd seen it live the way I had. The artist had captured it so well that it seemed poised to leap on its prey.

I shifted position.

From the side, I could see every last bit of musculature under the hide of the damn thing. And, yes, it was set to spring on its prey. Every inch of it just about vibrated, right down to the shadow of stripes across its haunches.

I let out a whistle of pure admiration.

Leo said, "You got it right, Bethany. See if you didn't."

Which reminded me Leo was there, not that I ever really forget. I turned to find him grinning and pushing a pixie in my direction. "Bethany, meet Annie Jason Masmajean. Annie, this is Bethany Carver Barandemaje."

She was as tiny as Leo is big, but the resemblance was unmistakable. "One of your kids, yes?" I stuck out a hand and got a tiny but very wiry and very callused hand in return.

"One of my three favorites," Leo said. He was still grinning shamelessly.

"Good thing you've only got three," Bethany told him, "or we'd be forced to take matters in hand."

"And I'd find myself sandblasted into the shape of a chimera and spending the rest of my life pouring water down on the world."

I couldn't help myself. "Why put Dragon's Teeth—even one based on Leo—on a cathedral?"

"Oh," she said, "it's traditional. Only on earth they called them gargoyles. I thought a Mirabilan cathedral ought to have Mirabilan gargoyles. It's part of the drainage system. After a rain, they spout water from their mouths. Come on up and have a closer look before we lose all the light."

The closer look was even more impressive. I laid my hand on the kangaroo rex's flank and discovered that I could feel every one of those bunched muscles. It was almost disturbing that the only difference between Bethany's kangaroo rex and the live ones I'd touched was that there was a chill to the stone one. "I'd hate to mess with that," I said, which set both Leo and Bethany off in chuckles.

Still laughing, they dragged me up entirely too many flights of stairs to the belfry. "Belfry" is another guild term, I take it—it means the spire they were to hang Leo's bell in. If I'd thought the view from RightHere was beautiful, the view from the belfry was a stunner. The entire town and harbor was spread out below us. As cold as the prospect might be (the windows weren't glassed in), I promised myself I'd stop back in the winter to see what RightHere looked like under a mantle of snow.

Now we were losing the light, so Bethany lit a torch—a real torch, straight out of historical dramas, which gives you some idea how seriously the guild takes its play—and led us back to the stairwell.

I said to Leo, "D'you suppose she felt obligated to do all this carving with a hammer and chisel?"

He snorted with laughter. "That torch is gasoline fed, Annie, burns a lot cleaner than wood. And she uses state-of-the-art to do her carving. No way she could have done so much in so short a time without it."

We followed Bethany all the way back to her house. Turned out Leo had arranged for us to stay there as long as we were in town. I suspect this is Leo's way of introducing me to all his kids and grandkids. Who am I to object? I was beginning to like Leo's genes as much as I like Leo. I hadn't actually looked at them, mind you, but the results seemed to be consistently good, even to the grandkids.

Bethany had two bouncing around the household, which meant I had to tell about the kangaroo rex all over again. Leo made eyebrows at me all through the telling.

When I finished, Arkady asked, "What did you give him for a courting present, Annie?" "Yeah!" demanded Vassily, "What did you give him?"

"Nothing yet. I don't know what to give him for a courting present. Maybe you two have some ideas?"

"Oh, yes!"

I hushed them instantly. "Not in front of Leo! I want to surprise him! We'll talk about it when he isn't around."

So Bethany hustled them off to bed amid conspiratorial whispers and giggles and promises of tomorrow.

"Hope they come up with a good idea," Leo said with a grin.

"Me too." I grinned back. "Oh, well. Hold that thought, Leo. I still have work to do tonight." So Leo wound up looking over my shoulder while I went through the hard copy on birds one more time.

Not that it did me any good. Staring at genes wasn't going to make them viable. If we knew what was killing the birds off we might be able to twitch the genes around a little. For all I knew, the Earth-authentic birds were eating something Mirabilan and dropping dead on the spot. Damnify knew what—maybe the swarming horrors. I dropped the hard copy in a heap on the table and only then realized that Leo had wandered off. "Deserter," I said.

"You've been talking about birds for months now," Leo said, looking up from the computer. "The only birds I've seen are ducks and quail and Cornish fowl. I want to see the kind you're interested in."

"Oh. Let me. I know where they're hidden in ships' records." I pulled up a chair and found some birds for Leo—not gene-reads but photos of the animals themselves. "There," I said. "That's a pretty characteristic bird."

I turned to find him frowning at the screen. "It's different from what you're used to, but I wouldn't think it deserves a scowl."

"Do ships' records include any photos of them in motion, Annie?"

When Leo asks a question in that tone, he's got a damn good reason for asking. So I tapped a little deeper and found him some motion pictures of various birds. He watched the birds, I watched him. The frown deepened the longer he watched.

At last he said, "Find me a motion picture of each of the birds you've tried to establish on Mirabile."

So I went down the list, both Sabah's and mine. It took about an hour to satisfy him, though toward the end less than a minute of film was sufficient before he called for the next one. "That's it," I said, turning off the computer. "That's the lot."

The frown wrinkled into pure sadness. "Shall I tell you why you couldn't get any of those established on Mirabile, Annie?"

"If you don't voluntarily, I'll sic your grandchildren on you!"

That brought a smile back to his face. He raised both hands and said, "I volunteer. Annie, all those birds move just like flurts." Then he waited.

I knew he was waiting for me to think about it, so I did. He was right. The Mirabilan flurt doesn't have feathers and it doesn't fly but it does move with the same bounce and hop as the birds I'd showed him. And it spent much of its time in trees. Its feet were built for climbing, not so well for walking.

Then I realized what Leo was getting at. "The whompems are eating them!"

"I'd bet money on it," Leo said. "The whompems eat your birds thinking they're flurts. Obviously, your birds don't poison the whompems either."

"We've spent years feeding the whompems. Hell."

"Sorry, Annie."

"Good grief, Leo, don't be sorry. We could have spent years *more* feeding the whompems. Now we have to think of something else."

I brought the computer up once more to leave a note for Sabah telling him what we'd been doing wrong (and giving Leo full credit). Then I dragged Leo off to bed to thank him properly.

NOTHING QUITE LIKE a good night's romp to clear the mind. If we'd been going at the problem wrong, then we needed to come at it from another angle. The very first thing I did (after breakfast) was to set Leo the task of looking through the file for any bird that wouldn't attract the predatory attention of a whompem. The Cornish fowl hadn't been eaten by whompems, so I had some hope for the project—and Leo seemed enthusiastic about helping out.

Then I hunted up Bethany's kids. "Okay," I said, "you promised me a suggestion for Leo's courting gift."

"Right," said Vassily. He gave a glance at Arkady that made me instantly suspect mischief, then the two of them glanced around furtively—checking, it seemed, where their dad had gotten to. Dad was out of earshot. Still, Vassily beckoned me closer.

By now I was curious as all hell to find out what the two of them were up to. I bent down and turned an ear close.

"Bats!" Vassily whispered. The whisper was loud enough to bring a vigorous nod of agreement from Arkady.

Bats. Where had I heard about bats, and just recently too? Ah, from Sabah. I was not to let the guild hassle me for bats.

"Bats," I said aloud. "That's it? Last night you had 'lots' of suggestions."

Arkady drew himself up and said, "Bats is best."

"And you think Leo would like this bats thing?" I'd spoken in a normal tone of voice. The two of them hastily shushed me, drawing a curious look from dad.

"Oh, yes," came the answer, still whispered. "Leo would like you-know-whats best of all."

"All right," I whispered back. "I'll look into it and see if I agree with you. Thanks for the suggestion."

I left the two of them hugging each other in what looked to me like triumph and headed out for another look at the cathedral. That day I could have found it from the noise alone or from the cloud of rock dust Bethany's carving raised.

When I got within view of what she was doing, I didn't interrupt her at once. For one thing, I wasn't sure I should distract her while she was carving. For another, it was a treat to watch as she freed another Dragon's Tooth from its chunk of rock. I didn't recognize this one, so it must have been something from the local EC that Sabah and his team had taken care of. Even now, it was in the act of raising a club-like foot as if to bash in a skull.

The foot raised, there was a sudden startling silence. Bethany had turned off her carver and doffed her elaborate face mask. "Annie! You shouldn't be hanging out here without a mask. This stuff is hell on your lungs."

"I didn't intend to hang out. I got suckered into watching you . . . find the Dragon's Tooth."

She looked enormously pleased at that. One hand went up to the stone. She meant, I think, simply to brush away the stone dust, but the gesture turned into a caress. I couldn't blame her. All her creatures wanted patting, even the ones that looked like they'd take your hand off for trying.

After a minute, she turned. "Did you come to watch us install the bell? If so, you're about an hour early."

I shook my head. "I came to ask about these bat things you folks seem to want."

"Oh, no! The kids!" She looked stricken. "Annie, I'm so sorry. Leo made us promise not to hassle you for bats. I made the kids promise. . . . Wait till I get my hands on those little monsters!"

I had to hold up both my hands to stop her. "The kids didn't ask me for bats for your guild! I won't have you punishing them either—when all they did was suggest that I give Leo bats as a courting present." And I couldn't help laughing. "Clever pair, too. Wish you could have seen them at it. You'd have been proud of them."

"I'm afraid I can imagine." She laughed. Through her laughter, she managed to get out, "I am sorry, though, Annie."

"Don't be. Tell me about the bats."

"There's nothing much to tell. Besides bells, belfries are reputed to have bats. They're *supposed* to have bats. I did the next best thing. Come on, I'll show you."

So it was up the stairs to the belfry all over again. This time, she pointed up to the ceiling. First time there, I'd been so caught up by the view outside that I hadn't seen the view inside: the entire ceiling was carved.

"That's what they look like—the bats. We couldn't talk Sabah into making us some, so I carved them in. But that won't satisfy most of the guild members."

The bats wanted petting too, or at least a much closer look. The buttressed ceiling was covered with them, hundreds of them. At first it wasn't easy to make out individual details, then I realized they were all hanging by their feet, faces downward. And it was the damndest collection of faces I'd ever seen—huge, outsized ears, noses that looked more like leaves than noses. There were even a dozen or so that seemed to have Pushy's old-boot head. Most of those with their mouths open showed needle-sharp teeth. They had wings too, it seemed—not like birds' wings, though—more like, well, broken umbrellas. Hard to believe something like that was Earth-authentic.

"You sure these aren't Dragon's Teeth?" I said.

Bethany grinned. "I got the pictures I worked with straight out of ships' records, Annie. They really do look like that. The only artistic license I took was, well, ordinarily you'd see only one kind of bat in a belfry. I put them all in. I liked their faces."

"I can see why. I'll see what I can do, Bethany. Mind you, I don't make any promises. First, I have to take a good look at what they'd do to the ecology. . . ." I suspected Sabah had already done that, since he'd warned me about the request. But a double check never hurt anything, and it would be something to take my mind off the birds long enough to give it a rest.

"Good enough, Annie. Uh—okay if I tell the rest of the guild members you're looking into it?"

"Why not? At least it will keep them from finding devious ways to mention the subject."

As long as I'd already climbed the stairs, I stuck around to watch them hang Leo's bell. Carved bats and cast pansies. Made me wonder what the folks back on Earth would have thought— d'you suppose they appreciate bats and pansies as much as Leo and his kin?

"We took a vote, Annie," Bethany said. The workers around her nodded agreement. "You get the first ring."

"Thanks," I said, "but it seems to me Leo ought to have the privilege. *I* haven't done anything yet."

There was some disappointment, followed by a moment's discussion, then Bethany said, "She's right. Leo made the bell. He ought to get first ring. How about just at dusk? You'll bring him, Annie?" At my nod, she said, "At dusk, then."

So I headed back to Bethany's to tell Leo his plans for the evening. He was still at the computer. When I laid a hand on his shoulder, he said, "No luck so far, Annie, but I'm still looking."

"Take a break, Leo. Let me at the computer for a while."

"I can do this. I'm not bored; I'm fascinated. I had no idea how many kinds of birds there were!"

I made shooing motions. "I have no intention of spoiling your fun. I just want to have a look at these bats."

That got his attention. "Annie, they didn't! They promised me!"

"They didn't," I said. "It was Sabah who told me about the bats. Anybody else, I had to ask. Now will you let me at the computer?"

He gave me his chair and drew up another. I went hunting for bats. The very first reference I found made my jaw drop. Tagged onto the description, almost as an afterthought, were the words,

"Most bats are economically valuable because of the volume of insects they consume."

"But . . .?" I did a quick test. No, asking the computer for a list of "insectivores" did *not* give you "bats." "Leo," I said, "we lost part of the index!" We knew we'd lost information from ships' records, but that we'd lost indexing. . . . God alone knew what was in the computer files—things we might need badly that we'd never know existed!

The first order of business then was a general bulletin to let everybody know there was information in the files that wasn't properly indexed and cross-referenced. Nobody was going to be happy to hear that. Still, a general bulletin meant that whenever somebody found something unindexed in the files, they'd tell library so it could be added.

When we'd done that (and dropped a note to the ships' librarians to cross-reference "bats" to "insectivores"), I went back to sort through the various kinds of bats. And I did it manually, file by file. After a while I had a goodly number of insectivorous bats that would do just fine not only in RightHere's EC but in the Loch Moose EC as well. In theory, at least.

In practice. . . .

I found motion pictures of each of the Earth-authentic species that interested me. Some of them weren't very good—bats being largely nocturnal—but they'd have to do. "What do you say, Leo? Do these get eaten the minute we turn 'em loose?"

"Not by whompems," he said. "Not if they're nocturnal."

"So far so good," I said. "You keep thinking about it while I read up on bats."

But I didn't do that immediately. Instead, I dropped a note to my own team which said, in its entirety: "Bats. Love, Annie." I knew that would be enough to get them started. That's why they're my favorite team. I also left a note for Sabah. That one said: "Bats, dammit, Sabah!" I signed it "Ann Jason Masmajean." I can't pull rank on Sabah, but I made sure the graphics underscored the "Jason." Sabah hadn't even looked at bats; he'd simply decided they were "frivolities" and let it go at that. Just goes to show—if you don't have time for frivolities, you're not doing it right.

Then I got to the reading. The more I read about them, the more I liked them.

I admit the vampire bats gave me a momentary turn . . . until I found out they didn't much bother humans. Real pretty bioengineering—all designed to keep its prey from noticing it was being bled, which was more than you could say for the human culture back on Earth I'd once read about that bled cattle for their favorite beverage, a concoction of blood and milk. Curious, when Earth humans were doing that, that the vampire bat should have given all bats such a bad rap, the way it seemed to have. Maybe the problem was just that bats are nocturnal. If nobody knows what you do for sure, everybody suspects you.

Anyhow, I was interested in insectivores, which was the largest group. And when I found one that was noted for its mosquito catching, I knew in my heart I'd found my insectivore of choice. I turned the computer over to Leo and headed out for Stock.

That was Ashok Saver Ndamba's province. He'd turned the landing skiffs into a combination storage bin and museum, and he ruled his territory with an iron hand. It always surprised me that he knew where everything was. Random access filing of the most eclectic sort. Luckily, there was nothing wrong with *his* indexing.

"Bats," he said. "I see the cathedral-builders got to you. You always were a softie."

"Who, me?" I said. "You must be thinking of somebody else. You know how badly we need insectivores?"

"Yes?"

"Bats," I said.

He looked up from his screen long enough for me to grin once and nod, then he shook his head and whistled. "I've got about five hundred kinds."

That didn't gibe with what I'd been reading. "Supposed to be twice that, according to the references I've been reading."

"Did you check the dates of the references? A lot of species went missing in the Bad Years. If it was extinct, they didn't send it with us."

I had to admit I hadn't checked dates. He was only partially right. By the time of the Mirabilan expedition, the geneticists had been reconstructing some of those extinct species. "Let's see what you've got. Here—this one—*Myotis lucifugus*. Let's start with that."

"At least you picked one we've got," he said and wandered off humming to himself to find the embryo stores. He wasn't humming when he came back. "Annie, I've got bad news."

"How bad?"

"Those idiots back on Earth stiffed us. I've got a sum total of forty embryos and even I know enough about jasoning to know that's not enough for a viable population."

I was not about to give up my mosquito-eaters without a fight. "Spare me what you can, then, Ashok. If I have to build 'em by hand, I will."

"For you, Annie, the whole batch, if you're willing to take them a few at a time. I also know enough to know that'll take some of the drudgery out of it."

"I accept."

WE STAYED just long enough in RightHere to give Leo first ring of the bell. I wasn't about to work in somebody else's lab when I could be home and surrounded by my own team. The message had done the job. By the time I walked in with my bat embryos, half the team was expert on the subject of bats.

This was not necessarily a good thing—it meant each and every one of them had a favorite bat to promote. "I brought *my* favorite," I said. "Anybody wants vampire bats can go get his own embryos."

Susan brightened perceptibly. "Really, Mama Jason?"

"Not really. That'd be a tough call. You'd have to do a lot of convincing. Any of the insectivores, fine. And somebody might think in terms of fruit bats for Encarnacion—it'd save them all that hand-pollinating. Talk to Leo before you do anything though. He can tell you which ones will give you the best shot at viability."

In the end, Leo'd had only one problem with my mouse-eared bats and that was the way they hung when they were at rest. He was worried they'd be attacked by stickytoes. So the moment I'd stored my embryos and the rest of my gear, we went out into the woods to watch the stickytoes in action, something I hadn't done since I was a kid.

A stickytoes is about a foot long and doesn't really have sticky toes, not in the gluey sense. It has a burr-like pad on each of its feet which lets it climb like nobody's business. The best part is that the burrs are so effective, the damn thing can come down a tree headfirst.

What Leo wanted me to see was the amount of damage a single stickytoes could do to the fruits of one of the local trees. The fruit wasn't human edible so the tree hadn't acquired a common name among the adults. When I was a kid, we'd called it "critterfruit" because of the resemblance to some sort of small furry brown animal.

Having taken a fresh look, I was ready to revise that to "batfruit." I could see Leo's point. That could be a problem. I watched the stickytoes hang from the bottom of a limb to eat its way along the branch. Batfruit after batfruit vanished into the stickytoes's gullet. Those teeth were sharp enough to crack the protective shell inside the hairy covering.

"Wanna bet the tree can't propagate without a stickytoes to crack the seed open?"

"Annie, I never take that sort of bet—not with you!" Then he said, "How much of a problem is it?"

"A bit," I said. "Am I remembering correctly that stickytoes are omnivorous?"

He nodded. "You are. And they have no problem with Earth-authentic meat either. Down at Loch Moose I've seen them eat mice."

"A taste for mice is altogether too close for comfort. It's not going to be easy to build up a sizable population of bats. They only have one offspring a year on the average. Ordinarily they live about twenty years but—"

"But not if the stickytoes try them and like them."

"So I'll have to make damn sure the stickytoes won't try them. Hell, if I have to make bats by hand, I might as well go all the way. Let's head back. You can spend the afternoon telling me all the things a stickytoes wouldn't touch on a dare."

FIRST OFF, we cloned the hell out of the few embryos we had. That gave us a working base and enough space to screw up one or two without causing a disaster. Then we built our bats by hand, splice by splice. It's time-consuming but no big deal.

Would have been boring as hell if Elly hadn't brought the whole troop of kids into town for a look-see. They'd gotten as worked up about bats as the team had. As long as they were around, I let Ilanith try her hand at a couple. She did just fine and couldn't have been prouder if she'd designed them herself.

"Mama Jason?" Jen came over to lean against my hip. "Are you going to let Susan make vampire bats? When *they* sprout Dragon's Teeth, the Dragon's Teeth look like people!"

It took us some time to sort that one out. Turned out she'd found *Dracula* in ships' files and she'd made the best sense of it she could. Which was that a vampire was a Dragon's Tooth that gave birth to bloodsucking bats and wolves and who knows what all else.

Elly, bless her many talents, made short work of straightening the kid out. I sure wouldn't have known how to field that one!

"Oh," said Jen at last. Then, turning her face up to me, she added, "It was your fault, Mama Jason. You told us to read fiction to learn about Earth-authentic species."

"So I did," I admitted. "And you're right. I'd have thought the same as you, if somebody hadn't told me better."

"Oh," she said again. "Okay, then."

Leo caught her eye and said, " 'Okay'?"

"Sure. If Mama Jason says it could have happened to her, it's not so bad if it happened to me. When I get as old as Mama Jason, I won't get mixed up about vampires."

I couldn't help but laugh. "Not about vampires. But you'll get mixed up about something else, I guarantee. Old as Mama Jason is no magical protection."

Jen eyed me sadly. "Too bad," she said.

"Keeps me from getting bored, though. So don't feel too sorry for me."

"Right," said Jen.

"Done," said Ilanith. "What next?"

"Next we pop them into the incubators and we wait. The real work starts when we pop them out of the incubators. Raising mammals is a pain in the butt."

"I'm a mammal," Jen said.

"My point exactly."

That brought a giggle from her. "Well, then," she said, after a moment, "you should ask Elly. She knows all about raising mammals."

Which wasn't such a bad idea. With everybody and Aklilu contributing, we told Elly everything she hadn't already heard about bats. When we were finished, Elly gave it some serious thought.

"They need dark and they need to hang upside down and they need to be warm." Elly ticked the requirements off on her fingers.

"*And* they need to be fed oftener than this troop," I said, raising another of her fingers.

"You'll need help tending them, then," Elly said, nodding. "I can recommend any number of bat-sitters." She looked around her expectantly.

The kids caught on even before I did. Elly got mobbed by enthusiastic volunteers. She made sure each and every one of them knew what kind of responsibility they were taking on. When she was finished, I had extra help by the handful.

"That takes care of the feeding," Elly said, as pleased with the kids as she was with herself. "As for the warm, dark and upside down—how about pockets?"

"Pockets?"

"Sure. A baby bat can hang upside down inside your pocket, where it's warm and dark."

"Elly, you're a genius."

"No. I'm just good at raising small mammals."

So by the time we were ready to pop the baby bats out of the incubators, we had patch pockets on all our shirts. Out of the incubator, into the pocket.

Half of Elly's kids flew home to Loch Moose Lodge with their pockets full of baby bats, all safe and warm.

There was only one problem with that, but it would have been a problem wherever the baby bats were. That was the bat shit. Yes, I know bat shit has its very own name. Call it guano all you like, it's still bat shit to me. And it was everywhere.

The bats survived only because they were, in Ilanith's words, "incredibly cute."

WHEN ALL THAT CUTENESS took to flying, things got pretty exciting around the lab for a while, until we realized bats—even baby bats—never run into anything.

By that time, they were on solid food. We set the local kids to catching bugs for them, but they'd already made some forays at hunting for themselves. Toss a bug and they'd catch it on the wing nine times out of ten.

The acid test came quite by accident. One of our bug-catchers left the door to the lab open. It was dusk, one of those beautiful clear nights. Next thing I knew, we had the swarming horrors by the millions.

Mike swatted the air like crazy, trying to fend them off, cursing a steady stream at the negligence of the kid. I settled for covering my eyes and cursing just in general. My pockets stirred and, before I could stop them, both my bats were in the air.

"Annie! My bats! Stop them!"

I blinked a dozen or more horrors out of my eyes and peered through my fingers. Mike's bats—Thorn and St. Germain—were in the air too. What with Tomato Surprise and Sulpho, that seemed to make more than four.

I had to lower my hands to watch. I'd have dropped my jaw at the aerobatics but that would have gotten me a mouthful of the swarming horrors. As I stared, Sulpho zigged, snapped up a dozen of the horrors, zagged to snap up another dozen, then did a full somersault in mid-air for yet another mouthful.

Tomato Surprise had an even neater trick. She dove into a cluster and scooped them up with her wing. Then she flipped up her tail to eat the ones she'd netted—all without losing so much as an inch of altitude.

I got it from the swarming horrors' eyeview once, too. Thorn aimed straight for my face, teeth first. For all of a quarter second, I thought I was about to get an explanation for the bad press bats had on Earth. Then, with a flick of his wing, Thorn hung a right so sharp I could only gape. I felt a riffle of air along my temple and then all the horrors that had been buzzing around my face were gone.

Mike grabbed me by the arm. "Dammit, Annie—what if they get poisoned?"

"If eating swarming horrors kills 'em," I said, "we have to start over. We might as well find out now."

He sighed. "Yeah, but. . . ."

"How many times do I have to remind you not to make pets of the laboratory animals?"

"Don't get snotty. You named yours first. And you look just like I feel."

"Yeah," I admitted, "but it's too late now, and if they've got such an instinct for eating swarming horrors, you know as well as I do they're gonna eat 'em sooner or later."

In this case, it was sooner. They'd settled into a routine now, all four making graceful sweeps of the lab. With each pass the number of swarming horrors lessened. Now *that's* what I call efficient!

They made unbelievably short work of the swarming horrors. Some fifteen minutes later, my bats landed on my shoulder and climbed back into their pocket, twice as fat as when they'd left it. I could have sworn I heard Tomato Surprise belch contentedly.

It was a week before Mike and I were willing to admit the bats had come to no harm. Then we did everything short of jumping up and down to celebrate. Jumping up and down would have disturbed the bats' sleep, you see.

Later that week, Susan went back to Ashok for another set of embryo samples to start the cloning of a second batch.

CAME TIME to release the first batch of bats, we decided to make a ceremony of it, which was nice because—for once—that fit in so well with my own plans. The first batch went to Loch Moose, and never mind how many guilds screamed. The mosquitoes were still on my mind. Besides, Elly and the kids had had as much a hand in raising the babies as my team had.

So every last one of us trooped up to Loch Moose, our pockets full of bats.

First thing we got was a tour of the lodge's attic. Elly'd enlisted the neighbors. They'd raised the roof two feet, put in a couple of bat-sized openings, and covered the floor of the crawl space with a tarp. "According to Ilanith, bat guano is great for gardens. We thought we'd better find a way to, uh, harvest it once we get them moved in."

I eyed Ilanith. "As long as you keep an eye on the vegetables to make sure the change in the EC doesn't change *them.*"

"Will do, Mama Jason," said Ilanith, snapping me a nod.

The kids had been making bat boxes to hang in the trees as well, just in case the bats preferred to leave "home." I could see where this had gotten to be a major project. And I never turn down volunteer assistance.

We had one helluva dinner, then we went out on the porch and settled in to wait for nightfall.

"Or the swarming horrors, whichever comes first," Ilanith said. "Akililu left the door open one night and a bunch of them got in, but the bats made short work of 'em."

Aklilu made chomping movements with his hands to demon-strate.

There was a stirring in my right pocket. Tomato Surprise climbed to my shoulder, seemed to test the air, and clung there for a moment.

Jen, who was sitting on my lap, said authoritatively, "He's clicking it out." Aklilu stopped "chomping" and nodded. To me, Jen said, "I can hear 'em sometimes. Aklilu, too."

This time Elly nodded. "The younger kids are more likely to be able to hear them. Glen Sonics Dollery got curious enough to check it out with an oscilloscope. The bat's lowest calls are just at the upper range of Jen's and Aklilu's hearing."

"I'm sorry I'm missing it," I said to Jen.

She gave my hand a squeeze. "Me, too. I like the way it

sounds. It means he's checking everything out. . . ." She cocked her head a moment. "Now he's gonna launch."

And with that he did. Moments later, Sulpho and the rest of the bats did the same sort of routine. Jen and Aklilu giggled. Soft fluttering filled the air around us.

The bats were on their own at last. Now it was only a matter of wait and see if they'd survive—and if they'd thrive. We'd done the best we could to give them a Mirabilan twist. Now it was up to the bats themselves.

"All gone!" said Aklilu, happily. "Raise more bats, Mama Jason?"

"You betcha," I told him. "Susan's incubating them now. You wait a few weeks, you'll have a new bat to feed."

"Good," said Elly. "I was a little worried what would happen when their pets left home."

"Were you, Elly?" Ilanith stood up suddenly. "If I'd known, I'd have told you— No, watch." She held out her index finger and made a sort of chirping sound. She waited patiently for a moment, then chirped again.

"She's coming," Aklilu announced.

Next thing I knew, Ilanith had a bat clinging to her forefinger. She offered it a grub which it ate with relish. Then it launched back into the air and vanished again.

Mike said, "Now why didn't I think of that?"

"Some people just aren't as bright as others," Susan told him, with a wink at Ilanith.

"Don't fight!" said Ilanith. "I can show you how, Mike. It's easy! They're bright—you can teach 'em all sorts of things."

Jen giggled. "You be careful if you teach it 'sic 'em' though. Ilanith did and didn't have a grub ready so it chomped her finger instead."

"I didn't hear about that little incident," Elly said, her voice ominous.

"Oops," said Jen.

Ilanith spread her hands. "Don't worry about it, Jen. We'd have had to warn Mike and he'd have told Mama Jason and she'd have told Elly anyhow."

"Dead on right," I said. I cocked a finger at Ilanith, though, and said, "Next time, I want to hear about it on the spot. When we're gearing up for the release of something, we need to know all their behavior patterns."

"But, Mama Jason," Ilanith's voice took on that exasperated-with-adults tone, "it was *my* fault it bit me."

"Have I suddenly lost all my wits? What on earth made you think I wouldn't take that into account?"

Ilanith found something terribly interesting around her feet that needed close observation. "Sorry," she mumbled, just about as audible as bat clicks. "I didn't think." Then a bit louder. "I didn't mean to insult you."

"No offense taken, so long as it doesn't happen again." I hoisted Jen into my arms and stood up to stretch my back. "Now, if you'll all follow me, I've got a bit of a ceremony to perform."

If I'd meant to take my time ambling back into the lodge, I lost that notion quick. The level of curiosity led to a jostling which led to minor pushing which led to a stampede into the dining room. Chie-Hoon, the only one who knew what this was about, grinned at me. I put Jen down to let her join the mad race. And took my time getting there so I could make an entrance.

Nothing like an attentive audience to put you on your best behavior, I thought. Damned if I knew what they expected me to do. . . . Took me a minute to find Leo in all that crowd. Chie-Hoon grabbed his elbow and thrust him to the fore, rearranging some of the smaller kids so they could still see.

I made Leo my deepest bow and said, "Leonov Bellmaker Denness—I, Ann Jason Masmajean, beg you to hear my petition. . . ."

It brought the house down. Elly outright whooped, then dropped to one knee to explain to Aklilu, "That means she finally thought of a courting gift for Noisy."

"About time, too!" commented Susan.

"So hush up and let her finish," said Leo, which brought instant quiet. He made me a return bow to get the ritual back on track.

"I have brought you a gift in symbol of my intentions," I went on.

Another exchange of bows. Leo was pulling out all the stops. He did it with such flare that Aklilu had to try it, too. Aklilu fell over, giggled, got up to try again, and the second time succeeded. I think I managed to keep my face straight; Leo didn't.

By the time I was halfway through my list of reasons for loving Leo, ritual got shot to hell. There I was on: "Because you're the only person I've ever met with hands as big as mine" and "Because you volunteered to carry baby bats in your pockets"— and the kids started calling out suggestions. . . .

"Because he can shout louder than anybody in the *world*," suggested Jen.

The hell with ritual. "Because you can shout as loud as I can," I told Leo.

"Stories!" said Aklilu. "Because he tells the best stories!"

"Because you tell the best stories," I echoed. Sometimes it's hard to talk when you're grinning that hard.

"Because he gene-reads his own pansies," Susan contributed.

"Who's proposing to this man, you or me?" I said, at last. Took me a minute to catch my breath, but while I did, they settled down to a dull roar.

"Because I like necking with you better than any other sport known on Mirabile or on Earth, and because you can reasonably out-stubborn me any day," I said, "I hope you will accept my gift and consider my suit."

We went through another round of bows and Leo said, "Ann Jason Masmajean, I, Leonov Bellmaker Denness, am sufficiently intrigued to view your gift."

A cheer went up, followed by shouts of "What is it?" and "Let's see!" and "*Where* is it?" I had to wave them into silence. "It's not a thing you can put in a pocket," I said to Aklilu, who was patting at my hip in an exploratory fashion.

"It's this, Leo: I'm offering to take you on as my apprentice."

Leo's jaw dropped practically to his chest. For one horrible moment I thought I'd gotten it wrong, then he said, "Me? You'd let me be a jason?"

"Only if you want. We could use you, Leo. You've got expertise we haven't."

He eyed me suspiciously. "You're serious?"

Helluva thing to ask. "As serious as your kangaroo rex courting gift was," I said. "I need somebody to specialize in Mirabilan wildlife. I've got the funds for it—ask Chie-Hoon if you doubt me!—all I need is the body."

Leo spread his arms wide. "This body is all yours."

That was a load off my mind. I stepped into his embrace. Behind me, I heard Susan say, "Yup. She got it right," and I heard Elly's answering chuckle.

NOT EVERYTHING works out as neatly as you'd like—at least, bats don't. We took the second batch to RightHere, but it was Bethany we took them to, in private.

"You've got a choice to make," I told her. "You can have Leo's bell or you can have the bats. You can't have both in your belfry."

It was Ilanith who'd discovered it—in her supplementary reading. Despite the guild's enthusiasm, "bats in the belfry" was not, by Earth-authentic standards, a particularly good thing. It certainly wasn't the compliment they'd taken it for. Bats are associated with *dis*used belfries only. Good reason for that: Leo's bell would deafen the poor things and next thing you know they'd be flying into walls.

"Why are you asking me?" she said. "Seems to me the whole guild—"

"You're the artist," I said. "A flock of real bats would, for one thing, cover up the bats you carved into the belfry's ceiling. If the choice were mine, I'd suggest you build bat boxes all around the town and leave the bell where it is."

Leo raised an eyebrow at me. "If they're so set on the bats, the bell can just as well come down. Or we could take the clapper out." To Bethany, he added, "I can't make out whether she's more interested in saving my bell or your carvings. Probably both, if I know her."

He took my hands in his. "Let's get the priorities straight. We *need* the bats. We don't need the bell."

"Or the carvings," Bethany put in. "I'll put it to the guilds, Annie, but I can tell you right now what the decision will be: bats in the belfry."

She was right. The only thing made me feel better about it was that they moved Leo's bell—right to the middle of the town square. There, at least, everybody could—and did—appreciate the work Leo'd put into the design. Leo seemed pleased by it all.

Then we saw the second round of bats settled in their new home. I was still sorry they covered Bethany's carvings.

Bethany had the damndest expression on her face, though, as if she might break into giggles at any moment. Half an hour later, once we'd gotten away from the guild, she leaned close and said, "Annie, what the hell kind of bats are those? I thought you were bringing us mouse-eared bats."

I hadn't expected that from anybody but another jason. As deadpan as I could, I said, "Red bats and yellow bats."

"Right," she said, and then she *did* burst into laughter. "You can't con me, Annie. I did my research for the bat carvings. Red bats are brown. Yellow bats are brown. *These* red bats are poppy red and *these* yellow bats are dandelion yellow. And I won't even bring up the pumpkin orange bats."

Not bringing up "pumpkin orange" set her to laughing all over again.

When it simmered down a bit, I said, "I had to do *something* to make them look unappetizing to the stickytoes."

"Oh!" Bethany's eyes lit up. "I get it. Nothing in its right mind would mess with a killquick, so you made them killquick colors."

I nodded. "I won't tell if you won't. Other than that, they're Earth-authentic."

Leo put an arm around my shoulders. "They're not Earth-authentic. They're Mirabilan, like Bethany's cathedral."

"Lord, Annie, I won't say a word," said Bethany. "They really brighten up the belfry. All that gray stone was a little grim before we moved the bats in. I think your Mirabilan bats are a work of art!"

Better than that, I couldn't ask for.

Sabah managed to keep his mouth shut too, even though it took some effort. With only a hint of smile, he (and the rest of his team) admired our Mirabilan bats and stuck to the term despite an occasional outburst of chuckles.

It was Vassily who named them, though. He stared up at the clusters of bats hanging from his mother's carvings and said, "Oh, wow! Tulip bats!" And from then on nobody called them anything but.

And Leo and I got the privilege of being the first couple to join hands in the new cathedral. So much to-do was made about it that it took us three days at Leo's cabin out on Loch Moose to recuperate. Elly restricted the kids to the other side of the lake for the duration, bless her, and there was nary a crisis to interfere with our pleasure, though we both suspected that the team had strict instructions not to call us even if there was one.

We were out on the loch at dusk, snuggled together at one end of Leo's boat, breathing in the night air and simply appreciating the sounds around us in the flickering shadows made by the nova light. And watching the lightning bugs twinkle.

The lightning bugs had been our wedding gift from the team. They'd worked like dogs, and all in secret too, to have some fifty of them to release the night we arrived at Leo's. Sweetest present.

"There's one," said Leo and lifted a hand to point it out to me. The lightning bug blinked closer and closer to the boat in its characteristic erratic flight pattern. Real pretty—just like the descriptions I'd read in ships' records. That was just about all it took to make Loch Moose perfect, as far as I was concerned.

Then I heard a soft flutter of wings, felt a rush of air ruffle my hair and the lightning bug was gone. I sat up, rocking the boat.

"Annie? What—?"

"Damn bat!" I said. "A damn bat ate our lightning bug!"

Leo started to laugh. "You are never satisfied. You wanted something that would eat insects; you got something that would eat insects!"

Well, it *was* funny when he put it that way. I couldn't help but laugh along with him. But—"As for never satisfied, you're wrong about that!" And then to clarify my meaning I kissed him—a lot. Let the damn bats eat the damn lightning bugs. Leo and I had better things to do than worry about the wildlife.

"Tell a scary one tonight, Mama Jason," Jen commanded.

"How scary?"

She thought it over. "Not too. Not the one—you know." She drew a finger up her ankle. "Gives me nightmares." She thought a bit longer, then she said, "Tell the one about how you met Nikolai."

"Go ahead, Annie," said Nikolai. "I haven't heard your version of that."

Ilanith grinned at him. "Yeah, then Nikolai can tell us how much of it is really true."

I did my best to look injured. "Would I lie to you?"

"No," said Ilanith, "but you'd tell us stories."

"Well," I said, "every word of this one's true."

5

Raising Cane

So FAR, it looked like spring as usual. The Cornish hens were hatching everything from chickadees to lizards—with the occasional frog on the side. Two of the ewes at Last Edges had given birth to angora goats. (Susan had taken the lambing off my hands this year. Gave her an excuse to see Janzen. I hadn't warned her lambing would leave her too exhausted to do more than wave to him in passing, on the way to the next birthing. She'd get me for that when she got back, no doubt.)

Three new stands of forsythia had flowered tulip red. Likewise, an entire field of dandelions had gone red on us, which meant we had to check every one to see what it had in store for us when it seeded.

If they hadn't been so eye-catching, I doubt a single plant would have lasted out the first flowering.

So it didn't surprise me much when Lalique Cowboy Imbamba called. Lalique's in charge of that Guernsey herd we've been trying to stabilize for the last thirty years or so. Once we get a decent-sized breeding pool built up, we can parcel them out around the colony for milk and cheese production, not to mention the occasional chop. We want to parcel out cows that pretty consistently produce calves, though, rather than goats or musk oxen or, worst case, Dragon's Teeth.

The look on Lalique's face said Dragon's Teeth. Well, at least it'd be a change from grubbing in the dandelion genes. I'd gotten to the point where I was doing gene-reads in my sleep—and they were all dandelion.

"Give me the worst," I said. "I could use the change."

"Uh, Annie? It's complicated. Let me tell you the calving results first, okay?"

Okay by me. I told the lab computer to save the rest of the dandelion gene-reads for later and nodded to Lalique's image. Then I hauled up a chair and settled in to listen.

"We've had thirty-four live births so far. Only three stillbirths. Of the three stillbirths, two were genuine calves, the third was a Dragon's Tooth."

"Not a viable Dragon's Tooth, then," I said. "What's the tally on the live births?"

"Calves—every last one of them. Except—"

Here it comes, I thought. Tell you the truth, I was looking forward to it.

"Except two of them were so underdeveloped that we're bottle-feeding them. When I did the gene-read on them, it turned out they were some kind of cow other than Guernsey. Both mothers birthed them prematurely, even though they were the same size as the rest of the calves."

Could have been worse. I had her shoot me copies of the gene-reads for the new batch of calves so far. Printed 'em up hard copy for the luxury of it. (Paper—now that's one we owe to the thoughtfulness of whoever back on Earth included kudzu genes in the honeysuckle.) At first glance, there was nothing on paper worth the frown she'd been frowning.

When I looked back at Lalique's image to see if the frown was still that bad it went from bad to worse.

Her finger all but jabbed out of the screen, pointing some-where behind me, and she shouted, "Annie, look out!"

I dodged and turned at the same time. Neither action saved me from a blast of foul breath in the face and a "GRONK!" in both ears that nearly deafened me.

"Gronk to you, too," I said, when I'd gotten my breath back. It was only Mabob.

Mabob was so pleased I'd talked its language that it rattled its scales all over and let out a second airhorn *gronk!*

A faint "Annie?" from the screen reminded me that Lalique didn't know it was "only" Mabob. I turned back. "Nothing to worry about, Lalique," I said, then I bellowed for Leo.

"What the hell is it?" Lalique wanted to know.

I took a look at "it" from her point of view. It was over three feet tall and had a beak that could probably take your hand off at a snap. If you've seen parrots in ships' records, think of it as an oversized parrot without the wings. Or better still, a dodo—same outsized head on a stubby body. And then forget all about birds, because it isn't.

Its scales (which are actually fur fused hard as chiton, like a pangolin's) were striped—that they were all shades of green didn't keep them from clashing with each other. On the top of its head the fur was unfused and actually fur-like to the touch, but it stood out in spikes, as if the thing had just stuck one of its talons into the electric wiring. The eyes (and I mean the whole eye, not just the pupil) were pumpkin orange, which didn't help its looks any.

Come to think of it, nothing would help its looks any—probably Lalique was seeing the Giant Killer Bird, straight out of her granddaddy's scariest tale.

At the moment, it was peering around my shoulder, both orange eyeballs popped and fixed on Lalique's image in utter fascination.

"It's not a bird," I said. "Lalique, meet Mabob. That's short for Thingamabob. You know Leo hired on with us to study the Mirabilan wildlife? Well, he brought this one home as an egg. Mabob, this is Lalique."

"Uh," said Lalique. "Hi, Mabob."

"GRONK!" said Mabob, rattling his scales happily. The image may not have smelled human, but being talked to was good enough for Mabob.

"Leo!" I bellowed again, with Mabob taking up the call for Leo enthusiastically. "Come collect this damn thing! You promised me you'd keep it out of the lab," I finished, as Leo opened the door.

"I didn't let him in," Leo said. "Somebody must have left the door unlatched. Sorry. I'll get him out of your hair." Leo let out a *gronk* that pretty much lived up to Mabob's decibel level, and Mabob charged out to greet him at the same level.

"Annie," said Lalique, "that's weird!"

I couldn't help but grin at her. "Any weirder than a cow?"

She grinned back. "Not when you stop to think about it, no."

I nodded to her. "Now, tell me what the problem is. I don't see anything unusual in this," I said, flapping the hard copy at her.

"Is it possible for cows to, uh, give birth to seeds that grow plants?"

"Technically, yes." I looked at the hard copy again. She'd only given me the gene-reads on the calves, not the cows that had birthed them. "I'd need the gene-reads on the cows in question to say for sure."

Before she could volunteer to get the cell samples and analyze them herself, I added, "Tell you what—I'll come up for a look-see."

"Sure, Annie. You'll want to see the plants anyhow. Maybe you can give us some suggestions about how to get rid of the damn things."

"Or about how to get along with them."

"You haven't seen them yet. They can't be Mirabilan and if you don't need them for anything, I need them gone."

Cows with encrypted plant genes didn't sound likely to me, but I wasn't about to bet on it after some of the Dragon's Teeth I've been chewed by. Personally, though, I didn't care if the damn things had fangs eight feet long—all I needed was a change from dandelions.

*   *   *

I PALMED the next hundred dandelion gene-reads off on Mike and went outside to hunt up Leo.

Found him watching Mabob stalk a whompem. I kept my mouth shut and watched as well, a little surprised that Leo didn't intervene—whompems run about a foot long, with a full set of predator's teeth and claws. This one was no exception.

The other thing that surprised me was that Mabob was actually keeping its mouth shut, something I didn't think it was capable of doing for more than three seconds at a time. Despite its size, that green-stripe camouflage really worked. When Mabob froze, it vanished into the background as if it had never been there.

It had worked its way between the whompem and the edge of the forest. Took me some hard looking to spot it. Then it started to inch toward the whompem. Those huge clawed feet were absolutely silent.

Maybe *I* thought it was absolutely silent, but something tipped off the whompem and it ran like hell. Like hell wasn't nearly good enough. Mabob had long legs and a flat-out gallop I wouldn't have believed unless I'd seen it.

Mabob chased the whompem the length of the street and overtook it in front of Mike and Selima's house, where it rolled its talons into a club and swung at the whompem's head. Even at that distance, I could hear bone crack. The whompem went flying. Mabob dashed after it, and before the whompem hit the ground, Mabob had sunk a footful of talons into its spine.

Mabob let go with a triumphant *gronk!* (Been nighttime, it would've waked the entire town.) Then it picked up the whompem in its beak and trotted back to us. It laid the dead whompem at Leo's feet and gronked again.

"For me?" said Leo.

Mabob nudged the carcass closer to Leo with its foot. Leo stooped and, after checking to make sure it really was dead, picked the carcass up. Mabob rattled its scales in pleasure.

"What do I do now?" Leo asked me, out of the side of his mouth.

"Same as with a cat, I guess. Tell it it's a mighty hunter. Thank it. Then say you're not hungry right now and give it back."

So that's what he did. Mabob took it in good spirit, rattling like a dozen maracas all through the compliments Leo paid it and rattling even harder when Leo rubbed it affectionately where the spiky fur was soft, making it still spikier.

Mabob didn't seem put out when Leo returned the gift, which was just as well. It clamped a foot on the carcass and began to rip chunks off with its beak and swallow them, bones and all.

"Good thing it thinks you're its mother," I said to Leo.

"That's the first time he's ever done that," said Leo, putting just enough emphasis on the "he" to catch my attention.

"I'll call it a he if it makes you happy, Leo. But I don't know it's a he and neither do you. And I can't tell from the gene-read unless you bring me enough other samples that they include one of the opposite sex. If, that is, this is one of Mirabile's two-sexed types and not something else altogether."

"It'd simplify your syntax."

"'He' it is, then. At least until we find out different. And you'd better get *him* out of Selima's snap peas unless you want Selima to remove *his* head."

Mabob isn't too particular about what he eats. He'll try just about anything, animal or vegetable, and he thinks most of it is perfectly good. The one time he'd refused to try something Leo offered him from the table, I got curious enough to do a little testing. Turned out that particular Earth import *would* have made him sick—that's pretty efficient hard wiring.

Leo had managed to hustle him out of Mike and Selima's garden. No real problem. I'd already learned that Mabob would do just about anything Leo asked him to. Meanwhile, I got around to remembering what I'd wanted to talk to Leo about in the first place.

"I'm headed up to Lalique's," I said. "She's got a problem plant. She says it's my bailiwick, but it could be yours. Want to come along?"

"That's Haffenhaff Island, right? I was just about to head up there myself—"

"Perfect."

"I was planning to take Mabob along."

"So you get me instead."

He smiled and spread his arms. Anything for an excuse to neck, I always say. (And we always do.) Mabob thought we were fascinating and rattled his scales furiously while he stretched his neck to try to peer between us. To my relief, he didn't gronk once.

When we broke the clinch, Leo said, "How about both?"

"Hunh?"

"I want you to meet Nikolai and I want Nikolai to meet you *and* Mabob."

Nikolai's the third of Leo's kids, the only one I hadn't met yet. Takes after Leo, which is why he hadn't even made it to our wedding—he'd been off opening new territory at the time. If Leo wanted him to meet Mabob, too, who was I to argue?

"The things I do for love," I said. "What are chances you can keep Mabob from gronking the entire trip? I hear one of those trumpet blasts in a closed hover and I'm likely to lose what hearing I have left."

"We'll open the windows. If we're lucky, he'll gronk at the scenery." He turned to Mabob. "Want to go for a ride, Mabob?"

The answer was obviously "yes," and there went the rest of my hearing. Damn Thingamabob *didn't* gronk at the scenery—he gronked at Leo, and the entire hover rang with the sound. On the second gronk, I grounded the hover in the nearest clearing. "Hush!" I said to Mabob. "That's enough! Out!"

Mabob rattled his scales engagingly, but I wasn't having any. No point doing this if it wasn't a break from the damn dandelions. "Leo, open the door and shove him out."

"We can't just leave him here, Annie!" He sounded a lot like kid defending pet, which I suppose he was.

"I'm not. I'm just putting him out for gronking in a closed space. Do it."

He did it grudgingly but he did it. I twiddled my thumbs and waited until Mabob shut up and started to peer wistfully through the window. Then I had Leo let him back in—anxious but subdued.

It was some twenty minutes before he relaxed enough to give us another air-horn squawk, at which point I grounded the hover on the spot and threw him out all over again. This time he shut up a lot faster.

By the third time, he shut up the minute he was out of the hover. Leo raised an eyebrow at me.

"I'm taking a leaf from Elly's book," I said. I'd once seen her use a similar ploy for misbehavior. "He's quiet. Let him back in."

After that, the rest of the ride was quiet, if you don't count the maracas as noise. Compared to the gronks, I didn't. Five minutes later we came to the Omigolly, turned the hover downriver and there was Haffenhaff.

Haffenhaff's a good-sized island smack-dab in the middle of the Omigolly River. Granddaddy Jason picked it as the right place to start raising a herd of Guernseys because, he figured, it was big enough to support the size herd he had planned, but small enough we could police the EC pretty well. Had the added virtue there wasn't much place for the herd to wander off to. Sooner or later, they'd hit the Omigolly and that'd stop 'em wandering further. He was right: in all my years, I'd never seen the Omigolly low enough to walk across.

From the upstream end, the island looked barren. Scarcely enough vegetation to make an environmental run-up seem worth the trouble—mostly shale and prickles. The prickles were interesting though, being an epiphyte with the damndest set of equipment for clinging to bare rock you ever saw.

The downstream end was already lush and green, with a spring overlay of reds and yellows. Granddaddy Jason told me once that his mother had been tickled to death that first spring to find that, "just like Earth, Mirabile thought of flowers too!"

A lot of the firstfolk seemed to have felt the same relief. Damnify I know why. They couldn't have had much experience with flowers after so many generations shipboard.

As far as I was concerned, I could have done without—at least without the dandelions. But it was hardly fair to hold the dandelions against Mirabilan evolution. Couldn't even hold them against Gaian evolution. I could—and did—hold them against a bunch of long-dead genetic engineers.

Leo'd been giving the island the same once-over I had. "Now I see why it got dubbed 'half and half,'" he said, grinning at me. Then he pointed. "That's where we're going, Mabob."

Catching Leo's excitement, Mabob rattled his scales. He looked like he was working up to another gronk.

"Don't you dare, Mabob," I said. "Hush!"

He didn't gronk. I was impressed. Telling him three times seemed to have been enough.

"How about that," Leo said. "It worked."

"He's brighter than he looks. Question is, will he remember when the time comes to head home?"

"We'll see," said Leo, scratching Mabob around the eyes.

Would be interesting to know. That Mabob took no for an answer made him a lot brighter than I'd originally thought—especially that he took the 'no' from me rather than from Leo, who'd raised him from an egg. He surely didn't think of me as his raiser. He'd only known me for a few weeks, since Leo'd brought him home half-grown, but maybe he'd lumped me in with official adult, worth learning survival techniques from.

I grounded the hover next to the main house, looked first, then stepped onto the ground. "Watch out for cow pies," I said to Leo. "Lalique doesn't usually let the Guernseys into this area, but that doesn't mean they haven't been here."

Cow pies—the bane of my life for five years. Nothing native to Mirabile would touch the things, so they'd just piled up and up and up. For a while it'd looked as if we wouldn't be able to keep the cows. I got stubborn and dug through ships' files until I found a truly obscure reference. Turned out they'd had the same trouble with cows on some island on Earth until they'd imported a particular kind of dung beetle. Three months later, I'd matched the reference to the right beetle in the ships' cell stores. Three months after that, a lot of beetles were eating themselves into oblivion and I got treated to my first slice of rare roast beef. Now *that* was an experience I'd like to repeat sometime!

I was about to try to describe the indescribable to Leo when Lalique came waving and hollering up. Mabob went running to greet her. Leo took off after Mabob, bellowing as he ran, "Don't shoot, Lalique! He's friendly!"

Mabob stopped, honked happily at Leo, waited for him to catch up. Then the two of them went to meet her together. By the time I ambled along, Mabob had already won Lalique's laughing approval. She greeted me with, "You're right, Annie. He's not that much funnier than a cow. And he's a damn sight more responsive. Cows don't pay you much attention."

I grinned at Leo. "His raiser taught him some social graces. Not many, but more than the average Guernsey."

Usually I get met by half a dozen kids, plus the rest of the cowboys. Today there was no sign of Lalique's brood. I looked around, wondering at the silence. "Where is everybody?"

"Keeping an eye on the last few births. I got 'time off' because I was up all last night. I got a few hours sleep waiting for you."

I snorted. "Your 'time off' sounds a lot like mine. Let's get to work then."

"Do you want to see the gene-reads first or the Dragon's Tooth?"

I'd have opted for the gene-reads first, if only because Lalique could get a bit more sleep while I worked on them, but I didn't get that choice. The walkie-talkie at Lalique's hip squawked and she answered it. All I could make out was that they had "another one stuck" and "Bring your machete."

Lalique said, "You get to see the Dragon's Teeth first, and you get to see them in action."

We followed her to the house and armed ourselves with machetes. Didn't even occur to me to get my shotgun out of the hover—if Lalique said best dealt with by machete, I believed her. Dragon's Tooth or not, she'd had experience with it and I hadn't.

If it was a Dragon's Tooth, it belonged in the slower-than-molasses family. We took a long leisurely hike across the pasture. (Mabob got a chance to stretch his legs. Leo got a chance to find out what a cow pie was.) Once we got close enough to hear the calf squealing, I'd have stepped a little more lively, but Lalique just plodded along as before.

Leo glanced at me, frowning at the sound. I shrugged. We stuck with Lalique. Mabob gronked and made a short gallop ahead but the minute he saw Leo wasn't following he did a hasty about-face and galloped back.

The squeals had attracted the attention of a good-sized part of the herd. They were all standing about, watching anxiously, doing nothing—pretty standard cow behavior. From the far side of the herd, a skinny kid in a splashy red shirt waved and shouted. "Over here, Lalique!"

Had to be Jibril, Lalique's third. He'd gotten two feet taller since the last time I'd seen him, but he was still as skinny as ever. Skinnier, if that was possible. But it was beginning to look good on him. If Mirabile didn't already have a Masai Guild, he'd have been the kid to start one up.

Behind him, the stand of canes that edged the pasture looked like somebody'd planted them just to make Jibril look good. They were as straight and slender as he was but a good deal taller— framing him. The stand was maybe a hundred feet long and I couldn't see how deep it went. The canes themselves were a rich dark green with splashes of red and orange flower throughout. The red ones matched Jibril's shirt precisely.

"That's our Dragon's Tooth," said Lalique, pointing in Jibril's direction.

"Real pretty ornamental," I said, not meaning Jibril any more than she had. If the canes were the problem, I hadn't seen enough to worry me yet. Lalique grunted a reply and pushed forward.

Getting through the herd was a lot like slogging through hip-high water—except that the water complains at you for shoving and, once in a while, especially if the herd's antsy, like this one was, tried to shove back.

Mabob had been sticking behind Leo—cows were new to him and he wasn't taking any chances—but one of the bulls took serious offense at the color of his beak and made snorting noises.

Mabob got defensive and glared at it. Mabob being a half foot taller (if only because of the spiked hair) had the psychological advantage, I think, but the only thing dumber than a cow is a bull.

It snorted again and pawed the ground threateningly. I was about to go over and clout it, the way I'd seen Lalique do often enough, but Mabob knew a threat when he saw one. He answered in kind. He drew himself up to full height—standing on his toes to do it—and bristled his scales. They made a rasping sound and Mabob suddenly looked twice as big as he had before. At the same time, he bugged out his bright orange eyes—"eye-blazing," they call it, when a parrot does it. Those orange eyes blazed all right.

Stupid bull didn't give an inch. So Mabob escalated. He arched his head over the Guernsey and said, at the top of his lungs, "GRONK!"

All around us, the cattle started. The calf in distress even stopped its squalling. "Annie," said Lalique, with a note of warning in her voice.

"I know." If Mabob rattled them too much, they'd stampede, and I didn't want to be in the middle of it if they did. Grant you, it's not the kind of stampede you see in ships' records, but I, for one, prefer my hips unbruised and my toes untrampled.

"Mabob, hush!" I said. Leo was already pushing back toward him.

But the single gronk seemed to have done the job. The bull was backing away. Mabob, delighted by his newfound power, followed . . . until even I could see that he was deliberately stalking the bull. Step by step, and for the pure pleasure of it. Because each time he forced the bull back another step, he paused to rattle his scales before he stepped forward again.

About the third step, Leo caught up to them both. "That's enough, Mabob. Don't bully the damn thing." Mabob rattled scales at Leo and invited him to play with the bull too. I swear I could actually see the offer made.

"Thanks, but no," said Leo. "Come away." It took a bit of coaxing, but he managed to lead Mabob away. The bull vanished into the herd, probably to find somebody lower in the pecking order to take it out on.

The calf took up squealing just about where it had left off, so we pushed on. Finally we'd all slogged through to Jibril.

"Hey, Annie!" he said. "Come to slay our Dragon's Teeth?"

"Depends," I said. "Do they need slaying?"

"Well," he said, "I dunno. We've got to cut enough of them down to get the calf out, at least." He pointed into the canebrake.

All I had to do, really, was look where the calf's squeals were coming from . . . the poor thing was thrashing about wildly, and the canes thrashed with it. Looked for all the world like a sheep caught in brambles, just tangling itself deeper the more it struggled. Only the canes didn't have any thorns that I could see.

"You must be Leo," Jibril was saying. "Boy! Do you ever look like Nikolai!"

My ear appreciated Leo's chuckle at that. ("Wrong way around," Leo said. "Nikolai looks like me.") But mostly I was giving a close look at the canes nearest me.

Close up they looked messy as all hell. The stalks were covered, top to bottom, with something clear and gelatinous. It reminded me a lot of the waterproofing on the stems of a water lily, but embedded in it was the damndest collection of insects I'd ever seen.

Not just insects, either. Bits of fur and scales were stuck to it as well, along with here and there a small animal.

Dragon's Tooth or not, the plants were unquestionably carnivorous. And they didn't seem any pickier than Mabob about what they ate—a number of the insects looked Earth-authentic to me.

I had just about stuck out my finger to poke one into position for a better look—at least enough to confirm my suspicions—when Lalique grabbed my wrist.

"Don't touch it, Annie, or you'll lose skin."

"Wasn't going to touch it. Just the bug." I pointed with my chin at the calf. "If it'll tangle something that size, I know enough not to touch it."

"Okay," Lalique said. To Leo, she added, "Getting loose is a lot like having surgical tape ripped off your body."

"Gotcha," said Leo. "Let's get that calf out before it tangles itself worse."

Lalique shook her head. "You watch while Jibril and I do it. This takes technique and practice. Next time you can help, I promise you."

The technique was tricky at that: without grabbing the cane to steady the cut, cut *away* from you, then lever the cut cane against the ground to snap it off the blade of your machete. And hope you don't get hit by any flying bits. If anybody on Mirabile needed a good source of high-quality glue, Lalique had found it.

Things got even trickier when they made it to the calf—they literally had to shave the canes from its body before cutting them down. The calf, of course, did nothing to help, just kept squalling and struggling.

Mabob got nosy and went in for a closer look before Leo or I could stop him. Leo made to call him back but it was already too late. Mabob had brushed against one of the canes. "Okay, Mabob," Leo said, "Hold still and—"

Mabob glared over his shoulder—not at Leo but at the cane holding him captive—and made a quick swipe with his beak. The cane sprang free, taking a single scale with it.

From then on, he picked his way through the canebrake as gingerly as a waterwalker—and not once did he brush against another stalk. Nor did he step on any of those Lalique and Jibril had cut down.

"Wonder why it took him three times to learn not to gronk in the hover," I said to Leo.

"The connection wasn't as obvious."

"Okay," I said. "I'll buy that."

Lalique glared at Mabob, but he didn't notice, being too busy checking out the calf. The calf took one look at Mabob and froze.

That made the job easier. Still in all, it took 'em close to twenty minutes to free it up.

Finally, Lalique emerged from the canebrake carrying the calf, followed by Mabob, who looked so smug you'd have thought he had performed the rescue work. Jibril followed with the machetes. Lalique let momma cow check her baby over, then she picked it up again, said, "Come on back to the barn. I've got to put some salve on the little idiot. See you later, Jibril."

"Hang on a minute," I said. "I need a sample, Lalique. Any suggestions?"

"Take your sample with something you won't mind having the sample permenently stuck to," said Lalique.

Jibril laughed. "It's not that bad, Annie. Take one of the leaves. The cows eat them all the time and it doesn't seem to gum up their mouths or their guts."

So the cows had learned something about the canes. That was worth knowing. They're not utterly stupid, just mostly. Momma cow followed us all the way to the barn, lowing at baby, who bleated back. Eager to get into the conversation, Mabob gronked at momma cow, who promptly shut up for the rest of the trek.

Leo and I got the door to let Lalique through. I stopped Mabob before he trotted after Leo. "Listen, you," I said. "One gronk out of you and you get yourself chucked out on your—" I was going to say 'ear' but it's not as if he has external ears "—ass."

Mabob paid me careful attention—at least, it looked that way, as he kept his eyes on me the entire time I was laying it on the line to him.

"So, hush!" I finished. "Got that?" Mabob rattled at me, for all the world as if he'd understood every word. I'd have settled for his understanding the "hush." It was worth a try though, so I let him in and closed the door behind us.

Inside, about a dozen people were flopped on bales of snapgrass. (Lalique's family—if some of them aren't blood, they're family still. Lalique's that sort of person.) Most of them looked about as dried out as the snapgrass did—from little round Brehani to long tall Gunnar, they had pouchy bags under their heavy-lidded eyes.

One of them—Villamil was his name if memory served, though he too had grown a lot in the last two years—found the strength to raise his head and say, "Last one done, Lalique. That's it for this year."

Orlando—Lalique's husband—his face darker than ever in the shadow of the arm thrown over it, just snored.

Having helped with the calving any number of years (come to think of it, this was only the second year I hadn't), I could remember how it felt. Give 'em each twenty-four hours of straight sleep and they'd be ready to celebrate. Until then they weren't up to feeling anything more than relief.

I went to the cupboard they kept the vet supplies in. Only one of the salves didn't look familiar. I held up the pot.

"That's it," said Lalique.

So while Leo kept Mabob from scaring the daylights out of Lalique's family, the two of us doctored the calf. The surgical tape analogy didn't quite make it, I saw from the damage. The calf had actually ripped at least one strip of skin off its hide in its struggles. "Is that common?" I said, pointing to the wound.

Lalique shook her head. "Mostly it's just a bit of hair here and there that they lose. The older ones anyhow. It's the calves that get the most damage."

She salved up the ripped patch. "At first, we thought they'd been burning themselves somehow—see here." She pointed out a long stripe on the calf's flank; no skin missing, just the hair. I might have guessed a healing burn too, if I'd seen only that one.

"But when we started seeing the flayed bits, we were sure we had a new predator. Or an old predator that had recently acquired a taste for the Earth-authentic." Lalique finished the last of the wounds, wiped her hands clean on the calf's side and shooed it back outside to its mother, who promptly began to lick the salve off the calf.

Lalique sighed. "It wasn't until Brehani found the first calf caught in the canebrake that we found out what we were up against. We came off worse than the calf did, to tell you the truth." She managed to grin. "Figured we were human . . . we could handle a plant, for god's sake! We barged right into the canebrake. . . . Well, that was pure arrogance, and we learned our lesson real fast. We wound up just as stuck as the calf, or maybe worse. Damn things practically snatched me bald. You can still see where the hair's growing back out!"

She parted her hair just enough to let me see a long pinkish brown scar. Healing well but it must've hurt like hell at the time.

"I'd have called you about them sooner but—"

"Calving," I said. "You don't have time to think about anything else. Hasn't been all that long that I've forgotten what it's like, Lalique."

She smiled at me ruefully. "Let me put the worst of these to bed, and then we'll get the cell samples from the last few calves."

I shook my head. "Just point out the ones that haven't been done, and tell me which of the calves needs special attention and what kind. We'll worry about your canebrake when the whole troop of you is rested. I need more information and just now I don't think I could get a coherent word out of a one of them. Bed for you too. Leo and I will see to what needs doing for a while."

"Thanks, Annie. I appreciate it."

"Hell," I told her, "I'm the one who appreciates it. Best thing I ever did was request a gene analyzer for you. You've been doing enough of my work, seems to me I can do a little of yours."

"Sure it's okay with Leo?"

I looked around. Leo had roused one of the kids—or Mabob had. Even though I hadn't heard a gronk, the kid couldn't have been staring at Mabob harder if he'd air-blasted him one.

Leo'd obviously been following the conversation. He called over, "I volunteer, Annie. It's a matter of family honor. Nikolai's asleep on his feet, so somebody's got to take over for him."

I should have known. The resemblance was unmistakable. Nikolai's crisply curled hair was darkest black where Leo's was pure white, and his brown skin was smooth where Leo's was crow's-footed and laugh-lined, but when the kid smiled—well, I could see where Leo got his crow's-feet and laugh lines because the kid's face crinkled up in all the same places.

Nikolai came shakily forward and held out a hand—a huge one like Leo's. "Nikolai Opener Jembere," he said. "And you've got to be Annie Jason Masmajean. Sorry I missed the wedding."

I took the hand. He had Leo's handshake as well. "We can get acquainted later," I said. "I can see the family resemblance but just now you look a lot older than Leo. Get some sleep."

He burst into laughter and grinned at Leo. "Perfect! Makes perfect sense!"

Leo grinned and nodded back.

"You don't," I pointed out. "Go, get some sleep! Honest to god, you're a compulsive volunteer, just like your dad."

Nikolai turned to include Lalique in his grin. "Hey," he said, "they help me dig bones. The least I can do is help them birth calves!" Still grinning mischievously, he gave one last look at Mabob and stumbled off to the house.

"That was clear as mud," I told Leo, after he'd gone.

"Don't worry, Annie. He'll tell you *all* about it when he wakes up. In fact, you won't be able to stop him."

ONE THING Leo's a helluva lot better at than I am is patience. I'm always finding that out at the damndest times. He waited until it was just the three of us (I'm counting Mabob only because he shared our interest in everything new), and then he gave me a grin and said, "Out with it, Annie. Tell me all about these 'Earth-authentic' cows."

I couldn't help laughing. "Aha!" I said. "*You've* been watching the 'westerns' in ships' files." Mabob rattled too.

"I was hooked on them when I was a kid," Leo admitted. "Those cows were big! These cows are no bigger than sheep." He gestured at the mother of the calf we were taking the cell sample from. "The lady there barely comes up to hip high."

"But they are Earth-authentic, Leo—as much as anything on Mirabile is, anyhow."

We moved on to the next stall to check on its newcomer. Mabob was getting on remarkably well with the cows, now that he seemed to understand he wasn't to bully them.

"They were breeding miniature cows back on Earth well before the Bad Years," I said. "Early transgenic work—some of the earliest, I think. The idea was to breed a cow that needed very little grazing space but still produced a lot of milk. That's the idea here too. Sorry—"

The calf had bawled a complaint—I hadn't hurt it, it was just complaining—and its mother glared and snorted, threatening me with a bruised thigh if I didn't leave her pride and joy alone.

Mabob stepped over and gave her a ferocious eye-blaze. I was surprised to note she didn't rate a bristle, but Mabob had judged it right. The eye-blaze was quite enough to quiet her down. I shooed the calf toward her and she settled for washing it head to toe.

"Thanks, Mabob. You could be useful." I gave Leo a speculative glance.

He shrugged. "We'll see."

Mabob preened, making a quiet little whistling noise somewhere in the back of his throat. All of a sudden the noise cut off. He looked anxiously from me to Leo and back again. Not the slightest doubt in my mind what that was about.

"That's okay, Mabob. I don't mind if you whistle." I reached out and scratched him where he liked to be scratched, just to let him know I meant it. He rattled and went back to the quiet whistling.

We moved on to the next stall. "Those cattle you saw in the westerns—they needed acres and acres of range. Couldn't feed 'em otherwise. Not only were they expensive but they were damn hard on any EC you put them into. These Guernseys—well, you could keep one in your yard. There'd be enough milk for the baby and for cheese besides. Once we get the herd stable enough, we'll hand them out to whatever town wants one or two."

"I like most goat cheeses," Leo said. "What's cow cheese taste like?"

"Ask Brehani. He's been experimenting with different kinds. He's probably *the* Mirabilan expert on the subject of cheese molds. Selima's been getting him a few new ones out of ships' stock every time she makes the trek into RightHere. So far he hasn't poisoned himself—or anybody else."

"That's reassuring."

"I thought so." I gave him my best grin. Must have been good enough, because we got to necking for a bit. This time we didn't have an audience, unless you count momma cow and her baby. Mabob, if my ears were any judge, was rummaging in a corner of the stall.

A minute later there was a hideous squeaking from the same direction. Sort of broke the mood, so we broke the clinch.

Mabob had a good-sized rat by the tail. The squealing was pure fury—flail as it might, that rat was not going to escape Mabob. He brought it, dangling and shrilling, over to where Leo and I stood arm in arm. I'd never seen a kid look prouder of a catch.

With an arch of the neck and a rattle of scales, he offered it to me. If I'd had gloves, I'd've accepted the damn thing on the spot and happily. Rats are a major problem. Some idiot geneticist back on Earth must have liked 'em—stuck genes for 'em in too damn many other things. They're forever popping up. If it weren't for the fact that most of their offsprings are nonviable Dragon's Teeth, the whole of Mirabile would be overrun by now.

I made enthusiastic noises at Mabob, told him what a good thing he was, scratched him even more—did my best to encourage his newfound skill. Finally I did my best to convince him I wasn't hungry, but that I'd be honored if he'd eat it *for* me.

Leo looked doubtful. "Do you think that's a good idea?"

"Leo, I don't know what he can eat safely. But if he brought it as a present, *he* must consider it edible."

He considered it edible. He didn't let go of its tail, just bent his neck until the rat could scrabble at the ground, where he clubbed it neatly to death. Then he ripped it up and gobbled it down with obvious relish. When he was done, he preened smugly for a few moments, then stalked the corner of the stall—head down, eyes big as saucers—looking for seconds.

"Take him with you when you feed the preemies," I told Leo.

While Leo and Mabob made the rest of the rounds, I hunted up the analyzer to check out the cell samples I'd taken from the latest of the calves. Fed what I got into the computer, then linked up with the computer back at the lab to check out the few I didn't recognize off-hand. Not a dandelion among 'em, I was glad to see. And all of 'em were as stable as could be expected for Mirabile—more so, since we'd been working our asses off to keep them that way.

If the cows had been eating leaves from the canes, it hadn't hurt 'em any. Didn't poison 'em and didn't change the EC enough to encourage those hidden genes to produce something other than Guernsey.

Our problem with the Guernseys was that any EC good enough for Guernsey was likewise good enough for Holstein or longhorn. The Holstein would have satisfied Leo's idea of "cow," being the huge kind, and the longhorn was the actual article he'd seen in the westerns. We couldn't afford either kind, ecologically speaking.

So I checked the gene-reads on the preemies. One was the predictable Holstein. The other wasn't—predictable, I mean. Took me about five minutes to find a match in ships' records: bison. Like the Holstein, it needed more range than we could afford to give it. At least, we couldn't afford an entire herd.

I did a little scouting around ships' files, this time outside the genetics file. Only took me a minute to find out my memory served me correctly. If the bison lived, might be Lalique had a good trade item.

Then I got down to the most interesting item on the agenda: the canes. By the time I had a gene-read on the screen, Leo was back. He took one look over my shoulder and said, "One of mine, then. Not yours."

It was native Mirabilan, all right. No doubt about that. "You mean you're not even willing to *share?* I'll trade you half my dandelions."

"I'd share anything with you, Annie, including the dandelions. Let me get a chair and you can tell me what the gene-read tells you. I'm nowhere near as good at reading them as you are. Not yet, at least."

While Leo got a chair, Mabob paused for a look at the screen. Obviously, he wasn't impressed. A moment later, he was back to hunting rats.

"He's good at that," Leo said. "He's caught five already."

"Deserves a medal for that, Leo. Watch out, or Lalique'll want to keep him."

A frown of concern crossed his face. "I hadn't thought of that. Maybe I'd better not tell her how efficient he is."

"Don't worry. He's *your* project. Furthermore, I don't want anybody else raising one until you've cleared it. When I put you in charge of Mirabilan wildlife, I meant just that."

The frown vanished. "Good. Now tell me what you can about these canes."

"They're carnivorous, for starters."

"Great planet. Not only have we got plants that commit arson, we've got meat eaters as well."

"Mirabile's as Earth-like as they come," I said. "I grant you the vegetable life is a bit more enthusiastic here. . . . The canes don't restrict themselves to insects. They'll actually go for bigger game. But I'm betting they don't really mean to catch calves."

"They did."

"Sure, but even something that size might eventually struggle free. And damage the plants a good deal in the process. No, there's something we're missing here."

I waited for the horrible squeals in the background to die. Literally. Mabob had clubbed himself another rat.

That reminded me how quickly Mabob had learned to avoid touching the canes. "Maybe most of the Mirabilan wildlife knows enough to avoid the trap. The cows don't."

"The older cows do. They didn't go in after the calf—not even the calf's mother was willing to do that."

"Hmmm. But they eat the leaves off the canes, according to Jibril." I stared at the gene-read again, then I said, "I think staring at the gene-read isn't going to help us much on this one. We should be staring at the canes, to see what works in practice."

He nodded. "I wonder why Lalique was so sure they were Dragon's Teeth."

"Probably just because anything anybody on Mirabile doesn't appreciate *must* be."

The door opened. It was Roland. "Hi, Annie, Lalique says for me to take over and for you to come on up to dinner." He stared at Mabob, who downed a last bit of rat and then stared back. "Leo and—Mabob?—too, she says."

Mabob whistled and rattled and trotted over to offer him the tail end of the rat.

"Uh," said Roland, "is that what I think it is?"

I grinned. "Yup, and if you want him to keep hunting 'em, you'd better thank him for the present—and mean it."

Turned out trapping rats was practically a full-time job in this neck of the woods—and Roland was the full-timer. So he did an all-out job of thanking Mabob. Mabob was still whistling and rattling as we left the barn and headed for the main house.

Once the door was closed behind us, though, Mabob charged ahead and let out three gronks in a row. Then he charged back to whistle at me, anxiously.

I had to laugh. "It's okay, Mabob. Outside, it's not so bad." So he beat us to the house, gronking all the way.

Lalique met us at the door. She'd had a few hours more sleep than the rest of them—that the rest were able to sleep through Mabob's gronking said it all about spring calving.

"Uh," said Lalique, "is he housebroken?"

"Yup." I grinned at Leo. "But tell him to 'hush' before you let him in. I think that'll save your hearing."

She did, and Mabob instantly simmered down to a quiet whistle. He was happy as a lark (though I've never seen anything in ships' files that would explain why larks are happier than anything else) with a whole new house to explore.

Lalique said, "So what's the verdict on the preemies, Annie?"

"One of 'em's veal."

"I thought as much. Well, at least we get a couple of good meals out of it. How about the other?"

"The funny-looking fuzzy one's a bison. Ask the Sioux Guild if they're in the market for a mascot. On the clear understanding that one is all they get—they're *not* breeding up to a herd."

"Hey! I can use that! Thanks, Annie."

She ushered us into the main room and saw us settled around the huge old dining table and dished out stew from the steaming pot in its center.

Her great-grandmother'd made that table the first year on Haffenhaff, and Lalique's family made things to last. I expect her seven-times-great-granddaughters will be eating around the same table. One of the reasons I like Lalique's family so much—a lot of respect for continuity.

That's what made me stop in mid-bite and look all around the
room. For the first time in all the time I'd been coming out to
Haffenhaff for calving, something had changed. Once I'd noticed
the change consciously it wasn't hard to pick out just what.
Against every wall, there was now a cabinet with a glass front.
Must have been twenty of them, all made of the same warm
silver-gray wood as the table—ballyhoo wood, practically fireproof. Thing is, every one of 'em was filled with what looked for
all the world like rocks.

I swallowed. The stew was good, so I gave it a moment's proper
attention before I waved my spoon at one of the cabinets and
said, "Somebody take up geology?"

Lalique grinned. "Wrong field, Annie. Those aren't rocks,
those are fossils that Nikolai and the kids dug out of the shale end
of the island." The grin got wider. "And we're the Franz Nopcsa
Museum of Natural History—at least, that's what the kids tell
me. Of all the paleontologists they found in ships' files, they liked
him best."

I worked on my stew while I thought about that. When I
opened my mouth, what came out was exactly what I'd been
thinking. "I'm a damned idiot. Never occurred to me that
Mirabile would have fossils, too. The things you don't think of!
Any planet with life would have fossils." Which explained
Nikolai's comment about digging bones. "What sort of things
have you found?" I was halfway out of my chair.

Lalique motioned me back down. "Wait for Nikolai. He's
'curator.' He'll give you the grand tour." She looked across the
table at Leo. "Do you know? I think this has all the makings of
a new guild: the folks who are interested in it are fanatical, it has
a separate history with its own heroes, and it even has its own
language. 'Curator'—that's guild tongue for 'the guy that keeps
track of it all.' What more do you need for a guild?"

Leo smiled and raised his hands to shrug. That was enough to
bring Mabob to his side.

"Oh!" said Lalique. "I don't have any social graces. Should I
offer your friend a bowl of stew?"

Leo had already fished a bit of meat out of his bowl to offer

Mabob a taste. Mabob accepted with a delicacy I'd never have expected, given the ferocious aspects of that beak. He whistled quietly for what would have been several sentences' worth in a human tongue, then he laid the tidbit just as delicately beside Leo's bowl.

Leo scratched Mabob's eye rims. "'Thank you, but I'm not hungry right now,'" he translated for Lalique, though it couldn't have been plainer if Mabob *had* used a human tongue. Mabob went back to his exploring and Leo went back to his stew.

"Wouldn't be important to you, Annie," Leo said. "That's why you didn't think of it. You've got live Dragon's Teeth to worry about—what's a fossil to you?"

"You never know," I said. "I've got the interaction between Mirabilan life and Gaian life to worry about. Seems to me I've got a use for anybody who studies Mirabilan life, even if it's the rock solid kind. Besides, you know how nosy I am."

"Dragon's Tooth," said Lalique, changing the subject back to one of more immediate interest. To her, at least.

"Nope," I said. "It's not. That one's purely Mirabilan. Which is why I brought my Mirabilan expert along." I nodded at Leo and got back to my stew.

"But, Annie, it can't be Mirabilan," Lalique said.

So I asked Leo's question for him. "Why not?"

"Because it wasn't here before we settled here, that's why not." She pushed away from the table and darted into the next room. Over her shoulder, she called, "I can prove it."

Leo raised an eyebrow at me. I shrugged and took the opportunity to finish my stew. If Lalique had a bee in her bonnet, it sure as hell wasn't an Earth-authentic one.

When she came back, she was struggling under the weight of three enormous books. Leo hastily shoved the stew bowls aside and made a place for her to thump them down between us. "Granddaddy Renzo's 'botanizing' books," she said. "See for yourself."

I was impressed already. The volumes were hand bound. You could see the love that had gone into the work. I was almost afraid to breathe on them, let alone touch them. Lalique must have seen that in my expression, because she chuckled and said, "Built to last, Annie. Go ahead. They're not fragile."

Even so, I couldn't help but treat 'em with the respect they deserved. I opened the top one at random and found myself face to face with a sketch of a stick-me-quick plant, from the highest burr to most delicate bits of its root system. A smaller sketch to the right showed the flower, from three different angles. To the left, another sketch showed a cutaway of one of the burrs and a cutaway of one of the flowers. The drawing was so meticulous that anyone could have identified a living example from its sketch without the slightest doubt or hesitation.

I whistled my admiration and turned the page. Handwritten, this one was—neat and clear—and the text was as meticulous as the sketches had been. "STICK-ME-QUICK," it read, "called 'the nasties' in the town of Gogol. Grows only in areas with a great deal of sunlight."

It went on for a full page about the habits (time of year it flowered, time of year it seeded) and needs (sunlight, speculation on lime in soil) of the stick-me-quick, even to including a list of the animals (Mirabilan *and* Gaian) Lalique's granddaddy had seen carrying the burrs. Last on the list was "Humans." Right all the way. I'd picked enough of the damn things out of my hide to sympathize. Bet Renzo had found that out the same way the rest of us had.

I turned another page. The next sketch was a small flowering plant I'd never seen. The text on the following page included a note that crushed leaves from this one were a very effective salve for burns.

I'd've been just as happy to spend the rest of the evening leafing through the volumes. Luckily, there were more than one so I didn't have to fight Leo for possession.

"I've got seventy-five years' worth of botanizing books, Annie," Lalique said. "Renzo was a completist. Orlando took up the hobby as well and, between them, they covered the island. They even included any Earth-authentics that showed up."

She pulled out the bottom volume to show me some of

Orlando's work. It was a slightly different style but just as meticulous.

She closed the book and slapped the cover. "That's why the canes have got to be Dragon's Teeth. There isn't a sign of one until after we started raising cattle here."

Opening the volume again, she scanned the index, then displayed a page. There was the cane. The sketch was Renzo's work. "First I've seen," read the notes. "I looked for more but haven't found any." It was dated some twenty-five years back.

While Leo and I read the rest of it (it included five pages of sketches of the various things granddaddy had found stuck to the canes), Lalique opened yet another of the volumes.

"Twenty-five years ago," she said, "there was one cane. Twenty years ago, there were four." She thrust the open volume at us for proof. "Now, they're all over the place. And the only other new thing on Haffenhaff is the Guernseys!"

"Doesn't mean they're related." I laid the volumes aside— would have done so grudgingly if Leo hadn't been so eager to get them all to himself—and went to the computer. "Give a look at the gene-read. See for yourself."

While I called up the gene-read I'd done on the canes, the household was starting to revive around us. Brehani and Villamil peered over my shoulder at the monitor until Lalique shooed them off to eat. It was Orlando who said it though—he took one look at the gene-read on the screen and said, "Well, *that's* not Earth-authentic . . . whatever it is."

"That's your canebrake," I said.

"Damn! So how'd they get here—swim? And why hasn't anybody else I've asked seen one?" Orlando turned and said to Mabob, "Good god! You're real! I thought I'd dreamed you!"

Mabob whistled and rattled; it was a lot like static in the background.

"Maybe they floated," I said. "Or they might have been spread by, oh, chatterboxes. We'll have to take a closer look at their seeding habits before we can make any kind of a guess." I reached out to show Orlando where to scratch Mabob for best results. "It *is* odd that nobody's seen one before—did you mean that?"

Orlando took over scratching Mabob. "Maybe it's not so odd, Annie. I've never seen one of him before either."

"Lots of them—huge flocks of them—out by Roaring Falls," said Leo. Then he added, "But, you know, Annie, I've never seen canes like those before either. And I've probably seen more of Mirabile than most people will ever expect to."

"Except maybe me," said Nikolai. He was heaping stew into his bowl. "Tell you the truth, Leo: I've never seen any of those canes before either. I'd've bet anything they were Earth imports. That doesn't mean there aren't any, of course, just that they're certainly not common. They're not the sort of thing you'd forget—not after they've stripped hide off you, anyhow."

That reminded me. "Speaking of stripping hide off—Lalique, Orlando, somebody, tell me: Why in hell aren't these botanizing books in ships' files?"

Orlando blinked at me. "It's just a hobby, Annie. Granddaddy Renzo taught me when I was a kid. It's just something we do for the fun of it."

Hopeless. I shook my head, wishing I could get Mabob to give him one good gronk, rotten breath and all. "Right. It's a hobby. You do for fun what Leo gets paid to do—"

"Also for fun," Leo put in. "But Annie's right, Orlando. Every one of these books is worth its weight in gold to me. All this information ought to be in ships' records." He glanced at me. "Think we can get funds from Sabah for him?"

"Wait a minute!" That was Orlando again. "No, Leo. No, Annie. You want to turn it into a job. I won't have that. Take the information, fine. Load it into ships' files, also fine, but I won't have my hobby spoiled."

Savitri, who was all of eleven, and consequently already recovered from the ordeal of calving, said, "I could load them into ships' files." She looked up at Orlando. "I can't draw like you and great-granddaddy Renzo—loading your pictures in could be *my* hobby. I'd like that!"

Orlando laid a hand on Savitri's shoulder and smiled big. "It's settled then, Annie. My hobby is sketching, and Savitri's is loading."

"I take it," I said to Savitri, "that getting paid for the work would spoil your hobby too?"

She nodded solemnly.

"Expected as much," I said. "Like father, like daughter." That got me a matched set of smiles. "But there's something else I need done as well—and since it's not part of the hobby, you might consider asking a piece-work fee. If you're willing to do it."

"Tell me what it is."

Sensible kid. Find out what's up before you commit yourself. "I *also* need a gene-read for each and every plant in the botanizing books. Means you'd have to collect a sample of each one and run it through the analyzer and add that to ships' files as well."

Her eyes went wide. "You mean, be a jason? Like you?"

"An assistant jason, for a start. Leo can show you how to use the analyzer. If it turns out you're good at it, I can always use another jason on the team."

She stared at me for a long moment. Then she plucked at Orlando's sleeve. He leaned over and the two of them held a whispered conversation. I tried to keep deadpan, but with everybody else in the room grinning I didn't stand a chance.

A moment later, they broke the huddle, grinning themselves.

"Okay," said Savitri. "I've decided. It's a hobby for now. But if I'm good at it, Annie, then I get to be a jason and you get to pay me."

"Fair enough," I said, and stuck out my hand. "Shake on the deal." We did. I turned to Leo and said, "You just got yourself seventy-five years worth of research *and* an assistant, to boot."

"It's about time," said Leo. "You can't expect me to handle the whole planet by myself."

HE COULD HANDLE teaching Savitri how to use the analyzer, though, and he was clearly loving every minute of it, too. Nothing beats the feeling of having learned a thing so well you can pass it on. Unless it's maybe watching somebody you've taught teach the next one—too bad Susan wasn't around to see him.

Meanwhile, I got the grand tour of the fossil collection. Made me start grumbling about hopelessness all over again. To Nikolai, I said, "And why isn't all *this* in ships' files? Do I have to hold *every*body's hand around here?"

Nikolai chuckled. If I hadn't seen him do it, I'd have misheard it for Leo's chuckle and I just about forgave him right there. But not quite.

"I haven't had the time, Annie. I scarcely get enough time off to dig for them, let alone—"

"Right. You get savaged by a pack of grumblers your next trip out and all that information in that thick skull"—I tapped him, none to gently, just behind the ear—"is gone forever. Now, what kind of notes have you got on all this?"

"Private file on the computer. Sketchy notes."

I must've growled. He held up both hands, just like Leo does when I give him the same look.

"Okay. I'll dump my private file to ships' files first thing in the morning."

"And . . . ?" I got a look for that. Seems like I've got to spell everything out for this crowd. "And you will also read through the notes, adding explanatory glosses wherever they're needed."

"Oh," he said. "'And.' Yes, that too. Far be it from me to ruin our friendship before it gets off the ground. Leo'd have my ears."

"Only one," I told him. "I'd get the other. We share."

He chuckled again, and I had to grin back at him. Leo's got great genes. I like 'em wherever they turn up.

"Come on," he said. "Let me show you our best find so far."

He snatched up a flashlight (not that he really needed one, it being a nova-lit night) and led me out to what the Imbambas dubbed "the Behind House." When the family'd overflowed the house that Granddaddy Renzo built, he built a second. Pretty soon now, they'd need a third. Since I appreciate the Imbamba genes too, the sooner the better. The cheerups singing their nightly question-and-answer sounded as if they agreed with me, which is one reason I like to listen to the cheerups sing.

I took my time following Nikolai. You can't be in a hurry when the cheerups are singing and when every breath brings you the

smell of roses. Lalique's farm is the only place on Mirabile I get
to smell the roses. It almost made me sorry I'd missed the calving
this year.

Could be Leo's patience is something he came by later on in
life, because you'd have thought Nikolai didn't know the meaning of the word. By the time we reached Behind House, he was
fairly bouncing with anticipation.

The Behind House had grown as many fossil cabinets as the
main house had—all the more reason for a third, I thought.
Nikolai didn't stop at the common room, though. He marched
me on down to the room where he was guesting. No, I realized,
Nikolai was a permanent member of the family. The room was
purely his.

Smack-dab in the middle of the floor stood a—well, it was an
eight-foot-high skeleton. Nikolai swung out an arm toward it and
said, "There!" As if I might have missed something that size if he
hadn't pointed it out to me.

I got in close to look. Took me a minute to realize what I was
looking at. It was fossil bones—all strung together on a wire
armature—as if he meant to bring the critter back to life. Took
me another full minute to realize Nikolai's critter was some
long-dead relative of Mabob's. Or near enough.

"Now I know why Leo wanted you to meet Mabob," I said. I
kept looking at Mabob's thousand-times-great granddaddy.
Something was wrong. Could have been a change in skeletal
structure between then and now but. . . .

"Yeah," said Nikolai. "I'd give just about anything for a look at
Mabob's skeleton."

"Don't you dare," I said. "Lay a finger on Mabob and—"

He raised his hands again. "I meant: I'll ask somebody in that
neighborhood to save me the skeleton if they come across a dead
one."

Good thing we understood each other. I went back to my
puzzle. It needed closer examination, so I dropped to one knee to
look at its. "You've got it mounted wrong," I said, pointing to the
knee joint.

He dropped to a knee beside me so fast it was worth a bruise. "What?"

"Look here. Mirabilan animals, at least the ones I've seen the carcasses of, have ligaments the way we do. This is clear enough that these"—I stuck a finger on the most obvious of them—"must be where the ligaments attach. Follow that to here and you've got a critter that stands exactly like Mabob. No hunch, no pigeon toes. See what I mean?"

That made it even taller than before and the head wasn't nearly as large as Mabob's, but on the whole it would look even more Mabob-like than it did now.

"Yes! You're right! Annie, I could kiss you."

"Sorry, you're too young for me."

He chuckled again. "Here," he said, "hold this a minute."

He meant to take the damn thing apart and put it back together again that very moment.

Last thing I wanted to do was spend all night holding bits of bone together. I stuck my hands behind my back and said, "Not a chance."

He looked so brokenhearted, I almost gave in. "No," I said, as much to me as to him. "You're tired. You need sleep."

That brought out the stubborn in him. I should've known there'd be a lot of stubborn there, given the genes. I've got my share of stubborn too so I put it to work. "Never mess with delicate stuff when you're tired. You can do it *right* in the morning—after you've had a good night's rest and a good breakfast. And after you get those notes into ships' files for me."

"Reasonably stubborn," he said. "That's what Leo told me you were. Now I get it. As opposed to *un*reasonably stubborn. Okay. Sleep first, breakfast first. . . ." He grinned all of Leo's laugh lines and added, "After that, we'll argue."

"You're on," I said. I got to my feet. Couldn't resist giving him a pat on the cheek. Definitely Leo's kid—took it just in the spirit in which it was given. If he noticed I copped his flashlight so he'd have to settle for the night, he didn't say a word.

Or maybe he remembered he didn't need one. I didn't bother to turn it on.

Outside, I took another deep breath, appreciating all over again. Somewhere out in the field, Mabob gronked enthusiastically. The cheerups were startled into momentary silence. Then they took up their chant with twice the energy they'd had before.

Occurred to me suddenly that I'd misled Leo earlier in the day. Well, it was easy enough to correct. I stopped along the walk and helped myself to a single "Aimee Vibert." Its misty white petals were luminous in the nova light.

When I walked into the main house, Leo was alone in the common room. Guess the others had all gone off for their much-needed sleep—the ones that weren't on duty in the barn with the bison, that is. "Hello again, Annie," said Leo. "What have you done with Mabob?"

"Not a thing," I said. "He's outside terrorizing the cheerups. I assumed you turned him loose for a little exercise. Hope that means he'll let us sleep tonight."

"Somebody turned him loose but it wasn't me. I don't suppose he can get into too much trouble by himself."

"Unless he goes back to terrorizing the bulls."

"I doubt that," Leo said. "You seem to have put the fear of God—or at least the fear of Annie—into him, on that *and* the gronking."

"I'll settle for the fear of Annie." Damned if that man doesn't always bring out smiles in me. Content and smug, that's me. Then I remembered what had been on my mind only a moment or so before.

"Leo, I misled you earlier—"

"Right down the garden path," he said. "And there's no getting rid of me now."

"I refuse to bite. When we were talking about Earth-authentic cows . . ."

"That, what with the encrypted extra genes, nothing on Mirabile is Earth-authentic?" He held out his hand by way of demonstration. "I am."

It was too good to resist. I laid the rose in his palm, all velvety white against the tawny brown. "And so is 'Aimee Vibert.'"

"Beautiful," he said, looking from me to the rose and back

again. Leo has the damndest priorities, and don't think I don't appreciate them!

"When the Mirabilan expedition left Earth, each of the expedition members got ten pounds weight allotment for 'frivolous' possessions."

"I didn't now that! No, wait—I guess I did but I never thought about it. That would account for the Earth-bound copy of the poems of W. B. Yeats that's in my family."

"That would account for it, all right. In Lalique's family the ten pounds 'frivolous' were ten pounds of rose cuttings. Dunno how they did it but they kept the damn things alive the entire trip. And now they grow all over Haffenhaff."

I brushed the edge of one perfect petal with my fingertip. "The thing is, because they were cuttings, they don't have any hidden genes tucked away in them. What's more: that's a clone. That's what a rose grown from a cutting is. You hold in your hand not a descendant but an actual piece of the original plant that grew on Earth."

That made him look down at the rose again.

"Smell it," I said and, when he did, he smiled and so did I. "That's what Earth smelled like," I said.

Still holding the rose delicately in his huge hand, he pulled me close and inhaled deeply. "And like you," he said. "Earth must have been one hell of a romantic world."

MABOB WOKE US bright and early, gronking outside our window. Still, it was outside, not inside, so I could hardly complain—beyond the few obligatory curses, that is.

Leo woke enough to chuckle. "I do believe you're mellowing, Annie. You didn't throw anything at him."

"If I'm mellowing either it's a) because of you, or b) because I had enough extra hands on the team this year that I *didn't* have to help with lambing or calving."

"I vote for 'a,'" he said. "But, knowing you, more likely it's 'b.' I've heard you snarling over those red dandelions."

I snarled at the mere thought. I had at least two hundred more

dandelion gene-reads waiting for me back at the lab. Not to
mention any more that might have flowered red since I'd left.

Leo grinned. "See? Can't be me. Let's go look at the canebrake."

"Let's. Anything but red dandelions."

After breakfast, we headed out for the nearest stand of canes,
Mabob tagging along behind—*and* in front *and* to the side—
wherever the spirit took him. What with the gronking and the
rattling and the strutting and the preening and the occasional
hunt for small edibles in the grass, it was clear he was having the
time of his life.

We found the clearing Lalique and Jibril had cut in the
canebrake and eased our way carefully into it. Mabob hung
around long enough to make sure we were being careful, then
wandered away to do some exploring of his own. Just as well. I
wanted to watch the behavior of the animals in the brake, and
having a predator the size of Mabob around would surely have
given me a skewed view.

We spread a blanket (no need to sacrifice *all* of our comfort)
and settled down to wait and watch. With Leo, waiting and
watching is not just an art, it's a full pleasure. So hardship didn't
come into the job anywhere, except maybe for the lumps that
were etching themselves into my butt.

If I'd correctly identified the cane I'd been looking at the day
before, then the absorption process was spectacularly fast—the
Earth-authentic bug had vanished but for a bit of wing tip.

First thing I learned, watching the wind whip the leaves
around, was that the leaves didn't stick to the canes. A light
rain made it equally clear that the glue wasn't water-solvent.
Should've known that. If it had been, Lalique would have
washed the calf down to free it. Still, if the leaves didn't stick,
then might be we could make a solvent out of *them*.

Leo tapped my arm and pointed further into the brake. A
fuzzwilly was building a nest—first time I'd ever seen one build
on the ground. Fuzzwillies are strange even by Mirabilan
standards. They're ninety percent fluff and, ordinarily, they
"hatch" their eggs by rolling them out of the nest to drop them on

the ground and break them open. If you saw the thickness of the shells, you'd understand why. No way the baby fuzzwilly could make it through that shell on its own. Still, they lose a lot of young every year in the process. Looked like the fuzzwillies were headed up an evolutionary dead end.

But there was one of them building her nest on the ground. Damn straight I was interested!

I was even more interested when the fuzzwilly brushed against one of the canes, got pulled up short, gave a little shiver that made it look like a dandelion head about to blow away and then *walked away*, leaving only a long silky tuft of hair stuck to the cane.

Hair's protein too—mine *and* the fuzzwilly's. The cane could probably absorb nutrients just as well from the fuzzwilly's hair as from the insects it caught. Even Mabob's scale—

"Yike!" I said, startling the fuzzwilly back into the canebrake. "Up, Leo! Get up! Out, out!"

We scurried out. I checked the grass, then sat and patted a bit beside me for Leo to share.

"What did I miss, Annie?"

"Same thing I missed." I turned the blanket over. The underside looked like clothes moths had been at it. Sure enough, the lumps I'd been sitting on *had* been etching their way into my butt.

I made a rude gesture to indicate the canes. "I bet that's not a stand of canes. I bet that's all one cane—like Earth-authentic bamboo. The interconnecting runners may not be sticky, but they can digest whatever's lying on them. So if they do catch something big, they can absorb it."

"Pleasant thought," said Leo. "For once, I'm glad we didn't get carried away."

"For once, so am I." I grinned back at him. "I prefer a nice soft bed myself anyhow." I went back to watching the canebrake. "Now I believe Lalique when she says the canes have been here only since the cattle have. I don't know why, but it's a good bet she's right."

"I don't get it."

"The fuzzwillies. They're adapted to live in canes like these, *not* in trees. But when have you ever seen a fuzzwilly nest on the ground?"

"Never," said Leo. His brows knit ferociously and then, like sun coming out, all the laugh lines came back. "Good lord! I get it! The fuzzwillies are mostly hair, so *they* don't get stuck to the canes. They just shrug off the stuck hair and go on their merry way. Meanwhile, the sticky canes keep most of the predators away from their nests."

Not Mabob, though. He had expendable scales, the way the fuzzwillies had expendable fuzz. Made me wonder just how many Mirabilan critters would come apart in your hands. But for now it was the fuzzwillies that interested me most.

I said to Leo, "And . . . ?"

"And? You mean there's more?"

"Come on, Leo. . . . Think of those damn thick-shelled eggs."

His jaw dropped. "The canes—the canes digest enough of the shell so the baby fuzzwilly can break its own way out!"

"Bet you're right. We'll stop back about egg-rolling time and see if we can catch them in the act."

Leo rubbed his shoulder. "Better here than somewhere in the woods, especially if you're right."

I had to raise an eyebrow at that. And at the shoulder he was rubbing.

He gave me a chuckle. "Egg-rolling time always brings back memories of sore shoulder. A mama fuzzwilly dropped her egg on *me* once. My shoulder didn't so much as crack the egg, but I had a bruise the size of a fist for a week." The chuckle got deeper. "I had to take a rock to the egg to crack out the baby for its mama. It was hardly her fault something soft walked under her tree at just the wrong moment."

All I could do was smile at him. Damn but I love that man!

After a while, he said, "So tell me why you believe Lalique now."

"Oh, sorry. Look, I thought the fuzzwillies were going up an evolutionary dead end, what with shells so thick the babies can't hatch. But if the shells originally co-adapted to life in a canebrake, then where have the canes been all this time that the fuzzwillies had to learn a new trick to 'hatch' their babies?"

"You're saying the egg-dropping trick is the only thing that keeps the species going where there aren't any canes for them to live in?"

"I'm saying that's my best guess. Come on, let's ask Lalique what egg-dropping time has been like since her family's been on Haffenhaff."

I collected a handful of leaves from widely spread canes; I also wanted to check my theory that the stand was all one cane. Leo hollered up Mabob and we started for the house.

We hadn't gone more than a few yards when the ground started vibrating underfoot. I'd felt that before. "Stampede, Leo, headed our way. Grab Mabob—and watch your toes!"

Leo nodded, snatched up Mabob, and the two of us braced ourselves. Here they came, looked like the whole damn herd at once. And they were spooked, no doubt about it. There couldn't have been a single loose thought in one of those tossing heads. From somewhere behind them, I heard one of Lalique's kids bellowing, "Stampede! Watch your toes! Stampede!"

Two of the bulls, in lead of the panic retreat, of course, were bellowing even louder than the kid.

The challenge was too much for Mabob. He kicked his way out of Leo's arms and charged the closest Guernsey, gronking at the top of his lungs. Then Leo was after him, bellowing at the top of his, which is pretty impressive.

If you can't lick, join 'em. I charged after Leo and Mabob yelling at the top of *my* lungs.

I like to think that did it, but I suspect Mabob's fevered gronks would have been sufficient. The herd panicked all over again, split right down the middle, and flowed around the three of us like the Omigolly around Haffenhaff.

The moment they passed by, I got a taste of what had set them off. More than a taste. I spat out a mouthful of the swarming horrors and swatted another hundred or so away from my eyes. Damndest, most irritating—a huge cloud of the tiny insect-like natives swarmed after the herd. Over the plaints of the cows and the whirring of the swarming horrors, I could hear Leo cursing inventively.

Gunnar skidded to a halt beside us, spat out a mouthful of his own and said, "You folks okay?"

We did a quick check. Leo'd gotten a bruised shin and I'd gotten my foot stepped on, but aside from that and the damn bugs in our faces we were fine.

Mabob loved every minute of it. (The swarming horrors didn't seem to horrify him at all. In fact, they ignored him. Must've been the orange eyes that did it.) He was still gronking insults at the Guernseys long after they'd passed us by. If Leo had let go of him, he'd have chased them right into the Omigolly.

As it was, the herd came to a screeching halt just before the canebrake. The Guernseys weren't so stupid after all. "Come on, Leo. I want a closer look."

He spat a few dozen swarming horrors out of his mouth. "Sometimes, Annie, I don't know why I go along with you."

But he did, gave me a hand even as I hobbled into the thick of the swarming horrors. It was tough trying to look and keeping them out of your eyes at the same time, but little by little they stopped bothering us altogether.

I pushed my way through the now quiet herd (I wanted to step on a few feet myself by way of revenge, but I resisted the temptation) to the edge of the canebrake. Sure enough, those cows weren't all that stupid. And the canebrake was having a feast. The canes were black from top to bottom with the swarming horrors, all stuck and all on the way to being trace elements in the canes' diet.

I was betting the hole Jibril and Lalique had made in the brake would be filled with new growth in two weeks' time or less.

We stayed long enough to make sure none of the calves got themselves stuck, then we slowly made our way back to the house.

Savitri was in the common room, using her free time to load Renzo's notebooks into ships' files. Boundless energy, these kids. Made her happy enough to do it that she was whistling to herself as she went from page to page. Mabob perked up, strutted over and whistled back.

Surprised her. She looked up, grinning, then her mouth made a little tiny "o." "Hi, Mabob. I thought you were Orlando—he always whistles back at me, too."

Which earned her another whistle from Mabob. Any minute, they'd work up to flute duos.

I decided to get my question in while they were still tuning up. "Savitri, what's egg-dropping time like around this neck of the woods?"

"I dunno, Annie. I've never seen one."

"We saw a fuzzwilly down by the canebrake—"

"Oh, yeah. Lots of fuzzwillies down there. They nest in the canes. I meant I've never seen a fuzzwilly drop its eggs. I've never even seen one nest in a tree. Orlando and Lalique warned us all about egg-rolling time but"—she looked a little bit embarrassed—"I don't see why they worry."

That was better confirmation than I'd hoped. "Good," I said.

Startled her, I guess, because her eyes got huge. "Why good? That's mean, Annie."

So I'm an idiot. Doesn't usually take me that long to figure out why a kid should be embarrassed about a fuzzwilly's nesting habits. "Hey, kiddo! I didn't mean Orlando and Lalique were wrong. I think your fuzzwillies are different from everybody else's."

I laid a hand on the shoulder Leo'd been rubbing. "And if you want to hear about the hazards of egg-dropping time, just ask Leo. He got himself clobbered by one!"

If Leo'd been egged, that made it okay, to judge from Savitri's relief. That meant her parents still knew everything. And why should I be the one to tell her different? She was coming up on the age where she'd find out soon enough for herself.

"Would you tell me about getting egged, Leo?" Savitri said. "And would you check my gene-reads to see I did them right?"

"You go ahead," I told him. "I'm going to hunt up some of the older members of the troop and get myself a little historical perspective."

Easy enough to do, all right. And it fit my theory like a glove. In Lalique's childhood, egg-dropping time had been so hazardous you didn't dare walk in the woods without carrying a board to protect your head. "Even that wasn't enough," Lalique said. She held up a little finger. I'd never noticed before—it was as crooked as a griffbramble twig. "I was holding a board over my head, so the egg hit my hand and busted up my finger. It hurt like hell just about forever. I still get twinges when the weather's about to change."

"And now?" I asked.

Lalique and Orlando looked at each other, suddenly puzzled as all hell.

It was Jibril that answered. "Now the fuzzwillies nest in the canebrake, Annie. That's why nobody gets egged anymore."

Trust the kids to investigate a menace more thoroughly than the adults. I grinned at him. "Okay, Jibril—when was the last time you saw a fuzzwilly nest in a tree and what was the first year you saw them nest in the canes?"

"I never saw them nest in a tree. Orlando and Lalique are always talking about it but . . . you know how grown-ups worry."

After that, it didn't take me long to establish that the canes and the fuzzwillies went together. It had taken the fuzzwillies a couple of years to relearn ground-nesting but, once they had, you couldn't get 'em back in a tree for love or money.

Lalique eyed her crooked finger. "Maybe I don't want those canes done away with, after all."

"Maybe not," I agreed. "Cows use 'em to shelter from the swarming horrors."

"They do?" said Orlando. "I was going to ask you for some of those bats. It's not just about the swarming horrors, Annie. We've got a lot of biting insects that bother the Guernseys. Some kind of black fly that drives them nuts."

Which I'd also seen stuck to one of the canes, if he meant the kind I thought he did. "I'll put you on the list for bats," I said, "but meantime you ought to have a look at those canes. They're already doing some of the job for you."

"Uh, Annie?" That was Lalique again. "If the fuzzwillies prefer to live in the canes, maybe *they* brought the seeds."

"Nice try," I said, "but we've got fuzzwillies all over the place and nobody's seen canes like yours. You said so yourself."

"Besides," said Jibril, "the fuzzwillies don't eat the cane seeds."

"What does?" I asked him.

"The Guernseys." He laughed. "You can't keep them away from the canebrake at seeding time." He glanced at Orlando. "It doesn't seem to give us Dragon's Teeth, anymore than the fact they eat the cane leaves does."

Orlando nodded agreement.

"So what else eats cane seeds?"

The whole troop went at it, and I wound up with a list of maybe twenty critters, all Mirabilan, that did. With that many, the canes ought to have been able to spread themselves far and wide. Only they hadn't—and the fuzzwillies that didn't live on Haffenhaff were still dropping eggs on heads, hands and shoulders as a late-spring ritual.

"I think that's all of them, Annie," said Lalique, "but you could check the botanizing books to see if anybody spotted anything else eating the cane seeds."

"And I'll have to stop by next time they seed. I'll want a look at the seeds for myself."

"Oh, that you can do now. Get Savitri to show you where the samples are."

"Samples?"

"The ones that go with the books," Orlando explained. "Renzo and I kept a sample of everything we sketched. I never could figure out how to press a sample of the cane itself. It stuck to everything I tried. But there's a pressed leaf and a boxful of seeds."

Hopeless, I tell you. No point asking him why he hadn't mentioned it last night—he hadn't mentioned it last night because I hadn't asked him. Besides, it was a hobby, so how could it be important?

"I'll go look," I snarled. Stomped out before I took up a hobby of my own—wringing necks.

As I headed back to the house, I met up with Mabob. He was stalking something in the grass again, so I stopped to watch. Didn't want to interrupt his snack. Turned out it was another rat, so it was just as well I hadn't.

After he'd finished gobbling it down, he spotted me and gronked a greeting that sent me staggering back a step.

"Hello to you, too," I said. This time he whistled back at me, which was a pleasant change because whistling didn't involve a blast of rat breath. I unlatched the door and held it open, waiting. "Want in?"

Nope. He whistled, at length and earnestly, then he strutted off toward the barn. When he got about a hundred yards away, he turned back and gronked.

I laughed. "Okay," I called back. "Have a good gronk!"

"HI, ANNIE," said Leo. "Is Mabob with you?"

"Last I saw, he was headed for the barn, or at least for space to gronk in. Leo? You telling me *you* didn't let him out?"

He shook his head. "Savitri? Did you let Mabob out?" He had to ask a second time before Savitri looked up from her task and shook her head as well.

"Door unlatched?" he suggested.

I thought back. Shook my head the same way they'd both done a moment before. Lot of that going around.

Leo went over to the door and pushed it. It didn't unlatch. Then he turned the handle, opened the door and let it swing. Out, in—I heard the snick of the latch as it closed. "Aha!" said Leo. "That solves that."

"Maybe," I said. "Certainly enough Earth-authentic critters learn how to open doors. Keep your eye on him, though. If he can, I want to know about it."

Leo flashed me that best grin of his. "You're not the only one. I like a little privacy myself every once in a while."

I grinned back. Then I turned to Savitri and said, "Where do you keep the samples that go with the botanizing books? I need some seeds from the canes."

Leo gave me a wondering look. "Samples, too?"

I snarled in the affirmative.

Leo chuckled. "It's times like these that I understand your disposition."

Which was quite enough to make me chuckle back at him. Took me a minute to realize that Savitri was waiting politely at my elbow to show me the stores of samples. "Sorry, kiddo," I said. "Leo's always distracting me."

She giggled. "That's what Orlando says about Lalique. He says some day I'll get distracted too." She gave me a thoughtful look. "I hope so; it looks like fun."

"That it is," I assured her. "Now, let's go see those samples before it gets out of hand."

She giggled again and led the way into the bedroom Lalique and Orlando shared.

Every wall had a storage cabinet shoved up against it. The cabinets they'd made for Nikolai's fossils were a simple variation on the theme. Damned if the entire household hadn't been a museum of natural history long before their pet paleontologist had gotten into the act!

Savitri stuck a finger to her lips. "Canes," she said, pondering the rows and rows of small drawers. "They'd be . . . here!" Triumphantly, she pulled open a drawer, scooped out a handful of seeds and held them out to me.

Each was about half an inch long, wrinkled brownish red. The actual seed, I was betting, was inside the wrinkled skin of the berry. "You didn't give me all of them, did you?"

"Course not," said Savitri. "Do you need all of them? I could ask Orlando if it's okay."

I shook my head. "No need. I was just making sure you left enough for the collection."

"Absolutely. Always." She said it with that utter solemnity only a kid that age is capable of.

Couldn't help but grin at her. "I think you've got the makings of a *very* good jason," I told her, and got a grin in return.

"Then I better get back to work," she said—and did.

"Corrupting the young again, I see," Leo said.

"Ha! In a family with some seventy years of 'botanizing' books?

Who needs to corrupt? I'd put the whole bunch of them on the payroll tomorrow if they'd let me."

"I'm *on* the payroll, Annie. And you're hogging my seed samples."

I gave him half. Wasn't about to turn over the entire puzzle to him and he very well knew it. It was that or dandelions—and I wasn't ready to go back to the dandelions just yet.

After a bit of necking, we sauntered back into the common room, pulled chairs up to the dining table and started poking at the cane seeds to see how they poked back.

Interesting results. Inside the fruit, the cane seed was every bit as hard as a fuzzwilly's egg.

"That makes sense," said Leo. "If the seed drops on the ground, the cane will eat through it the same way. Once it's been etched, the sprout should have no trouble germinating, even through that thick a seed."

"Only one problem with that," I said. "The damn thing's got fruit, which means it's meant to attract animals to eat the fruit and spread the seed by elimination. And it can't expect the animal to eliminate all the seeds where it or another cane could do the necessary etching."

"Maybe that explains why the canes are so few and far between."

"Maybe. But not why they've suddenly become common enough to be a nuisance—if they *are* a nuisance, taken on balance."

"Mmmm." Leo put one of the seeds on the floor, stood and put his foot on the seed. He bent to look at the result. "Mmmm," he said again. This time, he raised his foot and stomped it a good one. He winced and drew in his breath. Then he retrieved the seed and gave it a good going over.

"Nope," he said. "Takes more than a stomping on to crack that thing. Obviously it's not the Imbamba kids spreading them."

That reminded me. I didn't want Savitri suffering burnout at all of eleven, and she'd been working her eyeballs out for the past few hours. I went over to her. I waited until she'd finished the plant she was currently loading and then I loomed. "Take a break," I said.

"But, Annie," she said. Sounded just like Elly's kids, and in the same circumstances, too.

"No buts," I said. "I need the computer for a bit. You can have it back after lunch."

Leo caught on instantly. "Savitri? Could you do me a favor and see that Mabob isn't getting into trouble? He's not familiar with farms or cows and there's no telling what he's up to. Especially if he's bored."

"Sure, Leo. Uh, if he's bored, I could play with him."

"That'd help a lot, Savitri. Thanks."

She darted out, pausing only to make sure the door latched behind her.

I jerked a thumbs-up at Leo. "Good move."

"I learned some mothering tricks, too—and not just from Elly. In fact, I may be ahead of you on points."

He wasn't going to get an argument from me on that count. I nodded and settled at the computer to gene-read the cane leaves I'd picked earlier.

Got another surprise out of that. "I lose my bet," I said.

"What?" said Leo. There was more than a little amazement in his tone. A moment later he was looking over my shoulder.

"About the canes," I said. "Have a look at this. I thought we were dealing with a stand of clones—but these are all different plants."

"Why should that be surprising?"

"Because it means they're altruists, which isn't all that common where I come from."

I could see by his expression that he didn't get it. "Look, Leo—one plant catches the critter, holds it till it drops dead. But when it drops, it lands on the etching runners of one of the other plants, so that plant gets the benefit, not the one that did the actual catching."

"Bet those runners interlace a lot."

"Bet they do too. But it's still odd enough to be surprising." I pushed back from the computer to give him a smile. "That's what

I like about this business. You never know when nature's going to do something truly interesting."

The smile back should have gotten an award. "That's what I like about *you*, Annie."

I stood up and we did some variations on that theme, including some on how much I liked him back. After a while, I realized we had an audience. I tapped Leo to let him know and we broke, both of us expecting to find Mabob, I think.

It wasn't. It was Nikolai. Damn if the kid didn't have Leo's ability for quiet appreciation of a scene as well as the other traits I'd already noticed.

Nikolai grinned at both of us. "I came to apologize to Annie."

Leo laid an arm across my shoulders and said, "You didn't tell me Nikolai'd been misbehaving."

"He hasn't," I said. "Unless he knows something I don't."

Nikolai made a wry face. "That's exactly what the apology's for. —Annie, I haven't been relating my fossils to Mirabile's current wildlife. Not sufficiently, at any rate. You didn't think of paleontology, I hear—but I didn't think of contemporary biology, so we're even."

He spread his hands wide and gave me the most engaging grin this side of Leo's. "I spent the morning as instructed: going over my notes to gloss them before I loaded them into ships' files. And I found—well, if you'll let me hunt through the fossil cabinets a minute, I'll show you what I found."

"You're on," I said. So he went rummaging, while I sat on my impatience as hard as I could. Given Leo's example, it was easier to wait, but not much.

By the time Nikolai said, "Ah," I was not just sitting on my impatience, I was bouncing on it. Nikolai carefully hoisted a foot-long chunk of shale from the cabinet and carried it over to the table. With me treading on his heels.

He held the slate to his chest a moment longer. "If I'd been paying attention, *I* could have told Lalique her Dragon's Teeth were Mirabilan."

With that, he set the slab of rock—carefully—on the tabletop. "This is a chunk of shale from the upstream end of the island.

You tell me, Annie—is that the same plant as the calf-catching canes or isn't it?"

I'd never had any practical experience at examining fossils, but I was willing to give it a go under circumstances like that. What I was looking at was the imprint some plant had made in long-ago mud. Must have been very fine silt, come to think of it. The detail was extremely fine—after I'd gotten the hang of looking sort of sidewise to catch the shadows—I could make out not just the canes themselves, but leaves and even the slightly pressed image of a flower as well.

And short of doing a gene-read on the thing, which I damn well couldn't, I was sure. "Looks the same to me," I said. "Leo?"

Leo'd been doing some sidewise looking of his own. "Dead ringer for the calf-catchers. See here." He pointed at the flower. "The detail's good enough to see the structure of the calyx—that's almost as good as a gene-read."

"So I apologize," said Nikolai. "I promise never to hold out on you again."

"Good," I said. "Now tell me how common they were and when that was."

"*When* is something I can't tell you. I don't have enough information yet, and I haven't been able to convince the factory I've need of a carbon-14 dating machine. But—how common? Annie, there's practically a stall-full of specimens just like it in the barn. We only put the best of them in the cabinets. In the interests of my baby science, we couldn't throw any of them away—"

"Thank god for that!" I said.

"I take it that means I get to keep both my ears," Nikolai said.

"Yes," said Leo and I simultaneously.

Both of Nikolai's hands came up to grab his earlobes, as if to reassure them they weren't to be parted. But he was laughing out loud, now, and so were Leo and I.

"Well," he said, "the cane was as common in that level of shale as Mabob's cousin was. If you like, I can show you every single one of those we've found."

"I like," I said.

"Me, too," said Leo. "Mirabilan wildlife is *still* my province, Annie."

Mabob whistled and rattled happily.

"And just where did *you* come from?" I asked him.

He whistled at me earnestly, for all the world as if he was answering the question. Too bad I don't understand Thinga. Then he swiveled his head to watch Leo, wide-eyed.

Leo was checking the door. "Latched," he reported.

Mabob whistled a few phrases at him, sounding smug.

"Right," I said. "We're going to the barn to look at Nikolai's fossils, Mabob. Want to come?"

Mabob strutted toward Leo, with a quick glance over his shoulder to see if we were following. We did.

I'd heard that door latch when Savitri left the house. Still, maybe she'd tired of playing with him and let him in before she went elsewhere.

Between the canes and Mabob—not forgetting Leo—life was getting damn interesting around the Imbamba place.

LOOKING AT FOSSILS gets easier with practice, and we got a lot of practice that afternoon. Nikolai hadn't been exaggerating one whit when he'd said a "stall-full" of them. And the most interesting thing of all was that Mabob's cousin kept showing up in the same geologic period as the canes. (So did the fuzzwillies; made my theory look better all the time.)

From the looks of it, cousin had the same eating habits as Mabob—if it moves, eat it; if it doesn't, eat it faster. Any fossil that gave us a bit of cousin's stomach area gave us the bones of small creatures of every description.

A lot of them I'd never seen live. When I said as much to Nikolai, he whipped out a pad and started taking notes and asking a stream of questions that would have put Elly's youngest in second place.

The ones I could answer, I did. The ones Leo could answer, he did. The ones neither of us could answer, well—"That's your bailiwick, Nikolai. You're the paleontologist. You tell me!"

I don't think I've seen anybody that excited since Leo took up reading genes. Nothing like enthusiasm to brighten your day.

Unless it's just plain good luck. . . .

"Here, Annie," Nikolai said, shoving yet another chunk of shale at me. "Tell me what you make of this one. It looks like it's been eating peas. Or maybe eyeballs."

"Pretty solid eyeballs to have lasted all this time," I said.

But the stomach was full to brim with round objects. If I hadn't held them in my hand a few hours earlier, it never would have occurred to me. I stared at the fossil. There were enough scales and enough to the rib cage to tell me beyond doubt that here was Mabob's cousin again, with a stomach full of what looked for all the world like cane seeds.

"Sacrifice one of the eyeballs for science?" I asked Nikolai.

He hesitated a moment, looked down as if counting the number of "eyeballs" and nodded.

I shoved the chunk of shale into his lap, got up and went to the next stall over, where Lalique was feeding the bison calf. "Two questions," I said. "Have you got a microlaser—and who's got the finest hand at operating it?"

Luck was with me. She nodded. "Orlando," she said. Saved me the trouble and impatience of having somebody from the lab fly one in.

"Where's he?" I said. And when she told me, I said, "Three questions. Third one: do you have to weed canes out of the vegetable garden?"

"God, yes, Annie, hundreds of them. How did you know?"

"Paleontology," I said.

As soon as Orlando could be spared from farm chores, I put him to the task of slicing open one of the cane seed samples and one of Nikolai's fossil eyeballs. "I don't know how much fine structure the fossil retains, Orlando, but do your best."

I guess some of my excitement had rubbed off. "You bet!" he said, with real enthusiasm for the job. You'd never know the man had had maybe twelve hours sleep in the last two weeks—and only eight of it the night before.

"You think those are fossil cane seeds, don't you, Annie," Nikolai said. Except for the twinkle, it would have been an accusation.

"Bet money on it," I said. "Orlando, you folks still use slurry for cooking gas?"

Orlando gave me an absent "Sure," without looking up. That's how absorbed he'd gotten in his fossil botanizing.

"Right." I headed for the door. Didn't realize till I was already out and around the house that both Leo and Mabob were right behind me.

Wondered why Nikolai was missing, but it only took a bit of thought to figure that one out—he'd stayed behind to protect his fossils from Orlando's zeal.

The methane slurry was right where I'd remembered it. I lifted off the lid, reeled a bit from the smell, then rolled up my sleeves and dipped in.

Before I knew it, Leo had his sleeves rolled up too and was up to his elbows same as me. "Might help," he said, trying to talk without inhaling, "if you'd tell me what I'm fishing for."

"Round hard objects," I said, trying to do the same. It didn't work but that didn't matter—my hands had found exactly what I'd expected them to. I breathed in happily, not caring a bit about the stench I got with the breath.

"Got some," I said. I came up with a handful, in fact, all just the right size and shape.

Leo brought up a handful more and between the two of us we got the lid back on the slurry.

"Right," I said, grinning and dripping.

"Right," said Leo.

"Gronk!" said Mabob—reacting either to our triumph or to the partial relief from the smell.

We headed back to the house at a quick trot. I wouldn't know for sure until I'd rinsed off the seeds for a closer look.

When we got to the door, I realized neither of us had a hand clean or free to open it. The two of us stopped, looked at each other and sighed in unison. The pause was just long enough for Mabob to reach the door ahead of us.

He cocked an eye first at Leo, then at me. Then, whistling cheerily, he caught the door handle with his beak, twisted it open, and stood there holding the door for us.

"That answers that question," I said. And I stepped through, followed by Leo, followed by Mabob.

Lousy lack of manners, I realized. Stopped and turned back—just in time to see Mabob catch the inside handle and pull the door to until it latched. Then he let go and whistled brightly at me.

"Thanks, Mabob," I said. "Leo?"

"I saw," he said, very quietly.

Mabob whistled another few bars and set to preening his scales, while Leo and I looked at each other.

Nikolai broke the spell, bounding across the room to demand, "Where've you been—?" He recoiled from our combined smell in almost comic fashion.

I'd forgotten we were both still dripping. "Up to our elbows in cow shit, if you really must know," I said. "How about turning on some water for us so we can get cleaned up?"

"Maybe we should ask Mabob," Leo suggested. "A handle is a handle."

"Better make sure he knows how to turn that off," I growled. "Otherwise you'll have water running forever."

Having missed what had gone before, Nikolai ignored that and led us in to wash up. The washing up made the seeds look all the more like cane seeds.

Except for one thing, which Leo had already thought of. He put one of the seeds he'd retrieved from the slurry on the floor and put his foot on top of it. He didn't step hard, either, but the shell gave way with a crackle.

"Dragon's Teeth," he said, smiling. "From cows."

"But hardly from their genes," I said. Then I got another thought. "One thing I do want to know: Nikolai, can you spare one or two of the sample cane seeds that still have the dried fruit pulp surrounding them?"

"Living samples are Orlando's department," he said. Which was perfectly true, so we all trooped back into the common room to make the same request of Orlando.

"Yes," said Orlando, before I could even open my mouth. "The fossil seeds and the cane seeds are identical, as far as I can tell. See for yourself: the structure of the—"

"I'll take your word for it," I said. "Spare me one or two of the newer ones, with pulp still attached?"

Orlando gave me a long look, then cast about the tabletop and scooped up a couple of uncut cane seeds and poured them into my outstretched hand.

"Here, Mabob," I said. "Hungry? Want a snack?" I held them out to him.

Mabob dipped delicately into my palm and picked up a cane seed. Touched his tongue to it. Looked thoughtful.

Then, using only beak tips and tongue (and the tongue *had* to be prehensile!), he peeled the dried fruit from the seed and swallowed it. A quick check of the tongue to make sure he'd gotten all the good stuff, and then he laid the cleaned seed back into my palm and rattled happily as he took a second.

"Won't eat eyeballs," I said. "Poor fuzzwillies." I dropped the cleaned seeds back on the table and rounded on Nikolai. "Given a choice," I said, "would you rather go on scouting new territory or be a paleontologist full-time?"

If Nikolai had had orange irises, he'd have given me as good an eye-blaze as ever Mabob had—and his jaw dropped open as well.

When he got it together what came out was: "That's easy, Annie. I'd rather spend all my time with the fossils but. . . ."

"But me no buts." I grinned. "Orlando, I can tell you where those canes are coming from—and after I've done that, I'm going to call Sabah and tell him why we need a full-time paleontologist on the team."

"Not without Lalique," said Orlando. "Wait right here. I'll get her."

I was laughing by then. I couldn't help myself. "I promise not to say a word until Lalique gets here." As he charged for the door, I shouted after him, "But hurry! I don't know how long a wait Nikolai can survive!"

IT WASN'T just Lalique that Orlando rounded up, but every free hand on the place. They crowded around, milling and muttering and generally working Mabob up into a state of such excitement that he forgot himself and gronked. . . .

After which he tried to make himself invisible, which wasn't easy, given that the background wasn't the right color for vanishing into. "It's all right, Mabob," I said, and reached over to rub his head. "You forgot, that's all. These guys aren't being particularly quiet either."

Reassured, he whistled at me very quietly.

The door slammed. A minute later Orlando thrust Lalique into the middle of the crowd. "Okay, Annie," he said. *"Now* tell us the story."

I can resist anything except temptation. "Once upon a time," I began. There was a shout of laughter from Leo; Mabob caught the spirit of the thing and whistled cheerfully. "Settle down," I told them, "or you don't get your milk and cookies."

Nikolai swelled to about twice his size and looked about to explode with anticipation, so I went on. "Once upon a paleozoic time—or whatever the Mirabilan equivalent would be—there were fly-catching canes all over Mirabile. There were so many of them in fact that the fuzzwillies *always* lived in canebrakes—it was good protection from some of their predators. They had to do a little adapting for the occasion, and you can still see the adaptation in the thickness of a fuzzwilly eggshell."

I gave the floor to Leo and let him explain about the fuzzwillies to everybody who hadn't heard that part of the story.

Then I took up again. "At that same paleozoic time, Mabob's cousins flocked all over Mirabile. They had a taste for cane seeds and ate 'em by the stomach-full. Now, remember, this is how seeds get dispersed. Mabob's cousin likes the flavor of the fruit and swallows it seed and all. The fruit is digested and the seed comes out the other end, ready to sprout where it falls."

"Alimentary, my dear Annie," said somebody from the crowd, drawing an impressive series of groans and hisses. Mabob looked at me with alarm.

I rubbed his head. "Dunno if I can explain that to you, kiddo, but it's nothing to worry about. Okay?"

He whistled me a few notes and relaxed.

"Now," I said, regaining the floor, "what happened to Mabob's cousins, I can't tell you. Maybe the bad puns killed 'em all off. At any rate, they vanished. Problem was, just as the fuzzwillies had adapted to life in the canes, the canes had adapted to Mabob's cousins—and in much the same way."

I held out the cut cane seed I'd picked up from the table. "The cane seed's so thick the sprout can't make it through the outer shell without help."

Savitri took the seed from my hand to peer at it, nod, and pass it around for the rest to see. "What kind of help, Annie?" she said.

"Well, there was no problem if the seed fell in the canebrake because the canes would etch through it, the way they do the fuzzwillies' eggs. But to spread the seeds the canes needed Mabob's cousins. My guess is they had the right kind of stomach acid to soften the outer shells without digesting them all the way."

Nikolai said, "But when Mabob's cousins died out, the canes could no longer spread!"

"And the fuzzwillies had to learn a new way to hatch *their* eggs," said Lalique. "Oh, my aching hand!"

"Exactly," I said. "Mabob eats the fruit but spits out the seeds, so he's no help. Eventually there wouldn't have been any canes anywhere—they'd have gone the way of Mabob's cousins."

I waited, fully expecting a eureka. When I didn't get one, I said, "What—nobody's got it yet?" I looked at Savitri and said, "How about if I tell you your mom was right: the cows are responsible for the canes."

That got me the eureka.

Savitri's eyes popped. "The cows are eating the fruit, seeds and all! And their stomach acid is strong enough to help the seeds sprout!"

I handed her one of the seeds Leo and I'd fished from the slurry. "Found this in a cow pie," I told her. "Give it a squeeze and see what happens."

It took her more than a squeeze—I'd misjudged the strength in her small hands—but once she put it between the heels of her hands and pressed hard, she got a very satisfying *pop!*

"The cows," said Nikolai, and his face wrinkled up all over with a smile that matched Leo's to the last laugh line. "The cows are filling an ecological niche that's been empty since Mabob's cousins died off."

Not having a medal, I pinned a finger on his chest instead.
"You got it. *Now* I'm going to call Sabah and tell him why we
need a jason who can't do a gene-read on his specimens."

Nikolai gave me a puzzled look.

"You don't *want* to be a full-time paleontologist?"

He jerked back. "Sure I do, Annie! But there's still something
I don't understand. It's a hell of a long time between the last of
Mabob's cousins and the first of the cows. So where did the first
cane plant come from?"

"Oh, that. Seeds can germinate after hundreds of years; check
ships' files and you'll find instances of seeds found in archaeo-
logical digs that sprouted. I imagine the first cane seed was here
on Haffenhaff all along. Eventually, the seed simply *eroded*
enough to sprout."

"So the occasional cane seed would have sprouted all along,"
Nikolai said. "Not enough to flourish but enough to keep the
species from total extinction."

"If you've got a better theory, I want to hear it," I said.

He grinned and shook his head.

"Well, work on it," I told him. "I'm looking forward to hearing all
about Mabob's cousins. I suspect they're not just Mirabile's idea of
a Guernsey." Mabob, hearing his name, whistled agreement.

"Wait, Annie," said Lalique. "That means wherever there are
cows there'll be canes."

"Yup. And wherever there are canes, the fuzzwillies won't drop
eggs on your head. *You* decide if you want to root 'em out."

We left her looking at a crooked finger. Didn't have to ask
again—I knew which way *she'd* decide.

LEO, AS ALWAYS, was as good as his word. Once we got back to
the lab, he even shared the dandelion gene-reads. Didn't let Mike
off the hook either. While Mabob strutted around town whistling
his adventures to anybody he met, the rest of us grubbed our way
through some four hundred more dandelions.

"Enough is enough," I said at last. Pushed back my chair,
stood. It took me a full minute to stretch the kinks out of my
back. "What have you got, Mike?"

He leaned back and glowered at the screen. "Lettuce, endive, chicory, sunflowers, artichokes—"

"Any bugs?"

"No bugs in this batch. That doesn't mean the next batch won't seed bugs, Annie."

"Leo?"

"No bugs. I've got the showy stuff over here—asters, dahlias, marigolds, chrysanthemums." He grinned. "A whole flower garden full!"

Had to smile at that. "Mine too. So I say we're done for the year—at least, as far as the dandelions are concerned."

Mike frowned at me. Should've known, for all his bitching, that he'd be the one to hang on longest. The younger ones will always risk burnout.

But it was a different kind of burnout that worried him. "Annie, the folks in town are likely to torch them all if we don't certify them safe."

"I'm ahead of you on that one." I turned to the computer and called up the file I'd been holding in reserve since the dandelions had first popped up. "Have a look at that."

He and Leo both did. "Dandelion wine? You can make wine out of dandelions?"

"So it says in ships' files. I found a dozen different recipes, all of which say the primary ingredient is dandelion *flowers*. So the ones we've checked, they leave strictly alone. The rest are free for the picking—and the fermenting."

Mike considered the screen. "I think it'll work, Annie. I think you're right."

"Then I leave the arrangements to you, Mike." I took Leo's hand. "Come on, Leo—you and I are gonna go out and join Mabob. I could do with a good gronk."

Surprised the hell out of Mabob, but the rest of the folks in town scarcely noticed. By then, they were too busy harvesting dandelions to pay us any mind.

"Gonna be one helluva year for dandelion red," I told Mabob.

"GRONK!" he agreed.

The baby's wail brought me awake and on my feet faster than any bellow from the Loch Moose Monster ever could've. "You can get the next one," I told Leo, and watched him drop back to sleep almost instantly.

Elly and Mabob had gotten there first, of course, but Elly let me take over the cooing while she went for the bottle. Mabob cooed too—a soft whistle.

"Annie?" Nikolai stood in the doorway. He was rumpled all over and he had the damndest look on his face.

Took me a minute to realize he was scared—and a minute more to realize why. "It's okay," I told him. "Just a hungry cry, that's all. Right, kiddo? Ye-es, just a hungry cry." I made goo-goo faces until I got a big toothless grin out of the kid, and an even bigger one out of Nikolai, most which was relief.

"I'm not used to this," Nikolai said.

"That's why you're here," Elly told him. Making an award of it, she presented him with the bottle. I presented him with the kid to go with. Between the two of us, we got the two of them settled comfortably.

"Tell you what, kiddo," I said. "We'll let Elly get back to bed and I'll hang around and tell you a story. How's that?"

Nikolai smiled. "Which kiddo are you asking?"

"Let's let elder brother pick. I think it's his turn."

"Okay," Nikolai said. "Tell the scary one, the one that gives Jen nightmares."

"You were in on one end of it. . . ."

"Then I'll know how much is true."

"Surely you don't think I'm making this stuff up, do you?"

6
Frankenswine

THE MESSAGE BOARD lit red, something it doesn't often do these days. "Susan," I yelled, "pack your gear!" Her turn to handle the emergency—good use for all that excess seventeen-year-old energy. I punched accept and the screen lit up with the even fiercer energy of the younger Ilanith.

"Mama Jason," Ilanith said, and there was enough relief on her face that I knew this one was bad. "Elly says come quick—a Dragon's Tooth tried to chew up Jen."

I know what my face did, because Ilanith added hastily, "She's okay! And Noisy's out there with a gun now, but you should see, Mama Jason. It's nasty! Jen was out—"

She meant to tell me the whole story, but I cut her off. "I'm on my way. You can tell me about it when I get there." Much as I hate to disappoint a kid with a story to tell, I wanted to *be* there, even if Leo *was* after it with a gun. I snatched up my pack, my persuader and was grabbing an extra box of shells for it, all the time bellowing for Mike to hold the fort while I was gone.

Susan, pack in hand and face set stubborn, said, "You're not going without me."

"You're right there," I said. "You drive." Want to get somewhere fast, let Susan drive—and close your eyes for the sake of your nerves. "Mike!" I bellowed again, but he was right behind me. "Dragon's Tooth at Loch Moose," I said. "Hurt Jen."

"And you want me to stay here? Annie, you damn well better call me the minute you know anything or I'll—" Luckily Mike's not truly inventive when it comes to revenge, but I got the general idea.

Remembering how I'd cut off Ilanith, I said, "Call Ilanith, tell her we're on our way and get the story from her. Then get it from Jen." Jen deserved a chance at the telling too—her story, after all. That wasn't enough for Mike, from the scowl. "You take me for a damn fool?" I said. "Hear them out—if you decide we'll need the rest of the team, bring 'em. Just make sure there's somebody here in case something *else* comes up."

There was a time when something else always came up. He knew that as well as I did. That simmered him down long enough for us to make a dash for the hover and get the hell on our way.

I waited till we hit the river—smooth hovering even at the speed Susan was pushing—and got to business. Dumped the rock salt out of my persuader and reloaded for bear. Elly Raiser Roget is not easily ruffled, and when she says, "Come quick," then the trouble is real and big and likely not the sort that's settled by a load of rock salt in its ass.

Susan slowed the hover—well, let up on it just long enough to pass me her shotgun safely—then gunned it again twice as hard. The trees on either side of the river fused into one long green smear. Susan kept her stare straight ahead.

Can't think when I've ever seen that kid's face grim but it was now. No surprise—anything messes with the kids growing up at Loch Moose Lodge, she takes it as personally as I do.

"Leo's there," I said. Which was the only reason I wasn't twitching.

"Yeah," said Susan. "But you never know what's gonna happen with Dragon's Teeth."

"The way you're driving, we'll find out soon enough," I said.
She snarled, "Want me to slow down?"

"Nope," I said.

I shouldn't have been surprised at the snarl—I do it often enough myself I set a rotten example—but I was, because it wasn't at me. Something in the snarl told me Susan was blaming herself, which made no sense at all.

Didn't get the chance to pry an explanation out of her, though. I'd barely finished reloading her gun when she swung left, up over the riverbank, to a tricky shortcut straight across country. No way I was gonna distract her when she held my life in her hands like that.

The times like these my grudge against that gaggle of geneticists back on Earth gets large and hairy and begins to resemble the worst of the Dragon's Teeth.

My grudge was probably shedding all over Susan—she was still snarling as she pulled the hover altogether too close to Loch Moose Lodge and dropped it to the ground with enough thump to crumple its skirt. I got out, both persuaders in hand, and headed straight for the front porch of the lodge.

Susan caught up with me at the bottom step and grabbed for her shotgun. I've picked up enough mother's radar from Elly that I didn't let go. "First, we get the story from Elly," I said.

"But, Mama Jason, suppose Noisy needs help?"

"Noisy can hold his own until we find out what we're dealing with." That didn't satisfy her, judging from the twist she was giving the persuader to wrench it away from me, so I said, "Since when did you take charge of this team? Leo's doing his part, you do yours—and the first order of business is information. I need some and you're holding up the show."

The twist untwisted on the spot. I let her have the gun and the two of us went into the lodge. The lobby was milling with people, kids and adults as well. I pushed into the likeliest-looking knot and found Jen, Elly and Doc Agbabian dead center. Jen had a bandaged leg but didn't otherwise look too much the worse for wear. She brightened all over when she saw me. "Mama Jason! Wait till you see it! It's an *ugly* sucker!"

"Thought I told you not to mess with ugly suckers," I said. I jabbed a finger in the direction of her leg. "Did you bite it first or did you bite it back?"

She made a face at me. "Neither," she said, defensively.

I nodded. "Okay, kiddo. Lemme see." I dropped to one knee, pried at the bandage for a glimpse of the wound itself.

Elly slapped my hand away. "Doc Agbabian just put that on—you leave it alone, Annie." Her smile of relief took the sting out of the command.

"What kind of wound?"

I'd addressed nobody in particular, but Elly shoved Agbabian at me. He held his fingers some three inches apart and said, "Two opposing slash marks. If there'd only been one I'd have taken it for a knife wound, but broader. She's lucky it missed the tendon. It was just a matter of gluing her back together."

I could feel my shoulders relax. "Okay, then. Tell me what happened, Jen—everything!"

She didn't need asking twice. "Mabob and I were out picking blueberries. You know where we pick blueberries, don't you?"

I nodded and felt my shoulders tense up all over again. "Hold up," I said. "Where's Mabob? Did he get hurt too?"

Jen said quickly, "He's fine—he's helping Noisy stalk the Dragon's Tooth. Lemme tell ya what he did, okay?"

"Go."

"So we were picking blueberries, only Mabob was eating more than I could pick, and we found this hole in the ground." Jen held her hands to describe a six-inch round. "*Big* hole. I never saw anything lived in a hole that big. So Mabob wanted to look in the hole. . . ."

Well, I've seen Mabob poke his beak down rat holes often enough I'd have believed it, if Jen hadn't ducked her head at just that point in her tale. Sounded to me like poor Mabob was going to take the rap for this one. I raised an eyebrow at her, but I didn't say anything.

Jen looked up at Elly suddenly. "It wasn't Mabob who wanted to look," she said. "It was me. I thought I was being careful."

She looked at me again. "I didn't get very close at all, that's the thing. Maybe as close as Susan is to me"—about three feet, that made it—"so *not* too close."

I nodded. "I'd have thought that safe myself. So what happened?"

Her face furrowed. "It made another hole—the Dragon's Tooth, I mean. It came right up out of the ground next to me and it grabbed my leg and it hurt something awful and I screamed and then Mabob pecked it right in the eye! And the Dragon's Tooth let go and we ran away!"

Then she took a breath—which she must have needed after all that—and leaned back in the chair, waiting for my reaction.

I gave her the proper one—I whistled. Then I said, "Did you get a look at it at all?"

"Yeah," she nodded vigorously. "It was ugly like I told you."

I snorted. "'Ugly' doesn't give me much to go on. I can think of lots of ugly critters—some of which are Earth-authentic."

"Okay, you win." She closed her eyes, then opened one just a slit, as if she didn't really want to look at it again. "It was hairy and it had little tiny mean eyes. Had kind of floppy ears, like the Bhattacharyas' dog does. Had these big long teeth, just here." She opened her eyes long enough to jam her index fingers to her mouth, like huge canines jutting up from the lower jaw. "But curly." She bent her fingers to demonstrate.

I made a face back at her. "Ugly, all right."

"Wait, Mama Jason—you haven't heard the worst part." She squinted again then opened her eyes till they bugged with excitement. "Two worst parts. It had these big squarish front paws, almost like flippers, but with long claws on them. And it had this nose—"

Words failed her. She made a circle of her hands again, this time holding it out in front of her face. "Only not like a real nose." One hand still circled, she moved the other to cut flat across in front. "Like somebody'd chopped it off flat—all raw grey and round, with two holes punched into it to breathe."

"If there's a prize for ugly," I said, "that wins." I got to my feet. "Now I think I'll have a look for myself. I need a cell sample." I grinned at Jen. "We'll see if its genes are as ugly as its snoot."

There was a tap at my elbow. It was Ilanith, grinning real hard. "I'm way ahead of you, Mama Jason. Its genes *are* as ugly as its snout." To Jen, she added, "And, yup, it's a Dragon's Tooth, all right."

That pleased Jen no end—extra points for getting chewed by something nobody else has ever been chewed by, I guess.

Didn't please me. At least, the implications didn't. I fixed Ilanith with the hairy eyeball I'd learned from Susan and growled, "How in hell'd you get a cell sample?"

Elly had fixed her with an even hairier eyeball. If that kid thought getting the sample was risking life and limb, wait'll she saw what Elly and I were going to do to her for risking it.

"Quit scowling, both of you," Ilanith said. "Mabob got the sample for me. He stripped a whole chunk off the Dragon's Tooth when he pecked it. After Jen said what happened, I cleaned Mabob's beak for him. That's where I got the sample I fed to the analyzer."

Much relieved, I grinned at Susan over Ilanith's head. "That's what I like," I said. "Somebody who's way ahead of me."

"Me too," said Susan. "Let's see it, Ilanith."

"Here?" Ilanith cast a glance around the room, taking in all the onlookers.

"They'll feel better if they know what we're up against, too."

"Yeah," she admitted. "Guess you're right."

I gave her too much smug (deliberately) and said, "Of *course*."

She giggled and headed for the lobby desk and swung the computer around so everybody could see the screen. A few taps at the keyboard brought up her gene-read.

Chimera, no doubt about it. Not often you see that much of a mismatch. Still, from Jen's evidence, the damn thing was all too viable.

Ilanith sprawled across the desk and jabbed a finger at the screen. "I found out where *this* part of it came from. Here, I'll show you." Another stretch and another tap and there was a second gene-read on the screen. She highlighted the bits in common.

"Right about that, too," said Susan. "What's that when it's Earth-authentic, Ilanith?"

"Disgusting," said Ilanith. By way of proof, she called up its photo from ships' files. The face was every bit as bizarre as the one Jen had worked so hard to describe.

"Lemme see," said Jen. Elly got a supporting arm under her shoulder, and she hopped over, wincing all the way. I moved aside to give her a clear view of the screen.

Jen nodded fiercely. "That's it, Ilanith!" She hopped two steps closer, staring. Elly, with a grunt, hoisted her onto the edge of the desk, where she peered at the screen a moment more and then said, "That's the face, but the feet are all wrong."

"Of *course* the feet are all wrong. You could have told that by the gene-read," Ilanith told her scornfully.

Jen deflated. "Could I have, Mama Jason?"

"Only after *lots* of practice," I said.

That mollified her. "Okay, I'll practice *lots*." She gave another look at the screen. "So what is it, Ilanith, if you know so much?"

"It's a wild boar, and even when it has Earth-authentic feet it can dig like a plough. It eats just about anything a human being will eat and then some, and it especially likes roots—so it's all adapted to dig stuff up with its snout."

"'Snoot,'" corrected Jen, with a glance at me.

"Ships' files say 'snout,'" Ilanith told her—then *she* looked at me, too, and both of them waited for me to arbitrate.

"Whichever," I said. I'd been reading the entry on the screen, which finally twitched my memory so I had some idea what we had here. "Pigs," I said, thinking out loud.

From somewhere in the crowd, Chris said, "Pigs? As in pork?" She shoved through for a look, her eyes wider than Jen's, which I hadn't thought possible.

"Yeah," said Ilanith. "The files say wild boar is edible, too—'pork' is the word they use."

I haven't seen Chris that excited since we made her official cook for the team.

"Pork! You wouldn't believe how many recipes there are in

ships' files for pork," she said. "Oh, you've *got* to keep them, Annie!"

Jen caught her eye.

"Oops," said Chris. "I knew it chewed you, Jen. But it seems to me only fair that you should get a taste of *it!*"

Jen shook her head. "The thing that chewed me *isn't* pork, Chris. It's a Dragon's Tooth. Maybe it's not edible at all."

"Oh." Chris's face fell.

Susan patted her on the back. "Don't worry, Chris," she said, "we'll see what we can do for you."

Good a place as any to get the show back on the road. "Ilanith, shoot a copy of your gene-reads back to the lab for Mike, then see if you can find out anything about the other half of the chimera. It's a mammal—"

"Hardly narrows the field," said Ilanith.

"—But from Jen's description of the feet, it's a burrowing mammal, which does narrow the field some. See what you can find. Maybe Mike will have some suggestions for you."

I made a shooing motion to set her about the job then turned to Susan. "You're the expert at tracking down the origins of newly sprung critters—think you might be able to do it for a Dragon's Tooth?"

She'd have preferred to stalk the beast in the flesh, but the challenge was too much for her. "If it can be done, I'll do it," she said. "Elly, what computer shall I use?"

Elly sent her off to the one in her own bedroom, after first disarming her. Susan gave her the hairy eyeball for that, but Elly was immune from long exposure.

"Aklilu's at the age he plays with anything," Elly said. "I don't want firearms unattended while you concentrate on a computer screen."

"Gotcha," said Susan.

As long as I had so many helping hands, I went right on making use of them. "Chris, if you'll make us up a collection of pork recipes, that'd be a help. Stick to things you've got everything but the pork for, though."

Jen had been looking increasingly anxious each time I parceled out a job, so I turned to her next. "Jen? You up to doing a computer search?" Her leg probably hurt like hell, but doing something might help take her mind off it.

She must have thought so, too, because she brightened and said, "Sure! What should I do?"

"You just learned how to read secondary and tertiary helices, right? Then you find out for me what's likely to be the next beast we get if your Dragon's Tooth breeds."

"Yeah! I can do that!"

"Then get to work, while I hunt up Leo and see what he's found out about your Dragon's Tooth."

I had a spate of offers of help to hunt down the beast, but I sidetracked 'em all into standing guard on the lodge, where they'd be more use and less likely to get in the way. Then I went out to track Leo.

I found him not far from the blueberry patch. Mabob bugged a brilliant orange eye at me but gave me no welcoming gronk. For Mabob to keep quiet meant he was stalking prey. I joined them on the skulk. Leo flickered a glance at me and pointed—the same direction he had his gun leveled.

I didn't see anything, not even the sort of hole in the ground Jen had described, but Mabob cocked his head and took a step in my direction. Leo shifted his aim.

I brought my persuader into the same line without even thinking about it. I watched where Mabob watched, which is easy enough to do, because those orange eyes bulge to cones and focus visibly on his target.

Then I saw the ground surge. Well, if the damn thing made holes, maybe it burrowed through the ground as a general practice. The ground heaved up again, a little closer to where I stood, and Mabob followed, soundlessly picking closer to it on his huge taloned feet. Every time the ground bulged, so did his eyes.

To let Leo know my policy on this one, I snapped the safety off my gun.

The ground at my feet exploded upwards—I got a flash of tusk and snout and claw—and squeezed the trigger full into its face.

Leo fired at the same time. Bits of Dragon's Tooth and dirt showered us all.

By the time I'd spit out the mouthful of crud, the critter was still twitching—but given that we'd blown most of its head away, it was no longer in the dangerous category. Mabob gave the remains a vicious clout with one clubbed foot, then cocked his head at me and said, "GRONK!" in hundred-decibel triumph.

"Gronk is right," I told him, my ears ringing.

"They react to sound above ground," Leo said. "Remember that next time, Annie: don't wait till you're close to take the safety off your gun."

I nodded and knelt for a close look at what was left of Jen's Dragon's Tooth. I'd seen those flipper-like front paws somewhere before, in ships' files if not in real life. You couldn't have built a critter better adapted for burrowing if you'd started from scratch—certainly *I* couldn't have and I'm not the least bit ashamed to say I'm good at what I do.

Leo said, "And you've got to step more lightly. Both that thing"—he gave it a tap with his toe—"and Mabob heard you coming before I did. The Dragon's Tooth shifted course to stalk *you*. If 'stalk' is what I mean when it's done from below."

I nodded again and rooted out what remained of the Dragon's Tooth. It had stopped twitching. I stood up, holding the critter by its twist of a tail, and gave Leo a kiss hello, never mind the dirt and all.

Mabob gronked again. He gets an enormous kick out of our necking for some reason I'll never know.

Leo's smile brightened up my whole day. Best thing about a well-worn face like Leo's is that it's got all the laugh lines well worn in for extra emphasis. After a moment, he turned to Mabob. "I know what you mean, Mabob, but you'd better hush before you attract a dozen more of those things our way."

He let go my shoulder to replace the spent cartridge in his shotgun. I took the cue and did the same. "*How* many more?"

"I don't know for sure. But I don't see how one could have done all the damage we found. We picked this one to track because it looked as if it were on its own. I was hoping to find a way to bring one back alive for you."

I shrugged. "I don't need a live sample and a dead husband. I won't quibble when it comes to something that seems to have a taste for attacking humans."

Leo nodded. "Then you'd better come see the extent of the problem. From a distance, unless you can be as light-footed as Mabob."

Mabob rattled his scales happily at the mention of his name and Leo scratched him around the eyes.

"From a distance," I said.

We trussed up the carcass (I wanted a good look at its innards when I had the time and place) and I slung it across my shoulders, careful to leave my hands free. Leo did a little extra tying, to make damn sure it wouldn't attract its kin by thumping against me as I walked.

Then they led the way and I followed, as tiptoe as I could considering the brush and the ground cover. Don't get me wrong. I've had enough practice that I can stalk most anything safely, but this one had already proved its senses outdid my stalking ability. *Extra* careful was the order of the day.

We skirted along the hillside, keeping Loch Moose to our right hand always. It glittered through the trees. In the distance I could hear the otters and their cousins, the odders, playing. Typical day—including the Dragon's Teeth—except that I found myself watching the ground more closely than usual.

Every once in a while, there was a soft patch in the earth. And where the soft patch neared vegetation, the vegetation was dying or dead—wasn't just people this Dragon's Tooth had a taste for. All in all, I counted some fifty different species of plant that had been tasted to destruction. Most of them had no visible marks above ground. Looked to me like the Dragon's Tooth was as much a root-eater as its wild boar kin.

I restrained my impulse to check, though. If the click of my safety well above ground had attracted one, my grubbing around in the dirt would sure as hell bring them—and in quantity. I'd save the digging for later, under more controlled circumstances.

Leo had stopped, so I did too. Mabob stalked a few feet beyond
us, but when he saw we weren't following he made a hasty silent
retreat. I looked where Leo pointed.

I didn't need the point. The state of the trees would have been
enough to make me sit up and take notice: an entire grove of
smoking pines would never smoke again.

And at the center of the grove I could see a dozen or more
holes in the ground, each the size and shape of the hole Jen had
made of her hands.

I was looking at an ecological disaster. Smoking pines make
most Earth-authentic species sick enough to leave them alone,
but they'd had no effect at all on this particular Dragon's Tooth.
Without protection. . . .

I had a sudden stark image of Loch Moose, still glittering,
amid an entire forest of dead trees.

Wasn't gonna happen. Not if I had anything to say about it. I
glared at the burrow holes.

Mabob's head swung sharply and suddenly to blaze into the
woods beyond. I couldn't see anything but, a moment later, I
heard it, too: the footsteps of clashings headed our direction. I got
ready to duck, but kept my eye on the burrows.

With a little luck, the clashings would distract the critters and
let me in closer. Leo had the same idea, and we edged closer in
unison. That was fine with Mabob, who did the same, his eyes
flashing from woods to ground and back again like bright orange
warning beacons.

Then something startled the clashings, and they aimed straight
for us at full gallop. Leo and I both dropped to the ground, trying
to land without a sound so as not to attract the attention of the
Dragon's Teeth.

Mabob watched the wood for a long moment, then returned
his very orange attention to the ground in front of us. Ordinarily
he'd have given the clashings a warning blast. As he didn't, I
knew he considered the Dragon's Teeth more dangerous than the
prospect of being bowled over and bruised by a clashing.

Leo drew the same conclusion from Mabob's behavior I had,
and we kept out guns aimed at the burrows.

The clashings burst into the dead grove, paused—likely the unfamiliar smell of the Dragon's Teeth—then charged ahead through. It was a disastrous mistake.

The first one made it across the clearing on luck alone. It was over us and gone before Mabob had a chance to blink up from his crouch.

The next two hit that soft ground—must have been riddled with burrows—and I head the bones snap. The otters in the lake probably heard the bones snap. The third—well, the ground heaved up all around it. It was like seeing dirt boil. And for every leg there was a Dragon's Tooth, with tusks. They dragged the clashing to the ground, with a frenzy of snorts and snarls.

I'd never heard a clashing scream, but this one did. The sound went right through me.

Some of the Dragon's Teeth went to work on the other clashings as well. I counted seven of them. Once they'd gotten the clashings in the throat, the screaming stopped, except for the echo in my head.

I touched Leo on the shoulder and motioned him back. As we edged away, one of the Dragon's Teeth spotted the motion and flopped toward us, not nearly so fast above ground as it seemed below.

We kept backing, while it snarled threats it could all too well carry through on. It gnashed those tusks at us for proof.

It might have just been warning us away from its prey, but it got too close to Leo for my taste. I blew its head off.

By the time the shot stopped echoing, every last one of the Dragon's Teeth had vanished into the ground.

Mabob, who hadn't been the least bit startled by my gunshot, jerked to sudden attention, eying the ground with fierce suspicion. Leo and I took the cue: they were more dangerous under ground than above. The three of us hightailed it into the bush.

Leo knew the territory better than I did and I followed him. After a hundred-yard dash, he came to an abrupt stop. I looked down at my feet and laughed. He'd brought us to a generous outcropping of rock.

"Good thinking," I said, once I'd gotten my breath back. "Give 'em all a headache, if we're lucky." I sat down and patted the ground beside me. Mabob stepped into the spot I'd patted, whistled cheerfully, and sat, his long legs seeming to vanish completely beneath his belly. "That wasn't quite what I had in mind," I told him, but I rubbed him till he rattled anyway.

Renewed snorts and snarls from the direction of the dead grove made him stop rattling and blaze his eyes. From the sound of it, the Dragon's Teeth had gone back to work on the clashings. Whether the grunts and snuffles and squeals were pleasant mealtime conversation or nasty family squabbles, I had no idea, but I was glad they were otherwise occupied.

Mabob obviously had the same reaction. He resumed his rattle and began to preen, for all the world as if nothing out of the ordinary had happened for weeks.

Taking his example, I leaned back and relaxed just enough to be pissed that I hadn't gotten a sample from the second critter we'd shot. Dragon's Teeth can vary wildly from tooth to tooth.

I looked Mabob over, but all that preening was just for the sake of preening. He was too damn clean to help this time. Luckily, I couldn't say the same for me—*I* was a bloody mess. I scraped all the most promising bits and gobbets off my pants and tucked them away to gene-read when we got back to the lodge.

Leo smiled at the two of us preening, sat down on the other side of Mabob, and did a little preening of his own. He handed me bits to add to my collection. Then he said, "How do you know that charge was anything more than a 'keep away from my clashing'?"

"I don't. But I sure as hell didn't like the way they brought that clashing down."

"Does this mean you won't let me catch you one to study?"

"Who am I to spoil your fun, Leo? But taking one of those alive is going to require some precise planning."

"And a lot of sheet metal, I think."

Sheet metal. "Well, that's your department. The carcass is mine. Think it's safe to head back to the lodge?"

"Better to do it while they're busy with the clashings," he said, "but let's tiptoe."

*   *   *

WE TIPTOED all right. And when we got back to the lodge, the first thing we did was warn the folks doing guard duty they'd better be sneaky about it. Second thing we did, once inside, was bellow out a "We're both *fine!*" into the now-empty lobby. Knew the sound of shots would've worried Elly, not to mention the kids.

Then I looked down at Mabob. Usually I don't encourage such behavior but, under the circumstances . . . "Give 'em a gronk, Mabob. Let 'em know you're okay, too."

I never know how much Mabob actually understands. Whether he got the words of my message or not—maybe he decided it was okay to yell because I had—he got the general idea and let 'em have it with a single ear-splitting, head-rattling "GRONK!"

Ilanith was the first to the bottom of the stairs. She grinned at Leo. "He's noisier than you are, Noisy."

Leo grinned back. "I agree. It just so happens, though, that noisy is not a good thing to be just now, not out in *those* woods."

"Likely story," she said. "Mama Jason, Mike wants you to call him soon as you get back—right now! The other half of the Dragon's Tooth is mole, but we still haven't found out what it came from." She darted her eyes back to Leo. "Sour grapes," she said.

I shook my head. "Nope, he means it. He'll tell you all about it while I call Mike."

Mole—that's where I'd seen those forepaws before. Not that I'd seen any moles on Mirabile, but in the photos in ships' files. Just because I hadn't seen any live ones, didn't mean they hadn't sprung up. Maybe they were the source of the Dragon's Teeth.

Mike had no new information for me. He just wanted the on-site report. He was still itching to come see for himself. By the time I got done telling him about it, he'd lost some of his enthusiasm.

And when I told him about the damage to the smoking pines, he dubbed them "frankenswine" on the spot—but his face was a little too grim for the joke.

"You named it," I said, and I told him what else they'd eaten. His face got grimmer. "Sounds like we can't afford them."

"You know me, Mike: I hate to throw anything away. You never know what might be useful in the long run." I wasn't convincing myself, though, so I knew I wasn't convincing him either. I heard myself sigh. "Damnify know. Leo's going to try to catch one. When I know more, I'll call you."

"Should I arrange rooms for Elly's kids?"

I shook my head. "The lodge is built on solid rock. It's not as if we'll have 'em coming up through the floor." I shook my head again. "No, I don't think it's necessary."

I did have to swear on Granddaddy Jason's genes I'd call him with anything new, but he finally let me sign off and get back to business.

First business was Elly, who'd been watching over my shoulder. "You heard?"

"M-hm. I've already told assorted parents you hadn't recommended evacuation of the kids. Now I can call them back and tell them why. You're getting Beate Opener Valladin, though, ready or not."

Valladin—that made her Jen's genetic mother. "Ready, willing and able to blow away frankenswine?"

Elly smiled. "I sicced Leo on her. She's going to help him trap you one."

"Leo's amazing." I couldn't help smiling at the thought.

"He is. Especially since I see *you* had no hesitation about blowing one away." She pointed.

The ugly carcass lay beside the computer, right where I'd left it.

"Sorry," I said. "Want me to do the dissection outside?"

"Not on your life! Take it in the kitchen. Chris will give you something disposable to cut on, just in case it's toxic. She'll want to kibbitz, too."

I can do with Chris's sort of kibbitzing any day. While I took the thing apart to see what made it tick, Chris ran samples through every toxicity test she could think of—and some she'd invented, as well, since Earth-authentic toxicity tests didn't cover a number of the Mirabilan possibilities.

By the time I got done, I had a healthy appreciation for the frankenswine. It was a beautiful job of bioengineering—couldn't beat that mole and boar combination—efficient as all hell. I was not happy.

Chris, on the other hand, was ecstatic. "Perfectly edible, Annie, if you peel off that layer of fat. The fat's got heavy-metal concentrations you wouldn't believe—"

Probably from the smoking pine roots it'd been eating. Which did nothing to improve my opinion of the beast.

"But," Chris went on, "the meat's not just edible, it's full of stuff that's good for humans to eat." She hovered over me, just waiting to grab the carcass and cook.

I laid a hand on the frankenswine's haunch.

"Aw, Annie. Come on. Frankenswine is good to eat!"

"Chris, *this* frankenswine may be good to eat but don't make the mistake they all are. You'll have to run through the whole set of tests on each one individually. Dragon's Teeth can vary wildly from one to the next in the same litter. One gene off and you could wipe out everybody at the table."

She looked serious enough that I knew she'd heard me. "Right," she said, "I test each one separately. But I'm still sorry you couldn't bring the second one back." She held out her hands. "Give. Except for the fat and the liver, this one's okay to eat."

"One thing more." I gave her a grin to let her know this one wasn't in the doom-and-gloom category. "Get me your best butcher knife. I think Jen ought to have those tusks for a souvenir."

Her eyes gleamed wickedly. Between us we defanged the frankenswine with a will. Might have been satisfying, except all I was thinking was if it could handle heavy metals without poisoning itself, how the *hell* were we going to get rid of it?

CHRIS WAS RIGHT, dammitall—frankenswine made a really fine tazhine. Stewed up with raisins and onions, it was enough to make even Jen think twice about wiping out the frankenswine altogether. Except it wasn't worth that dead grove. I kept chewing but I was chewing it over at the same time. Ordinarily, I give Chris's food the attention it deserves—but I was losing a taste for frankenswine even as everybody else around me seemed to be gaining one.

"Keep scowling like that, Annie," Leo muttered at me under his breath, "and Chris will never speak to you again."

Times I wish my face didn't show every damn thing that goes through my mind. I made an effort. It must not have worked because Leo grinned and tickled me under the table, which did earn him a grin back.

After I polished my bowl, I looked around the table and said, "Okay, who's got what to report?"

"Me!" said Jen, triumphantly, overriding the rest. So the rest let her have the floor without so much as a squabble. Being gnawed gives you certain proprietary rights, even in this lively a bunch.

"So," I said. "What do we get if they breed with each other?"

She pulled out a sheaf of hard copy. She'd been sitting on it, literally. It was still warm from her bottom when it reached my hands.

"It's hard to tell, Mama Jason, because it'll depend on which one breeds with which one. Maybe the others aren't viable. But the two you and Noisy killed would have been. You see if I'm right." She glanced at Beate and explained, "Better if somebody checks, so I know I'm doing it right."

Then she turned back to me. "The bad news is, chances are the rest of them can breed *more* little frankenswine."

"Just what we needed," I said, and Jen nudged Beate and said, "See? Told you she'd say that."

I was reading Jen's hard copy but I didn't miss the grin back that Beate gave her—or Elly's chuckle, either.

The hard copy was nothing to chuckle over though. She'd printed out all the steps she'd gone through to get to it, so I could follow along, fully aware that she'd gotten the procedure right. If the procedure was right, so were the conclusions, and she'd summed those up correctly, too. If the two frankenswine we'd killed had bred, they'd have bred *more* frankenswine.

"Leo? I counted about seven of them. Does that jibe with your count?"

"I made it eight, not counting the two we blew away."

"Any reason to think they're all from the same litter?"

"Statistical reason. That's an unlikely sort of Dragon's Tooth to happen twice or more in a season. Wild boar have large litters—up to twelve at a time."

I'd been thinking the same myself, but I hated like hell having it confirmed.

"Don't blame the messenger," Leo said—but the smile he gave me said he wasn't about to take my snarl personally no matter what my face did in his direction, which was enough to make me smile back, of course. "Maybe some of them *aren't* viable."

"Twelve in a litter," I said. "Jen, can you run a probability program?"

"Of course," she said.

"Then you take these"—I handed back the hard copy—"and you run me one. I want to know the odds on the next, oh, ten generations. How many frankenswine are we likely to wind up with?"

"Mama Jason?" That was Ilanith. I nodded at her and she said, "I read up on wild boar. They can have two litters a year. Maybe they won't on Mirabile, but they could back on Earth. So. . . ." She held out both hands in Jen's direction.

Worse and worse. To Jen, I said, "So plot probability for two generations a year. Worst case."

"Want a best case, too, Mama Jason?"

"Only if it makes *you* feel better," I said. "It's worst case we have to plan for."

She gave it earnest thought, then she said, "I'll run a best case, too. After all, I was the one got chewed—but Chris is right about how good they taste. Maybe we could just eat them all."

The damage to Loch Moose's vegetation said different, but I didn't say it—let her have her best case. I had a feeling it wouldn't look much better than worst case.

"Next up," I said, and turned to Susan. "Have you got a line on what produced 'em?"

She'd been awfully quiet through dinner and she didn't look like she much wanted to talk now. "Yeah," she said, grudgingly, "and you're not gonna like that, either."

"Worst case," I said, shrugging.

"They didn't come from moles."

"Meaning . . . ?"

"The gene-read says they came from Earth-authentic wild boar. Meaning we've got wild boar loose in the woods some-where, as well as the frankenswine."

And Leo and I had thought ourselves safe sitting on that rock outcrop. I looked at him and he looked at me. Either he whistled or I did. I rubbed the back of my neck, where the hairs had suddenly stood up.

"Elly," I said, "nobody's to go into the woods until we get this sorted out. And nobody so much as goes from the lodge to the hovers without a shotgun."

Elly frowned. "How is it possible we've had something that dangerous around long enough to have a litter—and nobody spotted it?"

"I think it's likely it shifted range. Maybe because of bad foraging conditions elsewhere. Maybe because it wanted a quieter neighborhood for its brood."

"A fifty-mile shift would be nothing to a wild boar," Ilanith put in. "And you wouldn't have seen it unless it wanted to be seen. They've got lousy eyesight, but they make up for it by being a lot better at hearing and smelling than a human. They avoid humans unless the human makes a point of it."

Glen Sonics Dollery, who'd been taking this all in from up the table, said, "Then they might have moved here from the area around Ranomafana. Don't know if you heard, Annie, but they're having a bad drought there. Lots of animals dead, lots of trees dying."

"Trees dying," I said. "They sure that's drought and not a brand new predator?"

He leaned back and considered the question. "The fellow I

stayed with said drought and I wasn't there long enough to disbelieve him. I haven't a woods' eye, Annie. Leo could probably tell you at a glance if the damage was lack of water or. . . ."

I eyed Leo. If memory served, he'd opened that territory.

"Drought isn't the likely explanation," Leo said. "Not in that area. I'll call around and see what I can find out."

Dollery said, "Are you folks still planning to trap one of the frankenswine? Even with this other thing loose in the woods?"

Leo nodded; so did Beate. "We'll keep our eyes on the undergrowth as well as the underground," Leo added.

"Maybe I can help, then," Dollery said. "I may not have a woods' eye, but I've got some equipment you could use as an ear for things happening underground. I might even be able to tune it to a specific creature."

"Your department," I said to Leo. He nodded at Dollery.

Elly said, "Maybe the wild boar isn't as dangerous as its offspring. If it's kept away from humans so long, why should it change its habits now?"

"Because we blew away two of its children this afternoon," I said. "If Ilanith's right about its sense of smell, it knows who was responsible. How did you feel about Jen? Double that for our wild sow. If she's bright enough to carry a grudge, she's carrying one helluva of a king-sized one against us."

LEO'S PLAN to capture one of the frankenswine awaited the arrival of some sheet steel, but we did make one last foray outside before we lost the light. Dollery'd done some tinkering, and we drove a series of sensors into the ground that would theoretically let us know if anything nasty tunneled close to the lodge. Finding out how far from the lodge we had to go for ground soft enough to drive them into was reassuring—at least, if you didn't count the possibility of mama boar showing up on the porch, tusks curled and ready for vengeance. I said as much.

"Quit growling," Leo told me. "The sensors will pick up anything that so much as pussyfoots this close to the lodge. That should hold us for the night. We can worry about the fine-tuning tomorrow."

I snorted. "Meaning nobody sleeps through the night. We get roused for every clashing or red deer in the neighborhood."

"Cheer up," he said. He grinned at me. "Maybe for once we'll get a good look at the Loch Moose monster."

"Ah," I said, "but do you really *want* a good look at the Loch Moose monster?"

We went in, still chuckling at each other, and packed it in for the night.

Turned out it wasn't the frankenswine or the wild boar or even the Loch Moose monster that disturbed our sleep.

"Wake up, Annie," Leo whispered. "We've got company."

"If it's a clashing, I don't wanna hear about it." I don't take kindly to being awakened in the middle of the night.

"It's one of the smaller Loch Moose monsters," Leo said.

There was enough of a smile in the voice that I caught on even before I heard the barely suppressed giggle of one of Elly's kids. I made an effort and came fully awake. Middle-of-the-night visits at Loch Moose Lodge are not out of the ordinary, but they're always interesting, one way or another.

"Shield your eyes, I'm turning the light on," I said. When I could see again, I saw that it was Jen. Despite the giggle I'd heard, her face was solemn. I planted an elbow on Leo's chest, peered across at her and said, "What's up?"

"I tried and tried, but I don't know enough yet, Mama Jason. How do I find out what the wild boar came from?"

"The automatic program only handles one step back—if it does that," I said. "We might be able to do it manually. But the easiest way is to get a cell sample from the wild boar and analyze that. Only way to be sure, anyhow."

She sighed heavily and the frown furrowed deeper into a forehead that was never meant to frown.

"Is this important?" I could feel my face slipping into a frown to match hers. "You should be asleep. I need you rested and awake for action tomorrow."

She gnawed her lip. "It's important. Will you get a cell sample from the wild boar tomorrow?"

I looked down at Leo, then back at Jen. "That's high on my priority list, kiddo."

"Will you tell me first? Where the wild boars are coming from, I mean."

"You can do the gene-read yourself," I said, "*if* you get enough sleep you can see straight."

That should have been enough to send her scooting, but it wasn't. She shifted her weight, enough to let me know her leg was aching. "It has to be right," she said. "Me first after you. Not Ilanith or Susan."

Not what I'd've called the usual request. I cocked my head suspiciously, but she didn't back down. If anything, the small face set stubborner. "Okay," I said, "I guess you earned it. You do it; I'll check it."

Relief spread instantly across her features. It hadn't been the leg that was hurting, after all. "Thanks, Mama Jason!"

"Now, off to bed with you, kiddo, before Elly catches you up this late and feeds you to the Loch Moose monster!"

"G'night, Mama Jason." She leaned across Leo to give me a kiss on the cheek. "G'night, Noisy." Leo got a kiss too and then she was gone.

I was still wearing an elbow hole in Leo's chest, thinking about it.

"'Not Susan or Ilanith'?" he said, shifting my elbow. "What do you suppose that's all about?"

"Damnify know," I told him. "But I'm sure gonna find out. In the morning. Or, at least, sometime when I'm awake. G'night, Leo," and I gave him a pretty thorough good-night kiss before I fell asleep again. Made up for the elbow hole some.

I DAWDLED over breakfast, knowing I was stuck with the computer for the rest of the day. The plates of sheet metal had arrived and Leo and Beate were gearing up to catch us a frankenswine or two.

I felt better that Beate was going along with the plan. No

offense to Leo, but the more I read about wild boar, the less happy I was having *anybody* in the woods. Younger, faster reflexes were in order. Dollery's probes would give them some warning and the sheet metal some measure of protection but still. . . .

I made Leo call Ranomafana before he got away from me though. Turned out they'd lost an entire bed of bulbs last spring and hadn't thought to mention it to anybody.

"The whole damn population's getting too lax," I said. "Need a good shake—each and every one of 'em."

Leo laughed. "I shook him for you, Annie. I left orders nobody was to go out unarmed—and told them why. I guarantee the next time anybody in Ranomafana sees anything out of the ordinary, we get notified immediately."

"Good. At least that's accomplished something."

I turned and put in a call to the lab. It wasn't Mike I got but Nikolai, one of my favorite examples of good genes in action.

Of course, that also meant he was mad as a hatter that Mike hadn't let him come charging up to Loch Moose the minute he heard what was going on.

"Down, kiddo," I said. "I want you and Mike, fully armed and all eyes peeled, up at Ranomafana as soon as you can get there without wrapping the hover around a tree. There may still be frankenswine or wild boar in the area. Be ready for either. I want a full workup on the EC, with special emphasis on the supposed drought damage. I want it yesterday."

He grinned and stopped trying to jump out of the screen at me. "What's the policy, Annie? You want them saved, right?"

That was the crucial question, all right, but I'd answered it the day before. I shook my head. "Shoot anything that charges you, Nikolai—above or below ground. Save a cell sample of each. We can always reconstruct if we decide they're keepers, but I don't want you or Mike taking any chances. You haven't seen how fast or how nasty these little buggers are."

He nodded as solemnly as Jen would have. Then he grinned a descendant of Leo's grin and said, "You've been hanging out with Elly too much—you're picking up her Voice of Command."

"Whatever works," I said, grinning back. "And, Nikolai, we haven't dealt with any wild boar yet. Judging from the information in ships' files, they're as fast and as nasty as the frankenswine, only they weigh up to three hundred pounds."

His eyebrows went up and he gave a short, sharp whistle. "We'll read up on the way. We'll be careful, Annie, I promise." He nodded again, this time over my shoulder. "I promise, Leo."

I passed a few more specific instructions to Mike, then I broke the connection and turned back to Leo.

"I heard what I needed: don't take chances with them. You don't think they're keepers, do you, Annie?"

"You saw what they've done to the smoking pines."

"I saw," he said, very quietly, and he nodded and turned to go. I caught his hand. "I haven't heard what I need to hear."

He smiled. "I'll be careful, Annie. I promise."

That earned him another kiss. Then we both got back to business. First thing I did was double-check Susan's backread on the frankenswine genes. Sheer wishful thinking. I knew she didn't make mistakes like that. Sure enough, the frankenswine back-read to wild boar and *damn* those geneticists back on Earth!

Because of Jen's late-night visit, the next thing I tried was reading a step further back, to see if I could figure out what the wild boar had chained up from. No luck there. Like Jen, I'd have to wait till I had a sample of wild boar to work from.

A CELEBRATORY "GRONK!" from the lobby told me the hunting party had returned and I took the stairs two at a time. Never heard such a cacophony in my life.

Leo and Beate had set their makeshift cage dead center and it wasn't just the nosey parkers exclaiming over their catch that made the room reverberate. Hideous snorts of rage came from the cage, now and again punctuated by the scrape of tusk on metal as the frankenswine tried to gouge its way through. Luckily, those flipper feet couldn't get much purchase on sheet metal, but nevertheless three people were very hastily trying to reinforce the cage where it had already deformed from repeated impacts.

Mabob paced back and forth excitedly and answered the frankenswine's grunts and snorts with challenging gronks of his own.

"Outside!" I bellowed over the noise. "Where's your sense, for god's sake?" I glared at Leo, who simply grinned back and swung a hand to indicate the gaggle of onlookers.

Elly did what I couldn't. "Outside," she said. She didn't even have to raise her voice to cut through the excitement. "Take that thing outside this minute!"

You never saw such an abashed bunch in your life. The cage and its squealing contents got hefted up and taken outside that minute. Even Mabob looked hangdog, thoroughly ashamed of his behavior. He whistled anxiously at Elly until she took pity on him and scratched his head.

"It's not your fault, Mabob," she told him. "I'd have credited Leo and Beate with more sense, though." She raised her voice and pierced the cacophony once more. "I want all you kids inside now! The same goes for any adult who is not armed." Elly, who *was* armed, put her free hand on her hip and glared. "Move."

There was no grumbling, no reluctance—we just moved, as commanded.

Which meant I had to dash upstairs for my shotgun before I could get a good close look at Leo's prize captive. I was coming down the stairs at a good clip (you don't run with a loaded shotgun in your hand) when I heard Dollery's alarm go off.

I ran the rest of the way, never mind the loaded shotgun. As I elbowed my way through the crowd at the door, I heard two shots, then a third. My gun was up and ready when I hit the porch. I got a single quick glimpse of something huge and grey charging Leo at incredible speed.

Ten yards—five yards— My shot and Elly's went off simultaneously—but it was Elly's that did the job. The creature dropped.

Momentum tumbled it head over heels and it slid to a stop scant inches from Leo. Leo, with perfect equanimity, lowered his gun and put a fifth round into its throat, just to make sure. It finally stopped moving.

"Susan!" Elly yelled over her shoulder into the lodge. "Bring your gun!"

I was reloading. "There's at least one more of them," I called down from the porch. "Don't relax yet."

They hadn't; they were reloading as fast as I was. Elly snapped her gun shut and nodded crisply. "That's why I called Susan," she said. "Next to Beate, she's the best shot here." Her brilliant smile returned. "I know you'll want to examine that thing, Annie, but I want you covered the entire time."

"Thanks," I said. "And thanks for saving Leo's butt for me. I appreciate it."

"Didn't want to lose Loch Moose's best bedtime story teller," she said. "The kids would never have forgiven me."

Susan pushed her way through the crowd of onlookers at the door, took strict instructions from Elly and took up her post. Beate stood by the frankenswine's cage but turned all her attention on the underbrush that surrounded the clearing.

I went down the steps to Leo's side. He didn't seem to be missing any body parts. Relief washed over me and I gave him a huge dopey grin just on general principles.

Then I went down on one knee to get a good look at the critter. I *didn't* lay my shotgun aside.

"Mabob heard it before the alarm went off," Leo said. "That was all the warning we got. The damn thing didn't even stop to issue a challenge, just came straight at us." He glanced at the caged frankenswine. "Straight at *us*, Annie. And at about thirty miles an hour!"

"I saw how fast it was. Lucky for us Elly was faster."

The corner of his mouth twitched up in half a smile. "And here I thought it was your shot that took it out."

"Disappointed?"

He gave me a full grin. "Not as long as it's dead."

Practical man—I like that.

The carcass was our wild sow, and I had no doubt she'd been the mother of the caged frankenswine behind us. She'd attacked the humans, not the cage. That made her altogether too bright.

And I really didn't like the looks of the wounds I found on her body. The first shot had taken her full in the face—and hadn't penetrated the skull. The second, at the shoulders, hadn't gotten through the thick hide.

Elly's shot had been the one that took her down, all right. She'd gotten it in the spine, from above. That had penetrated. So had the shot to the throat.

I took out my knife and started probing for places you *could* shoot it successfully. There weren't enough of them. The heart was low and behind the leg, which made it a tough shot when the thing was charging you face on.

Mabob came tentatively over to pick up scraps and swallow them down. I saw he was keeping an eye on the brush, too.

"Hey, Mabob! Leave some for the rest of us!" Chris, shotgun in hand, made shooing movements at him from the porch. "Annie, anything you don't need, I claim."

"All right," I said. "Send out four people to help us get this into the kitchen."

It took that many, too. It was big! I couldn't think of a single native Mirabilan predator that was big enough or fast enough to take one of those down. I wasn't even sure there was anything Earth-authentic that could do it either, short of Elly and a well-placed shot.

I gave the frankenswine some further consideration. After I'd gotten a cell sample from it, I said, "Leave it in the clearing—in its cage. If papa shows up to rescue it, shoot to kill. Best you watch from the porch and aim for the spine or throat. Leo—"

He nodded. "I'll call Nikolai and Mike and warn them what they're up against."

"Put out a general warning as well," I said. "We don't know how many there are or how far they may have ranged."

In the kitchen, I collected what samples I needed, plus a good hefty chunk for storage. You never know what you might need *some* day, so I saved the ovaries as well. Mirabile might never be ready for wild boar, but I don't burn bridges before I come to them.

Took the sample of the wild sow to Jen. "Here," I said. "You first, as promised."

"Mama Jason. . . ." She stuffed a sample into the analyzer, then handed the rest back to me. The worry hadn't left her face. "You'll check it, won't you? Make sure I'm doing it right?"

I nodded. "Sure thing."

"But tell *me* first."

Well, that wouldn't hurt any, as far as I could see, but it was still odd behavior coming from Jen.

I nodded again. "Trade you for your probability study. And you let me know the minute you find out anything."

She gave a sigh of relief. "I will, I promise."

I took the sheaf of papers she offered and headed back to my room to have a good long look.

Her "best case" promised ecological disaster. Worst case really *was*. If we were lucky, we'd wind up with frankenswine. If the wild boar bred true, we'd be overrun with them in five years. I believed her figures, but I ran my own set because I didn't want to believe her figures. Didn't help.

What with two litters a year—even if only one or two offspring were viable—and no natural predators, the wild boar could outbreed anything on Mirabile.

All my life, I've been grateful that those geneticists back on Earth hadn't included diseases on their list of keepers. Now I was almost sorry. If there'd been any disease that could cut the wild boar population to a manageable level, I'd have turned it loose in a second.

I stuffed a sample of wild boar into my analyzer. Jen was right: we needed to know what they were coming from. I didn't get right to it, though—got a call from Mike and Nikolai.

"Uh, hi, Annie," said Nikolai, looking a bit worse for the weather. "We had to kill one."

"Good," I said. "Are you two okay?"

"We're fine," he said. Then he caught up with me. "'Good'?" he repeated.

"That's what I told him," Mike put in. "He didn't believe me. Annie, these things make the damndest mess of the ecology. You wouldn't believe what they've done to Ranomafana, and everybody here was ascribing it to drought or to something Mirabilan."

"It's clever and it stays clear of people," Nikolai said. "Nobody ever *saw* one. We only found it because we tracked it."

"And we tracked it from the dead trees it left in its wake," Mike put in darkly.

"Our turn to warn *you*, Annie," Nikolai went on. "We stalked the thing for twenty minutes, chased it for another twenty—then, no warning, it turned and charged us. And you should see that thing move!"

"I have," I said.

There was silence for a moment, then Mike said, "You're gonna get an argument on this one, Annie."

He thought I meant to keep the wild boar. What with my reputation, I suppose that was fair, if only because he'd had such a close brush he wasn't thinking.

"I doubt that, Mike," I said and watched him stop and think. "Here's the probability run Jen did on future population."

He swapped me for his preliminary report on the EC at Ranomafana. It only confirmed what I already knew. The wild boar ate anything—Earth-authentic, Mirabilan, didn't matter. Stuff that would poison ninety percent of our Earth-authentics, the wild boar ate safely. The frankenswine ate same—with heavy metal sauce.

And I wanted to personally gnaw the roots of anybody in Ranomafana who hadn't bothered to report such obvious and widespread damage to their local EC.

Mike looked up from the probability study and said, "You can't keep these, Annie—"

"I know," I said, before he could work himself up into a real state.

He took a deep breath and visibly calmed. "So now what?"

I took a deep breath, too. "Order a hunt," I said. "We can't afford to keep them . . . but try for a cell sample from each one."

His hackles went up again. I could see his jaw set.

I threw up both hands to fend off protests. "I'm not asking you to save the beast, I'm asking you to save its potential. Suppose we don't have any embryos for pig in the ships' banks? We've been shorted before."

He nodded—grudgingly—but he nodded.

"I also need you to run a backread on *your* wild boar. I need to know whether we've got one source or two."

"Will do, Annie. And I'll save you a cell sample from it, too."

Relieved now, Mike was trying to make me feel better about the decision.

I gave him half a smile. "Save the whole carcass. Chris has a stack of recipes she wants to try while she's got the chance."

"She can try them on me," he said. Good humor restored, he broke the connection.

Problem was, making the decision—even if I knew it was the right one—had done nothing to restore my good humor.

"We hafta kill 'em?" said a voice from behind me. "Even if they're Earth-authentic?"

I turned to face Jen. She'd come in while I was occupied.

"Yeah, kiddo," I said. "We hafta. Otherwise they're likely to ruin Mirabile."

She nodded solemnly. "Then why are you saving their cells for the files?"

"Because maybe someday your great-great-grandchild might like a taste of pork. Maybe someday we'll need the wild boar or even the frankenswine genes, that's why."

She looked scornful. "Why would anybody need frankenswine genes?"

"Because heavy metals didn't poison the one we shot—and they also didn't poison us when we ate the one we shot. All the heavy metals wound up in the fat Chris stripped off the carcass, so the rest was safe to eat. That might be real useful someday or someplace."

She made a disgusted face at me, tongue hung out and disbelieving. "Someplace? Where?"

I grinned at her. "From what I read in ships' files about Earth during the Bad Years, they could have used a critter that could metabolize heavy metals and was still safe for humans to eat. Maybe we'll have Bad Years on Mirabile someday."

"Never," she said. "I won't let 'em."

There's nothing so fierce as a ten-year-old. "Remember that when *you* have to make a decision about keepers or not, then," I said. "So, what did you find out about the source of the wild boar?"

"Red deer," she said. "I checked it four times, but you hafta check it too."

I let her at the computer so she could call up her gene-reads. From where I sat there was no doubt she'd done them right—all four times—but she was so insistent that I ran my own as well. "No doubt about it, kiddo," I said when I'd finished. "The wild boar came from one of the red deer."

"Does that mean we hafta kill the red deer?"

"It means we hafta gene-read them all and try to stabilize the herd. Not easy with wild things. That'll keep us hopping for a few years." I grinned at her. "At least it'll give me a good excuse to spend a lot of time at Loch Moose Lodge. . . ."

She gnawed her lip. "But you'd be too busy with the deer to have fun," she said. She leaned against me for a long minute. "Better if you didn't hafta," she said, from somewhere in my shoulder. Then she pushed back suddenly and hugged. "I didn't mean that the way it sounded! I meant, better you don't hafta spend years stabilizing the red deer!"

"Yeah," I said, hugging her back. "Wouldn't that be nice—not having to spend years. Are you trying to put me out of a job?" I'd expected a giggle, but I didn't get one.

Her eyes went huge. "Would it really?"

She was so clearly upset by the idea that I had to get serious. "No, of course not. I was just teasing. Even if the red deer were stable, there'd be plenty for me to do. I could spend a lot of time with Leo, studying Mirabilan genes." The thought was pleasant enough that I smiled.

"Oh. Okay, then." She gave me one last hug, frowned once more and said, "I hafta talk to Susan and Ilanith."

"Good. While you fill them in, I'll go see what trouble Leo's gotten into without me."

"Noisy doesn't get into trouble without you," she said.

"Then I'd *better* find him, hadn't I? Together, I'm sure we can think of some kind of trouble to get into."

That got me my giggle.

IT WASN'T LEO I went looking for, though—it was Elly. I found her in her room at the back of the lodge, supervising Aklilu's forays into the computer. Nobody else was around, which suited me just fine.

Aklilu crowed, exchanged grins with Elly, and said, "Look, Mama Jason! I found the cat!"

I looked. Sure enough, there was a cat gamboling on the monitor. "Looks Earth-authentic to me," I told him.

For some reason known only to Aklilu that made it all the better. "Earth-authentic!" he caroled. "Want to show Jen!"

He slithered off the chair and onto the floor. Elly made a move to catch him, but I gave her a quick shake of the head—no point discussing things in front of Aklilu I didn't want discussed in public. He was too close to the parrot stage.

"Okay," Elly told him, "you go show Jen."

"Earth-*authentic*," he said again and scooted off.

Elly waited until he was out of earshot, then turned to me and said, "What's up, Annie?"

"That's what I wanted to ask you. Are these kids up to something I don't know about again?"

She laughed. "Probably. They usually are."

"Is it something I *ought* to know about?"

"You'll have to give me more of a hint, Annie. Which kids?"

I told her about Jen and all her haftas and threw in Susan's grimness for good measure.

She shook her head. "Susan's been grim ever since she got here. I thought it was because this is her first real emergency."

It wasn't. I shook my head, and Elly went on thoughtfully, "I can't say that Ilanith's been behaving differently than normal."

I spread my hands. "Not that I noticed, either. But it would hafta be all three." I'd heard the "hafta" on its way out of my mouth.

"Now she's got *you* doing it."

I grinned and nodded. "Come on, Elly. There must be something you can tell me."

"Contrary to what the kids think, I'm not a mind reader. The only thing that strikes me is the amount of time they've put into ships' files lately." She propped her elbow on the table and laid her chin in her open palm. "That's Jen and Ilanith. I can't speak for Susan because she hasn't been here often."

"And what were they researching?"

"Nothing specific." She raised her head and looked me straight in the eye. "Now that *is* odd—and it drops Ilanith right into the plot with the other two."

"Give," I said.

"For the life of me, I couldn't spot any pattern to their research, so I asked Ilanith what they were looking for. And she said, 'I'm not sure. I hope we know it when we see it.'"

Her eyes hadn't left mine, but she was looking at Ilanith in her mind. When she saw me again, she said, "At the time, I took it for a joke and wished her luck. But it wasn't a joke; she was quite serious. Should we worry, Annie?"

"No more than they do," I said. Then I thought of Susan's grim face and I added, "I'll see what I can get out of Jen. Sounds like she knows what they're looking for."

At that, Elly sat straight up, for all the world as if somebody'd pinched her. "They found it," she said. "Whatever it was, they must have found it. They *stopped* looking about a month ago."

"Maybe they gave up."

She shook her head, smiling. "They wouldn't have stopped unless they'd found what they were looking for—not those kids. They're too stubborn." She dimpled. "I think 'stubborn' is an inherited trait. I know exactly where Ilanith and Susan got theirs!" She pinned me with a finger.

"Inherited or not," I said, "stubborn improves with practice, which gives me half a chance to find out what 'it' is that they've found."

Elly's smile broadened. "I've been meaning to talk to you about that."

"About what?"

"Susan's grown and flown now. I never feel quite comfortable unless I've half a dozen kids around the place, and I'm short one child. Why don't you and Leo fill the gap for me? I can't think of a kid I'd rather raise—even if it would mean double the stubborn."

I guess my jaw dropped. I know I couldn't think of anything to say. Not every day you get a compliment like that. And Elly doesn't issue that sort of invitation lightly.

"You think about it." She rose lightly to her feet and gave me a hug. "I'd better see what Aklilu's up to. I should have had complaints from Jen by now." She paused at the door. "I'll mention the subject to Leo, if you'd prefer."

I'm not that shy, but the invitation should by all rights come from Elly herself. "Yes, you tell him," I said. "He'll be as honored as I am. Thanks, Elly."

She went off smiling, leaving me to stand there with grin spreading all over my face.

When I finally went back out to the porch, I found Leo, sitting with his feet up on the banister. The mere sight of him made the grin spread even wider.

He gave me an answering grin. "You figured out a way to keep them?"

Susan, standing guard beside him, said, "No!" The grim expression on her face wiped the grin from mine.

"Simmer down," I said. "No, Leo. Not this generation, anyhow. I've called a hunt."

"Oh, well," said Leo. He gave an easy shrug of his shoulders and stood. "Maybe Susan will figure out a way, one of these days."

Susan caught his arm. "I'm joining the hunt." Her eyes were dark and angry.

Leo said what I was thinking: "Sounds to me like you've a personal grudge against the frankenswine."

Susan stared at him and some of the grimness went away. "They gnawed Jen," she said—then she turned her stare back on the undergrowth, daring any wild boar to come charging out.

She wanted to join the hunt, all right. With or without the rest of us.

But I'd seen enough to recognize that she hadn't suddenly remembered her job. She'd turned those angry eyes on the undergrowth to avoid Leo's. And I could tell from Leo's expression that her explanation wasn't good enough for him either.

He gave me a thoughtful look, then stretched. "I'll go raise a posse," he said. "Up to you, Annie, whether Susan's included or not."

Susan's stare came back to me hard.

"We could use somebody with her reflexes," I said. Besides, maybe I'd get a clue if we took her along. "If we leave her out, she'll only get stroppier."

Leo nodded and grinned, with a twist for Susan. Another thing I like about Leo is that he thinks the way I do. I could see him studying her already. With a little luck, maybe he'd turn up what I couldn't.

He turned up the posse first: half a dozen folks, armed to the teeth and as ready to kill frankenswine as Susan, from the looks of them. But he'd chosen them for good sense as much as for their readiness.

Beate Opener Valladin proved as much. Despite her *very* personal grudge against the frankenswine, she made it clear that she'd go along with sample-taking. "Though I vote we do the killing first and the sample-taking after," she added. "It isn't just the frankenswine we have to deal with. We hafta keep our eyes out for the other wild boar, if there is one. That's the more dangerous of the two beasts."

At least now I knew where some of those haftas of Jen's had come from. The others still wanted investigation—after we saw to the frankenswine.

One of the onlookers said, "What about the Loch Moose monster?"

"Hey!" said Jen, from somewhere at the back of the crowd. "You leave our monster alone!"

Beate, who'd also recognized the voice, smiled and said to the hunters, "Leave the Loch Moose monster alone. If you don't bother it, it won't bother you."

"Which is not at all true for the wild boar," I said. I took the floor and told them what we knew about both frankenswine and boar. Then I said, "Let's get this show on the road."

We left Elly and two others to oversee the caged frankenswine from the porch. No matter how mad papa boar was about what we'd done to his kids, he'd be no match for Elly protecting hers. With that worry off my mind, I concentrated on keeping *my* ass intact as we stalked on tiptoe into the wood.

Mabob led the way. If he'd had any bird or any dog in him, he'd have been the ultimate bird dog that ships' files made such a big deal of. As it was, he was better at this than even the best of us.

He'd figured out exactly what we were after, too, because when he came to an abrupt halt halfway up the hill, even I could see evidence of the frankenswine's presence. More dead trees— popcorn trees, this time.

I remembered sitting under these very trees one summer evening with Elly and the whole passel of kids. At dusk, the blossoms opened with audible pops and the sound brought humming nudgems to pollinate the flowers. We'd had fun that night. Jen imitated the pop and got a nudgem to fly right up and nose *her*.

I wondered if Aklilu had been old enough that he'd remember that night . . . he'd never hear *these* trees pop again.

Mabob had found the frankenswine's tunnel. We followed, trying to be quieter than we had before. My face was probably as grim as Susan's by now. I was looking forward to getting even for the popcorn trees, and getting the specific frankenswine responsible would be a lot more satisfying than shooting frankenswine at random.

No such luck. Mabob was leading us straight to the communal burrows. Once that was clear, all the safeties came off all the guns, and we got so quiet you'd have thought not a one of us was even breathing.

The smoking pines looked deader than before.

Either we were so quiet the frankenswine didn't hear us coming—which I doubt—or they'd already learned to keep their heads down around people with guns. As we stepped into the dead grove and circled the burrows, nothing moved in all that expanse of subterranean workings—not so much as a ripple of earth.

For all of a moment, I wondered if they'd moved elsewhere. Then I looked at Mabob. He was sure they were there, and I was willing to take his word for it. If we couldn't get 'em to come out, it was gonna be hell trying to kill 'em, though.

I looked at Leo; Leo looked at me. Then he grinned and made a gesture that said, clear as day, *You aim and I'll bring 'em out for you*. I aimed my gun at the holes in the ground.

Leo whistled a tune and did a dance step, a rhythmic thump and pound sort of thing. Mabob caught on and danced, too. His thump and pound wasn't in the same time, but his whistle came pretty damn close to matching Leo's. Under other circumstances, I'd've laughed aloud. I'd heard of ferrets dancing to bring a rabbit out of its hole, and I guess Leo'd heard the same story. He was counting on curiosity to bring the frankenswine to the surface.

Whistle, thump . . . Thump, thump, whistle . . .

Beate stared at them both, aghast. I punched her in the shoulder and indicated the ground.

I was just in time. One more thump and pound and the ground was alive with frankenswine. The volley of shots was almost as deafening as one of Mabob's gronks. Even with my ears ringing, I could hear the screams and grunts of the ones we'd injured. A second scatter of shots put an end to most of that.

Squinting through the flying dirt, I saw one duck back into its burrow. I watched until I saw the ground bulge ever so slightly, then I put my gun to the bulge and fired into the ground. Wasn't sure that would get it, but it was worth a try.

I reloaded as fast as my hands could work and, meaning to follow if it moved again, I stepped into the burrowed-out area. The ground sank under my feet and I went down. Lucky for all concerned, my reflexes are still good enough: I kept the gun from going off.

Lucky for me, Beate's reflexes were even better. The ground bulged again—an inch from my buried ankle—and Beate put her gun to the bulge and fired. This time the shower of dirt came up wet with blood. She fired again, reloaded, then reached out a hand to pull me to my feet.

"Thanks," I said.

"Don't take your eyes off the ground," she said. *She* hadn't.

Everybody else had learned from my experience. We picked our way gingerly across the clearing. It was like walking on a sponge. Mabob was doing better than we were. Either he was light enough to walk on top of the burrows or he had a better sense of where they were.

Another shot rang out and the last of the squealing stopped. "Cover me," I said to Beate and I reached down and dug until I pulled out what was left of the frankenswine her shots had dispatched. I tossed it to one side, onto what looked more like solid ground.

Leo flung a second onto that. Somebody fired again and, when I looked, *that* frankenswine had stopped moving. It, too, got tossed onto the heap.

There were five carcasses when we counted up. Problem was, I had no way of telling if that was all of them. "Okay," I said. "Everybody freeze and listen for more."

Three people jammed probes into the ground and listened, but it was Mabob I was watching. He was picking his way delicately over the clearing, crisscross and then crisscross again, watching the ground with those huge orange eyes and cocking his head every now and again.

The people with the probes occasionally glanced his way to make sure he was all they were hearing.

Mabob stopped dead, cocked his head at a sharper angle and began to stalk. I checked to make sure my gun was fully loaded then I made my way carefully toward him. Beate followed in my footsteps—where I didn't sink, she wouldn't either.

Mabob gave us a quick glance—to make sure he had backup, I think—then resumed his stalk. So did Beate and I. Out of the corner of my eye, I saw Leo gesture to the rest to stay put. The less distraction Mabob had the better.

No doubt in my mind whatsoever: we'd missed one. It was burrowing away from the clearing as fast as its tusks and shovel feet could take it, which was pretty damn fast.

Burrowing deep, too. For all my watching, I never saw so much as a bulge in the ground. That meant my chances of killing it with a shotgun blast *through* the ground were practically nonexistent. But sooner or later it would come to rocky ground and, when it did, I was going to be there, gun pointed right up its ugly snoot.

We followed it into the brush and down the side of the hill at a good clip. We were out of sight to the rest of the posse when Mabob stopped dead.

He listened, then he listened some more. He looked up at me, orange eyes blazed, then he focused on the ground once more. He picked his way around a spot on the forest floor as if it were some kind of a trap, cocking his head first this way and then that.

Then he froze in place, body hunched as low to the ground as it would go.

The frankenswine had apparently stopped moving. Not a bad idea. Freeze in place and hope what's stalking you gets bored and goes home in disgust. But the frankenswine hadn't counted on Mabob—*he* knew where he'd heard it last.

I was prepared to wait as long as it took, and I didn't need a glance at Beate to know she felt the same way.

We hadn't counted on Mabob either, though. He made a sort of snorting noise—first time I'd ever heard him do that—then he balled up a fistful of talons and thumped the ground hard, right over the frankenswine's head.

Then he put his head down to the ground and gave out with his hundred-decibel challenge: "GRONK!" And before the air around us had stopped vibrating, he'd started digging. It was one-footed digging, but it was fast and effective. Dirt flew every which way.

The frankenswine got the picture. It erupted from the ground like something shot from a cannon, and Beate put both barrels of her gun into it. It squealed in pain and rage and flailed at Mabob. I couldn't fire without hitting Mabob, but Mabob was holding his own. He balled up his talons again and slammed the frankenswine so hard on the snoot that it went flying. I put two more shots into it, and it was dead before it hit the ground.

I heard Beate's gun snap closed and knew she'd reloaded. I took the hint and did the same before I joined Mabob, who was already standing over the carcass, appreciating his trophy.

He rattled his scales happily, ripped a good-sized chunk off the frankenswine, and gobbled it down.

"Yeah," I said to him. "You deserve it. Just save me one chunk for the cell stores. The rest is yours and to hell with Chris's pork recipes."

"GRONK!" he said, into my face. Frankenswine smelled as bad on Mabob's breath as everything else did, but I scratched the soft hair on the top of his head into spikier spikes. He went back to eating, rattling as he ripped and gulped.

"We got it," Beate called up the hill to the rest.

"Still checking here," came a faint reply.

Beate gestured up the hill with the barrel of her gun. "Should we go back and help?"

"In a minute," I said. "I need a sample. . . ."

Mabob ripped off another good-sized chunk and, whistling softly in the back of his throat, he held it out to me. Mabob's generous with his food. We share with him, he shares with us. If occasionally we don't have the same tastes, no hard feelings on either side.

"Thanks," I said. I scratched his head again and accepted the tasty bit he offered.

He looked a bit bemused when I stuck it in my pack instead of wolfing it down, so I said, "I'll save it for later. Thanks, again," and scratched his head once more. Rattling, he offered a second chunk to Beate, who grinned and politely turned it down. She'd seen enough to scratch his head as a thanks but no thanks. Mabob went back to eating.

"What if he poisons himself, Annie?"

"Unlikely. He's better at this than we are. He's avoiding the fat, same as Chris did, so I have to assume it's all right. I have no idea what he eats when I'm not looking."

But he'd stopped eating. His head shot up to stare into the brush.

Beate and I both followed his eye-blaze and raised our guns simultaneously. I couldn't see a damn thing, but I knew better than to ignore Mabob's warnings.

Then we heard it too. Pounding feet and a faint rustle in the brush some fifty yards from us. Then forty yards from us. I still couldn't see a thing. All I knew was it was moving too fast for a clashing *or* for the Loch Moose monster. That left only one possibility—wild boar.

It burst from the brush and froze, snorting angrily at us. Face on, it was twice as ugly as its mate—and twice as furious. It fixed its savage eyes on me, and I knew it was seeing the thing that was killing its children.

Beate gave it both barrels, face and chest. Instead of stopping it, that only made it madder.

It charged—straight at me.

Mabob let loose a challenging gronk, but the boar ignored him completely and pounded on.

I fired once. I know I hit it, but that shot had no effect either. Then time slowed down. I could hear Beate fumbling to reload. I hoped she'd make it in enough time for her. I *knew* it wouldn't be soon enough for me.

Still coming at me in slow motion, the boar clicked its teeth. It was an eerie sound, too quiet for the force of the attack. The sound of a clock ticking off last seconds. I raised my gun for one last shot.

It was ten yards and closing. . . . when one hind foot went suddenly out from under it, and it foundered and went down on its side. As it scrambled to regain its footing, it slipped ever so slightly sideways to me.

With one shot left—and thinking, "You'd better be right about this, Annie Jason Masmajean"—I aimed just behind its foreleg and pulled the trigger.

The boar spasmed and went limp. Beate put a shot into its

throat while I reloaded. When I snapped my gun shut, there was a sudden very loud silence.

"God, they're fast," said Beate, after a long moment. I let out a long breath and nodded—wasn't sure my voice would work just then. She took a single hesitant step toward the huge carcass and stopped.

Mabob had no such hesitation. He strutted over to the beast, bashed it once, ringingly, on the skull. "GRONK!" he proclaimed.

That was enough to rouse us both from our awed stupor. We walked the three steps necessary to stand beside him.

As we stood looking down at the wild boar, Beate said, "Sorry I didn't pick my shots better, Annie. I know where you told us it was most vulnerable—but, it came at us so fast, I shot without thinking."

I shook my head. "If it hadn't tripped, it'd still be coming, and you'd have had a chance to avenge me. I wasn't sure what would stop it either, all I had was an educated guess. And I wouldn't have had a chance to guess if the slip hadn't thrown it sideways."

She knelt beside the carcass. Mabob stopped pounding it with his balled talons and peered to see what she was looking at. When she started to laugh, I stooped to have a look for myself.

Then I was laughing too, partly out of relief and partly out of the irony of it. The same thing that tripped me up had tripped up the wild boar: it had put its foot right through one of the frankenswine burrows.

When the rest of the posse skittered down the hill to make sure we were all right, they found us clinging to each other, still laughing, while Mabob rattled like a dozen maracas and kept time by thumping a foot on the wild boar's ribs.

As FAR AS I was concerned, I'd had enough excitement for one day. (Not Beate—she grabbed two others to fill in for me and Leo and went out to scour the countryside looking for wild boar or frankenswine we'd missed. To the relief of my eardrums, she took Mabob with her.) I got down to the more mundane business of gene-reading the ones we'd killed.

The results came as a considerable relief. All of the franken-swine had come from a single litter, and we'd killed both parents.

"So, no more frankenswine," said Leo, looking as relieved as I felt.

I tilted a hand back and forth. "Maybe—maybe not. Now I need the gene-reads, forward and back, on the three wild boar we've got so far."

As I'd expected, Mike had left the gene-read for his boar on file for me. I laid all three side by side on the monitor, put my elbows on the desk, my chin in my hands, and gave them a good long study.

When I turned back to Leo, he was smiling. "Tell me if I'm reading this right, Annie. . . . All three of the wild boar came from the same two red deer. If we eat *those* two, our troubles are over." He tipped his chair back with a satisfied air and added, "I've always liked venison, especially the way Chris cooks it."

"Some of our troubles are over if we eat venison." I tapped the screen. "You are reading it right, but you're not reading between the lines."

"What am I missing?"

"The fact that any red deer in the forest may well be prepared to give birth to wild boar next time around. And since nobody's reported any *tulip*-red red deer, we won't get any warning beforehand. Most does simply abandon offspring that far off normal, which cuts down on the problem, but we will have to take care of the mother of our three." I pointed with my chin at the screen. "She's obviously raising them."

"So the next hunt will be to sample the red deer."

"Sample and tag, I think. That way we can keep an eye on any other potential problems."

He stood. "That's decided, then. Let's eat."

"Let's neck," I said, rising to my feet beside him. "That was a helluva close call this afternoon, and I could use the reassurance."

He grinned. "How about both?"

"Done," I said, and we did.

*   *   *

AFTER DINNER, he did me the favor of checking to make sure all the parts were still there and in good working order. (It was his considered opinion they were.) And then we eased down deep into the bedding for a well-deserved rest.

Loch Moose Lodge being the sort of place it is, we didn't get it, of course. For the second time in as many nights, I got dragged out of sleep by whispers just outside the door.

"It was my fault you got chewed, Jen. I'm telling her and that's all there is to it." It was Susan's voice.

"You don't hafta. I got chewed because I got chewed. It's not as if *you* bit my leg. We decided before—"

"Before doesn't count," Susan said.

"Why not?" said a third voice. "Just because Jen got bit doesn't change things any more than the Kinyamarios' cat did."

I sighed and nudged Leo awake. Then I got out of bed and opened the door. Caught in the act, all three of my suspicious characters—Susan, Ilanith and Jen—started and blinked at me.

"After the ear strain Mabob gave me this afternoon," I said, "I'm having a helluva time eavesdropping. Why don't you all continue this discussion inside and save me the trouble?"

Reluctantly, they all trooped in. "Light coming," I said to Leo. To the kids, I said, "Sit down and tell me what's to tell."

There was a long silence; all of them looked at their feet. At last, Ilanith heaved a sigh of pure exasperation and said, "Too late now. Either we tell her the truth or we make something up *real* quick."

Jen brightened momentarily, as if she were on the verge of making something up *real* quick. Then she looked at me and shook her head, resigned. "Okay," she said. "Tell her, I guess. After all, if something happened to you, Susan, it'd get lost all over again."

"You tell," said Susan. "You started it."

Leo groaned and rearranged pillows until he'd propped himself up to look at the three of them. "Could we compromise on this? *Somebody* tell us so we can go back to sleep." He gave me a sidelong glance with smile. "Maybe it's just a dream?"

"If it is, it's one of those frustration dreams." I nudged him over so I could sit on the edge of the bed, then I held out my hand, palm up, to the three. "Come on—spit it out in Mama Jason's hand. Susan?"

"It's my fault Jen got bit," Susan said.

Ilanith made a rude noise in contradiction.

"Was not," said Jen. "Tell her she's wrong, Mama Jason!"

"You're wrong, Susan," I said. Anything to oblige. "Now, could we get to the heart of the problem?"

"It's not a problem," said Ilanith. "It's a solution."

"It's a solution that makes problems," said Susan. Her face had gone back to being grim.

"Then we'll have to find a solution to the problem caused by the solution," I said. To Leo, I added, "I'm not sure I'm awake. Did that make any sense to you?"

"As much as anything they've said," he answered. He fixed an eye on Susan and said, "Let's have it."

"From the beginning," I added.

"It was Jen's idea," Susan said. Jen glowered, but Susan went on. "We all thought the geneticists back on Earth forgot to tell us how to stop the encrypted genes from activating. Or maybe we'd lost that part of ships' files where they did tell us . . ."

"Tell me something I don't know," I said, growling despite my best intentions.

Ilanith said, "You tell, Jen. It *was* your idea. And it was a really good one, too, Mama Jason."

This time around Jen was proud of her idea. "Okay, I will. My idea was maybe they didn't forget to tell us how to stop red deer from chaining up to wild boar. Maybe it just wasn't indexed! And, if it's not indexed, you only think it's not there."

I'm pretty damn sure I heard my jaw hit my chest. "Good god, I'm an idiot!" I said. (Me and three generations of jasons—but I'm the only one I can hold personally responsible.) "Never occurred to me. . . ."

Ilanith picked up the story from there. "So we figured, if we just kept looking, we'd maybe find it."

"Ah," I said. "That explains the random computer searches Elly was wondering about!"

"They weren't random," Susan said. "We did the popular science magazines—every article on genetics we could find and—"

And then it hit me. Elly said they'd stopped looking. "You found it!" I came up off the edge of the bed and tried to gather all three into one massive hug. "You found it!"

I backed off, grinning like a fool.

When I turned the grin on Leo, I knew he'd gotten the implications of it, too. He grinned even wider and said to Jen, "I guess it's *not* genes that make the jason good. Think maybe it's something in the water at Loch Moose?"

Jen giggled. "Yeah," she said, "probably the Loch Moose monster."

Susan grunted and scowled at her feet.

"Light is beginning to dawn," I said. "Susan, if you must have the world's worst case of the guilts, at least have them over something you actually did—like eating the last of the molasses snaps."

"Susan, you didn't!" said Jen, but it was clear from the look on Susan's face I'd gotten that right. "I thought it was Ilanith!"

"I never," said Ilanith. "I thought Mama Jason ate 'em. She likes 'em as much as we do."

"Now you have something *real* to feel guilty about, Susan," I said. "I do like molasses snaps as much as they do. And you can't blame yourself for what the red deer gave birth to three, maybe four, years before you found out how to stop them from breeding Dragon's Teeth."

I cocked an eye at Jen. "What say we forgive her for the frankenswine but not for the molasses snaps?"

"Right." Jen gave Susan a single definitive nod. "You owe me a bunch of molasses snaps."

Susan put an arm around her. "Yeah," she said, "I owe you molasses snaps." The smile still wasn't up to its normal standards.

"But?" I said.

"But," Susan said, "what's been born in the last month that'll come jumping out at Jen—or you, maybe—five years from now?"

I shrugged and grinned. "I'll let you know in five years."

She and Ilanith exchanged a dark look—then Ilanith gave a huge sigh. "I don't think we can win, Susan. Either the problem is a problem or the solution is a problem."

Behind me, Leo gave a sigh that outdid Ilanith's. "They've gone strange again," he said.

"All right, then," I said. "What's the problem with the solution?"

Another dark look passed between the two older girls, then Susan said, "Sit down, Mama Jason. This is hard to explain and I want to get it right."

I sat.

"It's not hard to explain," said Jen. "Mama Jason, the Kinyamarios' cat had another litter of stillborn kittens, and I asked Susan why she couldn't fix it up so the cat would breed true and then we could have our kitten next time. And Susan showed me in ships' files about an island where there were so many cats—*imported* cats, like an Earth-authentic cat is on Mirabile—that they were wiping out all the native birds. Susan says—"

"Susan says," said Susan for herself, "that if our Earth-authentic imports bred true, they'd mean total disaster for the native Mirabilan species. Look at the wild boar, Mama Jason. You saw Jen's probability study yourself. You should see what it looks like if all the wild boar breed more wild boar."

"And the rats," said Ilanith. "If the rats bred true we'd be overrun."

"If the damn dogs hadn't had encrypted rat genes," I pointed out, "we wouldn't have had the rats in the first place."

"True," said Susan, "but we wouldn't have had the odders or the Loch Moose monster either."

"We might *need* something," Jen said. "Don't you see? And if we got rid of all those things hidden inside—hidden inside the Kinyamarios' cat—well, who knows what we might lose? Maybe something we need tomorrow."

I nudged Leo further over in the bed, put my feet up and

leaned back with a happy sigh. "Think I'll retire, Leo. I could use the sleep."

"Mama Jason, you can't," said Jen, and that was an order.

"I can't," I admitted, "and I won't—but I *am* going to leave this decision up to you."

Jen made a little squeak sound somewhere back in her throat. The three of them locked eyes for a moment, then Susan turned back to me and said, "Let me get this straight, Mama Jason. You want *us* to decide whether to get rid of the encrypted genes in all the plants and animals we brought with us from Earth?"

"Yup," I said. "Or decide which of them we can safely let breed true. You've got it straight, Susan. That's exactly what I want you to do."

I pulled the quilt over me and snuggled deeper into bed. "I suggest you sleep on it. Lemme know—tomorrow, next week, whenever. And I need a good-night hug from each one of you on the way out."

I got three of the best good-night hugs going, and a fourth that topped them from Leo after I'd turned out the light.

"Annie," said Leo, from somewhere in the nape of my neck, "that's an awful lot of weight to lay on those youngsters."

"No," I said, "I know exactly what they'll decide: they'll file the information so it can't be lost again, and they may even tell me where to find it, but only one female red deer will get her genes clipped."

"The one that's been raising her wild boar offspring to maturity, right?"

"Right, and only the one. Like Jen said, we don't know what we might need tomorrow, and those kids are wise enough to recognize that fact. They'll keep all the options open."

I kissed the bit of his ear nearest to reach and couldn't help but add, "Elly sure raises some terrific kids!"

"Uh, Annie . . . speaking of which . . . Elly paid us the highest compliment in her book today. . . ."

"Yeah," I said, grinning into the dark. "What do you say we take her up on it?"

"I say, I'd be delighted."

"That's settled, then," I said. "Next question: boy or girl?"

He laughed. It made the best kind of tickle along the side of my neck. "Annie," he said, "surprise me."

"I'll do my best."

From somewhere off in the distance, the mating bellow of the Loch Moose monster drifted faintly across the water. *This* year, there was an answer.

Author's Note

One of the joys of writing science fiction is that the writer can read anything that appeals to her and claim she's doing research.

If you enjoyed this novel, try the following books. They're all "keepers" and I plan to reread them for the sheer fun of it.

Wily Violets and Underground Orchids: Revelations of a Botanist, by Peter Bernhardt
    William Morrow & Co., New York, 1989
In Search of Lost Roses, by Thomas Christopher
    Summit Books, New York, 1989
Their Blood Runs Cold, by Whit Gibbons
    The University of Alabama Press, Alabama, 1983
Wonderful Life, by Stephen Jay Gould
    W. W. Norton & Co., New York, 1989
    (and anything else you find by Stephen Jay Gould)
A Book of Bees, by Sue Hubbell
    Ballantine Books, New York, 1989
Carnivorous Plants, by Adrian Slack
    The MIT Press, Massachusetts, 1989

If you want to build a bat box of your own, *America's Neighborhood Bats*, by Merlin D. Tuttle (University of Texas Press, Texas, 1988), will tell you how.

Also, for the fun of it, I recommend you take the lifetime

subscription to *New Scientist* and that you snaffle copies of *The Wall Street Journal* from a yuppie friend (read the middle column on the front page).

Cheers,
Janet Kagan

P.S. Some of these will answer the age-old question, "Where do you get your crazy ideas?" Surely you don't think I'm making this stuff up, do you?